# Love for Hire

## NIKKI CASTLE

*This one is for the women who grew up being told that carbs are bad, that women should be seen and not heard, and that cursing is unladylike.*

*Fuck. That. Shit.*

# ONE
## NICO

"It was really nice to meet you. I had a great time tonight."

*I did not have a great time tonight.*

Rachel, the girl I connected with on Hinge two weeks ago and met for the first time tonight, smiles at me as I open the Uber door for her. "I had *such* a fun time. Maybe we can do this again next week?"

I sigh internally. I don't like lying on dates, but it seems like the best option sometimes.

"I might be pretty busy the next few weeks," I say with an apologetic wince. "I have a fight coming up." *A white lie.* "So training unfortunately takes up a lot of my time. I'm sorry."

When her face falls, I try to lighten the mood with a joke.

"Some days, I swear, I'll have to retire to have a social life."

*Shockingly, not a lie.*

She tries for an understanding smile, but it's obvious she's bummed.

Goddamnit, why can't I fall for a girl like Rachel? She's sweet, smart, has a good job; our humor isn't a perfect match, but whose is? She's exactly the kind of nice girl who any man would be lucky to settle down with.

But I don't feel *anything* for her.

"Well, good luck on your fight then," she says sweetly. "Maybe...give me a call when life slows down?"

I force a smile. "I definitely will. Have a good night, Rachel."

Her gaze dips to my lips for a split second, but I can't bring myself to kiss her. I already feel empty from our date, and I don't think I could handle any meaningless affection.

I step back, as if to give her room to get in the car. "Get her home safe, please," I say to the driver.

I wait until the car is pulling away from the curb to let out a gigantic exhale.

I've lost track of how many dates I've been on lately that have felt like this. Where I walk away at the end of the night feeling like there's something wrong with me, because *how is it possible I don't feel anything for anyone?*

Ironically, even my relationship of five years suffered from this affliction. Every milestone we reached was just because the appropriate amount of time had passed and it made sense as the next step. Making our relationship official, saying *I love you*, moving in together, all of it felt...logical. It's hard to end a relationship when nothing is *wrong*, per se. But I guess she got tired of us being the equivalent of roommates who have boring sex once a week because, in the end, she's the one who decided to break up with me.

I should've been more upset about it, but the truth is, I felt nothing. Nothing but a little bit of relief that I could start to date again and maybe, *finally*, find someone who sets my blood on fire.

And yet, even after dozens of dating app dates, blind

dates, overpriced matchmaker dates...I still feel room temperature.

I let out another exhale, this one more tired than the last. I should go home and get some sleep. I wasn't lying to Rachel about training taking up most of my time and energy.

But I also know that if I went home right now, my restless brain would continue spinning and likely keep me up too late.

My feet turn toward the gym before I even make the conscious decision.

It's a fifteen-minute walk to my MMA gym. Even though it's almost 9 p.m. on a Friday, there might still be some stragglers on the mats. But even if there isn't, I've had the key to the gym since I was twenty-one when I committed my life to the sport.

A few rounds of bagwork should tire me out enough to shut off my brain.

But when I walk into the gym, I realize right away that I won't be going straight into a workout. Because my striking coach is standing at the reception desk, phone to his ear and a downright giddy smile on his face.

I lift an eyebrow in a silent *what's going on?* He hurriedly waves me closer as he says, "Speak of the devil. He just walked in."

He pushes the button for speaker as I step around the desk and plop down into the office chair. "Alright, you're on speaker," he says.

"Actually, I'll let you deliver the good news." I recognize my brother Lucas's voice instantly. Which makes sense, because he's also my manager. "I'm running into a meeting with a client."

My coach frowns down at his phone. "At nine p.m.?"

"Lucas swears by his late night, scotch-fueled closures," I

explain as I reach for the phone. Then, to my brother, "Goodbye, Lucas."

I hang up before he can come back with whatever quip he was waiting with, looking expectantly at my coach. "So, what's up?"

His grin is gigantic. "Lucas got you a fight. *The* fight."

For the second time tonight, I have to swallow a sigh. I should've guessed that was the news, just based on his excitement level.

*I really am off my game.*

"Oh yeah?" I ask. "Against who?"

Somehow, his grin grows. "Pete Hanson."

I let out an appreciative whistle. Lucas has been working on that one for almost two years at this point. "Damn. When?"

"Two months. You're fighting at the Garden."

*Holy shit. Lucas really did work his charm.*

Fighting at Madison Square Garden has always been a dream of mine. Add to that a perfectly matched opponent and the fact that it's close to home, and it's pretty much the ideal matchup. Plus, it might be the most important fight of my career.

*But do I even care?*

I try to shoo that thought away. Now is not the time to go down that rabbit hole. Turning my attention to my coach again, I ask, "Knowing Lucas, I'm assuming he already set up some extra training sessions for me next week. Are we focusing on improving my wrestling like we always planned on for this fight?"

He snorts. "Pretty sure he was setting them up as we were on the phone. Your brother is another breed." Then, he pauses, thinking over my question for a moment. "Two months isn't nearly as much time as I'd like for your fight

4

camp, but Lucas said you'd want to make that sacrifice for the Garden."

I simply nod.

"I know I don't need to tell you this, but I'm going to anyway: you're going to need to buckle down for this fight, Nico."

Another stiff nod. "I know."

If he notices my lack of enthusiasm, he doesn't comment on it. Hopefully, he just thinks I'm shifting into work mode.

"You know the drill when it comes to your training, but..." His hesitation makes me frown. *What is he trying not to say?* "I think you should relax with the social life, too."

Social life...? I barely ever go out, even when I don't have a fight coming up. The only people I hang out with are my brothers and—

His unspoken comment suddenly hits me. "You mean with dating."

"I didn't know how to say that in another way," he says with a wince. Then he sobers and looks me in the eye. "Look, I get it, okay? You're getting older; maybe your friends are starting to settle down and get married... I get it. I don't blame you for wanting to leave the bachelor life behind. But it's clearly eating up more mental energy than you can afford with this fight lined up."

"That's not true," I argue, albeit weakly. "They're just dinner dates. There's zero energy expended."

He gives me a knowing lift of his eyebrow. "Yeah? Is that why you walked in here looking like someone just beat you five rounds to none?"

You can't hide anything from coaches.

I blow out a heavy breath. "Alright, fine. I had a shitty first date."

He sighs and leans back against the reception desk.

"Maybe a break from dating would be good for you. I mean, don't they say you find your person when you stop looking?"

"That's a stupid saying, Coach."

For a second, it looks like he wants to defend it, or say something else to make me feel better. But then he visibly gives up. "Fine, whatever. But you can't say I'm wrong about it being distracting for you. And that you *should* take the next two months off while you're training for this fight."

*Damnit.* He's right. Dating is only making me disappointed and depressed lately.

"Yeah, okay," I relent with a huff. "No more dating."

He nods. "Good." And maybe in an attempt to make me feel better, he adds, "But hey, feel free to keep the occasional booty call. You know they've debunked the 'no sex before a fight' thing. It's just the emotional shit you've got to stay away from."

*At this rate, that's all I'll have. I'm going to die a spinster with a roster.*

I try for an amused smile. "You know, you really take modern coaching to a whole new level."

He grins. "Most guys would be grateful. Have sex but don't catch feelings."

Most guys probably *would* be grateful.

Leave it to me to be the only one who reaches the opposite of a mid-life crisis at thirty years old.

# TWO
## SCARLETT

The lipstick slides over my lips, smooth as silk.

Most escorts wouldn't wear lipstick to an appointment, but I have a no-kissing rule that makes it a non-issue for me.

The fact that it acts as armor that hardens me against the world is just a bonus.

I lean back, taking in my reflection in the mirror of my vanity. I have a very specific routine before my appointments, a routine that takes me exactly two and a half hours to attain the perfect look.

My blonde hair has been expertly blown out, the volume offering the ideal grip for chubby, greedy hands. My makeup is flawless; there's not a pore in sight, and my eye look is simple but perfect.

I'm wearing a modest black dress today, because even though my red lingerie beneath it screams *whore*, I still need to be conscious of my appearance in public, given that my profession isn't necessarily legal. I need to be strategic about how I look and when. It's the reason I'm such a perfectionist.

Well, one of the reasons.

*It's a woman's job to always look presentable, Scarlett.*

My spine stiffens, my darkened eyelashes fluttering quickly as I try to blink away the memory of my mother's voice.

When I was a teenager, her voice was the thing that drove my actions—both consciously and unconsciously. Every time I looked in the mirror, every time I thought about food…any time a man was nearby.

When I left home, somehow, the voice got louder. To the point that I had to actively work on shutting it out.

Taking a deep breath, I shake my head, loosening some of my curls. I hurriedly reach for the hairspray, hands shaky from my trip down memory lane, and accidentally knock over another spray bottle.

*God, what is with me tonight?*

Her voice used to consume me. It took me months, *years*, to get to the point where I could shut her out—save for a few tiny moments when she slips back in.

*Like tonight.*

Directing all my focus to my hair, I spray and smooth the strands until there isn't a single one out of place. Unfortunately, the easiest way to erase her voice has always been to achieve perfection. God knows that woman was only quiet when she ran out of critiques.

Sure enough, when I confirm in the mirror that my appearance is perfect, the sounds of the city filter back in and the room fills with air again. I can breathe.

Glancing down at my phone, I realize I'm out of time. Gathering the purse with all my essentials—lipstick, condoms, wipes, and pepper spray—I quickly slip on my heels before walking out the door.

Once I get to the hotel where my client's waiting, I'll add a little curve to my spine and shorten my strides to avoid any attention, but for now, I settle into the confident façade that comes so easily to me.

It's the armor I feel the strongest with.

When I reach the driver waiting for me outside of my building, I give him a polite smile but nothing more. And once I'm sitting in the car, I wordlessly press the button for the partition.

The twenty-minute ride allows me to go through the mental checklist I've perfected.

*Appearance: flawless*

*Voice: low and sultry*

*Smile: appears genuine*

*Emotions: numb*

It's essential that I go into my appointments with every item checked off. The first two are for client satisfaction and job security—my job is far easier if I'm seeing repeat, satisfied clients. The third is vital for this job. And the fourth...honestly, I don't know what it's like to *not* be numb, but I imagine most escorts require some level of numbness for a job like this.

Who knows. I don't talk to the agency's other escorts—or to anyone, really—so it's not like I'll ever ask.

Regardless, when I knock on my client's hotel door—*room 521, just like the agency's email said*—my body tenses and stomach twists when I come face to face with my client.

But you'd never know it from the smile I give him.

"Hi, baby," I purr.

"Daisy," he greets excitedly, using my pseudonym. "You look beautiful."

*You look fuckable*, is what he means. But my smile grows anyway, the movement—and accentuation of my lips—making his pupils widen further. "Aren't you sweet. Thank you."

When he stands aside and gestures me in, I enter the room with long strides, making sure my hips sway. I place my purse on the dresser and begin to adjust my appearance. Now that we're behind closed doors, I can safely morph into the character the client needs.

That's the secret to being an escort. It's not just about letting men use your body; it's about figuring out what it is that each man wants. Some pay for escorts because they want the woman to leave right after. Some just want to be wanted. Some are lonely and simply want to talk to another person. Every client has a different *why*. And it's my job to figure out what it is.

For Tom Harris, it's to roleplay his daily life, but with a different ending.

You see, Tom is a Vice President of a very successful software company. He's married with kids and has a high-paying job. He has everything he *should* want.

The only problem is that his boss, the CEO, is a stone-cold woman who runs the company with an iron fist and has no issue putting men in their place when they mess up. So, every time Tom gets chewed out in front of the entire executive team, I get a call. I'm hired to recreate the scolding, just so he can get on his knees for a different ending.

Men are such simple creatures.

"So," I start in a cold voice, spinning around to face him. "Would you like to explain to me why you failed to hit this quarter's numbers?"

Predictably, his breathing becomes heavier. "We had some unforeseen complications—"

"Isn't it your job to *foresee* those complications?" I interrupt. "I was under the impression you were competent when I hired you." I take a step closer, my voice dripping with condescension. "Are you not? Competent?"

His mouth opens, then closes, then opens again. I can see the outline of his erection against his slacks.

"If I had more support, I-I would have—" he stutters.

I let out a mocking laugh. "*Support?* Did you want someone to hold your hand?" I take another step, now close enough that there're only a few inches between us. Ironically, I'm taller than Tom in heels, so I have to duck my head slightly to taunt him. "Do you need a babysitter, little Tommy? Are you a poor wittle baby, in need of—"

I see the moment he reaches his limit. Wincing, he grabs his crotch, the pain on his face evident. He's seconds from coming already. This week must have been bad, because I usually get a few more jabs in before he cracks.

*Oh well. This just means a shorter appointment.*

I point at the floor by my feet. "On your knees. If you're going to be a disappointment, we might as well find *some* use for you."

He drops to his knees with a thud. Relief floods his face as he looks up at me, waiting eagerly for my next instructions.

Slowly, I slide the hem of my dress up. I already took my underwear off in the elevator, so I'm exposed to him as soon as it reaches my hips.

His eyes widen and his mouth opens as he begins to pant, his hand flexing on his crotch again.

"No touching yourself," I tell him. Then I place one leg over his shoulder, opening myself up to him completely. "Now…make me come."

Ten minutes and a fake orgasm later, Tom stands to his feet with a wet spot on his pants and a blush on his cheeks.

"Sorry," he murmurs, embarrassed by how quickly everything happened. "It was a…rough week."

I smile warmly, and I barely have to force it. For one, I

only ever want my clients to feel satisfied. But for another, I'm never going to complain about an appointment ending early.

"I'm sorry to hear that," I tell him as I stand to study my reflection in the mirror. "Do you want to tell me about it?"

But I know the answer even as I ask the question. While some men like the company and actually want to talk, Tom only wants one thing. And he just got it.

"No, no, I don't want to bore you," he says, confirming my thoughts. "I…appreciate you coming by."

I turn and smile at him. "Anytime," I purr.

He becomes momentarily mesmerized by my lipstick, but with a two-day refractory period, his body isn't capable of doing anything about it. His eyes move up to meet mine, and this time, there's nothing sexual in his gaze.

He nods at the envelope on the dresser. "Your money is in there. I added a little extra as a thank you for fitting me in last-minute."

"You're too good to me," I say softly, placing my hand on his cheek before I step away. "Call me any time, okay? You know I love to see you."

I know I've done my job well when I see him buy the lie.

Ten minutes later, I've made myself publicly presentable again and tucked the money into my purse. Twenty-eight minutes after entering the hotel room, I'm leaving two thousand dollars richer.

As soon as the elevator doors close behind me, I pull out my phone to text the agency.

> Scarlett: Done early. Everything's fine. I just left the hotel.

Amara's text comes back immediately.

Amara: Enjoy the early night. Thanks for checking in.

My obligatory check-in complete, I slide my phone back into my purse.

I catch a taxi in front of the hotel without issue. It's New York City, after all. And it's easier than having my driver wait for an hour, which would clearly give away what I'm doing in the hotel.

Sliding into the backseat, I give the driver a polite smile and my address, then let out a heavy breath. I'm officially off work for another twenty-four hours. I could make more money if I saw more clients, but I have a strict one-man-a-day rule, six days out of the week.

When we reach my apartment building, I wordlessly pay the driver and climb out of the cab. With every step toward the lobby, I pray for the numbness to fade. For some life to return to my body after selling it.

This feeling is one of the reasons I schedule my appointments at night. Because the only way for me to shed the mask I don for my clients is to take a sleeping pill and hope the sunrise snaps me back to life.

This isn't the life I envisioned for myself.

# THREE
## NICO

The smell of sweat and Icy Hot is a comforting one. So is the sound of leather hitting leather, followed by the occasional gasp or cheer. It's a setting that's felt like home for as long as I can remember.

I pull on my boxing gloves and take my place at one of the heavy bags. And then I pummel the shit out of it.

Punch after punch, I lay into the bag, blowing right past the bell signaling the end of the round. It isn't until I've blown past the second bell without stopping that I even start to breathe heavy.

I slow only when I hear a whistle from behind me, followed by a murmured, "Damn, Nico."

Chest heaving, I stop throwing and turn around.

My two brothers, Lucas and Alexander, are standing at the wall. Lucas is in his perfectly tailored suit, so I know he came straight from court. Alexander is, surprisingly, wearing street clothes, so I know Lucas somehow convinced him to take a night off.

But none of that explains why they're both *here*, interrupting my workout.

"It appears I've called this intervention too late," I hear Lucas mutter as he pushes off the wall. "You look like you're attempting to punch your way through that bag."

Panting, I brace my gloved hands on my knees and give my brother a confused glare. "What intervention?"

"The one where we take you out to blow off some steam because you're wound way too tight," he says dryly.

My brow furrows. "I have a *fight* coming up."

"That doesn't explain why you haven't had a rest day in nine days."

Scowling, I look around to see who ratted me out. When my coach doesn't meet my eyes, I sigh.

I know I've been pushing myself too hard. But it's hard not to. My off days are when the restlessness hits the hardest, and when I would normally retreat to dating apps or the bar, I can't do that anymore.

So when the need to get out of my head gets to be too much, I find myself back here. Hitting the bag.

"Now go take a shower so we can get out of here. You're one round away from us dragging you out the door."

I let out a tired breath of defeat. "Alright, alright," I concede, ripping the Velcro off my gloves. "Just...gimme a minute."

"You have ten," Lucas says in a no-nonsense voice. "And then you're leaving with us, with or without clothes. You need a night off, little bro."

"Yeah, because *that* wouldn't start a riot in the gym," I grumble as I stride out of the bag room.

Eight minutes later—Lucas does *not* pull punches—I'm showered and dressed in clean clothes, following my two brothers out into the night air.

It's a Tuesday night in Philadelphia. The MMA gym was filled with fighters, but the bars and restaurants are packed. It takes a five-minute walk for us to find the one Lucas is looking for.

I quirk an eyebrow as I look around. "A taco bar? Really? I thought that would be below Your Highness's standards."

Lucas just rolls his eyes at me. "Just because I work with millionaires doesn't mean I'm not the same kid who shoved your face into Mom's bowl of guacamole on taco night. Now, come on. I had Lila save us a seat in the back so *Your* Highness doesn't get easily recognized."

Now I'm the one rolling my eyes. But I follow him anyway, because he's right.

I went pro in the MMA circuit about three years ago. And while I'm not anywhere near the top 10 in my weight class, I've made enough of a ripple that the city often recognizes me.

Doesn't matter. That was never why I fought, anyway. The fame, the money, none of that has anything to do with my love of fighting. It's the sport I love. The physicality of it, the competition—the *beauty* of it.

Sure enough, there's a table waiting for us in the back. Lucas gives the waitress a smile dripping in charm before taking a seat and immediately opening the giant menu. I sit beside him, and Alexander takes the seat that puts his back to the wall.

"So, what can I get you boys?" Lila asks sweetly, her eyes bouncing around the table. With our group being made up of a professional athlete, a dressed-to-the-nines lawyer, and a giant, bearded guy who's clearly ex-military, it seems like she's trying to decide who she wants to flirt with.

In the end, Lucas is the obvious choice. Especially when he turns to her with another devastating smile and says, "Can I get two shots of tequila to start us off? Normally, it would be three, but this guy"—he jerks his thumb at me—"has to treat his body like a temple, or something." He grins when Lila giggles. "And I'll take a Corona as well, sweetheart."

"Corona for me, too," Alexander says gruffly. That's three more words than I expected him to say.

I sigh and lower the menu. "Just a water for me, please."

The waitress beams at us as she nods. "Of course. I'll grab those right now, and then be right back to take your food orders or answer any questions."

When she's out of earshot, I drop the menu onto the table harder than I mean to.

"Alright, so what is this? What are we really doing here?"

Lucas gives me a pitying look as Alexander studies the cut-up wooden table we're sitting at. Clearly, this is going to be a fight with my louder brother.

"Exactly what I said at the gym," Lucas says simply, dropping his own menu. "You're wound up lately. I mean, *insanely* wound up. You're killing yourself at the gym, even *with* a fight coming up. You're going to burn out if you haven't already. So, what gives?"

I fidget with the saltshaker on the table, spinning it between my hands. "Nothing," I grumble. "I'm fine."

"Is it a fighting thing?" Alexander asks.

I look up at my oldest brother in surprise. It's rare for him to chime in on family discussions, or even to voice his opinion. The fact that he did has me studying him a little more closely.

He looks worried. I mean, he always looks worried, but that's a result of his days as a Marine. He's gotten better since he came home, relaxing more, jumping a lot less, but there's always a part of him that seems stressed. Tonight, though, that's amplified.

My shoulders immediately droop. I never want to stress my family out, Alexander especially.

I suck in a big breath. "It's just... I don't know. I feel restless. You'd think two-a-days would burn me out, but I don't think it's a physical thing. I feel *aimless*." I straighten, my words coming quicker as my desperate need to explain rises. "Fighting is great, and this isn't me saying I'm not grateful for this fight and how far I've gotten, but... I'm thirty years old. Shouldn't there be more to life than just my work?"

My brothers exchange a look. "*More* as in," Lucas starts slowly, "a wife and family? Is this you wanting to settle down?"

I let out a gust of an exhale and lean back in my chair. "No. I don't know. It sounds ridiculous when you say it like that. I don't necessarily want...*that*, I just want...*more*. I don't know how to explain it."

"You could date more," Alexander says with a slight shrug.

Lucas snorts. "I don't think that's possible. The man has more matches on dating apps than I would if I was on them."

"That's very helpful, thank you," I say, sending him a glare. Then I sigh and add, "And anyway, I'm in fight camp. Dating is off the table, regardless. If that's even the problem, which I'm not sure it is."

"And it's not a career thing?" Alexander asks. "Like a feeling fulfilled thing?"

"I doubt it," I mumble. "Fighting is incredibly fulfilling. It's not like I'm looking for a new hobby."

"We could try a pottery class, just to be sure," Lucas says helpfully.

My glare only narrows. He must sense I'm two seconds

away from standing up and leaving because he lifts his hands in surrender. "Sorry, just trying to throw some ideas out there."

I slump back into my seat. "I think I just need a change. Something new. Some*one* new. I don't know, it sounds stupid and vague."

My brothers share another curious look.

"We could plan a trip," Lucas suggests, turning back to me. "Get away for a little bit. Go to a random small town in Europe with no tourists."

A tired sigh escapes me. "Yeah, maybe."

"Think about it," Lucas says. "Even if we only go for a few days. You give me the green light, and I'll set it up, yeah?"

I nod, but my chest still feels tight. "Yeah, sure. I'll think about it. Thanks."

He claps his hands together. "Fantastic. Now that we've covered *that* topic, we can focus on getting drunk and sharing more of our feelings." He points a finger at Alexander. "Starting with how *you're* doing, Marine."

At that, Alexander's eyes turn to slits. "Don't make me hang you on the coat hook behind you," he growls. He looks to me for backup, but I just shrug.

"Hey, you sprang this intervention on *me*. This is all you two."

With perfect timing, the waitress returns with our drinks. She sets everything down on the table, then straightens with a smile.

"Alright, have we decided on any food? Can I get you a starter? Maybe some chips and guacamole?"

*"No!"* we all shout in unison.

It startles Lila back a step, so Lucas quickly reassures her.

"Sorry, darling. Guacamole brings back bad memories. No, we'll just take some nachos for now."

"Actually, I'll take an order of the carne asada tacos," I interject, feeling my stomach rumble after a too-long workout.

"Make that three," Alexander tacks on in a gruff voice.

Lucas's brow furrows. "Since when do you order for me?"

Alexander only blinks at him. "Who said it was for you?"

I hide my chuckle in a sip of water.

Lucas sighs and hands Lila his menu. "Fine. Make it four orders of the carne asada tacos for these animals." Once she's gone, he takes the shot of tequila in hand and lifts it into the air. "A toast. To…figuring out the point." He looks around our table with a thoughtful glance as we lift our own glasses. "For all of us," he adds quietly.

***

Two hours later, I'm making my way outside for some fresh air. Lucas and Alexander are still inside throwing back shots. Lucas, because it's his job to entertain, and Alexander, because he's a gigantic human being.

Finally outside, I pull in a deep breath as I lean against the brick wall. As much as I hate to admit it, I did need this tonight. It didn't solve my general restlessness, but it softened the edges.

I'm still leaning against the wall, my eyes closed, when the voices from inside get louder as the restaurant's door opens beside me.

"Nico. Whoa, how you doing, man?"

I peel my eyelids open and turn my head to see who called my name.

It's Tyler Hatchett, another MMA fighter in the Philly circuit. He fights out of another gym, and he's a different level and weight class than me, so our interactions have been limited but amicable.

"Tyler." I nod politely. "I'm good. You?"

He lets out a heavy sigh. "Better now that I'm out of there. I've got a date to get to."

I huff a laugh and melt back into the wall. "Oh, yeah? Who's the unlucky lady you have to pay for that?"

That earns me a laugh in return. "You have no idea how spot on you are."

Head tilting, I train my full attention on him again. "What does *that* mean?"

He chuckles as he places a cigarette between his teeth. "Relax. More people do it than you think." When I only stare at him, bewildered, he lights the cigarette and inhales before explaining, "It's not that bad. The high-end ones are like a match-making service: they interview you, figure out what you want out of it, then match you with the right girl. It's easy. And there's no pressure, no games, no expectations. Way better than dating, if you ask me." Taking another puff, he waves the cigarette around. "And you have that fight coming up, don't you? So you don't want the mind games that come with dating right now anyway."

It takes me a second to find the words. I never even would've *thought* of hiring a…a prostitute? Escort? What's the difference?

"Isn't that illegal?" is what I end up blurting out.

Tyler chuckles once more, clearly amused by how taken aback I am. "No. Not really. It's an escort agency. They're just setting up dates, that's it. Doesn't even have to include sex." He digs around in his pocket for a moment before pulling out a business card and extending it to me. "Don't believe me? Give them a call. They'll explain everything. Put your sweet little mind at ease."

I don't know why I take the card, but I do. And I stare at it numbly as Tyler blows out a final puff of smoke.

"Alright, I'm out of here," he says, putting his cigarette out on the sidewalk. Then he grins and claps me on the shoulder. "Don't look so scandalized, Price. They already debunked the 'no sex before a fight' rule. Go get your glorified orgasm."

I'm still staring at the business card when Lucas sticks his head out of the restaurant.

"Hey. You coming back? I think I finally got Alexander drunk. He's two seconds from wearing the sombrero one waitress keeps trying to put on him." He glances down at my hands. "What's that?"

I hurriedly shove the card in my pocket. "Nothing. Just… ran into an old friend."

Lucas nods thoughtfully. "Ah. That's cool." When I don't move, he quirks an eyebrow. "So…you coming?"

I shake the bizarre thoughts from my mind and grab the door handle. "Yeah. Yeah, I'm coming."

But that card burns a hole in my back pocket, and in the back of my brain.

---

My apartment is entirely too quiet.

Water bottle in hand, I sink onto my couch with a groan. After a long day of training, every muscle in my body is sore. I'm exhausted. I should be passing out the second I get home.

But I don't. I never do. Because my mind won't stop spinning.

I meant what I said to my brothers. At my age, shouldn't I

have already found the point of life? I mean, I love fighting, but realistically, it's going to be a very short period in my life. It's a short period in every fighter's life. What do I have beyond fighting?

Guilt sits heavy in my stomach at having these thoughts during a fight camp. I'm grateful for the fight Lucas got me, and this is probably the worst time to be spiraling, but...I can't help it.

I drag a hand down my face with a sigh. Is this what a midlife crisis feels like? Maybe I should've been more honest with my brothers about what's going on in my head.

About my recent thoughts of retiring.

Maybe I should take that trip with them. I need a change of scenery, if nothing else. Because once I'm past the fight, this feeling is only going to grow.

And just like it has for the past two days, my conversation with Tyler comes back to the forefront.

The curiosity has been eating away at me. Is it true what he said about escort agencies being common? I've never thought about them outside of TV shows, but he made it sound like professional athletes use them all the time. And not just for sex. Are they really like a glorified matchmaking service?

I take another sip of my water. Should I call them? If it's legal, and the boundaries are set for both parties, then it's just a no strings attached hour with a woman, right? That's not a *date*. There's no expectation for a future, no need for games —it takes out all the parts of dating that have been stressing me out. It removes the potential for a genuine connection, too, but that's off the table leading up to this fight anyway.

Have I really reached the point of wanting to hire company? Am I really *that* lonely?

*Fuck.* Maybe.

I pull the card from my pocket where it's already worn down to a creased piece of paper. It's just a phone call, right? Worst case, I'm skeeved out and rip the card up.

Right?

*Ah, fuck it.*

# FOUR
## SCARLETT

When I left home at nineteen, I thought I was breaking free of the chains of my past. I thought if I moved to New York City, I'd finally be able to find myself. I envisioned exploring, making friends, trying new things. I envisioned an *exciting* new start.

Three years later, very little has changed. I'm just as numb to the world as I was when I left home. The only difference now is the amount in my bank account.

Every morning, my alarm goes off at 7:00 a.m., same as it has my entire life. Not so early that I don't get my full eight hours of sleep, but not late enough that I could be considered lazy.

Then it's right to the kitchen for a glass of water and a banana; just enough to give me a burst of energy for my workout. When I feel like splurging, I'll add a dollop of peanut butter. Once I've finished the last bite, I change into my only non-work clothes—athletic wear—and jump onto the treadmill in my living room.

Five miles later, I blend the same green shake I make

every morning. Full of vitamins, and with just enough calories to get me through the first half of my day.

After that, it's straight to the bathroom to shower and get ready. I have to run some errands today, but even if I wasn't leaving the apartment until my client appointment tonight, I would still go through my whole process to ensure I look presentable. It's a lengthy process, but I've been doing it for so long that I don't even notice it anymore.

In the shower, I wash my hair, exfoliate my body, and shave every inch that might grow hair. Once I'm toweled off and mostly dry, I reach for the body oil that makes my skin feel like silk. A quick inspection of my nails tells me I need to add a manicure and pedicure to my list today.

Then it's back to my hair. It took me a while to learn how to do the perfect blowout, but now it's become my go-to hairstyle. Once my hair goes up in curlers, I start my makeup.

Makeup took me far longer to master. If it wasn't for Amara taking me under her wing and helping me get on my feet, I still might not know the shades that compliment my skin and eyes. You'd think my mother would've taught me, considering she stressed that makeup was a necessity for women—just not *too* much—but I guess she couldn't be bothered to actually teach the lesson.

It takes me an entire hour to perfect my face. Full coverage, a touch of life on the cheeks, subtle eyeshadow to complement my eyes; the only part of my routine I leave for later is the red lip that's become my signature. For now, I just swipe on some gloss.

By 10 a.m., I'm ready for the only part of my day that evokes any kind of emotion in me these days: class.

It took me a long time to convince myself I could—and should—enroll in an undergraduate program. Because when you grow up with your mother constantly telling you beauty is more important than brains, and shushing you whenever your brains made an appearance, your academic interests consequently dim.

But after a year of living in the city, too scared to do things on my own and very much realizing that New York City is *terrifying* compared to a small southern town, the boredom started to eat at me. Only working two, three hours a night, meant I had a lot of free time.

Apparently, Arizona State University's marketing really works, because after one too many ads and emails, I became curious. And when I looked up their programs, they sucked me in. Every class description looked similar to the things I was reading in my spare time anyway. So, I applied for their liberal arts program, made my first tuition payment, and started online classes three months later.

While I'm waiting for today's live session to start, I log into my school email and LMS dashboard to check my to-do list. I have class now until eleven, then nothing until work at 5 p.m. For my psychology course, I have some reading to finish, but technically, that assignment isn't due for two weeks, so I could put that off until tomorrow. Which means I have time to get my nails done after my hair appointment, because God forbid Dr. Schaffer sees me without perfect toenails—

The ding of the professor starting the session shakes me from my thoughts.

"Good morning, everyone. Hope you all had a great weekend. We'll get started in just a minute."

The lecture is an easy one to follow. I do most of the work ahead of time, partly because I'm fascinated by the subject and want to understand everything, and partly because I have all the time in the world to do supplemental research. I could zone out if I wanted to, but I'm so

27

relieved to have something to *do* that I don't let myself do that.

On the screen, my social psychology professor switches the slide and asks, "Can anyone tell me the difference between conformity, compliance, and obedience?"

As I twirl the pen in my hand, I mentally recite the answer to the question, waiting for one of my peers to volunteer.

When no one does, I suddenly hear, "Scarlett, want to take a stab at it?"

My head jerks up, my cheeks heating. I hate being put on the spot in class. I can never get the balance right with being a good student and earning the title of teacher's pet. I *hate* sounding like a know-it-all.

"Um…" I fidget in my seat, glancing nervously at the faces on my screen. "Well, conformity has to do with fitting into a group. I think." *I know.*

My professor nods. "Good. Go on."

"Compliance has to do with complying with a request, as in, the case of doing a friend a favor." Another nod. "And then…obedience is following orders?"

He's watching me as if he's trying to figure me out. After a moment of hesitation, he says, "All correct. Anything else to add? Your assignment last week was remarkable in its breakdown."

I try not to beam at the praise. Being complimented for my brain—instead of scolded—always hits harder than I'm prepared for.

Nibbling on my bottom lip, I debate my answer. But half the class isn't even paying attention, so I decide: *screw it. I'm paying hard-earned money for this education.*

"The most important differences have to do with the power dynamics," I start carefully. "For conformity, the influence comes from social pressure. For compliance, it's from another person. And for obedience, it's specifically from an authority figure."

*Is that amusement on my professor's face?* "Very good. Anything else?"

"Yeah." I continue, and he doesn't hide his grin anymore. "I think the motivation behind these three ideas is important, too."

"How so?"

I sit up straighter, a spark of excitement jolting me. "Well, as I said, conformity has to do with social pressure. So the motivation behind it is wanting to fit in. And with compliance, you're fulfilling someone's request. So the motivation is either wanting to help, or possibly to avoid conflict. And with obedience, there's an authority figure involved, which means you either fear being punished if you *don't* abide by the order, or you genuinely believe in their leadership. Either way, the motivations highlight big differences between the three."

By the time I finish speaking, my professor looks impressed—but not surprised. He gives an approving nod and says, "That's very insightful, Scarlett. And correct on all counts."

I duck my head to hide my smile.

"You should volunteer more. The class would benefit from your insights."

My head snaps up at that. Nervously, my gaze darts to the other students to see if that comment solidified the feared teacher's pet status.

But half are still nodding off, some look curious, and the rest are furiously typing notes.

I let out a relieved breath and nod at the professor.

The rest of the class goes smoothly. I'm not put on the spot, but I do offer two more answers. By the time the hour ends, there's the slightest sizzle of life in my veins.

Normally on my day off, I'd rot away in front of the TV and try not to think about the parallel universe where I'm happy, have friends, and I wake up with a desire to explore the city. But I don't want to do that today. Maybe I'll *actually* explore the city. I could take a walk and go shopping. I have plenty of clothes, but it's been a while since I've shopped for myself. Or maybe I'll finally take the ferry out to the Statue of Liberty—

My phone rings, stemming all thoughts of plans for the day.

Amara's the only one who ever calls me. And the reminder of my job is enough to make every ounce of excitement freeze in my veins.

"Scarlett," she says sweetly when I answer. "How are you today?"

I let out an unfeeling hum. "I'm okay."

"Class was good? How did you do on your exam yesterday?"

I hide my sigh as I slump back into my chair. Leave it to me to find the one madam who genuinely cares about her girls.

In an instant, my mind flashes back to the night I met Amara.

I'd been on my own for exactly one day and was already being slapped in the face by reality.

Namely, that the world was much more expensive than I realized and that I had zero marketable skills to find a job.

I'd spent all day searching, growing more and more defeated with every rejection. I barely had enough money for another night at a cheap hotel and I hadn't eaten anything all day, too nervous to buy anything more than a hot dog from a street vendor. By the time I ducked into a bar to ask for a glass of water, my hopelessness had grown to the same level it had been when I left home.

That's where Amara found me.

Apparently, she watched as I turned down a businessman's advances at the bar, in awe of the gentle way I did it. With the way she tells the story, I was so polite about it that he wasn't even offended by the rejection.

She pulled me aside after that, bought me a drink, and asked me what I was doing so far from home.

Maybe it was naïve of me, but I felt like I could trust her. Despite knowing she was a no-nonsense woman, there was also a softness in her eyes that made me think she genuinely cared.

Or maybe it just reminded me of motherly affection I subconsciously craved.

I told her all about my sob story. How I'd run away from a bad marriage and a worse family, and now found myself alone and broke in a city that I thought would be a fresh start. How I had no idea what I was going to do for money because I'd never had a job and had no skills.

The part of that night I remember the most is how Amara's eyes lit up when I said that.

*You have more skills than you think, mia cara,* she said.

When I asked her what she meant, she told me she owned an escort agency and that she thought I would be a perfect addition.

I was too shocked to even laugh. She wanted to hire me as a…hooker?

*Not as a hooker*, she corrected. *An escort.*

*What's the difference?* I asked.

*As an escort agency, we offer companionship for dinners, business outings, and other social events*, she explained. *Both parties are consenting adults, and at no point are sexual favors being exchanged for money.*

I must have given her a look of disbelief, because she followed it up with, *Think of it this way instead: what if a seventy-year-old man loses his wife of fifty years and grows lonelier every day? Does he not deserve to have dinner with a pretty woman? To have an adult conversation with someone who likes him? Or if a man doesn't want to go alone to a mandatory work event, is it wrong for him to pay for a date?*

I remember feeling silly for my assumption. But that still didn't explain why she was telling me all this.

It wasn't until she said *Basically, I own an agency that pays women to stroke a man's ego the way you just did without even trying* that I understood.

She really was trying to recruit me.

*You're gorgeous, charming, and you have an incredible read on people. You'd be every man's dream date. I really do think you'd be a perfect escort. But...I also want to help you.*

Sometimes, when I look back, a part of me wants to slap that version of myself that believed a stranger just because she had motherly eyes.

It was then that my predicament truly registered. If I couldn't find a job within the next day, I'd either end up on the street or on the train back home. And neither option was acceptable.

We made a deal then. For one week, she'd put me up in an apartment in the building she owned. Food, clothes, everything included. And in exchange, I promised to talk to some of the girls who worked for her.

*Talk to them,* Amara pressed. *Ask them whatever questions you want. They'll not only confirm what I'm telling you, but you'll also see how much they love the job.* She started to tick things off on her fingers. *They control their own schedule, they make five times the money on a quarter of the time, and the only thing they have to do is fake interest in a man.* Her lip twitched. *As if women don't do that for free already.*

It sounded too good to be true, but I was too desperate to turn her down. When I shook her hand, it was for the sole reason that I wanted to buy myself another week to figure out a new plan.

Three years later, I know three things for certain:

1. Amara's words were genuine. She truly wanted to help me.

2. Working for an escort agency *doesn't* mean you need to sleep with clients. But you make a hell of a lot more money when you do.

3. Whatever I was hoping would be on the other end of that week, I never found it.

I wonder if she senses that. If it's the reason she pushed me to sign up for college courses, to find something that excites me the way arriving in New York City did all those years ago.

Why she inquires about my classes before she asks me anything else.

"I got a ninety-six on the exam," I answer her question, shaking away the memories of our past. "I only got one question wrong."

"See? I told you there was no need to stress," she chides. I can hear the proud smile in her voice when she adds, "As if you don't get an A on everything in that class."

It's that hint of care that always softens me with Amara.

It's unfortunate that it's always snuffed out as soon as she brings up work.

"The reason I'm calling is because I have a new client for you."

*Back to reality.*

"I know you're not fond of picking up new clients, but I have someone who I think would be perfect for you."

My spine stiffens at the suggestion.

I don't like taking on new clients. As a matter of fact, I hate it. Walking into a hotel room with a stranger, knowing he's paying me and that he could very well think he has the right to do anything he wants? It terrifies me. It doesn't matter that I'm the best girl Amara has at those first-time appointments, simply because I'm the best at reading what men want. I just...don't like it. It's the only time I feel unsure of myself. Things are much easier once I know what they expect from me and I can mold myself into whatever persona they want a woman to be. *That* I can do.

Amara sighs. "Eventually, you're going to have to replace the two clients you lost when they moved. Your roster is getting a little light. Now's as good a time as any to fluff it up."

Even though she's right, I'm suddenly finding it hard to care. It's not like I'm wanting for money. Even with a college tuition, I still make enough with this job to live comfortably. I don't *need* more clients.

Which Amara knows. And which begs the question...*why is she pushing for me to add this one?*

"Why do you think he'd be perfect for me?" I ask.

"He's...young. And has plenty of money. I think he would be a slam dunk. If you're going to take on any new clients, he's the perfect choice, Scarlett."

I chew on my bottom lip. "What does he do?"

Her hesitation tells me everything I need to know. "He's a professional MMA fighter."

I let out a tired exhale. "Amara, you know I don't do pro athletes." I'm not interested in the publicity they get *or* the risk that comes with their physical strength. Been there, done that.

"I know, I know. But listen to me. I couldn't find a single red flag. His background check is spotless, he's never had a PR crisis, and even the ex-girlfriends I talked to didn't have anything bad to say about him. They all said he was a genuinely sweet guy and the only reason the relationships didn't work out was because the connection went stale."

I'm momentarily distracted by the amusing picture of Amara going undercover to dig up dirt on a prospective client. It's the main reason I trust the dates she sets up for me. Because she knows exactly who she's putting into a room with her girls.

I rub at my temples with a wince, debating the risk that comes with a new client.

"What did he say he was calling for?" I ask finally.

"He said he didn't know." Does she sound...fond? "Said he just needed a change, and that he wanted some new company. Honestly, it sounded like he might even make it a conversation. Nothing else. He sounded...lonely. And sweet." Her voice softens even more, and she's definitely smiling. "Perfect for you."

I let out a heavy breath, accepting my fate. She's right; I need to replace the two clients I just lost. And I'll have to start somewhere.

"I want security *in* the hotel that night," I demand. Needlessly. Because if there's one thing Amara does, it's protect her girls.

"Scarlett, you know I'd never put you at risk. It's already taken care of."

A headache starts to pound at the base of my skull. "Fine. I'll do it. When?"

"This Thursday. At the Ritz."

I wince. That's only three days away.

"Just wear your usual and go in with an open mind. Feel him out. I don't need to tell you how to get a read on him. You do that naturally."

"What's his name? I want to look him up."

"Nico Price." She sounds teasing. "You might not hate me so much after you look him up."

Doubtful, but hearing her say that eases my tension the tiniest bit.

"Okay. I guess...I'll check in with you Thursday."

"Before *and* after," Amara says sternly.

I roll my eyes. "Yes, mother."

After I end the call with Amara, I drop onto my couch with an exhausted exhale.

*Couch rotting it is.*

# FIVE
## NICO

*I'm nervous.*

It doesn't make sense. Not just because I never get nervous about these things, but also because this is the only date I *shouldn't* be nervous about. I'm literally paying for the guarantee of a good date.

And yet...

I arrive at our meeting spot a half hour early. To avoid traffic, I made the drive from Philly to New York earlier today, and I've already checked in to my hotel room. The agency strongly suggested a hotel bar for the first date—I'm assuming for safety reasons. I don't mind it, though. I want her to feel comfortable with me. Plus, a bar lounge makes for much easier conversation, too.

I take a seat at the bar and order a seltzer while I'm waiting. Ten minutes later, I realize I've nervously chugged the entire thing and decide to switch to still water.

Spinning my watch around my wrist, I look around the bar once more. The agency showed me a picture of my date, so I know what she looks like, but I have no idea if she knows what *I* look like. Does doing a background check mean they sent her my dating profile and picture? Does she even care about that stuff?

Meanwhile, I have her entire profile saved on my phone, and I've referred to it way too many times this week. I couldn't help it.

*Daisy. 22. From North Carolina, recently moved to the Big Apple. Plays the piano, loves animals, and her ideal date is listening to live music.*

Based on her profile and her picture, she seems like a sweet Southern girl who yearned for the city life. Ironically, I would've matched with her instantly if she were on a dating app. I've been a city boy my entire life and would've jumped at the chance to show her around NYC. Add in some dogs and the preference for a quieter, softer life, and I'm sold.

I tried to look at the matchmaking call as just that, a dating service, but knowing that it's not made the whole thing feel…weird. I just couldn't shake the knowledge that my money could include sex if I wanted it to.

*Fuck.* Maybe this is a bad idea. I'm not an escort guy. What am I even doing here? All I wanted was to not feel lonely for one goddamn night.

I should leave. I'll just call the agency, tell them I changed my mind. I'm sure they get that a lot, right? Guys with cold feet? I'm sure it would be—

But before I can so much as reach for my phone, my breath freezes in my lungs.

Because *there she is.*

It's not an exaggeration to say she's the most beautiful woman I've ever seen. I've been around plenty of beautiful women in my life, but there's something about *this* woman that makes it hard to breathe. It's her look, her walk, her smile… Everything.

She's wearing a little black dress that hugs every curve of

her body and black heels that make her legs look even longer. And she's *tall*. I watch as she enters the hotel and walks toward the bar, her hips swaying with every step.

Her hair bobs with the motion, too. It's blonde, long and flowing, and I immediately want to run my fingers through it. But then my gaze locks onto her lips, and I become singularly focused on what it would be like to kiss her.

She's wearing the sexiest shade of red lipstick I've ever seen. I watch as she smiles politely at a passerby, and I decide *yeah, she's definitely the most beautiful woman I've ever seen.*

It takes her locking eyes with me for me to get my shit together. By the time she reaches me, I've somehow managed to compose myself enough to not look like a bumbling idiot in front of her.

"Hi," she says with a smile. "Are you Nico?"

*Christ.* She has the voice of a siren. I'm tongue-tied all over again.

"Yeah," I manage to get out. "Are you Daisy?"

Her smile widens. "I am. It's so nice to meet you."

*It's nice to meet you, too.*

*God, you're beautiful.*

I don't say either of those things. I can't. I'm stuck on her lips again.

Either she doesn't notice, or she takes pity on me, because she glances toward the lounge area and asks, "Should we take a seat? Or are you comfortable here?"

*The date. Right. Talking.*

"Let's take a seat," I rush to say. When I reach for my glass, I finally think to ask her, "Would you like something to drink? I was a little early, so I took the liberty of getting a drink already."

She glances over my arm to the glass I'm holding. "Sure. What are you drinking?"

"Uh…different variations of water," I answer with a wince. "Sorry, I'm not very exciting right now."

An amused smile tugs at her lips. "Somehow, I highly doubt that," she purrs, and I swear to God, I could fall at this woman's feet.

She looks at my glass again, making her decision. "I'll take a water, too."

And then it hits me. "Oh. Uh, no, that's not—" I let out a laugh. "I'm not in recovery or anything. I'm just in training and can't afford the calories. Please, order a drink if you'd like one."

Her curiosity piques at that, but instead of a follow-up question, she says, "In that case, I'd love a glass of their Pinot Noir. Please."

I'm already waving down the bartender. I left him a hefty cash tip before she arrived so he beelines over to me, and less than a minute later, I'm handing Daisy the glass of red wine.

"Thank you," she says sweetly.

I nod, finally feeling myself loosening up in her presence. I even manage a smile in response. "You're welcome." Gesturing toward the lounge, I ask, "Should we sit?"

She leads the way and ends up choosing a pair of lounge chairs tucked against the back wall. There's a small table between them, but for the most part, they're right up against each other on a slight angle. I watch as she spins and settles gracefully.

"So," she starts, crossing her legs and taking a sip of her wine. "You're an athlete? What sport?"

I place my water on the table and take my seat beside her. "I'm an MMA fighter."

Her eyebrows lift. "Wow. That's an…intense sport."

I chuckle, used to the reaction. "That's putting it lightly."

"What made you choose that?" she asks, taking another sip.

I shrug, twirling my glass in thought. "I guess I kinda just fell into it," I answer honestly. "I grew up with two brothers, one of which ended up in the military, so my entire childhood was already fighting. Wrestling coach found me in high school, and then when MMA started getting popular, I switched to an MMA gym my junior year." I look up to see her studying me curiously. "I've been training ever since."

Daisy's forehead creases with the slightest frown. "But… you're in the UFC. Are you telling me you just *happened* to end up in the greatest martial arts organization in the world?"

Slowly, a grin forms on my face. *She looked me up.*

"I didn't realize you were a fellow MMA fan," I say casually.

The sweetest pink blush tinges her cheeks. "I-I'm not," she says. I secretly love the subtle shift from confident escort to blushing woman.

It makes this feel real.

After a moment, she sighs and says, "Okay, fine, I stalked you a little bit. I got curious."

My grin widens.

"And…I had to. To be safe."

All humor drops from my face and I nod once, stiffly. "Good. You should be safe."

But then the reminder makes something else occur to me. When I frown, her eyebrows narrow in confusion.

"*Are* you safe?" I demand. "I mean, do they really just send you to meet with strange men? What if I was dangerous? I punch men in the face for a living, for fuck's sake. What if I hurt you?"

I'm startled out of my rage when I feel her warm touch on my hand where it lies on the armrest of the chair.

The words die in my throat.

"I'm safe, I promise," she says softly. "We have all kinds of security measures. Background checks, panic buttons, that kind of thing. Don't worry."

I don't think my frown lightens even a little bit. I sound grumpy as shit when I say, "Still. You shouldn't trust anyone."

"I don't," she responds, amused.

I tilt my head in thought. "You should learn some self-defense. Have you ever taken a class?"

*Why does she think this is funny?* "I haven't, no."

"You should. Security or not, you should know how to protect yourself." I hesitate before adding, "I can teach you, if you want."

"That's very sweet of you," she says with a smile. "Not tonight, but…if you'd like, we can do it another time."

My frown returns. "Not if *I* like. If *you'd* like."

"Nico, I'm here for *you*," she says. "You make the decisions here."

*I hate the sound of that.* "I don't like having that kind of power over you. Especially knowing you don't know self-defense."

Her smile grows. It's only when she pulls her hand away that I realize she's been touching me this whole time, gently sweeping her fingers over the back of my hand.

I stare at my hand, at the absence of *hers*, wondering how to get it back.

"How about this," she starts. "If you decide you want to see me again, you can show me some of the basics next time."

"Deal," I agree. *Way* too fast.

That fondness on her face shines brighter. "I think you might be the sweetest man I've ever met, Mr. Price."

I can't stop staring at her. "Just Nico is fine," I say dazedly.

Because *Mr. Price* makes this sound like it's not a real date.

I look at her with new eyes, finally realizing something I should've picked up on when I was making the call to the agency.

"Your name isn't Daisy, is it?"

She might not even realize that the smile she gives me is a little sad. It's also the only answer I get.

"That wasn't me pushing for your real name," I hurry to add. The last thing I want her to think is that I'm an overeager client who wants to push her boundaries. "It was just an observation."

Coming face to face with the knowledge that this is a fake date bothers me.

"Can I call you something else?" I ask, desperate to take control of this night, to make things feel a little more real. I swivel my head to meet her eyes and find her watching me. "I mean, if that's offensive, then forget it, but—"

"You can call me whatever you'd like, Nico."

Thank God, she sounds like she means it. I would've called her Daisy if she wanted me to, but a part of me likely would've felt distant for the rest of the night.

*Why do I suddenly need this to feel real?*

*And why did I think picking a new name for her would make that possible?*

A nickname, I decide. In that sense, people pick names for others all the time.

"Can I call you Red?" I finally ask. With the way my

focus keeps going back to her lips, it's the first thing that comes to mind. It feels fitting, too.

I don't understand why she looks amused by the nickname, but I don't question it because it's followed by a flash of adoration. And *that's* real enough.

"I like Red," she says.

*Thank fuck.*

"Well, in that case…it's nice to meet you, Red."

Those red lips curl into a genuine smile.

"Likewise, Nico."

# SIX
## SCARLETT

*This guy is way too hot to be hiring an escort.*

I knew what he looked like, of course, but I wasn't prepared for what he *looked like*. I wasn't prepared for the way he would look at *me*.

He looks both sweet and rugged, somehow. It's clear his nose has been broken a few times, but even with the scars and crooked feature, his eyes are soft and he's wearing a half-smile. And the first time that dimple popped out on his left cheek, I just about melted.

He's dressed simply in jeans and a dark-gray Henley. Add in his wavy brown locks that I want to sink my fingers into and the intoxicating smell of whatever cologne he's wearing, and I've been lost in his aura since I walked up to him.

Normally, a good-looking man wouldn't make me question why he's calling me. Plenty of guys are hot *and* assholes. But not Nico. He's like a walking green flag.

*Amara was right.*

I want so badly to ask him why he called the agency, but I can't. I have to play the game.

"So…you're from Philly?" I ask instead, shifting in a way that makes Nico look at my legs. "Did you grow up there?"

Sure enough, his gaze drops, then quickly lifts to my eyes. His throat bobs on a swallow as he nods. "Born and raised," he says in a rough voice.

"I've never been," I say conversationally. "Would you recommend it?"

"I think everyone should visit," he answers with a shrug. "It's a great city. Great restaurants, fun bars, plenty of history. I almost like to think of it as a smaller, more manageable New York City." When I let out a thoughtful hum, he tilts his head and asks, "So, you're from North Carolina?"

South Carolina, actually, but I keep my agency profile close enough to the truth that it doesn't feel like a huge fib.

I nod. "Born and raised," I parrot with a smile.

"That's a big move, coming to New York," Nico comments curiously.

"Just a little," I tease with a smile.

He hesitates. "Can I ask what brought you to the city?"

"I just needed a change," I tell him honestly.

It took me a little while to figure out how to navigate the personal questions on the job. When clients don't want sex, they want conversation, and even though most of that tends to focus on the client, it's still natural for people to ask about me. There's a level of security in vague answers that I use to protect myself, but it's also essential to sprinkle some of the truth in. It makes it easier to weave the spell they're looking for.

"Was that a culture shock?" Nico asks me.

I blow out a breath. "Definitely. I thought I could prepare myself for it, but there's no preparing for this city. Especially at nineteen."

*Shoot.* I didn't mean to let that detail slip out.

I know Nico picks up on it because his eyebrows lift. Maybe he can even tell that I hadn't intended to tell him that, because he doesn't press it.

I hurry to shift the topic to something I can use to figure out why he called the agency.

"So, when you're not fighting, what do you like to spend your time doing?" I ask, casually dropping my hand to the side table so I can touch his hand again. "Any fun hobbies?"

I think Nico might be able to read me better than I was expecting because his gaze drops to my hand before looking out at the bar with a thoughtful expression.

"I can't remember the last time I did something fun," he muses. "I mean, outside of the occasional dinner with my brothers."

*Interesting.* Maybe I'm just some fun he's looking for?

"So you're close with your brothers?"

He nods. "I'm close with my whole family. They're my best friends."

*What does that feel like?*

I shake away the errant thought before it can sour my mood. I need the focus on *Nico.*

"That's sweet," I say, gently moving my hand to his. "It's really refreshing to hear that from a man."

His eyes drop to my hand and stay there. I'm half-wondering if he's going to pull away, he's staring so intently. But after a moment, he wraps his thumb tentatively around mine.

When he lifts his head and our gazes meet, there's a low simmer of fire in his eyes. He's affected by my touch.

*Good.*

"So…if dinner with your family is the only thing you do outside of the gym, it sounds like fighting doesn't leave time for much else in your life." I brush my thumb over the back

47

of his hand, momentarily distracted by the sight of them. They're calloused and rough; they look like a *man's* hands. "That sounds pretty stressful."

His gaze *burns*. "It— Yeah, sometimes it's a little stressful." Something flashes in his eyes, too quick for me to read. "In all honesty, it's one of the reasons I called you."

*Now we're getting somewhere.*

I lay my *escort* voice on thick, stepping fully into character. I'm here to do a job, after all. Not get distracted by a hot guy with an adorable dimple.

"I can absolutely help with that," I purr, sliding my finger up and down his forearm.

To my surprise, Nico stops my touch by gently grabbing my hand. My eyes dart up to his and widen.

"Do *you* have any fun hobbies?" he asks.

For a moment, I can only blink at him. I was two seconds from asking if he wanted to go upstairs, and he stops me to ask about hobbies? Who *is* this guy?

I can't remember the last time I tripped over an answer during an appointment. But right now, I can only open and close my mouth in surprise.

"I guess that means we both work too hard," Nico comments softly.

This is not how this conversation was supposed to go. There's nothing sexy about this, nothing that might make the client feel good.

*What am I doing?*

I need to redirect us. Get this back on track.

"If you could spend a rest day doing anything, what would you do?" I manage to ask.

A warmth lights in his eyes that I am entirely unprepared for. His lips lift in the barest hint of a smile.

"I'd come see you."

My cheeks heat at that. As does the rest of me. *He's… flirting with me.*

*And in a way that's making me feel like a teenager with her first crush.*

"I thought I was supposed to be the one doing the charming," I whisper, unable to take my eyes off him.

He doesn't look away either. "Trust me. You are."

I can feel my pulse hammering in my neck, my skin growing hot at his words and proximity. *Who's seducing who here?*

I glance at his lips before I can control the impulse. I don't ever kiss clients, but suddenly, all I can think about is what kind of kisser Nico would be.

*Would he be gentle? Take his time? Or would he flip a switch and become an animal?*

I have to clear my throat before I can bring myself to ask, "Do you want to go someplace a little…quieter?"

For the first time, there's a flash of indecision in his eyes. *Does he not want to include the physical aspect in his booking? Did I read him wrong?*

But then that heat flames right back to life. "Only if you do, Red."

Somehow, the nickname makes me even hotter for him. I've never before been excited to sleep with a client, but with Nico…

I stand from my chair and extend a hand to him.

"I would like that very much."

# SEVEN
## NICO

I'm in a daze the entire walk to my hotel room.

Once Daisy pulled me to my feet, she never let go of my hand. Even in the elevator, she kept a hold of it as we silently watched the floor numbers ascend.

The only thing I could think about was how good she smells, and how beautiful she is. I couldn't believe she was here with *me*.

Then she was pulling me in the direction of my room, the hotel key I'd given her in hand. And the only thing I could think about was how long her legs were, and how perfectly that dress hugged her ass.

I'm no longer in control of anything when she pushes the door open and leads me into my hotel room. I follow blindly as she pushes me down onto the couch.

I can't take my eyes off her as she takes one, two swaying steps toward me, until she's standing right in front of me.

And then she hikes her dress up an extra inch and plants one knee on the couch beside my hip.

I'm not breathing when she drops her other knee on the other side.

My hands go to her waist before I can think better of it. I don't know if I want to pull her closer or keep her at bay so I can stare at her for a little longer, but she takes the decision out of my hands a moment later. Instead of dropping her weight onto my lap, she sits back on my thighs.

"Tell me if I do something you don't want," she whispers, sliding the tiniest bit closer as her hands go to my shoulders.

Swallowing roughly, I nod. "You, too."

Now it's her that's swallowing. "They told you my limits?" she asks breathily.

I nod again. Nothing rough, basically. No choking, spanking, anything beyond a light slap to the ass. No bondage. No kissing.

*No kissing.*

My gaze goes to her lips before I can curb the instinct. Those perfect lips, that intoxicating color... I wonder if they'd leave a stain on me if I kissed her. I wish they would.

Suddenly, kissing her is all I can think about.

I have to force my gaze from her lips to her eyes. "Yes, they told me. You can trust me to keep them."

She smiles, and I see something flicker in her eyes. "Trust isn't something I know how to do," she says, almost to herself.

But then she shifts forward, coming into contact with my cock that's hardened to steel, and any question I have disappears into a wisp of smoke when she drops her head back with a throaty moan.

"Fuck," I grit out, unwittingly squeezing her hips in my hands.

My expression has her head raising, a seductive smile sliding across her lips. I feel like I'm missing something, like she's hiding something, and—*fuck*—if I could just *kiss* her—

She grinds forward, then back, the heat of her clothed pussy over my jeans making me incapable of thought.

"Jesus, look at you," I breathe, uncaring how I'm coming off right now. I'm powerless against it. "I could come just looking at you."

Humming thoughtfully, her hips circle, once, twice, three times, until I still her with my hands.

She looks at me with a smile. "I can make that happen, if you'd like."

I bark out a harsh laugh. "I don't doubt that. But no, I'd prefer to be a little more hands-on."

Her fingertips brush from my shoulder, over to my neck, then down my chest. They only still when I gently grip her hand over my stomach.

Her eyes are twinkling when she looks up and meets my gaze. "Whatever you'd like, Nico."

And there it is again. That…*something*.

Carefully, I ask, "What if I say I'd like to do something *you* like to do?"

That twinkle doesn't dim a watt. "I'd say I'm at your command."

My eyes narrow slightly. Then my hands fall to the cushions beside me. "Alright, then. Tell me what *you'd* like to do."

I don't understand why my words please her. But then she leans forward, close enough that I can feel the heat of her breath against my ear as she whispers, "I'd really like to suck your cock."

*Fuck.*

Every remaining oxygen molecule whooshes out of me. I *know* she's playing me, and yet—

She slides back until she's sitting on my thighs again, just far enough that she can reach between us and undo my jeans.

My head drops back against the cushions with another muttered, "*Fuck*."

"Let me take care of you," I hear, just as I feel her climb off me and tug my jeans down. I have no control over my hips lifting to help her with it. When I finally raise my head to look down, she's so gorgeous that I almost look at the ceiling again.

Instead, I watch as she settles on her knees between my legs, taking my leaking cock in her hand and stroking me. Her grip is firm, but I think she notices when my breathing grows heavier because it immediately tightens.

I don't even get a chance to wonder if I'm too dry for that kind of touch because a moment later, she rises on her knees, leans over me, and lets a wad of spit drip from her red lips onto my cock.

And then she grips me again and strokes. Hard.

"*Jesus fucking Christ*," I grit out. "That feels—"

She looks at me right as she takes me between her lips.

She knows exactly how she's making me feel.

I watch in silence, heart pounding in my ears, hands fisting the cushions beside me, as she starts to suck me. The same way she figured out how I like to be touched, she quickly figures out how I like to be tasted. She gives me long, deep sucks, moving slowly but consistently.

It's the greatest blow job I've ever gotten, and she's only been on her knees for about sixty seconds.

"Red…" I force out in warning.

She sits back, popping her mouth off my weeping cock. Her hand returns to my length as she brings her focus to me once more.

"What do you want, Nico?" she asks in that low, sexy voice. Her hand never stops moving. "Tell me. I'll give it to you."

For some reason, that's the moment that snaps me back to coherence.

*That's enough of that.*

I'm not blind to the fact that she's putting on an act right now. I don't even blame her for it. But I make a living out of reading people's micro expressions and seeing *hers* ignites something in my chest.

This might be transactional, but I'll be damned if it's not real.

I quickly pull my jeans up my hips, then lean forward to scoop her into my arms. She wraps her legs around my waist without hesitation.

I'm walking toward the suite's bedroom when she starts placing sweet kisses along my neck, down to the hem of my shirt. A shiver runs through me when one becomes a nip.

"Not fair," I growl, my steps quickening. "You're teasing me with that mouth, baby."

"I never said you couldn't have my mouth," she whispers into my ear.

Another growl rumbles through my chest, and this time, I stop in the bedroom doorway so I can fist my hand in her hair and bring her face to mine.

I don't kiss her, but *God,* do I want to. There's barely enough space for breath to pass between us, and I feel when her chest starts to heave. She's waiting to see if I'll cross her boundary.

No chance of that happening.

"I'm not going to kiss you," I say on a tight breath. "But I'm going to tease the fuck out of you."

I love the way her smile grows. "I hope you do," she says simply.

And because the urge to kiss her is becoming too strong, I take two big steps forward and press her into the bed.

I have to smother a groan when her legs stay wrapped around me, her hips already rolling against mine in a needy grind.

To keep another curse from slipping out, I stamp a hard kiss to the place where her shoulder and neck meet. But I'm so outmatched by this woman that I become immediately obsessed for a whole other reason.

Her soft skin. Her intoxicating scent. She's a goddess in human form.

Pressing kisses along her neck, her shoulder, the strap of her dress, I'm relieved to feel the beat of her pulse against my lips. She's not as unbothered as she wants me to think.

The realization triggers something in me. Desperation, maybe, but also a deep-seeded desire to make *her* feel good.

I slide my lips along her skin, over to the place right below her ear. "Can I touch you?" I ask. I won't even lie to myself about how much it sounds like begging.

"*Yes*," comes her breathless answer. "God, please, yes, touch me."

There's a tinge of stiffness in the words. As if it's a line she's used but has never meant before.

That's okay. As long as I can differentiate between her fake and real, I'm fine.

"I want to taste you," I murmur against her skin. "I want to taste *every* inch of you. I want to feel you come against my mouth. I want to feel you come on my fingers, too. And I'm *dying*"—I suck at the sensitive skin on her neck—"to feel you come on my cock."

I feel the shiver that runs through her. "That's quite the goal," she moans, arching her neck for another kiss.

"I'm a determined man," I murmur. "Whether it's tonight, tomorrow, or another time, I want to unravel every perfectly painted piece of you."

And now the stiffness is in her body, not her words.

*Fuck. Too far.*

I lift slightly, just enough that I'm not pinning her to the bed. I'm relieved to feel her legs don't drop from my waist.

"How about this," I start with a gentler kiss to her jaw. "Just let me touch you tonight. No tasting, no fucking. Orgasm or not, just let me learn your body." Another kiss. "I'm desperate to learn your body, Red."

I feel her hesitation in the way her hands on my back stutter in their path from my waist to my upper back.

"You don't want to fuck me?" she asks. I search for a hint of insecurity, but I find none. There's a wall here somewhere.

"I'm *dying* to fuck you, baby," I say, groaning at the admission. "But that's not the only thing that matters here."

She hums, her hands moving lightly over my back. "Okay," she whispers. "Touch me, then."

The way she says it... I think it might be a challenge.

She confirms as much when I start to kiss down her body, down her neck until I reach the curve of her breast, because I hear her muse in the silkiest purr, "But when you beg to fuck me, just know I'm going to say yes."

*Holy shit.*

My kisses become a little harder, a little more eager. I start to worry she might be right, and I find myself muttering as I slide one strap of her dress over her shoulder, "We'll deal with that if it happens."

Her laugh is throaty and the sexiest sound I've ever heard.

I slide the other strap down, and now I can tug the top of her dress down with her bra.

*Godfuckingdamnit. I've made a mistake.*

Because her breasts are the perfect round handfuls, but mostly because her nipples are pink and hard and *begging* for my mouth.

She must know what I'm thinking because she arches closer to me with a soft sigh, but only for a split second.

"Remember, no tasting," she purrs.

"You're going to kill me, aren't you," I croak, staring at her breasts.

"I'm just repeating your demands," she says, amused. Her fingers touch under my chin, guiding me to look up at her and also to lift my mouth. "What happened to touching me?"

A heavy breath rushes from my lungs. "Definitely going to kill me," I mumble, turning my attention back to her body. I can't taste her, but...

I cup her breast in one hand, absorbing the weight of it, the softness, before quickly pinching her nipple between my thumb and forefinger.

She sucks in a gasp, arching harder into my touch.

*Yeah. I'm not the only one who likes a firm touch.*

My other hand goes to her other breast. I squeeze, then pinch once more, this one a little harder.

She *moans*.

I have to bury my face in her neck to control the urge to bite her.

Which doesn't work because I sink my teeth into her shoulder instead.

My head spins when I feel her nails immediately dig into my arms, her hips grinding up against mine. "Fuck, I'm sorry," I gasp. I shouldn't be rough with her. *I'm being too rough with her.* "I didn't mean to—"

A groan steals my words when she rips my shirt to the side at my neck and sinks her teeth into my shoulder muscle.

"Fuck," I mutter, my hips punching forward on reflex.

I prop myself on one forearm in order to keep my position on top of her—close enough for her to bite again—but my other hand brushes down her body and fumbles with the hem of her dress. I rip it up, far too aggressively, but I'm hanging onto my sanity by a thread.

And I haven't even felt her pussy yet.

I drop my face to the bed, right beside her face, in an effort to control myself for a little longer. Even just the feel of her is enough to make me come in my pants like a goddamn teenager. I need to get my shit together.

But when my hand brushes over her hip, down to her bare skin, and over her thigh to the heat between her legs, I already know there's no keeping my shit together around this woman.

Sliding my hand up the inside of her thigh, it takes one graze over the soaked fabric of her underwear before I'm squeezing a fist in the sheets and groaning into the bed beside her ear.

I'm so focused on my own sanity that it takes me a second to realize her grip is also fisted in my shirt, that she's squirming underneath me and moaning something in my ear.

"Touch me," she begs. "Touch me. *God*, please, touch me—"

I don't need to be told twice. I smooth my hand down the front of her lace underwear, directly to her slippery clit.

We both moan at that.

Fuck, she's so *wet.* She can't be faking that, right?

"Inside," she begs. "I want—"

I sink one finger deep inside her.

"Christ, you're tight," I groan into her shoulder. "I can feel you squeezing down on me."

"More." She rocks into my finger. "Give me more."

*Snap.* There goes the hold on my sanity.

Ripping my hand from between her legs, I push onto my knees so I can reach for the underwear with both hands and pull it down her legs.

Thankfully, she seems just as eager to have nothing between us, because she sits up and impatiently pushes my shirt up my chest. I reach back with one hand and pull it off in one motion.

I almost miss her breath catching at the sight of my abs.

But I *don't* miss the way she leans forward to trace the V of the muscle with her tongue.

Groaning, my hand goes to the back of her head as my own lolls back. Suddenly, all I can think about is how her mouth felt on me.

"Do you want me to suck your cock again?" she asks innocently, looking up the length of my body to meet my eyes. My pulse jumps when her tongue peeks out to run along my skin for a split second.

"I want everything," I say dazedly, looking down at her. "I can't think beyond that." My hand brushes gently over her hair. "I *really* want to lick your pussy," I murmur, my eyes lowering to the place between her legs that's now only a shadow in this position.

My gaze shoots back to hers when I see her lips lift in a sensual smile. "Are you regretting your boundaries?" she asks sweetly.

I swallow roughly. "Very much so."

She leans forward to press a gentle kiss above my happy trail. "Do you want me to make it easier for you?"

My voice is like gravel when I ask, "Why do I feel like you're about to make it harder?"

She lets out a tinkling laugh, the sound mesmerizing. I don't realize she's reaching for the thong I just ripped off of her because at the same time, she's curling a hand behind my neck and pulling me back on top of her. It's only when I'm braced above her again, barely a few inches between us, that I hear her whisper, "Open."

This woman is a siren.

I don't think. I just do.

When I open my mouth, she stuffs her lace thong inside.

I *groan* as her taste explodes on my tongue. The lace is soaked. *She* was soaked. And she tastes like the sweetest thing.

"Easier or harder?" she asks, her sultry eyes taunting mine.

I can only groan again in response, dropping my face into her neck.

But when she reaches down between us, I snap out of it enough to remember what I was doing before she hypnotized me. Shifting my weight onto one forearm, I drop my other hand between her legs, right to the bare, wet center of her.

I'm rewarded with her gasp.

Sliding my fingers through her wetness, I force myself to slow just enough that I can tease her a bit. I touch her everywhere but where she wants me, if her hips lifting toward me is any indication. I circle around her clit but don't touch it. I slide down to her entrance but don't press a finger inside.

"Nico," she whines.

I want to lift up and look at her as I finger her to an orgasm for the first time. But I also don't think I'll be able to watch her without coming.

So I keep my face in her neck, pressing kisses along the skin as much as I can, and then I slide two fingers deep inside her.

"Ohhh God," she moans, her voice shaky. "That feels—"

She breaks off in a gasp when I finally press my thumb to her clit.

Slowly, I pull my fingers out, then slide them back in. And then I do it again. My thumb never stops moving in tight, firm circles on her clit.

And then she starts to moan.

I want to bottle the sound. I want to bottle this entire night. I don't think I've ever been this turned on in my *life*.

I hear the moment her breaths become shallow, can feel the moment her nails dig into my arms. But before I can revel in the knowledge that she's about to come all over my hand, she stiffens.

It's only for a split second, but I feel it. I pull my fingers from her so I can rip the thong out of my mouth and ask her what she needs.

Sure enough, something shutters over her gaze. She probably doesn't even realize it's there, because the moment we lock eyes, she pastes a smile on her face.

"How does my pussy feel?" she purrs, moving her hips once more. But the pattern is slightly different.

When I open my mouth to answer, she cups my face, brushing her thumb over my lip. "How does it *taste?*"

My head spinning, I can only suck her thumb into my mouth with a groan.

She smiles at that. "You feel so good," she whispers, her hands sliding down my neck, down my chest. Her gaze follows, her enjoyment of my body obvious. "I want to make you feel good, too."

"You do," I croak out. I clear my throat and try again. "Everything you do feels good."

She hums, still smiling. "I think we can make you feel better," she muses. And then she slides her hand into my pants and grips my cock.

It doesn't matter that she's already touched me. I might as well be a virgin experiencing a girl's touch for the first time.

"*Fuck*, baby," I groan, thrusting into her grip. I slide my fingers back inside her pussy at the same time. "That's going to make me come."

She starts to stroke me. "Is this how you'd like to come? Or would you prefer my mouth?" When my attention zeroes in on her red lips, her smile grows. "Since you don't want to fuck me tonight."

"I didn't—" My words break off when she brushes her thumb over the head of my cock.

And then they disappear completely when she lifts that thumb to her lips and sucks it into her mouth.

She lets out a hum of delight, her eyes closing with a pleased smile. "Delicious," she whispers.

I don't think I'm breathing anymore.

"You know, we could probably cheat just a *little* bit," she says, reaching between us again.

I don't understand what she means—don't have the brainpower to ask—but then she wraps her hand around my wrist and guides it up toward our faces. "Just a taste," she whispers.

It's not enough that she presses my fingers to my own mouth, drenched in her pleasure. That in itself would've short-circuited my brain. But she also chooses that moment to bump her hips up. And because she somehow managed to pull my cock free of my pants while she was touching me, the motion makes her wet pussy slide along my length.

Having the taste of her in my mouth and the feel of her on my cock is too much. It's too much for any man.

Groaning around my fingers, I pump my hips forward, wanting more of it. Wanting more of *her*.

"*Yes*," she sighs.

I look between our bodies so I can watch as I slide between her lips and over her clit. She's so slick. And it feels *so fucking good*. I just need—

"It's almost like you're fucking me," she moans. Once again reading my mind. "Almost, but not quite."

I have to bite back a whimper at the thought of sliding a little lower, changing the angle *just a little bit*—

"You could, you know." When I feel her hand go around my lower back to my pants, I lift my focus to her face.

She's pulled the condom from my back pocket and is holding it between two fingers.

"You could fuck me if you wanted to," she purrs, rolling her hips so her pussy glides along my cock. "No one would know. And you're almost there already. Just...a little... bit...closer..."

I reach the end of my rope before she's even finished her sentence.

Grabbing for the condom, my eyes lock on hers in shock when she doesn't let it go.

Her explanation is one simple word, said in the lowest, sexiest whisper.

"Beg."

My eyes widen as I remember our earlier conversation. Jesus Christ, how did I ever think I'd be able to stop myself from fucking her?

I never had a chance in hell.

"Please." The word slips out of me, unashamed, no hesitation. "*God*, please, let me fuck you."

A satisfied smile quirks her pretty lips as she presses the condom into my hand. I shred the foil with my teeth and slide the latex onto my throbbing cock with one swift motion.

And then I thrust into her with one drive of my hips.

I don't smother the shout she lets out. I *want* her to scream. I want her to voice whatever thoughts are spinning around in her head, anything that will let me know how she feels.

Because I'm losing my goddamn mind.

She feels *so. fucking. good.* I should've mentally prepared for how tight and slippery she'd feel just based on how she felt around my fingers, but part of me also wonders if there *is* any preparing for her.

I groan as I pound into her, hard and fast. There's nothing patient or teasing. I'm just…*fucking* her.

I smooth one hand up under her back until I can grip the base of her neck, partly to hold her close but also to hold her in place for my thrusts. My other hand hikes her thigh up over my hip so I can get a little bit deeper. "Are you going to come with me?" I growl into the curve of her neck.

It's only when she doesn't respond that I focus in on the details of her body. Her nails are digging into my arms once more, and her legs are no longer plastered to my sides. Instead, they've dropped to the bed, into the widest possible position.

Most importantly, her breathing is shallow.

On my next thrust, I grind down into her clit, just to test her reaction.

She *whimpers.*

And suddenly, I'm done with it all. Done with waiting, with reading between the lines, with everything. I just need her to fucking *come*.

Sliding my hand between our bodies, I press my thumb to her clit and start to rub.

I'm braced on one elbow, looking down at her when I watch it happen. I see the moment her eyes widen in surprise. I hear the way her breathing picks up, the way she desperately sucks in one small breath after another. I can feel the way she clings to me, as if needing me to anchor her.

Her whole body stiffens with a raspy moan, and then…

Her eyes slide closed, and she *shudders.*

I don't know how I fuck her through it. The sight of her coming is the most erotic, intoxicating thing I've ever seen.

But I somehow manage to wait until she drops, limp, onto the bed before I let myself come. With a guttural groan, I give in to the pleasure.

We're both gasping, trying to catch our breaths, when the silence of the room becomes obvious. I feel suddenly very aware of the fact that I'm completely plastered against her, panting in her ear as I try to put my head back on straight. I have *never* had sex like that.

I think that's the reason it takes me a second to realize she's gone stiff beneath me. She's not gasping anymore, she's...holding her breath?

I lift my weight off her with an awkward mutter of "sorry." I can't bring myself to look at her, to see whatever expression she's wearing, but that I know isn't "that was the best sex of my life, when can we do it again?" Instead, I focus on tying the condom off and righting my jeans that I'm still wearing.

She slides off the opposite side of the bed as soon as I create space between us. One glance at her tells me the tension is back in her shoulders.

*Shit.* I know first-time sex can be awkward, but this is beyond that. The speed she's dressing with screams *regret*.

It's...confusing.

I pull my shirt on, feeling like I need to be fully clothed for whatever comes next. Daisy is already dressed and adjusting her heels.

"Do you need...?" I ask stiffly, gesturing toward the bathroom.

Her smile is just as stiff. Shaking her head, she inches closer to the door, clearly wanting to get out of the bedroom.

I swallow a sigh as I pass by her and stride into the living area. The fall back to reality is harder than I expected it to be, but I grab the envelope from the desk anyway.

"Two thousand in cash," I say, hating the words—hating *myself*—as I hand it over to her. "And a little extra."

To my surprise, this is the moment she seems to relax. She takes the envelope from my hand with a smile, this one no longer tinged with stress.

"Thank you," she says softly.

I take what might be my last chance to look at her. She pulled herself back to being presentable fairly quickly, but there are tiny hints all over her body that give away what we did tonight.

Her red lipstick is muted, because she sucked my cock.

Her hair isn't as sleek as it was when she arrived, because I couldn't keep my hands out of it.

Her skin is still slightly flushed, and there are a few spots on her neck that might be the beginning of a mark, because I was going to die if I didn't taste her.

Secretly, I love that she's leaving here with reminders of me. Even if I was wrong to do it.

When her eyes shoot to the door, I'm seized with a jarring desperation to keep her here longer. *This can't be the last time I see her.*

"You don't have to rush out, you know," I say, sliding my hands into my pockets just to have something to do with them. "I could pour us another drink, or order some room service, or…"

Her pitying smile makes me trail off.

"I appreciate the offer," she says. As if we're discussing a business transaction. *Which I guess we are.* "But we're at the end of our time, and I can't extend tonight, unfortunately."

I nod, swallowing roughly. "Ah. I understand."

"But it was very nice to meet you, Nico." Another smile, and this one doesn't reach her eyes either. "The agency will follow up with you to ensure the experience met your expectations. Beyond that…" To my surprise, she extends her hand to me. "Maybe I'll see you again, Mr. Price."

I shake her hand, not because I want to breathe more life into this stupid transaction, but because I'm dying to touch her one more time.

"I'd like that, Red."

The second her hand slides from mine, she turns and vanishes from my room.

# EIGHT
## SCARLETT

A client just gave me an orgasm.

I just came for the first time during sex.

*A client just gave me my first orgasm.*

I can't seem to catch my breath during the time it takes me to ride the elevator down, walk across the hotel lobby, and hail a taxi. My chest is still heaving and my pulse is still spiked when I finally slide onto the leather back seat.

*What. Just. Happened.*

That entire appointment was out of the ordinary. *How* did I let this whole night get so out of control?

Typically, a first-time appointment includes a feeling-out process, me squashing the awkwardness by coming onto him physically, me figuring out what it is he wants sexually, and then him having the time of his life while I put on a poker face and pretend to have the time of *my* life. All the while, I'm either adding to my mental grocery list to pass the time or thinking about my high school gym teacher to stay wet. At no point have I ever been invested during sex with a client.

Until Nico.

The second he put his hands on me, I couldn't take my

focus off of him. The hotel could've shaken with an earthquake and I still would've been lost in the haze of Nico's touch.

I tried to put distance between us. I almost came when it was only his fingers inside of me. I thought redirecting his attention would make the orgasm go away, but it seems I underestimated him. Because that man *still* got me to finish.

When my phone buzzes with a text, I pull it from my purse with shaky hands.

*Amara.*

> Amara: Everything good? You normally check in as soon as you leave.

I press my fingers to my temples with a wince. I've been lost in my head for—

The taxi stops. We've reached my apartment building.

*Damn. More than twenty minutes.*

I slide the driver a hundred and quickly type out a response to Amara as he counts the change.

> Scarlett: Fine. Just needed a minute to recoup. I'm home now. Everything's fine.

By the time I'm in the comfort of my apartment, there's a string of texts waiting.

> Amara: Okay good. I was worried for you, cara.

> Amara: I'd like to hear what you thought of him.

> Amara: Can you come by the gallery tomorrow?

The headache that started in the car begins to pound. I don't usually mind my weekly trips to Amara's art gallery, but it's been a long week, and I still have an appointment with a client tomorrow night.

And on top of that, I don't have a shot in hell at hiding what just happened from her. That woman can read me like a book.

> Amara: We'll make it quick, Scarlett. I'll have The Palm Court cater an afternoon tea for us.

I sigh. In a way, she knows me too well; she knows my favorite cafe in the entire city, and she knows that I prefer it in private.

I type a response, feeling the exhaustion settle into my bones with every letter.

> Scarlett: Okay. I'll be at the gallery at 1.

That night is the first night I don't complete my fourteen-step nighttime skincare routine. I simply drop onto my bed and fall into a dreamless sleep.

---

I'm awake far too early the next morning. Too afraid to close my eyes again because Nico appears every time I do.

Throwing the sheets off my sweaty body, I decide I'm going to run my stress and confusion into the ground. Grabbing my sneakers, I don't even bother dressing out of my sleep shorts and tank before I lace them up and pull my fold-up treadmill out of the living room closet.

An hour later, I'm heading into mile seven, two more than is typical for me, drenched through my clothes.

Maybe if I feel skinnier, I'll feel more in control.

By the time my legs turn to jelly and I have to pull the emergency break after stumbling for a second time, there's a dull ringing in my ears that's loud enough to drown out the majority of my thoughts. I care less about my insane date last night than I did when I started, which I'll count as a win.

I drag myself into the bathroom to run a warm bath. Sinking into the water with a whimper, it takes me less than a minute to doze off.

Three hours later, I take one last look in the mirror before leaving my apartment. Despite the chaotic start to my morning, I'm still dressed to the nines, same way I always am when I leave my apartment. I'm wearing a pretty summer dress, my hair is blown out, and my makeup is perfectly done. I'm ready to face the world, red lips and all.

It's a half-hour drive to Amara's office. The art gallery is real, as is Amara's love of expensive paintings, but the business was opened specifically with the intent of laundering money for the illegal side of the agency. Since beauty is in the eye of the beholder, no one bats an eye if a painting is bought for what some might deem "too much" money.

Amara's assistant is on the phone when I walk into the gallery, but I'm assuming she was told of my appointment because she waves me in. I find Amara standing in the center of the art space, staring at one of her most prized paintings.

To this day, she's the most elegant woman I've ever seen. She's tall, taller than me, wearing a dark-green dress that perfectly complements her olive skin tone. Her brown hair is twisted into a coiffure and her makeup is so perfect, she looks like a real-life filter. No one would ever guess she's in her forties.

Or that she runs the most successful escort agency in New York.

"Pemberly still trying to buy it off you?" I ask as I stop beside her.

She sighs. "Yes. The man doesn't know how to give up."

I take in the gorgeous painting in front of me. I don't know much about art, but even I can tell this one is an artist's crowning achievement. "Can't really blame him."

Amara doesn't respond. Instead, she turns to me and asks simply, "How was last night?"

I can't bring myself to look at her. "Are you asking because of me or the client?"

"You know you come first, mia cara," she says sweetly, touching my hand.

I let out an unfeeling hum.

I don't know the answer to her question, so instead, I focus on the easy part and hand over the bag I'm carrying. Fifteen percent of my bookings, all cash, no trace. Amara sighs as she takes it.

"He was nice," I answer simply. "Clearly hadn't done it before, was a little unsure in the beginning, but ultimately just wanted a vanilla date." I don't mention that vanilla date was the most mind-blowing experience of my life. "He was a solid referral."

When Amara doesn't react right away, I finally turn toward her with a frown. She looks lost in thought.

"Why?" I ask. "Is there something I should know?"

Her gaze jerks toward me in surprise. "What? Oh, no. Not about him. It's the guy who referred him who I'm having an issue with, so I wanted to make sure I cut out the entirety of the rot. That's all."

"Hm. Well, whoever that guy was, I can't see how it

would extend to Nico. The guy's a nice guy, through and through."

Amara tilts her head. "Nico?"

I look away to cover my blush. I usually call clients by their last name; it helps make them feel like a nobody. "He's young. It feels odd calling him Mr. Price."

"He's not *that* young," Amara says with a chuckle. "It's one of the reasons he called us."

Part of me is bursting at the seams to ask her more about that. She probably got more information about Nico during her background check than I did during our date, so she's going to be my best shot at learning more about him.

But...I can't. I can't make Amara think Nico was a unique client. And I can't care.

"He spoke very highly of you," Amara says casually.

My head snaps toward her before I can control the impulse. "You called him? It's barely been twelve hours!"

She gives me a knowing smile. "I didn't call him, Scarlett."

My eyes widen. Nico called already? What did he—?

*He called for a second date.*

I turn my gaze forward, back to the painting in front of me. I don't know why I'm surprised. He did allude to future dates a few times. I just wasn't sure if he'd snap back to reality after I left and realize he was flirting with an escort.

I can't tell if I'm relieved it didn't happen or bummed that it hasn't happened yet.

"Are you okay with seeing him again?" Amara interrupts my thoughts.

"Why wouldn't I be?" I answer in a flat tone. If only I could adopt this emotionless shell around Nico.

"He asked for this Thursday. I know you typically put a week or two between clients, but since he's a new client, I thought you might want to hook him early." Her mouth twitches with a smirk. "Although it sounds like you've already done that."

I shouldn't say yes. I shouldn't feed into her suspicion, shouldn't encourage Nico.

"Thursday's fine."

Amara nods. "Very well. Should I put him before or after your appointment with Mr. Harris?"

"Give Harris to one of the other girls. It doesn't matter who's bent over in front of him. He just wants someone to tell him his cock is small."

Maybe I'll regret handing off one of my "easy" clients, but I can't find it in me to care.

I can feel the way Amara's studying me. Any other madam would probably scold me for thinning my roster instead of filling it, but not Amara. Not with me.

"If you need a break, cara, just say the word," she says gently. "I can cancel your clients, put you on a plane to an island, let you relax—"

A loud laugh bursts out of me. The idea of a vacation solving my problems is absurd.

My reaction only seems to worry Amara more. When the guilt starts to seep in, I let out a tired exhale and assure her. "I'm fine. Really. Just a little burnt out." I hesitate, then add, "Maybe a vacation at the end of the year wouldn't be a bad idea."

Seemingly pleased that I've at least taken her question seriously, she nods. "You tell me when, and I'll put it on our calendar."

I try for a smile, but I think I'm too drained. "Just schedule Nico for Thursday," is what I say instead.

I'm too busy mentally calculating if three days is enough to compose myself for another date.

# NINE
## NICO

Of course I called for a second date.

I would've called, regardless, but having to stay at the hotel and sleeping in the bed that I fucked Daisy in—the bed that smelled like her, that had her lipstick print on the pillow —made it impossible *not* to call as soon as I woke up.

The only sobering moment was discussing scheduling. Hearing "she's booked the rest of the week" wasn't just a slap in the face, it was a right cross to the jaw.

Which should *not* have been as disconcerting as it was.

When I first called the agency, I didn't think too much about what a date would be like. I figured the sex would be good, and maybe I hoped there would be some interesting conversation given the parameters of two people who don't know each other, but I didn't exactly have high expectations. I just wanted to spend *one* night not in my head, not depressed by the quiet of my apartment. I thought it would just be sex.

I never expected to feel…excitement. I never thought I would still be thinking about Daisy days later.

My entire drive home was spent with mounting

frustration. Because what do you *mean* I'm smitten with an escort.

It's the classic pathetic male response, isn't it? Man pays woman for a date, woman somehow convinces man that she's not there for the money, man falls head over heels, woman leaves as soon as man stops paying. It's a tale as old as the profession itself.

I should call the agency back and cancel. I should chalk this up to one crazy story and leave last night where it is.

But...I can't. Because my gut is *screaming* at me that last night was different. And the only way I can think to find out the truth is to see her again.

I just need to keep my head on straight next time.

It's the longest week of my life. I throw myself back into training, hoping to distract myself from thoughts of Daisy. I spar more than I ever have, because it's virtually impossible to think about anything but the shin coming at your face when there's a two-hundred-pound man in front of you.

After one particularly hard sparring session, I'm dead on the ground, trying to catch my breath, when my striking coach's face appears above me.

"You're looking good, Nico," he says with a pleased tone. "I was a little worried when we accepted the fight that your camp would be too short, but you've been working hard. I'm impressed."

I almost want to laugh. If only he knew that my motivation today has nothing to do with my upcoming fight.

*Hey, Coach, remember when you told me no dating during fight camp? Well, you never said anything about escorts. And it turns out, that's the one girl that will sufficiently distract me.*

"Thanks," I say instead, pulling myself to a seated position. "Yeah, I've been trying to get as many rounds in as I can. And actually—" I swallow thickly, hoping nothing weird is visible on my face. "I was thinking about getting an extra session in at Renzo's."

He nods his agreement. "That could be good for you. If you don't mind the commute."

I don't tell him that the commute is my reason for it. That even though it's common for fighters all over the Northeast to drive hours to train at the world-renowned Renzo Gracie's in New York City, it has nothing to do with my decision.

That's determined solely by a certain beautiful blonde.

I take the train up on Thursday morning, just in time for an afternoon training session. I've been here plenty of times, so the coaches and athletes welcome me the same as they always do. They're excited to hear I might be coming up here more often.

By 8 p.m., I've eaten, showered, and downed one of the drinks from the mini bar to settle my nerves. I don't even feel this way before my fights. Why am I nervous? This is a transaction. I know exactly what I'm putting into it and getting out of it.

All thoughts about this being a business arrangement fly out of my head the moment I hear a knock.

And just like it did last time, my breath escapes me when I open the door to Daisy.

*Christ*, what's her real name? I wish I knew.

I wish I could put a name to the goddess standing in front of me.

She looks gorgeous tonight. It's not just her physical appearance—although it would be insane to say she's not the most stunning woman I've ever seen. She's wearing a skintight dark green dress today, nothing too short or revealing, but the lace covering her neckline and arms is an enticing detail. Her hair is curlier than last time, but her lips are the same shade of red.

I'm just as desperate to taste her as last time.

"Hi, Red," I greet softly.

*Do I imagine the way she lights up at the nickname?* "Hi," she breathes, wearing a soft smile of her own.

I step aside and gesture her into the room. As she moves past me, her aura is every bit as commanding as it was last time. And when she speaks, she sounds every bit the seductress I remember.

"It's nice to see you again," she says over her shoulder. "I'm glad you called me."

I lock the door and follow behind her into the suite. "I told you I would."

When she reaches the couch, she turns and sits with the most demure movement. "And now I know you're an honest man, Nico."

A shiver runs through me at hearing her say my name. *Fuck.* She's turning it on early tonight.

I can *feel* the spell she's weaving around me. With every word, every look, all I want to do is sink to the floor in front of her and bask in her presence.

"So, how's your week been?" she asks. "Are we relieving any stress tonight?"

*This is far more stressful than anything that happened this week.*

I don't tell her that. I just pour us two glasses of water and walk over to where she's sitting. "My week was good. Busy. More training sessions than I can count."

When I hand her the glass of water, she looks surprised. Hoping I'm misreading the expression, I say, "I can get you an unopened bottle of water if you'd prefer that."

Her gaze shoots to mine. "Oh. No, that's not—" The

faintest bit of color touches her cheeks. She takes the glass from my hand and says softly, "Thank you. That was sweet of you."

*Getting a drink of water is sweet?*

"How was *your* week?" I ask as I sit on the couch across from her.

Last time I saw her, I got the sense that she tries to stay away from personal questions. I don't blame her for not being an open book with a stranger, but I'm also intrigued enough to want to know more about her. I'm just hoping if I stay away from personal details, that she'll be willing to make this more of a conversation.

Sure enough, she studies me before answering the question. Her answer is slow and calculated when she says, "It was like every other week."

She might believe that's a non-answer, but it tells me more than she thinks. Her days are structured, maybe even monotonous.

"What does your average day look like?" I press. And then, because I suspect she's constantly trying to remind me of what she does, I add, "Before...this."

She's trying to read me, trying to distance herself so she can make it all about me. "I work out, run errands, scroll social media. Same as most people's, I suspect."

I raise an eyebrow. "I spent the day punching men—and women—into the mats and then folding them into pretzels."

That surprises a laugh out of her. "Okay, fine, maybe not everyone's average day." A twinkle of interest appears in her eyes. "Do you really train with both men and women?"

"Of course. Some of the best training partners I have are women."

Leaning her elbow on the armrest of the couch, she props her head on her fist. It's the most relaxed pose I've seen her in. "Do you have to go easier on them? Since I'm assuming they're smaller than you?"

"Depends what I'm doing," I answer, adopting a mirror image of her pose. Even though we're not talking about her, I like that we're *talking* without innuendos or hidden agendas. "If we're sparring, I'm not throwing punches full force at a woman's head, because that doesn't help anyone." I frown. "Although to be fair, I rarely do that with men, either."

Her lips pull into a small, natural smile. I want to freeze the moment and paint it.

"So then when *do* you go full force?" she asks curiously.

"When we're doing jiu-jitsu. There's no striking, so you don't have to pull any power. It mostly comes down to strategy. It's like chess." I cock my head in contemplation. "To be honest, they probably have an advantage in that sense. A lot of men are used to throwing their muscles around in physical sports, but women get to rely on the thing they've spent their entire lives sharpening: their brain." I wave at nothing in particular as I finish the thought. "Plus, they're quicker, more flexible, and they don't know what the word tired means."

When I turn my attention back to Daisy, I find her frozen, staring at me. But I can't read a single thought in her eyes.

I smile awkwardly. "What? I can admit the truth."

That somehow makes her eyes go wider.

My gaze narrows on hers as I ask, "What part of that just threw you?"

She shakes her head, as if to clear it. "I just... I've never met a feminist before."

My bark of laughter startles her. "Sorry," I say with a chuckle. "I don't think I've ever been called a feminist."

Her confusion grows. "Really? What else would you call that?"

"That I consider women in the gym my equals?"

"Well…yeah."

"Being a decent human? And, to be fair, it's much harder to argue the fact when I'm smacked in the face with it on the daily."

Her forehead creases with a frown. "What do you mean?"

"I mean, I get my ass regularly handed to me by women. So I can't exactly say I'm better than them."

I haven't really thought about how sex workers might view men and women. I guess I assumed they would look down on men for having to pay a woman for her company. And it makes sense that they would assume men would think of *themselves* as superior, simply because of the stereotypes about sex workers.

Leaning back against the couch with a heavy exhale, she says, "I can't even picture it."

I only hesitate for a moment before asking, "Want me to show you?"

Her mouth twists with a smirk. "What, do you have videos of women beating you? I figured you liked being told what to do, but I wouldn't have guessed a masochism kink."

A flash of heat runs through my body, and before I can stop it, I nearly growl. "I might argue that giving you the power to put your soaked thong in my mouth makes me the opposite of a masochist."

All amusement drops from her expression, and I watch her pulse pick up speed in her neck.

But before she can make this sexual—that's not what I'm trying to accomplish with her—I stand from the couch and extend a hand.

"I meant I can show you how to kick my ass."

She looks at my hand, clearly wanting to take it, but first she says, "Starting to sound like a masochism kink, Nico."

I throw my head back with a laugh. "Just take my hand, Red."

I pull her to her feet, but I'm too forceful about it. She braces her hands against my chest, our bodies plastered against each other. She's close. Too close.

I hear the breath she sucks in, can feel the way it hits her chest. She might have a no-kissing rule, but her body is telling me she's at least thinking about it right now.

After a moment, she pushes off my chest and forces her gaze to mine. "So…how are you going to show me this butt-kicking?"

My lip twitches. "Butt-kicking? Do you not curse?"

She shakes her head as she smooths down her dress. "No. Cursing is unladylike."

Her answer is instant and monotone. It almost sounds like she's *repeating* it. And I find it as interesting as I do disturbing.

"If cursing is unladylike, then what is fighting?" I try to sound playful.

"I…" Her brow furrows, her mind clearly flying a mile a minute. "I didn't mean to offend you. It's just…a personal preference…"

"Baby, I don't think you could offend me if you tried. I —" I drag a hand down my face. "I'm sorry, I didn't mean to tease you. You just surprised me, that's all." I glance toward the open space in the suite, suddenly second-guessing my idea. "I wanted to show you a jiu-jitsu move, but if it makes you uncomfortable, then we can forget it. I don't want—"

"I want to try," she blurts out.

I think we're both surprised by the eager answer.

"I mean, if you want to show me, then I'd love to learn," she tacks on, backtracking. But I can see through the lie. She's trying to hide her interest by making it about me.

I'll let her hide. For now.

"Come on." I take her hand and lead her to the open area. "I'll warn you that it's going to seem a little weird in the beginning, but once you get it, it's really cool."

"That's not terrifying," she mutters sarcastically.

I turn to face her, chuckling. "Also, a dress is going to feel like an odd outfit choice for this."

"If I had known I was dressing for a fight, I would've made slightly different clothing choices."

Curious, I ask, "What's your everyday clothing choice?" I'm suddenly dying to know if she's a jeans and tank top kind of girl, or if she's always dressed like she's headed for the runway.

But for some reason, she clams up at that before joking, "What do you mean? I'm always dressed in cocktail attire."

I decide to move past the question. "Regardless, cocktail attire wouldn't be my go-to for this activity. But we're just going to ignore that. Can you—" I feel my face heat with a blush, realizing for the first time how weird this request is going to sound outside of the MMA gym. "Can you lay down? I need to be on top of you."

She tries to hide her smile but fails. "I thought that came later. But okay." Moving gracefully, she lowers herself to the carpeted floor and lies flat on her back. "This doesn't feel conducive to self-defense, Nico."

"I told you it was going to feel weird at first," I grumble, questioning this decision as I lower to my knees beside her. Especially when I have to clear my throat and gesture toward her legs. "I…uh, I need to kneel between your legs."

She props herself up on her elbows and raises an eyebrow. "This is sounding more and more like foreplay…"

"Yeah, all of a sudden, I kind of understand why keyboard warriors call me gay when I do this with men," I mutter.

She chuckles, the sound easing some of my tension. But then she spreads her legs, her dress inching way too far up on her thighs with the movement. And all that tension returns.

I refuse to look down. That's not what this is about. This wasn't a ploy to fuck her, and I need her to understand that. So I keep my focus trained strategically on her neck as I shuffle between her legs, then lean over her and plant my hands beside her ears.

"Now what?" she asks, but she sounds slightly more breathless than before. Thank God, I'm not the only one affected.

"Now you—" I clear my throat and try to get my shit together. "One thing first. From a self-defense standpoint, the worst position you can be in is on the ground with someone on top of you. Right?" I wait for her nod to signal she's taking this seriously. "So, I'm going to show you something that's called a sweep. It's basically using leverage to get your opponent off balance so you can sweep them onto their back. Make sense?"

She nods again, her eyes wide and mesmerized.

I pull in a deep breath for courage, because now's the part where I have to look down at her legs—and try not to think about the space between them, wondering if this is making her as wet as it's making me hard.

"Okay, so, you have to get on your side for this," I start. "One leg can stay on the outside of my body, but for the other one, I want you to bring your shin directly across my chest."

Slowly, focusing on my directions, she shifts onto her left side and slides her right knee up.

"Good. Now, I want you to trap my arm with your left hand and grab behind my neck with your right."

"I feel like I'm being put through a Thai massage, not beating you in a fight," she mutters.

Chuckling, I tell her, "Trust me, it won't feel that way in a second. Now the last step: since your right shin is across my chest, you're going to bring your left foot up and essentially kick my knee out from under me. Since you have my arm pinned, I have nothing to brace with, so if you kick my knee out while also knocking me over with the shin that's across my chest, you'll—"

I let out a surprised yelp as she follows my instructions to a T, taking my leg out and driving her shin into my chest at the same time. I fall onto my face beside her, forced to roll out of the move.

"Does unladylike mean you're a natural?" I groan from my back. "Because that was perfect."

She seems *delighted*. Sitting up, she looks down at me with sparkling eyes. "That didn't even take any muscle! I thought that would be hard."

"You're bruising my ego, Red." But I'm smiling as I say it. "Let's try it again, but this time, I want you to roll with the throw so you're on top of me at the end."

She hurriedly lies back down, and I go to my knees again, resuming the original position.

As I open my mouth to talk her through the steps again, she's already moving through each step, her brow furrowed in concentration. She shifts onto her side, brings her shin across my chest, traps my right arm, and then—

Once more, I go flying as she takes my knee out from under me and pushes me onto my back. But this time, she follows through on the sweep like I told her, which means she ends up straddling me.

I'm chuckling as my hands go to her hips. "Good girl. That was perfect."

Bracing her hands on my chest, she beams down at me. "That's so fun. Weird, but fun."

"And also proved my point," I add. "You said it yourself; you didn't need strength to do it."

"It probably helps, though," she muses. "I'm assuming you could throw me off with all strength and no leverage."

Wordlessly, I trap her hand and bump my hips up, flipping her over and reversing our positions. Her squeal turns into another laugh.

"Leverage makes it easier," I tell her with a wink.

Before I can guess what she's about to do, she goes for the sweep once more. But she's a little overzealous and tries to do all the steps at one time.

She brings her shin up at the same time that she kicks my knee out, and I go face first into her knee.

The momentum automatically finishes the sweep, but by the time she's sitting on top of me, I'm groaning around a fat lip.

"*Oh my God*," she cries, cupping my face in her hands. "I'm so sorry! It was an accident! Are you okay?"

"I get hit in the face a hundred times a day," I say, chuckling. "Of course, I'm okay."

"But I kneed you in the face! Oh my God, I'm so sorry."

She seems so distraught, I start to rub a soothing path up and down her thighs. "Red, I promise I'm fine. This really is nothing. *And* it was my idea to show you the move."

"I'm sure you never intended for me to *beat* you."

"That was exactly the point I was trying to prove."

She lets out a heavy breath, seeming to finally accept that I'm truly alright. Then she leans over me and plants her hands next to my head. My hands freeze on her body as she looks down at me.

"Should I get anything?" she asks softly, her eyes scanning my face. "Do you need ice?"

I can't breathe, can't talk. I just shake my head in answer.

I watch, mesmerized, as her gaze tracks over my lips. I can feel the slight swelling, although I'm not lying to her that this is nothing for me.

When her eyes meet mine again, there's a flash of uncertainty in them. I don't know why until she whispers, "Don't kiss me."

My eyebrows pinch. I open my mouth to tell her I'd rather die than cross her boundaries, but before I can, she lowers her head.

And barely, just barely, brushes her lips over the swelling.

Terrified to move, yet desperate to feel that again, I lock every muscle in place.

Slowly, she does it again, her kiss—is it a kiss?—lingering for a moment longer and sending my heart into overdrive.

# TEN
## SCARLETT

*I'm kissing Nico.*

*Why am I kissing Nico?*

Okay, so it's not *really* a kiss. It's just…when I saw his lip swelling, I felt a sudden and overwhelming urge to take care of him. I still do.

But when I pull back and take in the sight of him below me, that urge morphs into something else. Something different.

Something I'm far more familiar with.

Nico's eyes are wide, his breaths coming in short bursts. His grip has latched onto my hips. He's turned on. And I bet if I shifted back just a little bit, I'd feel the proof of that.

It takes me a second to realize that I *want* to have sex with Nico. Maybe it's the primal, empowering feeling from his lesson, maybe it's the feel of his body below me, maybe it's a combination of everything. Whatever it is, I'm more turned on than I've ever been.

When I lean down this time, I slide my hands from his chest, up to the side of his neck, and I press another kiss to the corner of his mouth.

Too powerless to fight the urge, I flick my tongue out to trace Nico's lip.

A groan rumbles up his throat, into my kiss. His hands tighten on my hips. I expect my teasing to be what snaps the thread on his control, but...

He doesn't move.

When I lift up again, I can't help whispering, "You didn't kiss me."

He's still panting, still looking like he's teetering on the edge. "You asked me not to," he rasps.

And then it's no longer *his* control snapping, but mine.

I slide down his body until I'm sitting on his thighs, then immediately set to undoing his belt. My hands are shaking with the need to touch him. Right as the button on his jeans pops open, I slide the t-shirt up his body so I can press another kiss to those intoxicating muscles.

I hear Nico's groan as I feel his hand cup the back of my head. "You don't have to—"

My lips still on his skin, I look up the length of his torso and into his eyes. "I want to," I promise.

He holds my gaze, his throat bobbing on a rough swallow. "I feel like you're lying to me," he croaks.

Another light kiss, another swipe of my tongue. "I'm really, really not," I whisper breathily.

His head falls back to the floor with a dull thud. "You're going to be the death of me." But his hand kneads the back of my neck in a silent sign of consent.

So I tug his pants down his hips and set to worshipping him.

I've never been a fan of oral—giving *or* receiving. To be honest, there are few sexual activities that I see the appeal of as a woman. But right now, after the past half hour...all I want to do is see how much pleasure I can bring Nico.

I didn't get a chance to do much of this on our first date, so I start with the intention of taking my time. Licking the length of him, I leave wet, teasing kisses along the skin as I search for the areas that will drive him crazy. It doesn't take me long to discover the place where his shaft meets his balls is the most sensitive. As soon as I brush my tongue over the spot, every single one of his muscles tenses under me.

Smiling, I let out a contemplative hum as I do it again. The vibration only drives him crazier, his hands turning to fists by his sides.

"You can touch me, you know," I purr, moving my touch up to the head of his cock. "Unless you're planning to make up rules again?"

He looks down at me, his pupils blown completely black. "I don't think there's a man alive that could fight the temptation to touch you."

And yet, he still doesn't reach for me. After a moment, I take his hands and gently lead them to my head, smiling when they immediately sink into my hair.

Then I start to suck him.

It takes three strokes to get his entire length in my mouth, and with each one, Nico's hands tighten in my hair. By the time the head of his cock is tickling the back of my throat, he's groaning like he's in pain.

"Shit, Red. Your mouth is the sweetest thing I've ever— Oh, fuck. *Fuck*."

His words cut off when I take him deep into my mouth again, pausing long enough to brush my tongue over that sensitive spot underneath.

Suddenly, my head is being lifted. When I look up, Nico's chest is heaving, and his eyes are crazed. Still holding the sides of my face, he gasps, "I've never wanted to come so quick in my *life*."

I smile, my hand drifting over to his cock so I can loosely stroke it. "You can, you know. You can come as many times as you want."

*There's no limit to how many orgasms you can have in the hour you pay me for.*

I *want* to remind Nico that I'm an escort. To establish boundaries, keep things clearer and easier—I *should* remind him.

But at the same time, the idea of interrupting this moment makes my stomach twist. I like the way I'm feeling too much to stay logical right now.

So, I don't say it. But I wonder if Nico still sees it, because suddenly, there's a look of determination in his eyes. And then he's flipping me onto my back and covering my body with his.

"You first," he murmurs, pressing his lips to my neck and laving kisses along the skin.

I let out a happy sigh and bare my neck for more kisses. "Fine by me."

Although I am very much planning on *not* coming.

I know some escorts who prefer to orgasm with their clients; in their minds, if they're having sex, they might as well be enjoying it. But for me, I have a rule for exactly the opposite. Without an orgasm, it's easier to differentiate between "real" sex and "work" sex.

*Not that I've had any "real" sex since moving to the city.*

With clients, it's all about faking orgasms and focusing entirely on their pleasure. With personal intimacy, I can be selfish with my pleasure. The clear-cut boundary between the two is my orgasm.

Until Nico.

I didn't plan on coming the last time I slept with him. In fact, I specifically tried to steer away from it. When I got close while he was touching me, I changed positions and guided him to a new rhythm. I thought I was safe.

I underestimated him.

The second he slid inside me, he went right back to the same touch as before. And with his size, and me already more turned on than I've ever been, I didn't stand a chance of stopping the orgasm he was determined to fuck out of me. Clear-cut boundaries be damned.

This time, I'm not making the same mistake. There will be no orgasms tonight. I'm determined to keep that distance between us.

"Can I—" Nico's voice shakes me from my thoughts. He's still pressing kisses along my neck and shoulder, still lying with his weight completely on top of me. "Can I taste you?"

A small chuckle slips out of me. "Baby, you can do anything you want to me."

I feel the vibration of his unhappy growl as he lifts up to look down at me. "Don't say that. I'm *asking*."

I can't help but soften at the earnestness of his expression. Placing my hand against his cheek, I nod my answer. "I *want* you to taste me," I whisper. And I mean it.

Some of the tension releases from his shoulders, and he quickly leans down to press a kiss to my jaw that feels suspiciously like *thank you.*

Then he slides down my body until he's settled between my legs, slowly pushing my dress up and over my hips.

Hunger flares in his eyes when he hooks a finger in my lace panties to tug them aside and sees that they're wet. I don't think he'll be able to make me come, but that look alone makes my heartrate pick up speed.

And then his tongue swipes through my center.

The gasp I let out is far too loud in the quiet room. Nico

chuckles a sexy sound as he slides his hands under and over my thighs, gripping me tight as he pulls me into another lick.

My moan is too loud. Jesus, he's going to think I'm playing at being a porn star.

But I can't help it. His mouth is warm, and wet, and whatever he's doing with his tongue feels *so. good.* He's flicking my clit, swirling in circles around it, never giving me a chance to catch my breath. The pleasure that started as a low simmer in my belly is growing, the wave rising higher and higher.

"Nico, I—" I hear myself panting but can't do anything about it. Oral has never felt like this before. It's like he knows exactly where to touch and how hard, and he never deviates as he takes note of every positive response I give him.

I need him to deviate.

I *can't* let myself come with him. But I'm pretty sure he noticed the last time I tried to redirect his touch, so I can't do that again.

I'll just fake it.

Being an escort, you learn to perfect your acting skills, inside and outside of the bedroom. Learning to fake an orgasm is essential. Not every client cares about a woman's pleasure, but enough of them have a better experience if the woman *does* come. Faking it is basically Escort 101.

Not that I have to fake much right now. The gasping, the rapid heartrate, all of that is Nico's doing. I just have to concentrate on arching my back, moaning a little bit louder, and reaching down to grip his shoulder. Then after one particular swirl of his tongue sends a shudder through me, I squeeze down on my pelvic muscles and fake a few tremors.

Nico's tongue slows as I collapse back onto the carpet. The fact that I'm vibrating from still being keyed up works perfectly as post-orgasm aftershocks.

The hand on his shoulder slides up into his hair as I let out a purr of satisfaction. Nico rises up to brace himself over my body once more.

My focus goes immediately to his glistening lips. "Feel good?" he asks in a deep growl.

I nod, a lazy smile on my lips. "Very good."

I don't notice his pause until he says, "Good. Now let's do a real one this time."

My eyes shoot up to his, heart stuttering, all sex dropping from my smile. "A— What?"

There's no judgment in his eyes, but there's also no bullshit. "You can't fake it with me, Red," he says in a slightly softer tone.

My mouth opens, then closes immediately. I've never been called out on faking it; never been with someone who cared enough to discuss it. But Nico not only *noticed*, he—

That thought cuts off the moment he slides down my body and settles between my legs again.

Without another word, he goes right back to eating.

And this time, he doesn't take it easy on me.

Another too-loud moan bursts from my mouth as his lips suction around my clit. My hand slides into his hair, this time to hold on for dear life. I must've been delusional to think Nico wouldn't be able to read me. It took the man one hour to figure out how I liked to be touched, and much less than that to figure out the best way to taste me. I'm clearly at his mercy.

Sure enough, I'm already on the verge of coming when he slides two fingers inside me. A full-body shudder ripples through my body as a whimper slips from my lips.

"There it is," I hear Nico murmur against my skin.

With the dual sensation of his mouth on my clit and his

fingers repeatedly hitting my G-spot, I don't have a chance in hell at stopping this orgasm.

It washes over me like a wave, overwhelming in one moment and soothing in the next. It's the most intense sensation I've ever felt.

I'm still trying to catch my breath when Nico rises over me once more. I would assume he'd look arrogant, but he just looks…relieved.

"Much better," he says with a tender smile.

And while giving in to an orgasm that's sure to blur the lines will probably hit me harder later, right now, all I can think about is staying close to Nico for a little bit longer.

Wrapping my legs around him, I pull him closer. We're both still entirely clothed, though I don't think either of us cares. I fist my hands in Nico's shirt and beg in a breathless whisper, "I want you inside me."

His breath leaves him in a rush. Shifting onto one elbow, he reaches into his back pocket to grab his wallet.

Watching him shred the condom wrapper with his teeth is the most erotic thing I've ever seen. I've only ever felt impatience when I've seen men do it in the past, but with Nico…

Everything feels different.

He reaches between us to slide the condom on. And then, in one smooth thrust, he's inside me. I let out a shaky exhale and tighten my legs around him.

"*Christ*, baby," Nico groans, slowly starting to fuck me. "You feel fucking perfect."

A smile lifts the corner of my lips, contentment thrumming in my chest.

Suddenly, an idea occurs to me.

I can't quite use the exact move he showed me earlier, but…

Scissoring my legs, I knock Nico to the side and roll on top.

I can't stop a grin from forming. My hands propped on his chest, I look down at his shell-shocked expression and slow blinks as he tries to make sense of what just happened.

And then he laughs.

"I don't think I've ever been prouder as a coach," he says with a chuckle.

"I'm just glad this one didn't come with a bloody nose."

Nico's eyes drop over my body. "I wouldn't have even noticed."

Usually, a gaze like that makes me feel leered at. Like my body is a piece of meat, with no soul or value inside of it.

With Nico, I'm finding that I *want* him to admire me.

In one motion, I reach for the hem of my dress and pull it over my head.

I watch Nico as he watches me. I see the way his throat moves on a swallow, can feel the way his hands go back to my hips and tighten.

"You're so beautiful," he says in a rough voice.

Warmth fills me at his praise. Then I once again lean forward onto his chest and start to ride him.

His eyes slide shut on a groan as I work myself up and down on his cock. I know how to move my hips when I'm on top, I know how to squeeze his shaft with my inner muscles, when to swirl and how to bounce. I know exactly how to ride Nico to make him lose his mind. It's my job, after all.

And he does lose his mind, fairly quickly.

"*Fuck*, wait— Baby, you have to slow down, that's going to make me—"

I smirk down at him and squeeze hard on his cock, just for good measure. "I thought we were trying to make each other come?"

A pained wince crosses his face. "Don't remind me about you coming. I'm going to lose my shit in two seconds over the memory."

I let out a laugh and lean back, never stopping the movements of my hips.

But when I feel his thumb press against my clit, all amusement fades.

"Yeah, that's what I thought," he grumbles. "Two can play that game."

And that's how we end up fucking each other into oblivion. With both of us desperately trying to make the other come, it takes no time at all before he's thumbing my clit as he fucks up into me, and I'm riding for broke as I feel my orgasm bearing down. The moment it explodes into a blissful firework of pleasure, Nico groans below me, his hips stuttering in their movements.

My last thought before I collapse on Nico's chest, out of breath, and more sated than I've ever felt, is: *He just* had *to be good at sex.*

# ELEVEN
## SCARLETT

"So, Daisy, what are you in school for?"

I force a smile at my client's boss across the table. "Hospitality," I lie, deciding on a major that doesn't usually get a lot of follow-up questions.

He smirks, giving me a judgmental once-over. "And what do you plan on doing with a hospitality degree? Party planning?"

I keep the smile plastered on my face. "Maybe. I haven't really decided yet."

I weather the look he gives me, a look that's equal parts lecherous and condescending. He might not know I'm an escort, but that doesn't mean he doesn't have sex in his eyes. Even with my "boyfriend" sitting next to me.

I glance at my client, a forty-five-year-old balding businessman who's trying to climb the corporate ladder by showing off his hot girlfriend to his shallow boss. In a way, he's one of my best clients, solely because I don't have to touch him, but I do wish he'd man up just a little bit and at least look ashamed that his boss is a leering jerk.

He doesn't look ashamed. He's excited to have something his boss wants.

"Daisy throws great parties," my client says. And the undertone is obvious when he adds, "She really knows how to have a fun time."

The sound of their chuckles makes my skin crawl. You'd think I'd be used to men talking about me like this, but the truth is, you never get used to it. You simply get better at dealing with it.

I double check my smile before placing a hand on my client's arm. "I can't take all the credit. It's almost impossible *not* to have a good time with Mark."

Delight flashes in his eyes. And I can tell that the moment we leave this restaurant, he's going to ask me if he can extend our booking with a visit to the hotel next door.

Waiting for that moment makes the rest of the lunch tense. I have to be diligent about the attention I send him after that, because even though I need to sell my role well for *this* job, I also need to be careful that my inevitable rejection doesn't offend him. Bitter clients are the most dangerous clients.

I'm so focused on *my* client that I forget to worry about his boss. But the moment Mark excuses himself to the bathroom, my spine stiffens.

"So, Daisy," he says, brushing a single finger over the back of my hand. "Is this thing with you and Mark...serious?"

I glance pointedly at the wedding ring on his finger and smile anyway.

"A girl can only hope," I simper.

Something calculating flashes in his eyes that puts me on higher alert than I already am. "You know, I could've sworn I heard Mark asking one of our interns out on a date last week," he says with faux innocence. "It can't be that serious if he's seeing other people, can it?"

I study him for a moment, wondering if all men are this obvious or if my job has just made me smarter. Because he's lying. Mark could barely stutter his way through asking for a date he was *paying* for, so there's no way he's hitting on women at the workplace that triples his insecurity every day. Which means his boss is trying to sabotage his direct report in order to create an opening with me for himself.

I wave him off. "Oh, I'm sure he was just trying to help her with work. Mark and I agreed to be exclusive."

The boss gives me a pitying look, then shakes his head as he leans back in his chair. *Fine by me. I'll take pity over creepy.*

"I hope for your sake that you're right. But if he ever *does* turn out to be…not the man you expected…" That perverse smile curls his lips once again. "I'm always happy to be a listening ear."

I'm saved from having to come up with an answer—that isn't vomiting all over his shoes—because Mark reappears beside our table.

"You two doing okay?" he asks with an uneasy glance between us.

I smile and reach for his hand. "We're great. Just chatting. You ready to go?"

Mark nods and shifts his attention back to his boss, though that tension doesn't dissipate. It seems Mark isn't as clueless as he appears. "Thanks again for lunch. I'm going to walk Daisy out and then I'll meet you back at the office?"

"Sounds good. Don't be late for our team meeting." He turns to me. "It was very nice to meet you, Daisy." And he waits until Mark is reaching for my coat before he winks at me behind his back.

My skin is still crawling from the interaction as Mark leads me outside to catch a cab.

And I barely suppress a shiver when I hear, "So…any chance you're free for an extension? I've got an hour to kill…"

It takes more than my usual willpower to squeeze his hand and lean forward to press a kiss to his cheek. "I would if I could, baby. Maybe another time?"

His face falls, but I must have been gentle enough because he nods and says, "Worth a shot. Thanks for today. You were a huge help with my boss."

*Your boss who would clearly stab you in the back any chance he gets—girlfriend or otherwise.*

"Of course," I say in a far-too-bubbly voice. "It was my pleasure."

Once I'm in the cab, I have a choice. I can either go home and scrub the touch of Mark and the gaze of his boss off my body, or I can go to the gym to work off my frustration.

Today, I decide on a bubble bath.

But as soon as I get home, I realize I should've chosen the gym.

Because there's an issue with my plumbing. Something must be going wrong in the building because my bathtub is backing up with brown water and throwing all dreams of a bath out the window.

I call the building's maintenance man, trying not to tense at the fact that a strange man is about to be in my apartment. Which might be bizarre, considering what I do for a living, but it's harder for me to justify being in close quarters with a man I haven't heavily vetted.

When the maintenance man shows up an hour later, I try to adopt my work persona to cover my nerves. I open the door with a smile and welcome him in, immediately asking if he'd like a water.

"No, thank you, miss," he says with a smile. I try to read what kind of smile it is. "I'll just take a look at the bathroom. Is the bedroom suite this way?"

If he notices my hesitation, he doesn't let on. But it takes me a second to gesture down the hallway to the bedroom.

He disappears into my bedroom without another word. I *hate* that he has to walk through my bedroom to get to the bathroom. But since I'm not willing to leave him alone, I follow him in, one hesitant step at a time.

He's digging around in the tub when I finally walk in. He hears me come in and smiles, then jerks his chin at the too-big bubble bath collection I've started.

"I never could get into baths," he says casually. "I always get bored in two minutes. But I do wish I could like them. They seem…relaxing."

*Is he flirting? What man talks to a woman about baths?*

"They're pretty nice," I say absentmindedly. "Can—can you fix the plumbing?"

He sends me a curious glance but answers, "Yeah, I should be able to fix the issue. I should have the…" He digs around in his toolkit and pulls something out. "We had this happen a few weeks ago, unfortunately. Should only take me a few minutes."

I give him a stiff nod and decide to give him some space. I only go so far as my bedroom, though, and even then, I end up pacing the entire time.

Fifteen minutes later, he comes out. "Well, it's all fixed. No more faulty bathtubs for you. I'll let the building owner know what happened and to keep an eye on it. But you should be good now."

Twisting my hands in front of me, I send him a shaky smile.

"Great, thank you so much for coming out so quickly." I glance around the room and toward the bathroom. And then, because one of the weird stipulations in my lease is having to front the cost for my own repairs, I ask, "How much do I owe you?"

He waves me off. "This one is on the house."

I freeze. *Please don't say that. When men say that, they always expect something in return.*

"Oh, you don't have to do that," I rush to say. "Really, how much do I owe you?"

He frowns. "No, really. No charge. This was nothing."

And maybe it's because my nerves are already raw from my date earlier, but panic starts to swell. I'm suddenly very aware of the fact that a strange man is standing in my bedroom, pressing to do me a favor.

*Please just let me pay you. At least if there's money involved, it's a straightforward transaction.*

I open my mouth to *insist*, but before I can say a word, he says, "I need to get going. I have another job to get to." He smiles, and despite being wired, I automatically return a polite smile of my own. "Hopefully, it doesn't act up again, but if it does, call the maintenance number. We'll get you sorted."

"Will do." It comes out as a squeak. "Th-thank you."

Another glance I can't read, but thankfully, he leaves right after. Once he closes the door behind him, I flip the deadbolt and collapse onto my couch with haggard breathing.

That should not have been as stressful as it was. At twenty-two years old, and after three years of living on my own, a regular service call like that shouldn't be making me hyperventilate.

I jump when my phone pings with a message. It's Amara's notification sound, and I know what's in the text before I even check it.

Amara: Date number three with Mr. UFC tonight. I'd say check in with me afterwards, but it looks like things have been going well.

The reminder of my date with Nico brings a wave of relief. I try to tell myself it's only because it'll be the first male interaction today where I know exactly what I'm getting out of it, but I'm not as convincing as I should be. I know it's because it's *Nico* I'm meeting.

Looking toward my bedroom, I debate taking that bubble bath to scrub the nerves from my skin. But I can't get the sight of that guy in my bathroom out of my head, so that effectively scraps that idea. I'll probably have to bleach the entire bathroom before I can use the tub again.

I glance toward my treadmill.

*Guess I'm sweating it out instead.*

———

Five hours later, I'm knocking on Nico's hotel room door.

The moment it swings open, every ounce of tension leaves my body.

"Hi," I whisper, almost shyly.

His smile is sweet and genuine and better than I deserve.

"Hey, Red."

He steps aside and gestures me in. It occurs to me that he never touches me when I walk by him. Actually, he doesn't touch me until *I* initiate it.

"How are you?" I ask, pulling off my thin cardigan. I'm wearing a thin blue dress, more casual than usual for a client.

But when I spin and see a look of awe cross Nico's face, I know I made the right call.

"Uh, good," he says, his gaze snapping back to my face. "Good. How are you?"

I sink onto the couch with a smile. "I'm great."

I'm not even lying.

"Did you train today?" I ask him.

He nods and takes a seat on the chair beside the couch. "I got two sessions in today. So if I seem a little tired, that's why."

"We could've postponed," I offer. Though I hate the idea. "You shouldn't have to be tired when you see me."

His lip quirks. "Red, I'm *always* tired. And besides, I didn't want to go another week without seeing you."

*Why does my stomach flutter at that when, coming from any other client, it would turn me off?*

"Would it help if I gave you a massage?" I ask. Partly because it's an obvious way to flirt, but also because I'd really like to touch him.

He shakes his head with a smile. "Honestly, I'd rather give *you* a massage. You look tense. Is everything…okay?"

It should alarm me that he can see me so well. But instead of shaking him off with a lie, I find myself telling the truth.

"It's better now."

He seems to believe me because after a moment, he smiles. Then he relaxes back into the cushions with a yawn and says, "It sounds like both of us could use a more relaxing night."

He has no idea how right he is.

"What does relaxing look like for you?" I ask.

"Depends," Nico says with a shrug. "After a fight it means devouring all the food and rotting on the couch for a few days. But on an average rest day during the week, it could mean grabbing a drink with my brothers, or going to the movies with a teammate." He turns toward me. "What about for you?"

"I like bubble baths," is the first thing that pops into my mind. I feel my cheeks heat at the confession, but Nico only smiles with amusement. "Sometimes I'll watch reality TV to destress and turn my mind off."

"Can I tell you a secret?" he asks. I nod too eagerly. "I got really into watching *Dancing With The Stars* recently," he whispers.

A laugh bursts out of me at the image of Nico being riveted by celebrities dancing. The thought is adorable.

"Have you seen the latest episode?" I ask.

He shakes his head. "Not yet. I'm caught up except for that one."

I only hesitate for a moment before asking, "Do you want to watch it?"

He seems surprised but excited about the idea. "Hell yeah."

I watch as he stands and moves over to the couch I'm sitting on, the one that has the best view of the TV. He keeps a respectful distance between us, but I manage to move a few inches closer when I shift into a more comfortable position. If he notices, he doesn't comment on it, but I think I see his mouth twitch.

"Have *you* seen it?" he asks as he turns it on.

I shake my head, but I'm lying. I don't want to say anything that will make him change the channel.

And as the familiar intro starts to play, I relax for the first time all day. All *week*, maybe. I don't know what it is about Nico, but...

A few minutes later, I'm fast asleep on his shoulder.

# TWELVE
## NICO

I let her sleep.

The show's been over for a while now, but I can't remember a single thing that happened. I've been too busy staring at her.

She looks…peaceful.

There's no tension on her face, no stress lines visible anywhere. And there's a soft smile on her lips, one I've never seen before.

Her head rests on my shoulder, her body tucked into my side with her hand wrapped around my arm, and I can hear the tiny sounds of her snoring.

She's adorable. I could stare at her for hours.

I can't reach my phone from here—not that I'd want to— so I click the guide on the TV to check the time. 9:37 p.m. She got here at 8:00. Our appointment tonight was for an hour.

Should I wake her? Am I supposed to wake her?

But also, *why* did she fall asleep? Was she that tired? I would've noticed when she walked in if she was exhausted. She just looked a little tense.

I can't help brushing a hand down her hair, taking in her features and the way she's curled into me. I don't even know if I *can* wake her up.

Before I can help it, my thoughts start to shift.

Is this…normal for her? Not just the tiredness, but feeling comfortable enough with an essential stranger to fall asleep on them?

And as much as I hate to even think about it, it's definitely not normal for an escort to go past a client's allotted time without discussion.

…right?

Is it possible she's more comfortable with me than anyone else? That she actually likes me? That I'm not alone in this attraction toward her?

*God, I hope that's possible.*

I can't stop looking at her, can't stop stroking her hair. I've been dying to ask her out—on a *normal* date. I want to get to know her, want to ask her questions that she'll answer for real. I want to take her on a date that's not inside this hotel room, that doesn't have a time limit, and that doesn't need to include sex or intimacy or anything that she's used to being paid for.

But she's so closed off that I'm nervous to ask, too terrified to ruin any semblance of a connection I have with her.

My worry is interrupted by her stirring in my arms. I quickly pull my hand from her hair, but I can't bring myself to move away.

She wakes with the sweetest little moan, her body stretching free of sleep before she's even opened her eyes. When she finally does, she smiles up at me.

My heart stops at the sight.

And then it all goes to shit.

I watch the realization enter her eyes, and the smile drops from her lips. Suddenly, she's crawling backwards to the other end of the couch, shock and regret on her face.

"Oh my God, I'm so sorry," she breathes. "I-I didn't mean to fall asleep on you, I'm so sorry."

I hold my hands up in a gesture of *there's nothing to be scared of.* "You're fine, I promise. I'm not mad." *Far from it.*

She leaps for her phone on the coffee table. When she sees the time, her eyes go impossibly wider.

"Oh my *God*," she nearly yelps. "I slept for over an hour! Why didn't you wake me up?"

I frown, suddenly worried that she missed something because I let her sleep. *Another client?*

I try to fight down the jealousy. And fail.

"I didn't wake you because you looked like you needed the rest," I tell her carefully. "From my end, it's not a problem. Are *you* okay?"

Now that shock morphs to horror.

"No, I-I didn't mean it for me. I just... Oh my God, I'm so sorry. I can't believe I wasted your time like this." Her head whips around, searching for something. *An answer?* "Obviously, there's no charge for tonight. This was completely my fault."

"Red..."

"No, I mean it." She grabs for my hand, looking desperate. "I can't charge you for this. This was completely unprofessional, and I can't apologize enough."

"It really is fine—"

"I hope you won't hold it against the agency," she continues, not hearing any of what I'm saying. She's in a panic spiral. "If you'd like to see another girl, I can get Amara to comp your next appointment."

I wonder if the horror is showing on my face. "Uh…no. I want to see *you* again."

Finally, that gets her attention.

"You… You what?"

I take a chance and shift her hand in mine so I'm holding it, my thumb brushing over her skin. "I want to see *you* again. I'm not mad that you fell asleep." Another risk, but I take it. "I actually really enjoyed our night." I give her a lopsided smile to break the tension. "It was relaxing."

A small fraction of her tension disappears, her shoulders dropping.

"Well…" She gives me a look of uncertainty. "If you'd like to see me again, then I'll comp your date. No charge."

Still smiling, I shake my head. "No deal. Tonight counts just as much as the other two. Red, I had *fun*."

She doesn't believe me; I can see it in her eyes. *Jesus, does she only think she's worth spending time with if there's sex involved? Or is this an escort thing?*

"I'm really going to insist," she says after a beat. "Tonight *shouldn't* count. All I did was say hello and then fall asleep." I open my mouth to push back one last time, but she talks right over me. "Call the agency for another date. One you can pay for."

I hate paying for any of them. Not because I'm cheap, but because I want to *date* her.

But I can tell now's not the time to have that conversation. She's too on edge after waking up, too scared of something I'm not seeing. So I simply nod my agreement. "Alright."

When she seems relieved by my answer, I know I made the right call. I'll fight her insecurities, or whatever this is, another day.

Our conversation over, the air fills with awkward tension.

I'm not sure she wants to stay, and I don't know how to ask her. But I also don't want to kick her out.

"Just so you know, Andy survived eliminations," I say casually.

Thank God it works. She lets out a soft laugh and says, "I assumed he would. That man is the people's princess. I love him."

Encouraged by her answer, I take a chance and ask, "Want to watch it again?"

*Whoops. Too much too soon.*

Her lips purse and she glances at the door. "I should probably get going." But she sounds regretful.

I nod. "I understand. I'll get your sweater."

Standing, I reach for the sweater she laid on the opposite couch and hold it up for her to slip into. She sends me a grateful smile before turning her back and letting me slide it on.

When she turns to face me, she's far closer than I anticipated.

Do I imagine the hitch in her breath? I don't know, but I'm not imagining the way her gaze drops to my lips.

"Thank you," she whispers.

I swallow roughly. "You're welcome," I respond, my voice like gravel. *God, she's so beautiful.*

But I can't kiss her. I shouldn't even *touch* her right now.

Thankfully, she takes the decision out of my hands. Because she reaches up slowly and pulls the collar of my shirt to the side.

"Did you get a new tattoo?" She's barely breathing as she asks the question.

I'm barely breathing as I *answer* it. "I did. Last week. Just a small one."

She tugs it farther to the side. "What is it?"

I hesitate for a beat, then say, "It's easier to show you if I take my shirt off."

There. The ball is in her court now. If she's truly thrown off by our boundaries tonight, she'll say no and leave.

Instead, she meets my eyes and nods. "Okay."

Slowly, I reach back with one hand to grip the collar of my shirt and pull it over my head.

"Why is it so sexy when guys do that?"

My lip twitches at her question. I don't think she meant to say that out loud, especially when her cheeks pinken. I don't tease her about it, I just point at the tattoo and explain, "They're paw prints from my childhood dogs. I've been wanting to get it forever."

Her gaze zeroes in on the ink, awe in her eyes as she lifts a hand and gently traces over the raised ink above my collarbone. "They're beautiful," she whispers.

"Do you have any tattoos?" I ask.

She shakes her head.

Taking a guess, I ask, "Are they too unladylike?"

The *yes* is obvious in her eyes. "Has there ever been a design you've really liked?" I try instead.

She lets out a noncommittal hum. "To be honest, I've never even considered the question." Her hand continues to trace over my skin as she adds, "But this is a very sweet tattoo, Nico."

I can't stop staring at her. "Have you ever had a pet?"

She shakes her head. "No. My parents weren't fond of animals. And even living on my own now... I don't know, I've never really felt like I'm ready for one."

"You could foster," I suggest. "Those are temporary. You could get a feel for pet parent life."

I can't read her expression. I touched on something, I just don't know what.

112

"Maybe," she says, pulling her hand away. I wish she hadn't.

"So I'll…call you?" I ask, my voice too high. Maybe I'm just overcompensating for the fact that I know I won't be calling *her*, but the agency.

The smile she gives me is a mask. I know it, and she knows it. "I'll be waiting."

And then she quickly leans up to press a kiss on my cheek before rushing out the door.

I don't move from my spot for a while.

---

The next morning, I'm still in the hotel room, bleary-eyed from sleep, when my phone rings.

*Lucas.* I answer it with a groan.

"Why are you calling me this early," I croak out.

A pause. "Brother, it's 9 a.m. I've already won two cases in court. Why are *you* still sleeping."

I blink my eyes open. "Because sleep is more important than making rich bastards richer?"

"Sounds like something a not-rich bastard would say."

I roll my eyes. "Lucas, you're my manager. With full access to my bank account. What's your definition of rich if not that?"

"*My* bank account."

I let out a heavy breath and drag a hand down my face. "Dude, why are you calling me?"

"Ironically, in manager capacity," he says dryly. "Your PR girl called me because she had an idea." A pause. "She said you're in New York?"

I hesitate. I haven't exactly shared with my brothers *why* I'm in New York. "I am."

Another pause. "Okay... Why?"

"I've been training up here," I answer simply.

I should've known that wouldn't be enough to convince Lucas. The guy's like a bloodhound. "That doesn't explain why you're sleeping up there."

Wincing, I tell him a half-lie. "I've been...seeing a girl here."

"Ah," I hear through the phone, his smugness obvious. "That's the big picture I was looking for. Is she hot? Does she have any friends?"

I roll my eyes, knowing he can sense the action. "As if you don't have enough dates lined up yourself. I'm not setting you up. And anyway, this is...new. I don't want to risk it with anything."

He chuckles. "Alright, alright, I'll let it be. For now. But you know this is eventually going to call for another night out with Alexander, right?"

*Yeah, for once I'm not looking forward to that.*

"Lucas, what's the idea?" I ask impatiently.

I can hear him clap his hands together, can imagine him pacing in his too-fancy office with the beautiful view of the Philadelphia skyline. "Here's what I'm thinking," he starts. "Socials absolutely *loved* the pictures of you at that *yoga with puppies* event. I think we should capitalize on it. Videos of you training are great for marketing this fight, but it's the after-hours that people love to see."

I chew on my bottom lip as I mull it over. I usually hate the PR stuff, but Lucas knows the best way to get me to do them is to involve animals. It's hard to hate a marketing gig if it involves puppies.

"There's a shelter in NYC that's getting all kinds of traction on socials right now," Lucas continues. "But somehow, it's still struggling to find fosters and adopters. You should attend one of their rescue meet-and-greets. Just spend the afternoon there, help out, and record a few videos with the dogs. Boom. Perfect non-fighting content to balance out the training videos we're using to market your fight."

Is it fate that I mentioned fostering last night?

More importantly, is that why I'm saying yes?

"It's a good idea," I find myself saying. "When's the next meet-and-greet?"

"Next week, on Sunday. I can set it up if you're good with it."

My brain's already thinking about whether or not I can get Daisy to see me on a Sunday night. "I'm good with it," I respond absentmindedly.

"Good. And I'll just put it out there: if you can get your mystery girl to come with you, it'd be even better for pictures…"

"Lucas," I groan.

"I'm just saying! You were just telling us you haven't had any luck with dating, and now suddenly you're driving up to New York once a week for some new girl. It makes me curious."

"*Everything* makes you curious."

"It's what makes me a good lawyer," he retaliates. "Anyway, plan for Sunday afternoon then. And if you feel like fostering by the end, even better."

I roll my eyes. "I'm hanging up now. I hope you get murked in court today."

He's still laughing as I hang up.

# THIRTEEN
## SCARLETT

Three days later, the autopilot I'm used to running on feels more depressing than usual. Even my classes aren't enough to bring me out of the haze I've sunken into. Instead of them being a flicker of excitement on my usually drab days, they just make me feel...desperate for more.

I think that's why Nico's comment about fostering continues to roll around in my head. I don't think I'd be ready for a pet in my apartment just yet, but there are temporary fosters, right? I'm pretty sure I've seen videos of people taking dogs out of the shelter for an afternoon. That could be fun...

A quick search tells me there's a meet-and-greet hosted by a local rescue this weekend. It's only a two-hour event, and they're desperate for volunteers. If they needed people to work hands-on with the animals, I don't think I'd be able to talk myself into it, but when I see they need a few people to assist with admin duties, it's less of an inner debate to make my decision.

It only takes a few clicks to register as an assistant.

And now I have three days to panic about this commitment I've made on a whim.

By the time Sunday morning rolls around, and I'm sitting in a taxi on my way to the event, my nerves have only tripled. *What was I thinking? Why would I step out of my routine like this?*

Sundays are normally my off days. Not that they look much different than my other days—besides the not seeing clients part. But knowing what I have to look forward to has been a comfort. Today's shaking me more than I thought it would.

When the taxi stops at the event, I'm breathing heavily and about to ask the driver to turn around. I shouldn't be here. I add no value here. I'm not even wearing the right clothes, *why* did I think I should wear a sundress to an event like this? I need to leave. I—

And then I see him. Nico.

He's kneeling in front of a golden retriever whose tail is going a mile a minute, who can't stop licking Nico's face long enough to let the man get his balance. Sure enough, he goes down with a loud laugh, disappearing behind a cloud of yellow fur.

My breathing slows. So does my heartrate.

"Thank you," I tell the driver, passing some cash over his shoulder. "Keep the change."

My feet carry me to Nico before I can think better of it. I stop thinking about how I should be questioning why a client is in the same space as I am, or that I need to check in to do the job I signed up for—I just need to be around him. Just for a second.

Nico's managed to right himself to a somewhat standing position, still bent over and petting the golden, when he spots me. His eyes go wide.

"Red," he says, straightening. "You're... You're here."

"*You're* here," I say in an accusing tone. But it's playful. "Should I be worried you're stalking me?"

His eyes go wider. "What? No!"

I gesture around the parking lot where there are two dozen dogs and their foster parents. "So dropping a foster idea last time I saw you was pure coincidence?"

*He's adorable when he blushes.* "It is. I swear. My brother set this up as a PR thing." That blush deepens. "Not that I don't do this at home, too. I love dogs. I help rescue organizations all the time. This has nothing to do with you."

I give him a small smile to let him know I don't actually think he intended for this to happen. "I believe you. But it *is* a funny coincidence."

Something occurs to him, and he frowns. "Wait. Have you done this before? Or did you really come here because of what I said?"

Now it's my turn to blush. "I really came here because of what you said," I admit quietly.

He practically *beams*. "Amazing. Are you planning to foster? Because if so, I've got the perfect good boy for you right here..."

I let out a laugh at that. "I should've known you'd be good at this. That dimple is far too persuasive." Proving my point, he flashes me a crooked smile. "But no, that's not why I'm here. I signed up to help."

"Ah. Well, that's good, too. Do you know where you're stationed?"

I shake my head. "I just got here. I need to check in."

Nico looks around the parking lot. "I think the organizer is at the front desk inside the shelter. I can come with you to —oh, here she comes."

I turn to see the woman whose face is plastered on every

post for the rescue organization. When our eyes meet, she smiles.

"Hi, there. Are you here as a foster parent, adoptive parent, or volunteer?"

"Volunteer," I tell her. "I'm—"

Suddenly, my gaze shoots to Nico.

I registered under my real name for this. The name Nico doesn't know.

I could probably pull the lady aside, make up some lie about needing to change my name for security reasons. I doubt they'd care, or even ask any questions.

Or I could give her my real name. With Nico standing right here.

I've never given a client my real name. It's always been an easy level of protection, one I've never even thought to reconsider. But with Nico...

*Do I want to keep hiding myself from him?*

The answer comes in the split-second it takes these thoughts to fly through my head. I hold Nico's gaze as I tell the organizer, "My name is Scarlett. I registered as a volunteer."

Nico's eyes widen as understanding dawns.

Then...he grins.

"Oh, perfect, we were just finishing assigning positions," the organizer says, oblivious to us as she looks down at her paper. "The foster parents are fine as holders, and I think we have the front desk covered to handle signups, but..." She looks up, searching for something, and immediately brightens when her gaze locks on Nico. "Oh, Nicholas! There you are. How's it going meeting the dogs?"

I quirk an eyebrow at him when he stops beside me. *Nicholas?* I mouth.

He shrugs, that damn dimple making another appearance.

"It's great, Mrs. Ross. I think I managed to introduce myself to everyone."

"Perfect. In that case…" She turns her attention to me. "Would you be okay with helping Nicholas conduct interviews of our harder fosters?"

My brow furrows in confusion. "He's *interviewing* the dogs?"

I turn when Nico chuckles beside me. "I'm just shooting some videos for socials. It's basically a few minutes per dog, petting them, telling viewers about them, that kind of thing."

I look back at the organizer. "Do I need to be on camera?" Because that's a giant no.

She's already shaking her head. "No, of course not, dear. We just need someone holding the camera." She seems to finally clue in to my hesitation—I thought I'd be handing out papers or something, not spending more time with a client—so she adds, "Or I could put you at the front desk and ask one of the other girls to help Nico?"

"I'll do it," I blurt out. Too fast. "I mean, as long as I'm not in the video, I can help." Suddenly unsure, I glance at Nico. "If you're okay with that."

His grin couldn't be bigger. "More than okay."

*Why does that make me giddy?* "Okay," I whisper.

"Great," he chirps, grabbing my hand. "Then I've got the perfect little puppy to introduce you to…"

A minute later, I'm staring down at the biggest dog I've ever seen. "*This* is a puppy?"

Nico nods as he squats down to pet what I'm assuming is a Great Dane. "Yup. Nine months. He'll get even bigger, believe it or not." Looking up at me, he smiles. "Wanna pet him?"

I'm doubting if I made the right call coming here. I've never been around animals, never had a pet of my own. I just always liked how people talked about their pets. I liked the idea of how they love their human unconditionally.

Nico must sense my hesitation because he stands up, sobering. "Here," he says softly, reaching for my hand again. Slowly, he extends it toward the Great Dane. "Just let him smell you first. He's a good boy."

I wait with bated breath as the puppy sniffs my hand, seeming just as unsure of me as I feel about him.

"You can read their body language the same way you can read people," Nico murmurs. "If their ears are back, or he looks tense, or too still, then I wouldn't recommend petting them. But if they—"

A giant tongue shoots out to lick the entire length of my hand.

I shriek and jump back, but the shout quickly becomes laughter.

"He likes you," Nico says as I extend my hand again, this time to pet the dog's head.

"I like him too," I say with a soft smile.

It takes me a minute to realize I'm still petting the dog, and that Nico is watching me do it. Blushing, I pull my hand back.

"So... How do you want to do these interviews?"

Taking the phone from his back pocket—he's wearing jeans and a black t-shirt, looking entirely too delicious—he unlocks his phone and hands it to me. "Just press record and aim it at me and the dog. I'll do the rest."

Perplexed, I stare at the phone. "Did you just hand a girl your unlocked phone?"

He grins at me. "Dig through whatever you'd like, baby. I have no secrets."

My eyes narrow at him. "That's a little terrifying."

He shrugs. "I'm not interesting enough for secrets."

"Well, we know *that's* not true," I mutter, swiping open the camera app. I don't miss Nico's chuckle.

For the next five minutes, I record Nico as he pets the Great Dane and chats with the dog's foster parent. He's a natural, with both the dogs and the interviews in front of the camera. He gets the most playful side of the dog, and he asks the important questions of the parent. By the time I press stop on the recording, I completely understand why his fans love him. He's everything genuine and lovable in a professional athlete.

"Alright, who's next?" I ask when he leads me across the parking lot.

"This," he says, "is Bossman. Boss for short. He's forty-five pounds of lovable micro bully."

But for some reason, Boss doesn't go for Nico. He goes for me. He trots over on his tiny legs and presses his flat face directly into my thigh.

I hear Nico's loud laugh as I squat to better scratch behind Boss's ears. He sounds like a pig with the way he's breathing, but his little nub of a tail is shaking so hard it's moving his entire bottom half. With another snort, he launches himself at me.

I collapse on my butt with a delighted giggle.

"Looks like Boss more than likes you," Nico says with a chuckle. "You might have to be the one doing this interview."

I send him a half-baked glare even as I scratch Boss's butt where it's still planted in my lap. "Not happening, but good try."

In the end, the interview is mostly a bust, solely because Boss can't focus on Nico for long enough to stay in the shot. He keeps trying to escape his foster to get to me.

"Sorry, folks, I might have to edit some footage into this video," Nico says, amusement coating his tone. "It looks like

Boss has a big thing for our camera girl and can't seem to stay focused."

With perfect timing, Boss yanks the leash out of his foster parent's hand and bolts for me. I let out a shriek of laughter and drop Nico's phone as I grab for his collar.

I'm still laughing as I watch Nico pick up his phone and turn the camera toward his face. "Well, folks, there you have it. Boss is clearly a loverboy. He's escaped the interview in favor of kissing our camerawoman." A pause as he looks at me. "Not that I can blame him."

My jaw drops. Nico's cheeks pinken and he quickly shuts off the video.

"Alright, moving on," he mutters, handing Boss's leash back to his chuckling foster parent. Then he extends a hand to help me up.

"You're cute when you blush," I whisper.

"Thank God, because you seem to bring it out of me," he mumbles. When he meets my eyes, his expression softens. "Are you having fun?"

I smile, a real, genuine smile. "I am."

He looks relieved at that. "Good. We have a few more and then we're done."

For the next forty minutes, Nico introduces me to more dogs, and I film more interviews.

It's the most fun Sunday I've ever had.

"How'd it go, you two?" the organizer asks when we return to the front desk. "Get some good footage?"

"A lot of good footage," Nico confirms. "I'll have my PR girl edit everything tomorrow and then start posting them. Is there anyone we should tag besides the rescue?"

"Nope, that should be enough. We just want to get some eyes on the dogs available for adoption. We're nearing max capacity, unfortunately."

"Well, that's my cue," comes a voice from behind us.

I turn to see a pretty brunette woman wearing blue scrubs walking toward us. She sends me a warm smile as she slides her hands into her pockets and trains her focus on the organizer.

"I'm Nova," she says. "We talked yesterday about one of your medical fosters?"

"Oh, yes. You're from the Philadelphia Vet Clinic. Nice to meet you, dear." She opens the half-door to get into the building and gestures for the girl to come in. "This way, I'll introduce you to Cheesecake. You're going to *love* her."

I watch the pair walk into the hallway where I can see they have the kennels. For a minute, I can only stare after the girl, who's clearly a veterinarian, and wonder what kind of life she leads. About the value she brings to the world, and the good she does in it.

About the sense of accomplishment she must feel at the end of a long day.

*What would that feel like?*

*Could I do that with a psychology degree?*

The sudden thought is a shocking one. Maybe I should've had it when I first picked my major, but that was never why I registered for college. I did it because I was good at it, because it was fun and gave me something to do with my time. I didn't have a *purpose* with it.

Now I'm wondering if I should.

I'm shaken from my thoughts when another volunteer appears from the kennel and asks Nico, "I'm so sorry, would you mind shooting one more? I just had an idea that might really help the organization out."

Nico doesn't even hesitate. "Of course. What do you need?"

An excited grin appears on the girl's face. "How are you with cats?"

Ten minutes later, I, along with three other volunteers, are trying desperately to smother our laughter as we watch Nico crawling with kittens. There's one on his shoulder, one hanging from his shirt, two in his lap, and two in his hands.

"Ow! Motherfu—" He catches himself before we can let our laughter explode. With a glare at the offender, he gently extracts the kitten that just hooked onto his nipple. "We might need to hurry this up," he mutters. "I think I may have just discovered I'm not a cat person."

The girl who brought us takes two of the cats from Nico with a chuckle. "Maybe we just leave the one sleeping in your lap and give you one to cuddle."

Nico sighs. "That might be a good idea. My nipples thank you."

One of the volunteers takes the two orange kittens wreaking havoc on Nico's clothes, another one trying to climb on his head, and I grab the black one trying to escape from his hold. Once he's left with two kittens, he's able to record a somewhat peaceful adoption video.

When the volunteers take the last two kittens from him to put them back in their crates, I take the opportunity to sidle up to Nico and murmur in a voice only he can hear, "So does this mean pussy doesn't like you?"

His eyes widen as he turns to me. I'm trying to bite down on my smile, but I can feel that I'm failing. For a moment, he only stares at me.

"I'm still trying to figure that out," he finally says.

It's so obviously aimed at me that I duck my head with a smile and shift away.

*I'm trying to figure it out, too.*

# FOURTEEN
## NICO

By the time the cats are all put away, we've officially reached the end of our volunteer obligations. And as we walk back to the front desk area, I start to sweat.

Because I'm running out of time to ask Scarlett—*her name is Scarlett*—on a date.

This is the best opening I could ever hope for. Accidentally running into her, in public, in a setting that has nothing to do with her job or our previous interactions…it's the best chance I have. Especially now that a dozen animals have softened her.

Especially knowing she trusts me enough to give me her real name.

*I can't believe she gave me her real name.*

When we reach the front desk, I've reached a state of *fuck it*. I'm just going to ask her.

But just as I open my mouth, a girl walks through the front door who immediately captures everyone's attention.

It's not just the combat boots, all-black clothes, or fishnets showing through ripped pants—it's the *I don't give a fuck* attitude emanating from her. Which triples when she sees me staring, digs her hands into her sweatshirt pockets as she looks me up and down, and snaps, "Can I help you?"

My gaze shoots to the ceiling. "What? No, I'm good."

I hear a snicker beside me.

The girl trains her attention on the front desk staff, popping a large bubble with her gum. "I'm here to pick up a cat."

"Uh...okay. Any particular type of cat?"

"The spicy black one that no one wants."

I let out a snort of laughter that I hide with a cough.

It earns me a death glare.

"Oh!" one of the volunteers exclaims excitedly. "You're the one who just got approved for Milton. Hold on, let me grab him for you."

And then she's bringing out the black kitten that, not fifteen minutes ago, was trying desperately to get away from me. When it's handed over to the girl, not only does it not try to escape, but it sits regally in her hands, staring at her for a half-second before finally lying flat against her chest and closing its eyes with a purr.

Then *I'm* the one sending a glare.

"He's perfect," the girl says with the tiniest hint of a smile. "I'm assuming there's paperwork?"

The cat is still curled up in her arms when we exit the room to leave them to their adoption process.

"I guess some pets really do resemble their owners," I muse as I hold the door open for Scarlett.

"You're just mad it didn't like you," she says with an adorable giggle.

"You're damn right I am," I murmur. "I thought all animals liked me."

"Maybe it's just dogs," she comments as a German

shepherd rushes up to us. "Did you only have dogs growing up?"

I nod as I pet the fluffy pup. "Yeah, we were a dog household. We always had one in the house when we were kids, and then once I moved out, I started fostering. I work with their sister organization in Philly." I send her a hesitant glance. "That's why I mentioned it last week. I swear I wasn't stalking you."

Thank God, she sends me a sweet smile. "I know. I was never worried about that." Then, to herself, she muses, "Maybe I should be."

"Go out with me." It escapes me in a rush. Holding it back is basically impossible after that.

Except, the shocked and fearful look she turns to me with makes me wish I'd tried a little bit harder.

"What?"

I swallow and decide to keep going. "Go out with me. Please."

I try not to be offended by the disbelief on her face. "And...do what?" she asks.

I almost laugh. "Whatever we want. It's just a date. We could grab some food, or see a movie, or—"

"*Just* a date?"

Her sudden intensity makes me frown. "Uh, yeah. It's not like we haven't done them before, this time would just mean—"

"That you're not paying me."

My eyes widen. I open my mouth, but nothing comes out.

She sighs. "Sorry, but it's true. That would be the only difference."

My head is spinning. *Technically*, that's true, but—

"I can't, Nico," she says simply. But she doesn't say it like a rejection. She sounds almost...sad.

"Okay," I say slowly. "Can I ask why? Because if you honestly think I'm just trying to get out of paying you, then I've done a piss-poor job of showing you who I am."

"But that's just it," she says. "I *don't* know who you are. I mean—" She lets out a humorless laugh. "We've seen each other a few times. I have no idea who you are. And you want me to trust you with thousands of dollars? One free date is two *thousand* dollars, Nico."

I open my mouth, then close it right away. I never thought of it like that.

She sighs and steps closer. After a moment, she takes one of my hands. "Look. I *like* you. I have fun with you every time we're together. And yes, in another life, if you asked me out on the street, I'd say yes in a heartbeat. But that's just not my reality. I don't date clients." Her thumb brushes over the back of my hand. "I'm sorry," she adds in a near-whisper.

Inwardly, I sigh. I can't even blame her.

I'm not giving up, but I don't blame her.

"Okay," I say after a moment. "I understand."

And then before she can read this as a breakup, I add, "I'll keep paying."

Her brow furrows. "What do you mean?"

I wrap my other arm around her waist and pull her closer. "I mean, I still want to date you. I want the kind of date that this would be if we were in another life. But I'll pay for it. I'll earn your trust."

She still looks skeptical. "I don't understand. If this were a normal date, you'd still be trying to get under my skirt."

"I know this might sound stupid since we've already had sex, but...no, I wouldn't."

She doesn't even try to hide her disbelief.

"I mean it," I press. "I can guarantee that even if we'd

met the normal way, I would've been more caught up in the get-to-know-you part than anything else."

She's too polite to tell me she doesn't believe me, but her quirked eyebrow is enough to say what she isn't.

I try a different approach. "Okay, then how about this? We date. I still pay you. But we don't have sex."

Her nose scrunches at that. "Why would we do that?"

*Oh, my sweet girl. Who hurt you?*

I want so badly to ask her. To get her talking so I can finally understand why she sees the world—and men—the way she does. But she's clearly not ready for that yet, so for now, I don't ask.

I brush my thumb over her hand that I'm still holding. "Because I like you," I say softly. "Because it's not your body I'm after, but *you*."

My knees almost buckle with relief when I see a tentative hope flash across her face. She's scared and unsure, but it's the beginning of trust.

"So let's just…hang out," I suggest with what I hope is a casual shrug. "No pressure, no masks needed, just two people spending time together who want to get to know each other."

There's still a beat of hesitation, but after a moment, she says slowly, "Okay."

I grin and take a step back, still holding on to her hand. "Great. So…art or music?"

She blinks at me. "I… What?"

Patiently, I ask again. "Do you like art or music more?"

She still doesn't seem to understand the question. "Whatever you like is fine."

I have to focus on swallowing my sigh. "Red…" But then something occurs to me, and I turn fully so I can take both of her hands. "Do you know what I'd really like tonight?"

She shakes her head.

"I'd really like to learn what *you* like. No hidden motives, no catering to *my* likes."

"I don't know if I can do that," she whispers.

It's the most honest moment we've shared.

I can't help cupping her face in my hand. I know she's scared; I can see it in every inch of her. But I'm hoping I can coax her out of her shell anyway.

"I know, baby," I whisper. "But can you try? If not for me, then do it for yourself. I want you to have fun, too."

Her throat moves on a rough swallow, none of that fear dimming, but after a moment, she gives me the tiniest nod.

I know the moment my smile brings out my dimple because a huff of laughter leaves her pretty lips.

"Good. Now. Art or music?"

There's still a little bit of hesitation, and her voice is still quiet, but she says, "Music."

My grin widens. "Amazing. I have the perfect spot."

# FIFTEEN
## SCARLETT

Twenty minutes later, our taxi stops in front of a bar called the Cellar Dog Jazz Club.

"Have you ever been here?" Nico asks as we step out of the taxi.

I shake my head, taking in the lively bar in front of me. "I'm not super big on the party scene," I admit.

He lets out a thoughtful hum as he takes my hand. "What scene *are* you big on?"

To my surprise, I feel an urge to be open with him. Maybe because I feel safe with him. Or maybe it's because I know he took a risk asking me out.

"The academic one," I admit quietly.

While I occasionally tell clients I'm in school if it fits with the persona I think they want, I've never *really* broached the subject of school with a man. Not in a way I could be honest about it. I heard *no one wants a know-it-all for a girlfriend* so many times in my life that it's practically engrained in me. Amara is the only one who knows I'm even enrolled in college. But...I think Nico might be understanding of it.

I'm holding my breath for his reaction, but he sounds excited when he asks, "Really? Does that mean you're in school?"

I nod, my grip on his hand tightening.

He grins as he pulls me to sit on the stools at the bar. "Damn, Red, you're holding out on me. Now I want to know everything."

All tension releases from my shoulders with one relieved laugh. Of course, Nico wouldn't think college was a turnoff. The man is the least judgmental person I've ever met.

"But first," Nico says, waving the bartender down, "let's get you something to drink. What would you like? Wine?"

When I glance at the drink menu behind the bartender, I realize…no, I don't want wine. I want to be normal for once in my life and order what *I* want.

I want to order a beer without feeling like my mother is going to sneer at me for picking a "trashy" drink.

"Actually…" I start, looking to Nico for help. "Can you help me pick a beer? I'm not a big beer-drinker so I don't know what to try."

He looks surprised but turns to the bartender anyway. "Then let's get you a flight. I'm sure they have something basic and light, yeah?"

The bartender nods and immediately walks off, leaving Nico and I to our conversation.

"So…academics. That's a pretty broad answer. What are you studying?"

I have to tamp down on the giddiness that bubbles inside me at the question. I've never thought about how it would feel to tell somebody about this thing that I love so much that was never encouraged when I was growing up.

"Psychology," I answer proudly. "I'm doing an online program for my undergrad right now."

Nico nods at that. "Psychology makes total sense for you."

I tilt my head. "Why do you say that?"

When he grins, his dimple pops. "Because you can read people like a book."

I let out a loud laugh that I'd normally be embarrassed about, but I feel too free to care. "I can read *you* like a book because you have the worst poker face." Feeling cheeky, I nudge his leg with my foot. "Aren't fighters supposed to be good at hiding their reactions?"

He looks downright delighted by the question. "I'm sorry, are you *teasing* me?"

I shrug, feeling too happy to hide my smile.

"For your information, I have a fantastic poker face when I'm fighting," Nico says with a sniff. Then after a moment, he adds, "It's just you I can't hide my thoughts from."

Part of me loves that, because I feel the same way about him.

"So, what's the dream?" he asks. "Why psychology?"

"I haven't gotten that far," I admit. "I have no idea what I'll do with it, if anything. It's just…something to do for now."

"And you enjoy it?" Nico presses. "You like your classes?"

I nod, a small smile coming back. "I like them a lot. And…"

Nico latches onto the word. "And…what?"

I take a deep breath before admitting, "And I'm really, *really* good at it. I have the highest grades in every one of my classes."

I've never told anyone that. I never wanted to sound like I was bragging, or that I thought I was better than anyone. But with Nico…

With Nico, something else flashes in his eyes.

"Fuck, baby," he breathes. "You're sexy *and* smart? Are you even real?"

*I don't think I've ever been more attracted to a man.*

Nico might see the thought in my eyes because he sucks in a breath as heat flames in *his*. His gaze drops to my mouth, and he reaches for my chair to pull me closer—

"Here you are, folks, one flight of our light beers."

I jerk back as the bartender puts a tray of four small beers on the bar in front of me. "Th-thank you," I stammer, my cheeks warming as I lean away from Nico. "Which ones…?"

The bartender points at each beer as he lists out, "In order, you have the Pilsner, Pale Ale, Wheat Beer, and then—excuse the executive decision—I brought you a cider to try, too. If you don't know much about beer, you might prefer that one or a sour."

Nico slips a twenty into the tip jar in front of us. "Thanks, man. These are great."

Once again, excitement bubbles inside me. "Should I just try them in order?" I ask Nico, studying the beers. "Or is there a specific process for this?"

"You can try them in whatever order you want," he says with a chuckle, resting an arm along the back of my chair. "I'm curious to see which one you like the most."

I pick up the far-left glass and take a tentative sniff before lifting it to my lips.

"Well? What's the verdict?" he asks as I let the flavor sit on my tongue before swallowing.

"It's…not bad."

But Nico must see the lie on my face because he grins and says, "Beer in general might be an acquired taste. At first, it kind of tastes like ass."

I take another sip. "How old were you when you had your first drink?"

"Fourteen, I think. I'm the youngest, so I started everything a little too early."

Lifting the second beer to my lips, I take a sip.

And immediately make a face.

He throws his head back with a laugh as I slide the second beer back. "Did you also think that beer tastes terrible?" I ask with a wince.

"Yup. I took one sip of the Coors Light I stole from Lucas and immediately dumped it."

"That's not making me excited about these other beers," I grumble, reaching for the third one.

"They're not all bad, I swear," Nico says as he nods at the one in my hand. "That one's a little fruity, so you might like it."

Sure enough, when I try the wheat beer, my eyebrows shoot up. "That's not bad. Definitely the best of the three."

"One more," Nico says, sliding the last beer in front of me. "Then you can decide which one you want to order for when we tear into some of these games."

I frown at him. "We're playing games?"

"Mhmm," he says with a smile. "The live music starts in an hour, so I figured we could try your hand at some bar games while we wait."

And maybe a tiny buzz is already hitting my system, or maybe it's *Nico's* presence that I'm drunk on, but I can't hide the giddy smile that pulls at my lips. "Okay," I whisper happily.

His smile grows, his gaze dropping once more to my lips before quickly lifting back up. "Go on," he encourages.

As soon as the cider hits my taste buds, my eyes widen. "Oh my God."

Nico grins. "Yeah, that's what I figured would happen. It's good, right?"

I take another, bigger sip. "*So* good. It's like spicy juice."

He waves the bartender down again. "An accurate description. Now let's get you a real glass so I can start to school you on those games."

———

I can't remember the last time I had this much fun.

Maybe the first time my mom took me horseback riding. I was twelve years old and had finally worn her down about signing me up for lessons. It probably wouldn't have been as fun if she went with me, but then again, that was never a real worry. She'd rather pay for a private and pawn me off on some instructor. Thankfully, the instructor was more lenient about taking me out on the trails instead of just having me ride in circles around the arena.

It was the first time I ever felt truly free.

Until now.

"You're *cheating!*" I shriek at Nico. But I doubt he can hear me over my laughter.

"You're just mad I keep beating you," he says with a grin, spinning the foosball handle and scoring his tenth goal.

I straighten with a groan. "They should make it against the rules to spin the handle blindly like that."

"It is," says some girl as she walks by me.

My head whips around to stare open-mouthed at Nico. "You *are* a cheater!"

"You're cute when you're outraged," he says with a chuckle. Gesturing around the bar, he asks, "So, what's next?"

We've been here for over an hour at this point. I was

worried he was going to want to talk the whole time, but we've mostly been playing games. I learned how to play shuffleboard, a couple of arcade games, and I even got to try ping-pong for the first time. The only one I couldn't bring myself to attempt was pool, but maybe another time.

*Another time?*

I'm snapped out of the foreign thought when there's movement on the stage. Chairs are being carried out, instruments are being moved around. It looks like they're setting up for the musicians.

"Want to find a seat?" Nico asks.

I nod, so he leads us over to the left side of the room, into a slightly more secluded area. He grabs us two more waters on the way.

I have to fight the unladylike urge to chug it. I think I've been laughing to the point of dehydration.

"Okay, so…question for you," I start once we're seated, waiting for the music to start.

He turns his entire body to face me. "Shoot."

"If I had picked the art option, where would you have taken me?"

"I was wondering if you were going to ask me that. We would've gone to the Banksy exhibit. Have you seen it?"

Slowly, I shake my head. *I've barely seen anything in this city.*

Somehow, I think he reads that on my face. Because his next question is gentle. "Would you say you haven't done much exploring in the city since you moved here?"

"I thought I was supposed to be the one who's good at reading people," I try to joke. But when he only gives me a knowing look, I sigh and give him a real answer. "I would say that, yes. I'm basically a hermit."

Nico's brow furrows as he mulls over my answer. "So

then why'd you move to New York? I understand wanting to try a big city if you grew up in a small Southern town, but… why *this* city? If you weren't going to explore it?"

It's a valid question. One I've asked myself more than once over the years.

"I had every intention of experiencing the city when I moved here," I admit. "I wanted to see the world, so of course New York City was the best one I could think of." Lost in my own naïve memories, I look out toward the stage. "I had grand visions of going to the best restaurants, finding the coolest bars, living in the city the way the movies always portray. But…I don't know, I guess reality hit pretty quick. I grew up a spoiled rich girl, so finding out the world is way more expensive than I thought was a big shock." Sucking in a big breath, I turn back to Nico. "And then once I *had* money, I no longer had any interest in doing anything."

The unspoken part of that—that once I started working as an escort, I no longer had the energy to romanticize my life— is loud. When sadness flashes across Nico's face, I know he at least understands the sentiment.

I try for a smile. "So yes, my goal when I moved here was to explore. But that's not how life worked out. Instead, I work a part-time job and spend the rest of my time attending an online college."

"And helping at rescue organizations."

My head jerks back in surprise. Then I laugh.

Leave it to Nico to put a positive spin on things.

"And helping at rescue organizations," I agree.

"*And* taking a chance on a guy by letting him take you to a really cool jazz club."

My laughter softens as I study him. From any other guy, it would sound like he's fishing for a compliment. But with Nico…he's just being honest.

"It wasn't that big of a chance," I whisper.

He smiles softly at that and opens his mouth to say something else, but before we can chat any more, the music starts, the first notes of a saxophone sounding through the speakers.

I stare at the musicians, in awe of the soulful magic they've created. I've never heard anything like it. It doesn't matter that I grew up in the South, where jazz is prominent. Anything besides classical music was beneath my parents.

"It's good, right?" Nico whispers. I don't even look at him as I nod.

He doesn't speak again, but I can feel him smiling beside me.

Somehow, we stay for the entire concert.

It isn't until roaring applause breaks out after the band's last song that I realize we've been sitting here for more than two hours. Far longer than I'd intended to stay out tonight.

Clapping politely, I whisper, "We should probably get going."

He doesn't argue, just grabs my hand and guides me through the establishment and out to the street.

Suddenly, I'm nervous all over again. Because I'm so far out of my element.

For one, this date wasn't scheduled through the agency. It wasn't planned. And it went on far longer than the agreed upon time, with no conversation about an extension.

But more importantly, there hasn't been any sex.

Panicked, I look around. This is New York; there has to be a hotel around here somewhere. If we can find a hotel, if we can just have sex, I can at least feel like this date was normal, that it was worth it for him. I just need to—

Nico's whistle and wave for a taxi startles me from my thoughts. "What are you doing?" I ask in shock.

"Calling you a taxi," he answers, as if I'm not having an existential crisis.

"But—" I look around again, my head whipping in every direction. "Shouldn't we find a hotel? I'm sure there's one nearby."

"Not a chance, Red."

Frowning, I face him again. "What? Why not? You said you were paying for this date."

"I *am* paying for this date," he says simply.

"But—" I shake my head, at a loss for words. "But you didn't get anything out of tonight!"

The look he gives me is soft, even tender. "I got exactly what I wanted out of tonight."

I think I'm gaping at him. "How is that possible? We didn't even do anything."

He smiles now, his hand lifting to brush my hair away from my face. "You are so, so wrong, Red."

Just then, a taxi pulls up at the curb. I stare at it, not computing what's happening. Especially when Nico pulls a wad of hundreds out of his pocket and slips it casually into my purse, hiding the movement with his body.

"I don't know how much that is, but it should be at least two thousand."

Now I'm definitely gaping, eyes wide. "You just walk around with thousands of dollars in your pocket?"

He grins and winks at me. "I can fight, remember?"

"You're insane," I breathe. *For more than one reason.*

"Go straight home with it, okay?" he says, serious this time.

I nod, stuck in a stupor. He guides me into the taxi, then claps his hand against the driver's door. "Wherever she's going, get her there safe, yeah?"

And then he comes back to my window, that damn dimple

141

making an appearance. "Just so you know," he drawls, "this is the kind of date you can expect with me from now on."

My brow furrows as I search his eyes. "What do you mean?"

He straightens and slides his hands into his pockets. "No more hotels. No more sex. Just fun and conversation."

*I'm not going to survive this man.*

# SIXTEEN
## SCARLETT

Nico's question about exploring New York City rings in my head for days.

I had all these visions about what my glamorous life would be like in the Big Apple. But after I started working for Amara…those visions died quickly. Because when I *was* doing city things, they were always with clients. And that soured my desire to do anything.

The more clients I saw, the more disconnected I became.

But ever since Nico brought it up, I've felt this itch to do more, experience more. Ever since I met him, this feeling has grown. It's like he's awakened something in me, something that's making me want for a life outside of clients and classes.

I want to experience something *new*.

Maybe even find the girl who jumped on a train to run away from a life she didn't want and run *toward* the life she always dreamed of.

So on a day when I have no classes and only a late dinner date client, I lace up my sneakers and leave my apartment. I have no idea where I'm going; I just want *out*. I want to explore the city the way nineteen-year-old Scarlett never got to do.

I have no idea where to go first. It's insane to think I've lived here for three years and have never seen the city in its full glory. All that time, I've been looking at it from behind the muted and ugly shade of cash. But thankfully, a Hop On Hop Off bus passes me and takes the decision out of my hands. After buying a ticket, I climb on and step unashamedly into the role of tourist for the day.

I *love* it. I love walking around the Museum of Modern Art. I love strolling through Times Square in the daytime and shopping at stores for no reason other than that I want to. I even love taking the elevator 102 floors to the top of the Empire State Building and looking out over the entire city.

Even the bus ride home is fun. Sitting on the open top deck, watching the city flash by, I feel…free.

I feel the way I wish I could've made my younger self feel.

The only thing that puts a damper on it is hearing my phone ding with a notification and seeing I have a text from Amara.

> Amara: Are you ok if Francesco makes his appointments every week instead of every other week?

Immediately, my stomach roils.

Francesco is one of my least favorite clients. If he didn't tip so generously, I would've dropped him a long time ago. He's a guy who pops a little blue pill before every appointment because he "needs to get his money's worth and go for the full sixty minutes." Because of that, he's one of my most physically taxing appointments.

Lately, he's become emotionally taxing as well.

I don't know if it's because sex with Nico is so different, but for the past few weeks, *all* of my sex feels different. I'm just not able to stay as numb as I usually do. And if I'm not numb, then I feel more of my appointments. I feel shame when I'm put on my knees and sick when I'm bent over. It's no longer something I can just get through, like I used to.

Now, I feel on the verge of breaking every time I'm penetrated.

Before I can think about it too hard, I type out a text to Amara.

> Scarlett: No. Give Francesco to one of the other girls. He tips well, they'll love him.

Fifteen seconds later, my phone is ringing.

I answer her call with a sigh. "He'll be fine, Amara, don't worry. Just make sure he gets a blonde."

"I know *that*," she says with a sniff. "I just wanted to make sure *you're* okay. What's going on? And why does it sound like you're in a wind tunnel?"

I look around at my view, smiling despite myself. "I'm on one of those double decker buses. I'm touring the city today."

"Uh…why?"

Her shock is evident, and it makes me huff a laugh. "I just wanted to do something different for a change."

There's silence on the line. This is very abnormal behavior for me, and I can tell Amara is itching to ask more questions.

"Okay," she says slowly. "But you're good?"

I tilt my head back with a smile, enjoying the sun on my face. "I'm great."

The sound of papers rustling sounds through the phone. "Okay, so I'll take Francesco off your schedule. Any other changes I need to make?"

I think she means it as a joke, but at the question, I sit up straight, my smile sliding from my face.

"Yes. Give Phillip and Professor Jenkins to someone else, too."

That she *has* to ask questions about.

"Scarlett, what's going on?"

"I just… I need a break," I admit. Maybe it will be more than a break. "I'm tired, Amara. I might need to tailor my schedule a little bit for the next few weeks."

Which translates to: *I need a break from the clients who want to aggressively fuck me.*

Thankfully, Amara understands what I'm saying. She knows everything about every client of the agency, and as someone who did this job herself, she can read between the lines and doesn't fight me on it.

"Alright, mia cara, I'll take care of it. Enjoy the rest of your day, okay? Maybe next time, I'll join you on your adventure."

I almost laugh. I feel affection toward Amara, but the idea of hanging out with her for a whole day… I'm not so sure about that.

"Thanks, Amara. I'll talk to you later."

*After I'm done sleeping with a different client who isn't as bad as my other ones but whose appointment I still need to grimace my way through.*

I deboard the bus with an exhausted sigh and head home.

# SEVENTEEN
## NICO

Three days later, I'm still catching myself randomly smiling at the memory of my date with Scarlett.

I'm shocked she agreed to the date, especially without knowing what I had planned. Hell, *I* was nervous for what I had planned. I had no idea if she'd enjoy it or ask to leave as soon as we got there.

I don't know which one of us was more surprised when she *did* enjoy it.

I want, so badly, to know how she ended up where she is today. What scarred her so badly that she ended up as an escort in NYC? Not that you have to have trauma to be a sex worker, but hers is so obvious that it's not a question. Was it some kind of abuse at home? Or did something happen when she got to the city?

Every time I see her, I have to fight the urge to hug her and beg her to tell me everything. Just so I can fight her demons.

I let out a shaky exhale as I turn back to the meal I'm cooking, trying to move past my troubled thoughts. I have no right to save her. No right to be worried about her. All I can do is appreciate the time I'm given with her.

*That* thought adds a little pep to my movements.

I've just pulled the steak off the cast iron pan when I hear my front door unlock and swing open. I turn to look, but I already know who it is.

"I gave you that key for emergencies," I grumble at Lucas before turning back to my food.

"Trust me, this is an emergency I needed to be in-person for," he retorts, strolling into my condo and immediately throwing himself down on my couch. I see the moment he notices the shift in my usual atmosphere because he frowns and asks, "Are you listening to jazz music?"

I don't bother answering that. "So, what is it that couldn't be a phone call?"

When he doesn't answer right away, I turn to face him. He's looking out the window, bouncing one foot that's crossed over the other.

"I heard the most interesting thing today," he says after a moment. Finally, he turns to look at me. "I called your PR girl to see how the foster footage turned out, and she seemed pleased with how things came out. As in *very* pleased."

"So? Isn't that what you wanted?"

He nods. "It is. But I was curious about *why* it was so good. So I asked her to send it to me."

My mind starts to spin. *Scarlett wasn't in any of the videos, right?* I figured she wouldn't want to be, so I wasn't surprised when she made the request. I'm pretty sure I kept her out of everything.

*Didn't I?*

Before I panic, a video sounds from Lucas's phone.

*"It looks like Boss has a big thing for our camera girl and*

*can't seem to stay focused."* A loud burst of Scarlett's laughter. *"Not that I can blame him."*

Lucas puts the phone down and quirks an eyebrow at me. "Anything you'd like to tell me, little brother?"

I fidget with the salad tongs in front of me. "No," I say gruffly.

"You sure? Because either you *did* bring mystery girl with you, or you're officially so lonely that you're flirting with everyone."

I send a glare over my shoulder. "I'm not lonely."

"So it *was* mystery girl."

I drop way too much cheese on my salad. "It wasn't on purpose. I didn't plan it that way. She just happened to be there."

I can *feel* Lucas's surprise. "So she just so happens to work with foster dogs? Where did you find this girl again?"

There's not a chance I'm telling him the truth. Not yet. Not when it's still so delicate.

"It was just some random dating app," I lie.

I hear his sigh from behind me, followed by the rustle of him standing from my couch.

"You know you can talk to me, right?" he says as he stops beside me. "I am actually capable of cutting the teasing for a few minutes." When I don't respond, he sighs again. "Or at least talk to Alexander. I know he's not a wordsmith, but—" I snort at the understatement. "You know he'll listen. And be honest."

My shoulders droop, all tension and fight going out of me in an instant. I *want* to tell my brothers. I want to confide in them about how much I like this girl, and how confusing it all is. That even though I still feel a little restless from all the uncertainty, somehow, she makes me feel more grounded.

Less worried about my future and more comfortable in the present.

"I will," I finally say. "I'm just not ready yet. But I will."

Lucas must know I'm telling the truth because he nods and claps me on the back. "Alright, good. And if I can help with fight camp, if I can take some stress off somehow, just say the word."

I manage a grateful nod. "Sounds good. And…thanks."

He waves me off. "Yeah, whatever." And then he steals a giant handful of dried cranberries and starts to pop them in his mouth.

I glare at him again. "I was just about to ask if you wanted to stay for dinner. Now I don't want to."

"Oh, shut up. You know you have two more giant bags of those things hidden in this kitchen somewhere. Little weirdo. What *is* it with you and cranberries?"

I slap his hand away when he tries to take another handful. "They're delicious. Now get your dirty, money-grubbing fingers out of the salad and set the table."

"Hey, these money-grubbing fingers are about to pay way too much money to DoorDash some Isgro's pastries for your weekly cheat meal."

I turn to him with a frown. "Isgro's closes at two and isn't available through DoorDash. How are you going to manage that?"

He just winks as he pulls two plates from the cabinets. "You have your secrets, I have mine."

---

My next date with Scarlett starts at the hotel.

I meant it when I told her no more hotels, though. No more sex, either. But I don't have her number and still need to go through the agency, and I realized when I called them that they might not like the idea of the kind of date I'm planning.

Hell, she might not either. But I'm willing to try.

I hear a knock on the door at exactly seven o'clock. I swing it open with a grin I couldn't control even if I wanted to.

She looks stunning. Same way she always does. She's wearing a light blue dress with long sleeves, some kind of strappy black sandals, and her blonde hair is pinned up with a clip. Plus, a red lip, of course.

It takes me a second to realize it's not what I asked her to wear.

I'd never tell a woman what to wear. But this is a unique instance. One of the questions the agency asks is if I have any preferences for my date's outfit, and since I couldn't talk to her directly, I made a request. Solely because I know what she normally shows up in, and I have different plans for tonight.

"You're not wearing jeans," is what comes out of my mouth. Instantly, my cheeks heat. "I mean, you look beautiful."

She seems amused at the sight of me tongue-tied. Stepping into the room, she asks, "Do I look like I own jeans?"

*She doesn't own jeans?*

But then something occurs to me, and a smile tugs at my lips. I stop her as she's passing me, close enough that I can breathe the words into her ear.

"Are you going against a client's wishes?"

I see the way her red lips curl. "I guess I am."

I can't contain a smile of my own. "Good girl," I whisper.

After I close the door behind her, I spin to see she's sitting on the couch. She doesn't look surprised, or disappointed, that we're in a hotel room again. I guess she didn't believe me last time.

"So," she starts, crossing one leg over the other. "How was your week?"

I don't answer. I simply walk over to her and gently pull her to her feet.

"Already?" she asks with a chuckle, brushing a finger down the front of my shirt.

I stop it in its path. "How do you feel about going out tonight?"

She freezes, just as I knew she would. Her eyes shoot up to mine. "What?"

"I didn't exactly want to ask you through the agency," I explain patiently. "I wasn't sure how they would feel, or even how *you* would feel about them knowing. I didn't want to ask about policies and things. But I meant what I said."

When her eyes go wide, I realize she was hoping I was lying last time.

"I don't think that's a good idea," she says, clearly unsure. "Any new locations or date types need to be cleared with the agency."

"The way you cleared it with them last time?"

"That was different," she says defensively, head tilting up to me with a little sass. "And a unique situation. I've never done that before."

"I'm glad to hear it," I say as I smooth a strand of hair behind her ear.

Her eyes go wide again. And then the fear comes back, and she looks around the room.

"Anyway, why would you want to leave? We're already here, the bed is right there. We could just—"

"Scarlett," I interrupt gently. "I meant what I said last

time. No more hotels. No more sex. I'll pay you, but I want dates. Real dates."

Her eyebrows pinch. "These *are* dates."

"Not real ones," I say, shaking my head. "Not ones that matter."

She doesn't understand.

"And where exactly do you want to go that matters?" she demands.

*Okay, that's progress.*

"I'll give you a choice. Physical activity or sightseeing?"

"A physical activity? Is that why—?" She looks down at her legs, lips pursed. "Is that why you said jeans?"

I shrug. "Yeah, but you're actually fine in that dress. I was more so suggesting something casual. Which I have a feeling is what this is for you."

She seems so unsure of herself, looking down at her dress and shuffling her feet, that I find myself stepping forward and pressing a gentle kiss to her exposed shoulder. "You look beautiful," I whisper. "You always look beautiful."

I can *feel* the way the tension leaves her body.

It drives a bolt of warmth through my chest.

"Umm, in that case… Physical activity."

I pull back with a grin. "Amazing. We're right around the corner. Come on."

# EIGHTEEN
## SCARLETT

Fifteen minutes later, I'm standing ten feet from a giant target with an axe in my hand.

"You have *got* to be kidding me," I say in the driest tone possible.

Nico's laugh booms behind me. His hands go to my hips, and I find myself melting back into him.

"Just try it," he says. "It's fun, I promise. Grab it with two hands"—he gently guides my grip to the handle—"lift it over your head, and chuck it as hard as you can. We'll tweak your technique after."

"Nico, I can't do this," I whine.

"Of course, you can. You're strong. And haven't you ever wanted to throw something at a wall? This is like that."

I shoot him a confused frown over my shoulder. "That might just be the fighter in you talking."

"Doubtful," he retorts, nipping at my shoulder. His playfulness warms me up inside. "Everyone has a beast in them. Now come on, throw it."

"If I take your eye out, you still owe me two thousand," I grumble.

And then I throw the axe, the sound of Nico's laugh loud behind me.

I'm shocked to see it hit the board head-on, even if it's nowhere near the target circle, before bouncing off and dropping to the ground.

Nico whistles and passes by me to grab it. "Good throw, Red. Now try it again, but let it go a little later. I think it'll stick then."

Taking the axe from him, I scrunch up my face in concentration, get into the stance he showed me, and throw it again.

This time, it burrows into the board.

I let out a shriek of excitement. When I spin to jump on him, Nico is already there with open arms.

"Good throw, baby," he says fondly into my hair. "How did that feel?"

"Exhilarating," I breathe, sliding down his body. "I want to do it again."

He gestures at the table of axes. "Have at it."

Twenty minutes later, I've fine-tuned my technique to the point of landing four out of five throws in a five-inch diameter on the board. I'm almost as good as Nico.

"Well, that didn't take long to get good at," he says with a chuckle. He's been leaning against the high top at our section, looking way too sexy in a casual stance and with a water in his hand.

*I want to jump him.*

The thought isn't a surprising one, but it's definitely a unique one. I've never had a client I've *wanted* to have sex with before.

"Do they do this with knives, too?" I wonder out loud in an effort to distract myself. "Or just axes?"

Nico's eyes go wide with surprise. Then he lets out a

laugh. "You sure you're a piano-playing good girl? Between this and the self-defense lesson, I'm starting to think you're a Russian spy just playing the part."

I grin and skip over to him. "Hardly. You just bring out the Russian spy in me, I guess."

His smile softens. "I'll take anything I can bring out of you, baby."

I don't pull away when he nuzzles into my neck. I might even close my eyes and lean into it. "Smooth talker," I murmur.

He just hums in answer. "Do you want to keep playing? Or are you ready for a break?"

I look around and try to guess what he might have in mind next. "What's a break for you?"

He tugs me over to the high tops in the bar area in answer. "Just some food. Figured I'd feed you before I have to take you back."

I follow behind him, albeit begrudgingly. This looks like the kind of place that only serves greasy, calorie-filled bar snacks. "I'm...uh, I'm not really hungry," I lie. In reality, the only reason he hasn't heard my stomach growl is because it's so loud in here. "But I'll take a water if you want to eat something."

His frown deepens. "There's no way throwing axes for an hour didn't make you hungry. Come on, we'll just get an appetizer or something."

I don't know how to argue without making him suspicious, so I let him tug me along.

"Looks like they have the usuals," he says once we're seated with a menu. "What do you want? Pretzels? Nachos? Sliders?"

*Carbs. Carbs. Carbs.*

As I look over the menu, the only thing I can think about

is my mother calling me chunky when I was thirteen and asked for pizza for dinner. "Uh, I'm really not that hungry," I argue weakly.

Nico notices. Of course, he notices.

He doesn't press, like I thought he would. He doesn't judge, like I knew he wouldn't.

And whether he guesses the reason or not, he asks gently, "How about some chicken wings? We can get them plain, if you want."

*So...protein. I can do protein.*

I give him a careful nod. "Okay. Wings would be good."

I stay at our table, sipping my water, as Nico puts our order in. When he comes back, he smiles and asks, "So, what's your favorite food?"

For a moment, all I can think is, *this shouldn't be a hard question.*

But the truth is, I can't remember the last time I ate something I *wanted* instead of the low-calorie diet that was drilled into me. I can't say eggs are my favorite food, that's ridiculous.

I shrug and give him a small smile. "I don't know, it changes constantly," I lie. "Maybe pizza?"

"Oh, yeah? What's your favorite New York pizza spot?"

*Shoot.*

*I can't think of a single pizza place name.*

"I haven't found a spot that's better than my hometown pizza." Another lie. My mother never would've allowed pizza in the house. "It was a little hole-in-the-wall spot."

He nods, spinning his beer bottle on the table. "I feel that. Philly has some great undiscovered spots." His eyes meet mine. "You should come visit me. We could plan a date there."

I've never before agreed to an overnight date with a client, but with Nico, I know I would break that rule.

"Would we stay at a hotel?" I tease.

"Are you kidding me?" he asks incredulously. "I would *kill* to see you sleeping in my bed."

"Possessive," I purr, naturally trying to seduce the conversation. "Would you like to fuck me in it too?"

I watch his throat move on a rough swallow. His gaze drops to my lips, the same way they always do when he's turned on.

"I said sleeping, not fucking," he says. But his voice is deep and gravelly, like he had to force it out.

*We'll see about that.*

I don't believe Nico that he's not interested in sex anymore. I felt our connection during our previous dates; I know how good the sex is. No man is capable of not wanting more of that.

I don't know why he's started fighting that part of our arrangement—especially since he's still paying me—but I fully intend on making him reconsider. Not just because I'm made for sex and need it to make sense of my dates, but also because *I* want it, too.

Just then, our food arrives at the table. Plain chicken wings, and…a giant pretzel?

I gape at Nico as he rips off a pretzel chunk and dips it in whatever yellow sauce came with it. He makes a sound of enjoyment and rips off another piece.

"Are you even allowed to eat that?" I ask bluntly. "Don't you have to lose weight for fighting or something?"

He lets out a huff of laughter and reaches for a napkin to wipe his mouth. "Did you just fat shame me?"

My eyes widen. "What? No! I just thought— I mean, all

the videos I watched said you have to make weight or something—"

Chuckling, he pulls my chair closer to him and presses a kiss to my shoulder. The touch makes electricity spark over my skin. "Relax, Red, I'm teasing. Yes, fighting involves weight cuts."

"Then why…" I stare at his plate. "*How* are you eating carbs right now?"

"Two reasons," he explains, tearing off another piece of the pretzel. "For one: I always time my rest days for the days I'm with you."

I bite down on my bottom lip in an attempt to hide my giddy smile, but I don't think it works. *He plans his week around me?*

"For another, you should always have carbs in your diet."

The comment is so ridiculous that a snort bursts out of me.

Mortified, I slap my hand over my mouth. "Oh my gosh, forget that just happened."

His lips curl into an adoring smile. "Not a chance. That was adorable." But he sobers just as quickly. "But also, I have questions. You don't eat carbs?"

I don't answer, but he reads the truth on my face anyway.

"You work out," he says, eyes traveling over my shoulders and down my body. "A lot, if your muscle tone is any indication. How could you keep your energy level up if not with carbs?"

I laugh without humor. "Sheer will and fear of my mother?"

*Shoot. That wasn't supposed to come out.*

We both stare at each other, eyes wide.

"Scarlett…you can't *not* eat carbs. That's unhealthy." He hesitates, then adds, "The old-school 'carbs are bad' way of thinking has been debunked. It's not true. Obviously, some carbs are better for you than others, but you need *something* to fuel you properly."

I quirk an eyebrow and try to deflect. "Are you seriously telling a woman what she should and shouldn't be eating?"

He exhales a heavy breath and drops his head between his shoulders. "No, of course not," he grumbles. "I'm sorry, it's just the athlete in me. I'm pretty sure my nutritionist has burrowed his way into my psyche or something."

I huff a laugh at that. *He's adorable.*

He takes that as a sign to say more, I guess.

"Okay, let me just say one more thing, and then I'll shut up," he blurts out. I roll my eyes but don't answer. "If you're going to add any carbs to your diet—and I strongly recommend it, for everyone, not just you—do it in the morning. Whole grains, fruit, that type of thing. Do a parfait or oatmeal or something. Your body needs it. And then it can burn it for whatever workouts you're doing."

"Pretty sure the point of a workout is to burn fat, not food," I say with a quirked eyebrow.

His eyes widen again. "Uh...*what* fat? You have none."

"Then I'm doing it right," I say proudly. I point at the pretzel. "Because I don't eat things like that."

He doesn't look like he knows how to respond to that.

*Fine by me.*

Unrolling the silverware I snagged from a passing server, I place the paper napkin in my lap and grip the utensils in my hands.

"Please tell me you're not about to eat wings with a knife and fork..."

I try to ignore the way my cheeks heat. I *know* this isn't how people eat wings, but I have a better chance of sprouting my own wings than I do ignoring the manners that were instilled in me.

"What's wrong with that?" I challenge, stabbing my fork into one of the wings and delicately placing it on my plate.

"What's *wrong* with—? Scarlett, I'm pretty sure there's a commandment about this."

I laugh despite myself. "Don't judge me just because I like to keep my hands clean when I eat."

"They're wings. It's pretty much a rule that you have to get your hands dirty. Face, too, if we're being honest."

Without any hesitation, I dip a finger in the ranch that came with the wings and swipe it across Nico's cheek. "There, we've covered the dirty part."

His expression goes from shocked to heated in half a second.

"The fuck we have," he growls. Then he's grabbing my finger and sucking it into his mouth.

A tingle ripples through my body, and I squirm in my seat, unable to take my eyes off him. "Do you—" I clear my throat and try again. "Are we walking back to the hotel after this?"

He stares at me in a way that makes me think he knows exactly why I'm asking.

"Yes," he says carefully. "But not yet. Eat your wings first."

"Bossy," I grumble.

"Hey, you're the one with the habit of ordering me around."

I shrug, looking down at my plate. "And you're the one who listens and pays me for it."

I can feel him studying me again, but I'm not sure if it's because of my comment or the way I'm reaching for my knife and fork again.

"Here," he finally says, grabbing a wing with his hands. "If we take the finger-dirtying aspect out of it, will you eat it?" And then he holds it in front of my mouth.

My eyes lock on his. I shouldn't. I wasn't raised like this. And what if I get grease or something on my face? *No man wants to see that*.

Maybe it's the sound of mother's voice that makes me open my mouth. Or maybe it's just Nico's presence.

Either way, with my eyes still on his, I lean forward and take a bite of the wing, gently ripping the meat off the bone.

He seems weirdly thrilled. "Atta girl," he says with a grin.

Flavor explodes on my tongue. Even without sauce, the wing is delicious, so much better than the barely seasoned chicken breasts I typically make for myself.

I cover my mouth with my napkin as I chew so that as soon as I've swallowed, I can say, "That's delicious."

"See? I know my bar food. Now eat up, I might order another batch."

But suddenly, I'm not as interested in food.

Holding Nico's eyes, I place my hand on his thigh under the table and slide it up the slightest bit. "Are you ready to leave soon?" I ask in a silky voice. "I'm kind of dying to get you back to the hotel."

I see the flash of desire in his eyes, confirmation that I'm still in control here. Thank God.

"Yeah, let's—" He clears his throat. "Let's get out of here."

# NINETEEN
## SCARLETT

The walk back to the hotel is a quiet one. I take Nico's hand as soon as we leave the axe-throwing place, comforted by his presence in New York's streets. And when he sees me shiver, he doesn't say a single word; he just pulls off his zip-up hoodie and settles it over my shoulders.

I give him a grateful smile. "Thanks," I say softly, tangling our hands again.

I don't quite understand why he seems on edge, or why he's not hustling me back to the room, but we're so close to the hotel that I don't bother asking. I'll just seduce it out of him.

Sure enough, when we reach the room and he closes the door behind us, he practically melts into the wall to get past me without us touching.

"Do you want anything to drink?" he asks, everything in his body screaming with tension. "I figured we could watch the newest *Dancing With The Stars* episode if you haven't already seen it, but if you want to watch something else—"

His words cut off with a sip of air when I move behind him and place my hands on his shoulders. "Why are you so tense all of a sudden?" I ask, massaging his muscles. "You know you can talk to me."

The only answer I get from him is a humorless laugh as he slips away.

Still not understanding, I sidle closer. Now that he's facing me, I can approach him with more intent, a sultry smile on my lips as my hands go to his belt buckle.

"I can help with that tension," I purr only centimeters from his lips.

But when his hands still mine, I look into his eyes with a confused frown.

"I don't want to have sex," he says in a rough voice.

I quirk an eyebrow as I look down at the giant bulge in his jeans.

I want to lick his blush away as he covers it with his hands.

"Okay, fine, you make me hard," he admits, taking another step back. "Constantly, *insanely* hard," he adds in a mutter. I try not to preen under the compliment. "But that's not the point here."

Since this is clearly about to be a conversation, I back against the counter so I can plant my hands behind me and lift myself up onto it. Crossing one leg over the other, I ask, "What's the point then?"

He rips his gaze from my legs with a head shake and focuses on my face. "The *point*," he stresses, "is that I told you we're not having sex. That's not why I want to spend time with you."

My brow furrows. "You can't be serious."

He doesn't look away from me. "I meant it, Scarlett. I *do* mean it. I'm not hiring you for sex."

I blink at him in confusion. It's not that I don't believe Nico when he says he wants to do non-sex things on our dates; it's just hard to believe that he doesn't want sex during *this* part of the date. When we're alone in a hotel room and he's so attractive I want to rip his clothes off.

*Why doesn't he want it to involve sex?*

Suddenly, a memory flashes through my brain. I can still feel my ex-husband's touch on my skin, can still see the sneer that flashed at me when I said no. Can still feel the crippling weight of worthlessness that came with the silent treatment in the weeks after that.

My resolve hardens, if for no other reason than to never feel that way again. I might not fully understand why Nico enjoys spending time with me, but I *do* know why he enjoys me physically. With sex, I have something to offer.

"I know how to be worth your time," I say as I uncross my legs. My dress naturally sits mid-thigh, so I place my hands on my thighs and slowly brush the fabric up higher.

Nico freezes in place, his eyes going to my legs. "Scarlett…" he warns.

"We don't need to argue, baby," I purr, leaning back against the cabinets behind me. "Wouldn't it be so much better if we just made each other feel good?"

His chest starts to heave with his breaths. "Scarlett, don't do this," he begs.

"Do what?" I ask innocently. I keep pulling up my dress, finally exposing the simple white thong I wore for Nico tonight. "I'm just trying to help."

"This isn't—"

But his words cut off, because I'm reaching for the sides of my thong so I can pull it off under my dress.

And then I spread my legs.

"Christ," Nico bites out, pressing his thumbs to his eyes. But he can't look away for very long. In an instant, his gaze is back on my cunt.

"Is this what you wanted?" I ask, arching my back and sliding one hand between my legs. "You could've just told me if you preferred to watch."

Holding my dress out of the way, I touch myself.

I'm already wet. Being around Nico basically guarantees that. It makes it easy to swirl the pad of my finger around my clit, slower than I need it to come, but that's not the point of this, anyway. I know how to put on a good show.

"Did you know that I think about you all week?" I moan without thinking.

But despite that being a truth I shouldn't have admitted out loud, I can still use it in the fantasy I'm weaving. *I say it to every other client, anyway.*

I've just never meant it before.

"Most nights, I dream about you," I say, eyes closing as I move my finger down to my opening. *Another truth.* "Then when I wake up in the morning, I swear I can still feel your hands on my body." Slowly, I slide one finger inside, then another. "And every morning, I have to touch myself just so I can hold on to the memory for a little while longer."

"Scarlett…"

I open my eyes at his pained plea. He's collapsed against the counter across from me, his eyes wide and crazed and locked on the space between my legs.

It's all the confirmation I need to continue, to pull him into this vortex of desire where we belong.

"I wish you'd touch me," I whisper, sliding my fingers back to my clit. I'm so turned on that even a slight brush sends sparks along my nerves, the urge to come growing.

"Don't you want to touch me?" I ask. It sounds too much like begging to my ears, but I can't stop. My fingers swirl faster and faster, my body arching into my own touch.

Suddenly, Nico's hand stills my own. I open my eyes to

see his forehead pressed against the cabinet beside my head, taking one heavy breath after another.

"Scarlett," he croaks out. "Please, don't. Not like this."

And that's when everything comes crashing down.

My entire body freezes. My breaths start to come quicker, my lungs desperately trying to suck in oxygen and stop my head from spinning.

*He doesn't want to fuck me.*

*He doesn't want* me.

Nico must notice my panic because he pulls back to look at me. He looks wrecked. *Why does he look wrecked if he doesn't want me?*

"Scarlett." *I wish he'd stop saying my name like that.* "We need to talk about this."

I hurriedly pull my dress down, avoiding all eye contact. *Mortified* at being rejected like this. "We do *not*. If you weren't interested in me, I have no idea why you'd keep booking me through the agency."

"If I'm not… *What?* Scarlett, I just said I *am* interested in you."

My laugh sounds self-deprecating. "Clearly, you're not."

I try to jump off the counter, but Nico locks me in place with his hips. He's still hard, which just makes this embarrassment even more confusing.

"Jesus, just…give me a minute." His hands plant beside my hips without touching me, his head dropping between his shoulders. "Just let me *think*."

I stare at him. "What on earth do you need to think about? You just clarified things perfectly."

"I need to figure out how to explain this in a way you'll understand," he says. After a moment, he straightens with a deep breath. "Okay. Can you promise me something?"

The escort in me knows to make any promise he wants.

But that's not why I nod.

He looks relieved. "Okay. I want you to promise that you'll hear me out. That you won't try to leave before we talk through this."

That sounds awful, but...

I nod again.

Another relieved exhale, but then he tenses up as he straightens. "That wasn't a rejection," he starts. "Even if it felt like it. I need you to understand that."

I don't answer. It *did* feel like it.

He sighs, seeing that on my face. "I'll tell you the truth. Even at the risk of it biting me in the ass at the end of this." When that piques my curiosity, he admits, "I don't just dream of you, Red. I *day*dream of you. I'm constantly thinking about you. Whether I'm training, sleeping, resting, anything, you're on my mind. In every sense of the word."

My eyes widen. And maybe it's because it's not my usual reaction of freezing in fear, but Nico latches onto it. It amps him up.

"Of course I think about fucking you. I'd have to be dead to not think you're the sexiest goddamn woman in the world. But it's more than that. I think about your lips, about kissing them, not just because I want to know what you taste like, but also because I'm dying to have the touch of your lips imprinted on mine."

His vulnerability has my stomach fluttering in a way that feels foreign. With my eyes on his, he continues.

"I think about calling you, just to see what you're doing. To ask your opinion about little things, like what movie I should watch when I get home. To watch a movie *together*, on the phone, like we're high schoolers or something." When that startles a laugh out of me, he smiles and brushes my hair back. "I think about seeing you more than once a week, more than *twice* a week, just so I can hear you laugh and find all the things that make it happen." He pauses, his hand brushing over my hair again, his eyes searching mine with a soft smile. "*That's* what I think about."

I soak up his touch, his words. I want so badly to believe him. I *want* to believe that I'm more than just my body. I spent my teenage years being conditioned to think my only worth is in my ability to be a wife, and I spent my entire marriage learning that my "wifely duties" were centered around my ability—and availability—in the bedroom. Hearing Nico say he likes me for *other* much more meaningful reasons is...everything I've ever wanted.

But the voices of my life before him are just too loud, too eager to tear me down and leave me in the gutter. Those voices are what keep me from responding to Nico in the way that he wants.

He sees it, because he sighs and takes a step back. "So no, I don't just want sex. I want the rest of it, too."

And *God*, I want so badly to believe him. I *like* spending time with Nico. I like him and I like how he makes me feel and I *want* to explore this with him.

It's just...hard.

"I don't—" I swallow and try again. "I'm not sure what that looks like," I admit in a shaky whisper.

And Nico being the brave, beautiful man he is, simply smiles and says, "I know, baby. That's okay. We can figure it out together."

"It's hard for me to trust men," I say quietly. "The *no dating clients* rule is common sense, but...that's not the only reason."

I take another breath, this one for courage. To be honest with him, the way he's been with me. "I was married. Before

I moved to New York. And I know it's cliché to say a bad relationship gave me trust issues, but—"

"You were *married?*" Nico asks, his eyes going wider than I've ever seen them. "But—" He shakes his head with a confused frown. "You were nineteen when you moved here." His jaw goes slack again. "You were married at *nineteen?*"

I laugh softly, though nothing about this is funny. "It's a long story. And not one I want to get into right now. I was just trying to explain why I have a hard time trusting men." *Trusting everyone*, I add mentally.

"I *want* to believe you," I hurry to add. I need him to understand. "I'm not against the idea of dating because I don't want to date *you*. I swear. I just…" I blow out a heavy breath. "It's…hard."

For a moment, Nico studies me. I can tell he wants to ask a million more questions about my past, but he can also sense that I'm not ready to talk about it. So instead of pushing me when I'm not ready, he simply nods and says, "I understand." Then he tucks my hair behind my ear and gives me a small smile. "Thank you for being honest with me."

Just that reaction tells me I've done the right thing in trusting him with the truth. But even though my panic spiral melts away and the tension drops from my shoulders, there's still a small part of me that's holding back.

"Can we keep doing what we're doing?" I ask in a tentative whisper. "Just for now? I promise I won't pressure you for sex again, but…I think keeping it contained to an arrangement I understand might help me make sense of it." But when I realize what I'm asking, shame punches me in the gut and makes my eyes widen. "Not that I'm doing it for the money. I realize how that makes me sound. I just—"

But Nico just laughs and sweetly tugs at a strand of hair.

"Scarlett, you could charge me a hundred thousand and I'd gladly hand it over for a single date."

My mouth curves into a smile, everything in me melting at his words. "Would it include sex?"

Seeming to realize he's talked me off of whatever cliff I was standing on—and can now joke with me—he smirks. "Baby, if sex was involved, you'd have to charge me a million."

Giggling, I drop my face into the crook of his neck. I feel…warm. Safe. I let out a content sigh when I feel Nico press a kiss to my hair.

But when he shifts in a way that brushes his still-hard cock against my thigh, I pull back and ask, "So, now that we've had this clarifying discussion… Are you still saying no to sex?"

Chuckling, he angles his hips away from me. "Yup. I can't prove to you I want more than sex if we keep having sex, can I?"

"But I *like* sex with you," I whine.

He smiles and kisses me again, this time on my temple. "You're adorable," he murmurs.

"That is *not* what a girl wants to hear when she's trying to seduce a man," I grumble.

Nico studies me, serious this time. "Is this a rejection reaction? Or something else?"

I think about it for a moment, then answer, "It's an I'm-turned-on-and-you-didn't-let-me-come reaction."

At that, his eyebrow lifts. "Well, that I can help with."

"What do you—"

My words cut off in a gasp when he flips my dress up and drops to his knees.

"Nico, you don't have to—"

"You're goddamn right I do," he growls. And then he buries his face between my legs.

The second his lips touch my clit, I know this is going to be over too fast. I'm keyed up from him, this night, everything. Combined with how well he knows my body, it's not going to take much.

"Nico," I moan, arching into his mouth as my fingers sink into his hair. "Oh my God, *Nico*."

"Fuck, yes, say my name, baby," he groans. Distantly, it registers that his arm is moving, but when I feel two of his fingers slide inside me, I stop thinking altogether.

I chant his name all through my orgasm, however long it lasts. It feels like forever. My hand fists in his hair, my legs tighten around his head, and I explode.

When I finally come back to earth, Nico's breathing heavily, his open-mouthed exhales ghosting the inside of my thigh. I loosen my grip in his hair and run it through his locks.

"Okay?" I breathe with a sated smile.

Resting his cheek on my thigh, he looks up at me. "More than," he says.

I glance down his body, although I can't see much from this position he's in. "Will you let me touch you now?"

I don't understand why he laughs as he stands and tugs me off the counter into his arms.

"Baby, I just came all over the tiles. Now enough of this sex talk, let's go watch celebrities dance."

# TWENTY
## NICO

Lucas steps into the gym just as I'm finishing up a private lesson with one of the fighters.

I nod to let him know I'll be over in a minute, then turn toward the young guy who's been reduced to a sweaty, panting mess in the ring.

"Clearly, we need to work on our cardio," I tell him dryly. "You're not running as much as I told you to, are you?"

He only thinks about lying for a half-second before shaking his head. "Sorry, Coach," he murmurs.

I clap him on the shoulder with a focus mitt. "You're going to run every day?"

He nods quickly.

"And twice a week you'll do our sprinting drill?"

Another hurried nod.

"Good. You're done for the day. Go home and rest up."

When I turn toward Lucas, I find him looking over my shoulder, amused. I can only imagine the heap the kid just collapsed into.

"What's up?" I ask.

He jerks his head toward the door. "Let's go get dinner."

Which is code for: he had a bad day dealing with rich assholes and needs to talk to someone about something that has nothing to do with his daily life.

"You good with a burger?" he asks as we step out onto the sidewalk.

"That's fine. I can substitute the bun."

We don't talk during the ten-minute walk, or when we take a seat at a high top. It isn't until Lucas orders a Citywide that I snort and ask, "Rough day?"

He blows out a heavy breath. "Rough *week*."

"Want to talk about it?"

"Nope."

Chuckling, I shake my head. It's like clockwork. He does this once every three months. Alexander and I used to try to convince him to change jobs, but to no avail. Now, we just entertain the call with alcohol and a greasy burger.

But for the first time, Lucas changes the script. Lifting his beer to his lips, he sighs. "I need a vacation."

My eyebrows lift at that. "Yeah? When was the last time you left your laptop at home and took a real vacation?"

He blows out another breath. "I can't even remember. Too long."

"Where would you want to go?" I ask curiously.

"Anywhere that doesn't have service." He seems to snap back to reality because he shifts his focus to me. "What about that brother trip? You still in for it?"

I blink, thrown off by the topic change. I haven't even thought about our original conversation. And I definitely haven't thought about getting away from my day-to-day lately.

Not since I met Scarlett.

"Uhh...I don't know."

Lucas seems more and more into the idea as he leans forward and says excitedly, "Oh, come on, you were into the idea a few weeks ago. We should do it! You, me, and Alexander should get away to some luxury resort in Turks and Caicos, spend a week shark diving and hiking and drinking ourselves into the sand every night. It's perfect. Why not?"

"For one, that sounds expensive."

He shrugs. "So? It's not like you don't have the money."

*Yeah, but now I have something—some*one*—I want to spend it on.*

Lucas must read something on my face because he pauses the sip of his beer and frowns. "What? You having money problems?"

"Not *problems*, exactly…"

He tilts his head. "Then what? What's going on?"

I've never been good at lying to my brother. "Do you remember that girl in the shelter dog videos?"

He nods. "The one you didn't want to admit made you all gaga. Yeah."

"Well, she's kind of expensive."

He lets out a loud laugh. "So, she's a high maintenance girl? Weird way to word it, man. You make it sound like you're dating a hooker."

I wince at the word choice.

Lucas's eyes go wide.

"You *cannot* be serious right now."

"It's not as bad as it sounds," I rush to defend. "I met her through a highly reputable agency, so it's not like I just picked her up in Kensington. And…we get along well. *Really* well. Half the time, I forget I'm paying her."

I think Lucas's eyes might just fall out. "Nico, it's her *job* to make you forget that." He shakes his head. "You can't seriously be telling me you're developing feelings…"

I make a sound of frustration. "Look, I know how it sounds, okay? But I'm telling you: things are different with her. I *like* her."

*And I'm pretty sure she likes me.*

I don't say that part out loud, because I'm entirely aware of how it would sound. But it'd take too long to explain how my last date with Scarlett felt—how she finally opened up to me, and how we seemed to come to an agreement with the no-intimacy thing. And even if I tried to explain, the chance of Lucas understanding is still too small to bother.

"So, you're blowing your money on a high-end escort? As your manager and unofficial financial advisor, I really must protest, little brother."

"Noted," I say dryly. "It's not going to change anything, though. I'm still going to see her. I just don't want to spend money on a Turks and Caicos trip this year, is all." Then something occurs to me, and I add hurriedly, "And besides, I'm not always paying her. Case in point: the shelter dog date."

That seems to stun Lucas enough to cut off his brotherly scolding. He spent too much time teasing me about how smitten I sounded and how smitten *she* sounded to be able to use that as further proof of his point right now. Seems like he forgot the part about it being an accidental run-in.

Although, he looks like he wants to continue arguing. But after a moment, he simply sighs and says, "Just…be careful, okay? Keep seeing her, if you like her, but don't lose sight of the facts of the matter. Which is that you're *paying* her."

I roll my eyes in answer. I know that's as close as I'm going to get to an approval tonight.

But even as I mock him in return, there's a tingle of worry

in the back of my mind that I haven't been able to get rid of, no matter how many ways I try to convince myself.

Because even after my last date with Scarlett, as amazing as it was, as much of a breakthrough as it was…

She still wouldn't even consider the idea of us without payment.

# TWENTY-ONE
## SCARLETT

"Please, Daisy...*please.*"

I look down at the man kneeling at my feet, and I wonder if it's possible to feel any more disgust.

Every other Tuesday, I have an appointment at Dr. Schaffer's office. On his books, I'm just another patient there for therapy.

In reality, I go in to sit on his couch and let him obsess over my feet for an hour.

For half of the purchased time, I only let him look. Then, eventually, he receives permission to take off my heels, sniff my feet, and lick my toes. I don't have to do anything, and there's no penetrative sexual activity. Physically, it's one of my easier appointments.

But that doesn't mean I don't grimace when I finally tell the doctor, "You may taste."

He's so busy sliding my heel off, he doesn't notice the way I wince at his touch. When he presses his lips to my toenail, I start the process of distancing my mind from my body.

A process that becomes harder and harder with every

passing day.

The last fifteen minutes of the appointment feel like they take forever. By the time I'm sliding my feet into my second pair of heels and taking the cash from the doctor, exhaustion weighs down my bones. All I want to do is get home and scrub the day from my skin.

"I'll see you in two weeks?" Dr. Schafer asks with a smile. My heels that he buys for me so he can keep them afterwards dangle in his hands.

I give him a tight smile in return. "See you in two weeks, Doctor."

*I might not see you in two weeks, Doctor.*

---

The dates that aren't hard? The ones with Nico.

Even though our next one is a little different.

To my surprise, Nico requested an overnight date. I know he mentioned the idea briefly in the past, but I didn't expect him to organize it through the agency. I've never accepted an overnight date before.

It speaks to how much I trust Nico that I agree to this one.

After our last date, there was a small part of me that worried I would regret telling him about my past. That I would realize I only blurted it out in a strained moment, and not because he actually cares.

But those feelings never came. My honesty was safe with Nico.

If Amara is confused by the overnight request—or by me accepting it—she doesn't say anything. Ever since I changed my preferences, she hasn't commented on my client list. She just hums and sets my schedule the way I want her to.

This week, I'm going to Philadelphia.

I catch myself randomly smiling the day of our date. I have no idea what Nico has planned, but I also realize that I don't care. I'm just excited to be with him.

I take my time getting ready. When it takes me an extra hour to achieve the look I want, I tell myself it's because I want to look perfect tonight, not because of the exhaustion weighing on my shoulders.

*I must've worked out too hard this morning.*

At four p.m., I walk downstairs to the Uber black Nico said he called for me. We hit traffic on the drive, of course. It doesn't matter that it's Tuesday night, New York doesn't exist without traffic. The stop-and-go motion of the car makes me increasingly nauseous, which isn't normal for me. I attribute it to the fact that I didn't eat today in preparation for tonight.

By the time we're pulling up in front of Nico's building, I'm just about ready to throw myself from the car. I really hope he's not waiting outside for me because green is *not* a sexy color.

But I'm not that lucky. The Uber has barely stopped when Nico is ripping the door open and extending a hand.

"Hey, Red," he says in an excited voice. "How was the drive?"

The driver gives me an apologetic look in the mirror.

"Little bumpy," I croak out, taking Nico's hand.

Frowning, he looks me over. "Do you usually get car sick? I would've suggested the train if I knew."

"Not usually," I say as I sag into his embrace.

Once he's waved off the driver, he wraps one arm securely around my waist before leading me up the steps into his building. "Can I give you anything? I think ginger helps with nausea. Or maybe just some ice water?"

"I think I just need to sit for a minute," I groan. "I'm

sorry. This isn't how I wanted tonight to start. It's been a while since I've gotten car sick."

The truth is, I've never gotten car sick. But I don't know what else this could be.

"Don't be ridiculous, it's not your fault. Here, just relax." He pushes his front door open and leads me into his home. "I'll get you some water."

He seats me gently on his couch, taking a second to make sure I'm comfortable before he rushes off. It gives me a chance to look around his space.

It's neat and clean, but still looks lived-in. There are shoes scattered by the entryway and a cup or two on the kitchen island. It doesn't look like a bachelor pad, necessarily, but it's limited in décor. There's nothing on the walls and clearly no thought put into the color palette, but there's an oversized couch, a coffee table, and a big TV.

*I wonder if he's ever lived here with a girlfriend.*

It's the first time I've thought about Nico with other women. Which is ridiculous, because he's probably worried plenty about me with other men. But for some reason, I've never thought about his personal life outside of me. I just assumed the only thing he does is train and see his brothers, I guess.

*Wow. What a self-absorbed view of the world.*

Jealousy burns sudden and hot in my blood. I have no claim to him, no reason to ask about his dating history.

"Here, drink this," he says, handing me a glass of ice water. "Might make you feel better."

"Are you seeing anyone else?" I blurt out.

His lip twitches with a smile he doesn't let appear. "I am not, no."

My cheeks burn hotter. "Oh," I say weakly, bringing the glass to my chest.

But then his hidden smile falls, everything in his body going tense. I know he's thinking about reciprocating the question, but he already knows the answer.

I should tell him, anyway. He's done so much to put me at ease, the least I can do is return the effort. I could tell him I've cut back on my bookings, too thrown off by my dates with Nico to be able to stomach certain clients.

But...I can't tell him that. Because what would it accomplish? It's not like I'm quitting my job. I *can't* do that. What else would I do? And it's not like I'd be saying it to be *his* girlfriend. Who would ever want to date an escort?

"Can I get you something to eat?" he asks, still stiff. Still not meeting my eyes. "It might settle your stomach."

I cough into my fist to cover the rumble of my stomach at the mention of food. I should definitely eat something, but I'm still not letting go of the idea of going out tonight, so I'll pass for now. "I'm good, thank you," I say politely. I pat the couch next to me. "Just sit with me for a little. I'll drink this, and then we can go do whatever you have planned."

Seemingly soothed by my words, he drops next to me with a genuine smile. "Okay. Take your time; there's no rush."

I take a sip of my water. "What *do* you have planned?"

He grins. "Oh, I have big plans for us."

I smile into another sip. "So mysterious. Any hints?"

His excitement is palpable. "Well, *first*, we're going over to the Art Museum. Whether or not you want to go in, there are incredible views of the city from there." His voice drops to a whisper. "Also, the Rocky statue is right there, which is purely a selfish stop."

I chuckle at that, turning slightly in my seat so I can face him better. "And then what? A sports bar to watch the Phillies game? Will that give me the real Philly experience?"

"That and a Philly cheesesteak would undoubtedly give you the Philly experience, but no, that's not what we're doing. We have tickets to the Hans Zimmer concert tonight."

I perk up at that. "Oh my gosh, really? I *love* his music. I've always wanted to learn the *Interstellar* piano piece." But then my age-old need to please comes roaring to the surface, momentarily weakened by the roiling of my stomach. "Are you sure that's what you want to do? I don't want you to be bored. We could do something else; I don't mind."

Nico gives me a small smile in return. "Scarlett. We've been over this. I want to do things *you* want to do. Watching you enjoy them is why *I* enjoy it."

My brain is too foggy to fight him on this. I take two more big sips before putting the water down on the coffee table. "Okay. Let's go."

"You feel better?" he asks, clearly skeptical.

I nod and force a smile. "I told you, I just needed to sit for a minute."

In reality, I still feel exhausted and like my stomach is churning, but whatever; Nico is paying for a date, so he gets a date. Even if I don't understand *this* date.

After a moment, he stands and pulls me to my feet. "Okay. Wait here, I just need to grab my wallet."

I have to fight not to sag as he walks off. By the time he comes back and takes my hand, I'm channeling every bit of steel my mother instilled in me during my childhood. *Stand up straight. Smile. Don't bother a man with your problems.*

But on the elevator ride down, the metal box starts to spin. By the time the doors open, no amount of parental lessons could stop me from stumbling forward.

"Whoa, whoa." Once more, Nico wraps an arm around my waist. "I thought you said—" He tips my chin up, his eyes roving over my face. "This isn't from the ride here, is it? Are you sick?"

I start to go dizzy, a stupid smile appearing on my face. "Definitely not."

I hear his exasperated breath. "Scarlett, you're *sick.* Your entire face just went pale."

"Not possible," I mumble.

And then I can't say anything else. Because I'm rushing for the trash can in the reception and dispelling stomach contents that don't exist.

---

Miraculously, Nico manages to get me upstairs between bouts of heaving. I take the tiny bin with me—not that much is coming out. Since I didn't eat today, the only thing my stomach can get rid of is bile.

"Fuck, Scarlett," I hear him curse as he carries me into his condo. With my arms latched tight around his neck, he's carrying me with only one arm, the other hand holding the trash bin.

I whimper into his neck. "I'm so sorry." *I hate this. I hate letting him down.*

"What? No, that's not what I—" I feel his steps hurry. I have no idea where we're going until he sets me down on the softest bed I've ever laid on. His hand brushes my hair out of my face. "I just hate seeing you in pain, baby," he says softly.

"I'm okay," I try to say. But it's undercut by my desperate reach for the trash bin.

His gentle hands hold my hair back as I retch into it. When I stop heaving, I can't handle the shame at him seeing me like this. All I can do is let out another pathetic whimper as I fall back into his bed.

But my heart squeezes when I see how concerned he looks.

"It's probably the stomach bug," he says, continuing to brush his hand over my hair. It feels like he's looking for the contact. "I know you can't eat anything right now, but I think you should try to drink some Pedialyte so you don't get dehydrated."

I frown, my brain fuzzy. "Pedialyte? Do you have a baby? Why wouldn't you tell me that?"

I can make out his amused tone. "I do not have a baby. But fighters drink Pedialyte to rehydrate all the time. Didn't you ever use it for hangovers after a night of drinking?"

"I've never been drunk," I slur, my eyes sliding shut. "A lady never drinks to excess."

I might doze off for a second during his silence, but then another wave of whatever this is hits me, and I curl over the edge of the bed to vomit again.

I groan as I fall back into bed again. "Ugh, this is so not sexy. Why are you still here? Just send me to a hotel. You don't need to see this."

"Fuck that," he growls. "I'm not sending you anywhere. I'm going to take care of you."

At that, some of the haze clears, brought on by confusion-fueled anger. I force myself to a half-upright position on my elbows.

"You don't make *sense*," I spit at him with a glare. "Why on earth would you want to deal with this? Look at me, I'm disgusting. I can do *nothing* for you in this state. Not even the conversation you *claim* to love." I scoff. "Even if you're not paying tonight, it doesn't make sense why you wouldn't just reschedule and ship me off."

For the first time since I met him, there's a flash of frustration in his eyes. I watch as he leans over to open the drawer in his nightstand beside me, revealing a giant wad of cash.

"Here," he grits out, splitting half of it off and pressing it into my hand. "I told you I'm paying for *you*, in every sense of the word."

I just stare at the cash.

"Matter of fact, here." He smacks the rest of it on top of what's in my hand. "I'll pay you double what we discussed. I'll pay you anything you want. Whatever it takes to get it through your head that I don't want you as an *escort*, I want you as a *girlfriend*."

My eyes widen.

And then I keel over again.

I hear Nico sigh as he brushes a hand over my hair. "I'm not going to take that personally."

When I fall back this time, I'm trembling with exhaustion. I have no idea how long I've been here, or how long I've been throwing up. My head is pounding and I'm both shivering and sweating.

"Goddamnit, Red…" My eyes close as he pulls the blanket over me. "I'm going to get that Pedialyte."

I think I doze off because it feels like no time at all has passed when I feel a straw pressed against my lips. I try to take a sip. I've never felt this weak before.

"Good girl," Nico murmurs. "Do you think you can do some watermelon too? It's food and hydration in one."

When I only groan in answer, he says, "Okay, maybe later, then. Do you want to change clothes?"

I perk up at that. Sick as I am, the thought of wearing Nico's clothes is too enticing.

He chuckles and holds the straw to my lips again. "I'll get you a t-shirt and some sweats."

I should be embarrassed that he has to help me change out

of my clothes. I *do* hate that this is how he sees my lingerie for the first time in weeks. But I can barely summon the energy to lift my arms so he can peel my dress off, so I don't have many options here.

I lay there like a pathetic doll as he pulls sweatpants up my legs, but I hum in pleasure when he tugs his t-shirt over my head. It smells like him.

I sink into the bed with a happy sigh once his smell is all around me. This entire situation is atrocious, but at least I know what his bed smells like.

"If you don't throw up on it, you can keep that one," Nico says. He chuckles when I glare at him.

Unfortunately, he might be onto something. Because I throw up in the next second.

# TWENTY-TWO
## NICO

Two hours later, there's nothing left for Scarlett to throw up.

Four hours later, she's shivering with the dry heaves, tears running down her face.

And I'm starting to get really fucking worried.

It didn't escape my attention that there was nothing for her to throw up when she started vomiting. I guessed during previous dates that she might have a bad relationship with food, but I never would've expected that she eats nothing the day of a date.

I try once more to get her to eat some watermelon, but she only presses her lips together and shakes her head. She's white as a sheet and trembling. And she stopped accepting Pedialyte twenty minutes ago.

The only blessing is that she falls asleep between bouts of vomiting. For those twenty-minute periods, I cool her forehead with a damp washcloth, change the sheets she sweats through, and pace up and down the hall. I don't like that she hasn't been able to keep anything down in the past hour.

But it isn't until she spikes a fever that I truly panic.

Without any hesitation, I pull out my phone and make a call.

By the time Alexander walks through my front door, Scarlett has sweat through another t-shirt. I can't bring myself to leave her to meet him at the door.

"Nico?"

"In here," I call out, pressing a fresh washcloth to Scarlett's forehead.

I hear his heavy footsteps before I see him. When he stops in my bedroom doorway, I can feel the confusion radiating from him.

"Did you bring it?" I ask without looking up.

A pause, and then the thump of a bag beside the bed. "Yeah."

"Can you—" I clear a suddenly tight throat. "Can you take a look at her? I'm pretty sure it's just the stomach bug, but she spiked a fever, and she can't keep any fluids down. At the very least, she needs an IV."

Alexander appears in my peripheral, but when I look up, I'm surprised to see him studying me instead of Scarlett.

My nerves are too frazzled to deal with the questions right now. So I just stand silently and give him space to do what he needs to.

As a Marine, Alexander went through enough medical training to be the one I turn to for basic medical needs; God knows fighting has created enough situations where I've needed it. And calling my brother was always infinitely easier than making a trip to the hospital. So when I called him tonight and asked him for an IV and to bring his usual kit, he didn't hesitate.

And to his credit, he's not hesitating now, either. Even though I neglected to tell him that it's not for me.

I watch as he goes through some basic checks—

temperature, blood pressure, mouth and eyes—before starting to set up the IV drip. I've done enough of them here that I have a somewhat-setup for it, so it doesn't take Alexander long to have it ready. Barely a minute later, he has the needle in Scarlett's arm to start her rehydration.

"You're going to need to watch her," he says in a gruff tone. "If she tosses and turns a lot, or if she tries to jump out of bed to throw up, she might rip the IV out."

I nod, already worried about that. I'm not going to sleep a wink tonight.

"You're probably right that it's the stomach bug," he continues. "She'll be fine, but you did the right thing calling me. She was completely dehydrated." He sends a curious look my way. "Why didn't you just take her to the hospital?"

I've been thinking about that, too. I *should've* taken her to the hospital. But she looked so small, and in so much pain, and—for fuck's sake, she wanted me to ship her off. I couldn't bring myself to put any amount of distance between us, even if it was an ER and a waiting room.

"I didn't think it was worth it for just an IV," I lie instead. But then I feel bad about how that sounds and turn toward him with a guilty wince. "Sorry, I didn't mean I'd rather eat up your time than theirs. I just—"

"Nico. I get it."

I swallow thickly and turn back toward her. "Yeah. I… Thanks."

"Who is she?" he asks simply. With no judgment, no expectation.

"She's…" *Fuck, how do I describe Scarlett?* "We're dating." *Not completely accurate, but good enough. Worked with Lucas.* "She lives in New York, but she came down for the night. That's when she started throwing up."

Alexander nods once in understanding. He doesn't press for more details.

I turn toward him. "Thank you. For coming over so quickly."

He gives me a shrug that I've learned to interpret as *you're my brother, it wasn't a question.*

"Did I pull you away from work?" I ask him. Nowadays, Alexander works for a private security firm. Some weeks his hours are odder than others.

He shakes his head. "Not tonight. I'm not back on nights until next month."

"Shit, so I woke you up?" I didn't even think about how late it was. "I'm sorry. I can handle it from here, you don't have to—"

"Nico, it's fine. Are *you* okay?"

I nod as I sag against my dresser. "Yeah, I'm fine. Just tired. Sorry." I straighten with a groan. "Do you want a beer?"

He glances at Scarlett, taking in every detail of her current state before he turns back to me. "Sure. You should bring it in here, though. I want to make sure she's okay before I leave."

I clap him on the shoulder in a silent message of gratitude.

It's nice to spend time with my brother. We don't do it often enough. With my training schedule and his work schedule, I spend more time with Lucas than I do with Alexander.

We shoot the shit for the next hour, quietly chatting in the sitting area of my bedroom. Halfway through, Alexander gives her a second IV bag, and right before Scarlett rouses for the first time, he removes the IV entirely.

She's not throwing up anymore, thank God, and the color

is starting to return to her skin, but she's still sweating. The second she whimpers in pain, I shoot up from my couch.

"Nico?" she whispers, blinking her eyes open. Unfortunately, her gaze lands on Alexander before it does me, and her eyes widen. She tries to scoot away, but she's still so weak that she doesn't make it far.

"Hey, hey, no, it's okay," I soothe her, kneeling beside the bed. "It's okay, I'm here."

As soon as her eyes focus on me, as soon as my hand touches her face, she relaxes.

"I'm so thirsty," she croaks out.

I reach for the Pedialyte and hold the straw to her lips. "Here. Drink this."

I stroke her hair as she takes a few weak pulls. Then she melts into the bed with a sigh and falls asleep instantly.

"Christ," I mutter, dragging a hand down my face. I can't contain the sound of my worry as I ask Alexander, "She's getting better, right? I can't tell anymore."

"Much better," he answers. "You're just exhausted and worried. You should be getting some sleep, too."

I snort at that. "Fat chance of that happening."

When I sigh and turn back to sit on the couch again, he's watching me with that all-seeing stare of his.

"What?" I ask defensively.

"Don't you have conditioning at eight a.m.?"

I glance at Scarlett. "I'll probably push it to the afternoon. I don't want to leave her."

What I don't say is that I forgot I even *had* conditioning. It seems the more I think about her, the less I think about fighting.

Alexander's gaze tracks to Scarlett. He hesitates, then says, "You like her."

My chest twinges. I know what he means by that. "Yeah, I do."

Another pause. "I can watch her if you want to get some sleep."

I send him a grateful smile. "I appreciate that, but I'm okay. One night won't kill me."

He doesn't push me the way Lucas would. He just nods, drains the rest of his beer, and stands.

"Call me if anything changes," he says, clapping me on the back. And then he's gone.

Checking my watch, I realize it's almost five a.m. *Fuck. I really do need to get some sleep.*

Taking one last look at Scarlett, I decide Alexander was right about her looking better. She hasn't thrown up in hours, and since the IV isn't in anymore, there's no need to watch her like a hawk.

I cool her forehead one more time, refill the water on her nightstand, and then I crawl into bed beside her. I don't even care if I catch it from her, I'm staying right here with her.

Pulling Scarlett closer with an arm around her waist, I bury my face in her neck and fall into a dreamless sleep.

# TWENTY-THREE
## SCARLETT

I wake to the feeling of arms wrapped around me, a solid chest against my back.

I'm groggy, my thoughts swimming through mud. I'm also weak, thirsty, and my stomach is cramping. When I groan, the arm around me tightens to pull me closer.

And then I hear a startled breath and feel weight shift on the bed.

"What is it? What do you need?"

Sleepily, I blink my eyes open. It's daytime, the bedroom bathed in light and the sounds of the city loud outside the windows.

"Nico?" I ask with a yawn.

"Yeah, baby. I'm here."

Even the sound of his voice makes me feel better. With a content sigh, I turn onto my side and burrow into his arms.

I feel a kiss pressed to my hair and a hand brushed down my arm.

"How do you feel? Can I get you anything?"

At the repeated question, I sigh and try to focus. *Why do I need to focus again? Why am I being asked questions?*

And then the memories of last night hit me.

I jerk back, my eyes widening in horror.

*I was with Nico last night. I got* sick *with Nico last night.* On *him.*

"Oh my gosh." I try to put as much distance between us as possible, but since I sleep in a ball on the edge of the bed, there's nowhere for me to go. All I can do is hold the blanket up to cover my body.

My body that's clothed in Nico's sweats.

*God, they smell good.*

He lets out a giant yawn and wipes the sleep from his eyes. "What's wrong?"

I gape at him. And not because he's not wearing a shirt right now. "What's *wrong?* What's wrong is, I got sick last night."

Still rubbing one eye, he frowns. "I'm aware. Which is why I'm asking how you feel."

"I—" I feel like crap. But there's no chance I'm telling him that. It's bad enough I ruined our date. "I'm fine. Why are you in bed with me?"

He freezes at that, his frown deepening. "I didn't want to leave you unsupervised," he says carefully. He's watching me, cataloguing my reactions the way he always does. "But I can leave if you need space. *After* you tell me the truth about how you're feeling."

Just like that, all energy leaves my body. I drop into a seated heap on the bed.

"I'm okay," I say in a small voice. Truthfully, this time. "Just tired. And thirsty. And I feel gross."

I run my tongue over my teeth and feel the gritty remnants of a night spent puking.

*Mother would be so disappointed in me.*

Somehow, I can't summon the will to care.

About her, not Nico. I hate that Nico saw—is seeing—me like this.

"I need a shower," I admit. "Do you have a towel I can use?"

He nods and gets out of the bed. If I wasn't so dehydrated, I'd drool over the sight of him shirtless and barefoot, wearing light grey sweatpants.

"I have a bathtub if you'd prefer that," he says as he goes into his closet. "I think you mentioned liking baths."

I let out a groan I can't hold back. "I would *kill* for a bath."

His chuckle floats behind him as he walks into what I assume is the ensuite bathroom. "Coming right up."

Flopping back onto his pillows, I let out a big exhale. This is so not how I wanted last night to go. But I'm too tired to give in to the brewing freakout, so I try to just breathe and revel in the fact that I feel somewhat human again. Thank God, it was only—

*Wait, how long have I been here?*

I have no idea where I left my purse and phone, but Nico's is on the nightstand. When I tap it and the screen lights up, the time shines back at me.

2:53 p.m.

I jolt to a sitting position. *Shoot. It's been twenty hours.*

I don't have anything on my schedule today, but I have no idea what Nico's looks like. His date was technically only scheduled until eight a.m.

"Don't you have to go to the gym or something?" I call out. "Did I take over your entire day?"

Nico appears in the doorway, towel slung over his shoulder and a toothbrush in his mouth. When he leans against the doorframe and continues to brush his teeth, I nearly combust at the sight.

*Why did nobody tell me casual is attractive on a man?*

"I worked out while you were still sleeping," he says, his mouth full. "The beauty of having a gym in the building."

Guilt sits heavy in my stomach. "But you were supposed to go to *your* gym today, weren't you," I say, not a question. "I messed up your plans."

He leans out of my view for a second, and I hear him spit into the sink. "It was my decision, Scarlett," he says simply. "And I stand by it." Then he's walking toward me in all his half-naked glory. "Now come on, I'll grab some fresh clothes and make you some food while you take a bath."

"You don't—"

He pulls me to my feet and tugs me toward the bathroom. "I don't want to hear it, Red."

*Oh, God. My lipstick.*

For the first time, I get a look of myself in the mirror.

I look exactly as bad as I was scared I would.

Mortified, I turn and shove Nico out of the bathroom so I can close the door behind him. "Oh my *God*, don't look at me!"

I can hear his chuckle through the door. "Baby, you couldn't look bad even if you tried. But I'll leave you alone for a minute. I laid out a few things for you on the counter."

When I turn around, I see an unopened toothbrush, toothpaste, some mouthwash, and a separate glass of water. Next to the steaming bathtub, there's a fresh towel and a comb on the small side table.

*Are all men this thoughtful?*

I've never met one this thoughtful.

Sighing, I set to cleaning myself up. I look wrecked from a night of vomiting; my hair a rat's nest and my makeup is either smeared or nonexistent.

After I brush my teeth twice and rinse with mouthwash—

also twice—I drink some of the water before peeling off my clothes. Everything hurts. My *abs* hurt. My skin hurts to touch. But as soon as I sink into the too-hot water, I let out a deep groan of relief.

"Temperature okay?" I hear through the door.

My eyes slide closed. "It's perfect," I slur. "What did you put in here?"

"Just some Epsom salts. Figured you'd be sore."

"You'd be correct," I say through a light moan, sinking deeper into the water.

After a moment, Nico asks, "Can I come in?"

"I'm naked." But my tone is flat. I couldn't care less about being naked in front of him. This feels too good.

"Baby, I've seen every inch of you. *Tasted* every inch of you."

"Now is not the time to make sexual innuendos, Nicholas."

His huff of laughter makes me smile. "Yes, you can come in," I call out before I can think better of it.

I hear the door open and sense Nico stepping into the not very large space. When I crack an eye open, he's standing beside the tub with a plate in his hand.

"Feel better?"

I nod, eyeing the plate. "What's that?"

He doesn't answer, just pulls a stool over from who knows where and takes a seat beside the tub. Then he picks something off the plate and holds it out to me.

It's a strawberry.

"You brought me fruit?" I ask as I reach for it with one hand. When he holds the strawberry out of reach, I frown.

Then he holds it to my lips, and I understand.

"You *cannot* be real." But I bite the fruit from his fingers, letting out a content sigh when the flavor and much-needed liquid explode on my tongue.

He holds another bite to my lips—mango this time—and I take that one, too. After the third bite of watermelon, I sink back into the water. But it isn't until he reaches for a wet cloth that my confusion and insecurity come roaring back to the forefront.

"Nico…" My voice is small, and unsure. He knows what I'm going to say without me having to say it.

"Just let me take care of you," he says softly, brushing the cloth over my shoulders. "Stop thinking so much."

I swallow thickly, my eyes suddenly stinging. "I'm sorry we missed your plans last night," is the only thing I can bring myself to whisper.

And Nico, the sweet, beautiful, perfect man he is, just smiles.

"I'm not." When I frown up at him, he explains, "This whole time, I've been trying to come up with dates that a man wouldn't pay for, that you'd finally believe weren't for *me*, but because I wanted to date *you*. And you handed me the perfect one on a silver platter."

I let out a laugh, relief and giddiness washing over me like a wave. "What, me vomiting all night long and forcing you to cancel your life to clean up after me?"

He brushes a kiss over the back of my hand. "Exactly," he whispers with a smile.

My head falls back against the porcelain, my smile still firmly in place. "You're a hard man to argue with, Nico Price."

Something flashes in his eyes. Something I don't recognize.

But then it softens into something more familiar, a playfulness I've come to love.

"I hate to tell a woman not to argue with me, but…in this case, I think it goes without saying."

---

We spend the rest of the day lounging together.

We watch movies on the couch, cuddled under a blanket and sharing bites of the dinner Nico ordered: a nearby Mexican restaurant with arguably the best tacos I've ever had.

Slowly, my strength comes back, one bite at a time. I wouldn't normally let myself eat something like this, but between my sickness and this bizarre situation, it feels easier to make food decisions without so much overthinking.

*I'll run the extra miles tomorrow.*

Right now, I don't want to think about anything but Nico. I want to exist in this space with him, just for a little while. I want to enjoy him without the outside world and its pressures. I want to enjoy *myself* with him.

"You know what I was thinking about?" I muse, taking Nico's offered bite of chips and guacamole.

"What's that?" he hums. But he's looking at my lips as he says it.

"How didn't you get sick? Isn't the stomach bug highly contagious?"

He snorts as he scoops out a chip for himself. "Trust me, I had the same thought. I kept panicking that I'd catch it, and then you'd wake up out of your coma only to find me *in* one."

I shiver at the thought. "That would've been awful. I would've felt so guilty."

I don't understand why Nico gets quiet until he asks without meeting my eyes, "Would you have stayed to take care of me?"

At first, my eyes widen. *Of course, I would've stayed to take care of him.*

And then I realize why he's asking.

*He doesn't know how I feel about him.*

The entire time we've known each other, he's been killing himself trying to convince me that he likes me. That he's not here because of the sex, or because I can stroke his ego. He's here because he *likes* me. So much so, that he's continued to pay for things no man should be paying for on a date.

And I've been so caught up in my insecurities, I forgot to be honest with him about how I feel.

I know the answer to Nico's question, but I pause for a moment longer to analyze the deeper question. *Do I like Nico?*

Yes. Undoubtedly. Overwhelmingly.

"Of course, I would've taken care of you," I say, turning toward him and shifting closer on the couch. "I would've done exactly what you did for me."

His whole body melts free from tension.

Sighing, I lean my head against the back of the couch. "I hate that I made you question that."

He gives me a smile. "As long as it's a real answer, I don't care."

I look down, fidgeting with a blanket thread. "It's a real answer. And I'm glad you didn't get sick." But then a memory appears through the haze of last night and I look up at him. "Wait, was someone else here last night? Or did I dream that?"

Nico shoots me an unsure look. "My brother came over."

I blink at him. "Okay... Why?"

He nods at my arm. "He gave you an IV."

I look, wide-eyed, at the inside of my arm. I wouldn't

have noticed it among all the other aches and pains, but...there's a slight bruise on the inside of my elbow.

"I'm sorry I didn't ask your permission first," Nico rushes to say. "If you had been conscious, I would've. But you were so dehydrated, and you wouldn't stop throwing up, and I was getting really fucking worried. So, I called him."

"Does he work in healthcare?" I ask Nico.

He shakes his head. "Military. He was a Marine. But he has enough medical training that sometimes I call him for IVs when I'm dehydrated from training."

I nod. *That makes sense, I guess.*

"I'm fine with you calling him," I find myself admitting. I look up to meet his eyes. "Thank you for doing that. For taking such good care of me."

Another exhale of relief. I hate that I stress him out.

"And please thank him for me," I add. "Actually..."

I look around Nico's living room, reality intruding for the first time since yesterday. *Where did I drop my purse?*

When I spot it in the entryway, I rush to grab it. I carry enough cash that—

"Absolutely not," comes Nico's voice from behind me.

I spin, a wad of cash in my hand. "I can't *not* pay him. At the very least, I need to cover the cost of the IV."

But Nico is shaking his head as he stands from the couch. "Absolutely not. If it was mine, you wouldn't pay me for it, would you?"

My brow furrows. "But it's not. It's your brother's."

"So? We're family. We take care of each other."

*That doesn't clarify anything. My experience with family is entirely selfish.*

My confusion must be obvious because when Nico reaches me, he sighs and takes the cash from my hand. And then he slides it back in my purse.

"I don't know how your family operated," he says gently, correctly reading my reaction, "but in *my* family, we do everything we can to love and support each other. And that extends to the people and things we consider important."

My chest warms. *I'm important to him.*

"So no, you're not allowed to pay him for taking care of you after I asked him to. He wouldn't accept the money, anyway."

As Nico leads me back to the couch, something else occurs to me. "What does your other brother do? If you're a fighter, and the other brother is ex-military, what job does the third one have? Hockey player? Firefighter? What?"

I'm relieved to hear him chuckle again as he sets us down on the couch again. "I'm going to tell him you said that. He'll be butthurt for a week to know those are the jobs that match mine and Alexander's."

My cheeks heat. "I'm sorry, I didn't mean to offend. It was just a guess—"

"Baby," he says with another chuckle, "He's not even here, and you're worried about hurting his feelings. He's my brother; I have to mess with him."

I never would've *dreamed* of joking with my family.

"Lucas is a high-powered lawyer," Nico finally answers.

My head rears back. "How did that happen? That's a big difference in careers."

Shrugging, he relaxes into the couch and stretches his arms out along the back of it. "We have no idea. He was always a charmer when he was a kid, so the litigator piece didn't really surprise any of us. That boy could talk his way out of anything even when he was eight years old. Drove our mother crazy."

When he chuckles fondly, I find myself smiling at the story. I like hearing about his childhood.

"What kind of law does he practice?" I ask.

"He's a corporate lawyer," Nico answers. "Alexander and I like to joke that he makes rich bastards richer."

I frown. "That doesn't sound very noble."

He snorts. "Which is why the firefighter guess was so funny."

I look out at the windows for a moment, taking in the Philly skyline and the setting sun that's illuminating it. This city really is beautiful. This entire date feels like a fever dream.

And I never want to wake up.

# TWENTY-FOUR
## SCARLETT

We keep the conversation light for the rest of the night.

I manage to convince Nico to put some of his fights on. I want to know more about him, and I want to ask questions about the sport. It takes him a minute to agree, at first pushing for me to pick a movie *I* want to watch, but I'm adamant about it. Once he sees how invested I am, he relaxes.

It's…fascinating. I can't wrap my head around why anyone would want to do MMA. My mother would've disowned me for bringing home a fighter. She probably would've assumed he was a dumb, tattooed brute and kicked him out of the house.

But as I listen to Nico break down his strategy and some of the techniques, I realize he's far smarter than I'm sure people give him credit for.

"Do you enjoy fighting?" I ask, suddenly remembering our conversation that first night.

There's a thoughtful pause as he finishes cleaning up the last of our dinner trash. "I don't think enjoy is the word I would use," he answers, lips pinching. "There's a very specific type of fighter who *enjoys* getting locked in a cage with a man who wants to kill him. But I guess I enjoy the training."

I snuggle deeper into the cushions, wanting to know everything. "Do you ever think about retiring?"

He gives me that look from earlier again, that one I couldn't read.

Then he glances away as he clears his throat. "Sometimes, yeah." He fidgets with the napkin in his hands. "More and more, it seems silly to be doing something I'm not totally invested in. Dangerous, too."

That has me freezing, worry covering me like a cold blanket. "It's even *more* dangerous when your head's not in it?"

He shrugs and walks back to the couch. "Well...yeah. Any sport would be."

"Then you should definitely retire," I press. "You can't put yourself at risk like that."

He drops onto the couch beside me with a smile that has those damn dimples coming out. "You worried about me, Red?"

I answer with narrowed eyes.

Chuckling, he drops his head back to the couch. "I probably will soon. Actually—"

I straighten in my seat, eager for every bit of Nico that I can get.

"The fight I have coming up, it's technically the last fight on my contract."

"So you really could retire soon." Then the rest of his sentence registers and I frown. "Wait... you have a fight coming up? Since when?!"

"Since two months ago. The fight is next week."

I gape at him. "You have a *fight* next week? And you didn't tell me that?"

He shrugs, not meeting my eyes. "I kind of liked not having this part of my life be about fighting."

I soften at that. I can understand wanting to compartmentalize things.

Ever-so-subtly, I slide my hand closer so I'm touching his arm. The contact seems to release tension in both of us.

"I like being your escape," I say quietly. "But…shouldn't you be training around the clock for it or something? I'm surprised your coach lets you take days off to go to jazz clubs."

Nico winces. "Yeah, that wouldn't normally be the recommended rest day. But I'm not drinking or partying, and I *do* need one day every week when I don't have to train three times. So I'm telling myself it's fine." He huffs a laugh. "Although if I end up getting my ass handed to me, just do me a favor and leave out the *I told you so.*"

"I would never." Then, more carefully, I ask, "You won't, though. Right?"

He looks at me in surprise. "What, get my ass handed to me? No. I'm going to win." He lifts my hand to his lips and sweetly presses a kiss to the back of it. Then, in a careful tone matching my own, he says, "You should come to the fight."

For a moment, I only blink. I don't know why I never considered seeing Nico outside of a date setting. It would be…new.

And yet, I feel giddy at the idea of watching Nico in his element.

"Would you really want me there?" I ask.

His head shoots up, his eyebrows lifting as his gaze locks onto mine. "Are you serious? Of course I want you there." When he sees me contemplating the invite, his lips curl with a grin. "Red, if I haven't made it disgustingly obvious that I want you in my life, I'm clearly doing something wrong here. Yes, I want you at my fight. *If* you want to be there."

I nibble on my bottom lip as I mull it over. "Would I be in the crowd, or with you?"

He shrugs and twirls a strand of my hair around one finger. "Wherever you want to be."

"I don't think I'd like being in the crowd," I say quietly.

"Then you can stay in the dressing room and watch from there. Matter of fact, I could even have Alexander stay with you. He barely says two words, so you wouldn't have to worry about talking to him."

A small smile tugs at my lips. "Lucas is the talker, right?"

Nico snorts. "Lucas would make you wish you were in the cage with me just to get away from his incessant questions." When I giggle, his whole face lights up. "It's at the Garden, so right there in your backyard."

I'm surprised to realize how much I'm considering this.

"Can I give you a maybe? Let me just think about it a little."

Nico grows serious as he nods. "Of course. I'll leave a ticket for you at Will Call either way, and you can make the decision on your own." But then uncertainty flashes across his face.

"What is it?" I ask.

"I need to put your legal name down if I leave you a ticket," he says, sounding hesitant. "Since they check IDs."

Suddenly, this moment just got a lot bigger.

Giving him my first name had been a change, but not a huge risk. Scarlett is a common enough name that I could still hide in a city of eight million people. But giving him my full name… that's another level of trust.

*Do I want to trust Nico with it?*

The answer is louder and more obvious than I expected it to be.

"It's…Scarlett Adler," I tell him softly.

A loud exhale rushes from Nico. I wonder what he thought my answer would be.

"Scarlett Adler," he repeats. And just the way he says it, the *wonder* with which he says it, tells me I made the right decision. I want him to say my name over and over now.

And then a slow grin slides across his face.

"What?"

"I just realized something. Even before you told me your real name, I was calling you by your name. In a way." When I tilt my head in confusion, he says, "Red? Scarlett? It's the same thing."

Surprised laughter bursts out of me. "How did I never realize that? I guess that should've been my sign."

It's adorable how proud he looks. I want to tease him about it, but when he yawns, I realize how late it is. And while I slept for over twelve hours last night, Nico was probably up for most of it.

I try not to hate myself for the way Nico tenses up and purposefully keeps his focus away from the front door, because I know he's scared to ask me to stay for fear of me saying no. Little does he know, all I can think about is how I didn't get to enjoy sleeping in his arms last night.

"It's pretty late," I say simply. "Is it okay if I stay the night again?"

Guilt settles heavy in my stomach when the relief makes his shoulders relax. The desire to do something for *him* takes over, so I ask, "Can we take a shower?"

My wording makes him hesitate. "We?"

I nod and take his hand. "If you feel like joining me."

He watches me for a moment. "Always, Scarlett."

Smiling, I stand and pull him to his feet, then lead both of us toward the bedroom. Once we're inside the bathroom, I switch the shower on, then turn to lift Nico's shirt off.

He raises his arms and lets me pull it over his head, clearly skeptical about my intentions. But he doesn't stop me as I push his sweats down over his hips. When I kneel before him to tug his boxer briefs down and guide his feet to step out of his clothes, he watches me like a hawk, tension running through every muscle of his body. He thinks I'm trying to make things sexual again.

But when I ignore his hard cock between us and stand, his expression shifts to curiosity. He watches as I lift my own shirt off—his shirt—and then his sweatpants. When I step into the shower, he follows me without hesitation.

I reach immediately for the body wash. My intention for this shower wasn't to initiate sex, or to create another situation where he tries to care for me. It was to care for *him*.

At first, he doesn't react when I guide him under the water. But when I swap our positions and lather up his loofah to brush it over his shoulders, he says, "You don't have to do that. You never have to take care of me."

I press a light kiss to his chest before brushing the loofah over the muscle. "I know," I whisper.

I watch his throat move on a rough swallow. "Is this because I took care of you last night?"

Smiling, I press another kiss to his skin, this one to his throat. "No. It's because I *want* to take care of you." Peeking up at him, I add, "To repeat a very sweet—and very pushy— man, will you just let me?"

His relieved laugh fills the shower enclosure, the sound warming me more than the water hitting my back. "Yes, ma'am."

I take my time washing his body. Selfishly, I want to *look* at him. I want to appreciate every hard-earned muscle, every scar he's received from fighting and from growing up with two brothers. I want to see *him*.

I stay away from his cock, but he's still breathing heavily when I stand from washing his legs. I'm just as turned on as he is, but I don't give in to the urge to take him in hand. I just lead him to spin so I can wash his back.

"Can I wash you, too?" he asks, his voice like gravel.

I press a kiss to his shoulder, a foreign sensation growing in my chest. "Yes," I answer breathily.

And I realize as he brushes the loofah over my own skin that this feeling I'm experiencing is a sense of power. Not power as a superiority, but as a confidence I've never experienced before. It grows when I see the care Nico takes with me, and when I see the awe with which he looks at my body.

I wonder if it's a confidence I always should've had. As an escort, I *know* I can bring a man to his knees. But I've always faked it. I was channeling the woman they saw when they looked at me, not the woman I was.

With Nico, I can't fake anything. I don't want to.

For the first time since I was thirteen and my mother called me chubby, I don't hate my body. Not if Nico looks at it and thinks I'm the most beautiful woman in the world.

Eyes locked on his, I take a slow step back until I'm under the shower spray. I watch him watch me, how his pupils blow black as his hungry gaze travels over me. And then I tip my head back, my eyes sliding closed as I let the water slide in rivulets between my breasts and down my body.

"*Fuck*, baby," I hear Nico whisper. "You're the most incredible thing I've ever seen."

Without opening my eyes, my lips lift in a smile.

I'm not surprised when he doesn't initiate anything; he just waits for the soap to run from my body before reaching behind me to shut off the water. Pressing a kiss to my neck, and then my shoulder, he wraps me in a fluffy towel and carries me out of the shower.

*Why do I love the feel of him toweling me off?* I have to hide my smile as he does it. But it comes out full force when he asks, "Do you need a minute alone before we go to bed?"

I pull the towel up to cover my mouth and nod.

He probably meant for me to use the bathroom, or brush my teeth, or something along those lines. In reality, I spend it trying to tamp down on the giddy smile that Nico brings out of me.

When I have it somewhat under control—and once I've brushed my teeth and used the toilet—I step out of the bathroom. "All yours," I tell him.

Once again, he's shirtless and wearing sweats. And once again, I want to jump him for it.

He either doesn't notice or ignores my stare, because he gestures at the bed and says, "For the record, just in case it's not obvious, all bedding and sheets have been swapped out. No one is getting sick again." Then he points at the clothes he laid out. "I also pulled a t-shirt and boxers for you. Figured you'd be more comfortable in that."

*As long as it's yours, I don't care.*

I don't say that. I just nod and tell him thank you. But when he brushes another kiss over my bare shoulder as he passes by me, that giddy smile comes back full force.

I'm sitting in bed, comforter pulled up to my waist, when he eventually emerges from the bathroom. I shouldn't be nervous right now, but I am. It's been a long time since I've slept in bed with a man—last night notwithstanding. Do I snore? Did I take up a lot of the bed? Oh my God, what if I drool?

"Did I snore last night?" I blurt out.

Nico full-on jumps into the bed and lands with a flop beside me. "No. But then again, the sounds of vomiting may have drowned them out."

My mouth drops open as I stare at him. I shove him lightly in the shoulder, a mortified laugh creeping up my throat. "You couldn't have just spared my feelings?"

Grinning, he folds one arm behind his head. "Nope. Sorry." But then he softens and adds, "But I bet if you *did* snore, it would be really cute. Like puppy snores."

"It's not a compliment to compare a woman to a dog, Nico," I say with a sigh.

"I didn't. I said puppy. The cutest animal on earth."

I roll my eyes, but I'm still smiling. "I don't think I've ever been called cute before."

He shifts onto his side to gaze at me. "You are, though. Cute. And beautiful. And sexy."

My breath catches at how he's looking at me. "Nico—"

"And smart. And brave. And incredible."

For a moment, I can only stare at him. At this man who makes me feel so safe and cared for.

*What did I do to deserve this?*

In an instant, I feel exhausted. Nico sees the way my eyelids flutter with the need for sleep. Wrapping one arm around my waist, he pulls me into his chest and presses a kiss to my hair.

"You won't leave before I wake up, right?" he asks.

The feel of his embrace and his comforting scent lulls me to sleep before I can do more than shake my head.

I leave before he wakes up.

I hadn't intended to leave like this, but when my phone chimed with a text from Amara at 6 a.m., reminding me about a location change for my client tonight, the spiral that I was so scared of was immediately triggered.

This date with Nico has gone on for too long. In two days, I've managed to completely forget what my life looks like. It's just so *nice* being with him, I forget that this isn't my reality.

*My* reality is going back to my empty apartment, to my empty degree, and my empty clients.

I move around the bedroom as quietly as possible. Since I brought an overnight bag, I have casual clothes to wear on the train ride back—I don't think I can stomach an Uber for that long again—so I leave Nico's clothes folded neatly on his couch. Then I grab my bag and tip toe out of the room.

The guilt hits before I even reach the kitchen. He did so much for me, and I'm leaving like a regretful one-night stand. He deserves better.

I can't quite bring myself to turn around and crawl back into bed with him, though—as much as I want to. When I spot a notepad on his refrigerator, I do the next best thing and leave him a note.

> Nico,
> I'm sorry for leaving so early. I need to get home and I didn't want to wake you.
> Thank you for taking care of me. I'm sorry again for ruining your date plans.

I hesitate for the next part. I've been debating giving Nico my phone number, just to take the agency out of the equation, but I haven't worked up the nerve to do it yet.

Taking a deep breath, I add,

> *Call me if you feel like chastising me for the million apologies.*
>
> *xoxo,*
> *Scarlett*

And then I scribble my number and book it from the apartment.

It isn't until I'm already on the train that I realize I never returned the cash he stuffed in my purse that first night.

Regardless of my mental hang-ups over this relationship with Nico, the one thing that's become clear is that I trust him enough to stop accepting his money.

# TWENTY-FIVE
## NICO

Unfortunately, waking up to an empty bed doesn't surprise me.

Sighing, I roll onto my back and stare up at the ceiling.

I *know* I made progress with Scarlett. I *know* she likes me. The time we spent together, how relaxed she was, how playful, how she didn't push for sex. She let me care for her. Hell, even the fact that she didn't bolt as soon as she felt better is proof that I'm getting through to her about how I feel.

But it doesn't mean it doesn't sting that she left without waking me.

With a groan, I drag myself from my bed. Might as well get my day started.

When I see the note on the counter, it doesn't register at first what it is. But then I look closer and my heart beats faster.

She left me her number.

*She left me her number.*

At thirty years old, I should not be this excited to be getting a woman's number. But with Scarlett, it's so much more that I don't even bother to contain the giant grin that spreads across my face.

Lucas picks that moment to walk into my apartment.

I don't wipe the smile from my face. I can't. So when he sees it, he freezes.

"Do I want to know?"

I shrug, still smiling as I quickly save the number to my contacts. "Probably not."

He peeks at the note in my hand, of course. And then he sighs.

"This isn't being careful, Nico."

Turning toward him, I clap his cheeks in my hands. "Lucas, I mean this from the bottom of my heart. I don't give a flying fuck about being careful."

He's tense, more tense than I've ever seen him. He even hesitates for a moment, which I rarely see him do.

"Are you still paying her?"

His question stops me in my tracks.

I got so excited about the phone number, I didn't even think about the cash.

My eyes dart over the kitchen and living room, searching. I know I gave her six thousand for this week's date, but that was when she first arrived, when I was frustrated and trying to prove a point. She wouldn't have kept it, would she? Not when she left me her number. The number means something.

*Right?*

I dart down the hall to my bedroom, just in case she left it on a nightstand or in the bathroom. But when I don't find any cash laying around, dread grows in my stomach.

Lucas reads the answer on my face when I walk into the kitchen. To his credit, he looks sad to be proven right.

"As much as I should make the financial suggestion to stop seeing her, I won't," he says carefully. "Clearly, she's giving you something you need. But Nico, you can't fall in love with this girl. She's an escort. There's a 99% chance she's playing you. You see that, right?"

But I don't. All I can see is her phone number, and her smile, and that damn 1%.

*She's not playing me. There's no way.*

"Why are you here?" I bark out, harsher than I intended. Wincing, I drag a hand down my face. "Sorry. What's going on?"

Lucas sighs. "Alexander called me. Said your girl got the stomach bug and that we needed to keep an eye on you in case you got sick, too."

Immediately, shame floods me. My brothers have only ever wanted to have my back. I'm a dick for snapping at him.

I collapse onto one of the barstools. "I'm fine, but I appreciate it." When that only earns me a look of skepticism, I let out a tired exhale.

"Look, on paper, I know you're right. I know I'm paying her to seem interested in me. But Lucas...I don't think she faking. I really don't. I think she had a fucked-up childhood or a fucked-up life or a fucked-up *something* that got her into this career, and I know it sounds insane, but I swear, it feels like she's her real self with me."

Now is when I get pity from Lucas. "And the money?" he asks gently.

I let out a sound of frustration. "I don't know, okay? At first, she was taking it because it was the only way I could convince her I wasn't just fishing for a free date. But now..." I sigh. "Now, I don't know."

Lucas doesn't seem to have an answer for me. I don't have one, either. The high from receiving her phone number has dulled.

"Look, I only came over to check that you're okay,"

Lucas says. "Not to give you a hard time. Alright?" A pause pairs with a worried look. "We good?"

I nod. "Yeah, of course."

He straightens and claps me on the shoulder. "Good. I'm going to work, then. You have boxing today?"

Another nod. "Terry's probably going to put me through the ringer for skipping yesterday."

I should care more. I'm literally risking my life if I don't prepare for this fight.

And yet...

I wouldn't trade yesterday with Scarlett for anything.

But Terry *does* put me through the ringer. As understanding as coaches are about sickness, they're also firm believers in making up the work. Which means sparring the best boxers in the city isn't my only workout for the day. I also get put through a grueling strength-training workout and sent on a four-mile run.

I don't mind the busy schedule, though. It keeps my mind off Scarlett. And off of texting her. It isn't until I'm getting ready for bed and smelling Scarlett on my pillows that the urge to text her becomes too strong.

> Nico: If you could travel anywhere in the world, where would you go?

For ten minutes, there's nothing.

And then...

Bubbles appear. Relief floods my body. I didn't think she'd give me her number just to ignore me, but the past few days already feel like a fever dream and I can't bring myself to hope for more.

> Scarlett: It's a cliché answer

I stack my pillows against my headboard to get comfortable.

> Nico: The world needs clichés

> Scarlett: Greece

> Nico: Because of the beaches?

> Scarlett: That and the history

> Scarlett: I've always been fascinated by the Ancient Greeks

> Nico: Did I ever tell you I was a philosophy major in college for a brief time?

To my surprise—and delight—my phone buzzes with a call. When I answer, I'm greeted with Scarlett's tinkling laugh.

I manage to smother my own giddiness enough to ask in mock outrage, "I'm sorry, are you *laughing* at me?"

"You were a professional MMA fighter sitting in philosophy classes?" she asks, still giggling. "I'm sorry. I'm not laughing *at* you, it's just a funny picture."

"I wasn't pro yet, but…yes."

"I have so many questions. Why did you pick it as a major? And why was it for only a brief time? And how on earth did people receive you in those classes?"

I'm grinning as I shift to a more comfortable position. "Now don't get offended by this, but…I needed an easy-ish major. And Liberal Arts needed the smallest number of credits. And believe it or not, I'm actually pretty good at writing thoughtful ten-page papers."

"Why wouldn't I believe that?" she asks, all laughter gone. "You *are* thoughtful."

I shrug, even though she can't see it. "I don't know. Most people think fighters are idiots."

"Most people are idiots," she huffs.

*Is it normal to be smiling this much from just a phone call?*

"Speaking of school, how are your classes going?" I ask after a moment.

There's a pause this time, and her voice is softer, sweeter, when she answers. "They're good. I like my classes this semester. I got lucky with good professors."

*I want to know everything about her.* "What classes are you taking?"

She lets out a thoughtful hum, and I hear some rustling in the background. I want to ask where she is and what she's doing, but I don't want to break the spell.

She starts to list off classes. "For my major, I'm taking social cognition, behavioral neuroscience, psychopathology. Human anatomy and physiology for my science requirement, then ethical theory and creative writing for my electives."

"You're taking *six* classes?"

"Two of them are GenEds," she says humbly.

*Yeah, we'll have none of that.*

"Baby, just accept the fact that you're smart. It's sexy as fuck."

There's a pause. But I can *hear* her smile when she says, "If you say so."

"I do say so. I insist on it, actually."

She's quiet again, which lets my mind wander in a different direction. Toward something I haven't really let myself think about.

"Do you ever think about doing something with your degree?" I ask carefully.

But what I want to ask is: *do you ever think about doing something other than working as an escort?*

I wish I could ask her that. So badly. Not because I want her to quit and be with me—which I do, but we're not yet at that level of trust where we could have that conversation—but because I wish I could make her understand that she *could* do other work. She's smart and hard-working and could probably do anything she set her mind to, but I don't think she sees that. She's still so tied down by her self-worth issues that she won't *let* herself see it.

"I don't know," she says in a casual tone I can't read. "If you weren't fighting, do you know what you'd be doing?"

I smother my sigh at her deflection. I could push her a little, but I'm not sure it would get me a better answer. I'll settle for putting the idea in her head.

"I have no idea," I answer honestly. "Ask me in a week."

"I can't believe you have a fight in a week," she says, back to her normal warm tone. "And I can't believe you didn't *tell* me about it. Are you excited? Or nervous?"

"Honestly? None of the above. I don't feel much of anything."

It's the truth, too. Minus the day after Scarlett got sick, I've been putting in the same amount of work as any other fight I've prepared for. When I'm in the gym, I'm focused. I'm on weight. I have my plan for the week of the fight. I'm doing everything I need to do.

And yet...one day with Scarlett, even half-unconscious, made me feel more than any of this fight prep did.

"My next week is going to be a little chaotic, though," I say, bringing myself back to reality. "Fight week gets pretty busy. I meant to tell you that our date was going to be my last rest day."

Scarlett makes an *oh* sound. "So I won't hear from you. Got it."

"No, no, that's not—" I swallow roughly. "Actually, I was going to say the opposite. That I won't be able to make it up to New York to *see* you, but that if you don't mind the conversation, I'd like to be able to call you sometimes."

She hesitates, but I can hear the smile in her voice when she says, "I'd like that."

Hopefully, she can't hear my relieved exhale. *Lucas doesn't know what he's talking about.*

Feeling emboldened, I add, "And maybe after the fight, I could take you out on a real date."

This time, there's no hesitation.

"I'd like that, too."

It's a sign of the grueling workouts I was put through today that a yawn sneaks out of me after she says that. Thankfully, Scarlett only lets out a soft laugh.

"Go to bed. I can hear how exhausted you are."

I can't even argue with her. "Okay. Goodnight, Scarlett."

"Goodnight, Nico," she says sweetly.

# TWENTY-SIX
## SCARLETT

Texting Nico is easier than I anticipated.

What I didn't anticipate was how often the urge to text *him* would hit.

For the past week, we've been texting about the most random things. Our favorite movies, biggest pet peeves, which celebrities we'd invite to a dinner party. He asks me questions I've never even thought about.

I love it.

I find myself jumping for my phone when it vibrates. I love getting to know these pieces of Nico, and I love that he cares enough to learn them about me. I answer every question he asks, the need to connect with him now too great to hold back.

He keeps the conversations surface level, though. He even stays away from asking me if I've made a decision about coming to his fight. I think he senses that while me giving him my number—and full name—is a big deal, I'm not quite ready to divulge all of my secrets. Yet.

I'll give him the rest of me for now.

The day before Nico's fight, I wake up more restless than

normal. It's been over a week since I've seen him, and I think it's affecting me. Without a scheduled date with him on my calendar, I'm lost in my *own* life. And the emptiness is wearing on me.

It's early, too early, so I jump into a five-mile run on the treadmill. Soon, that restlessness I'm feeling turns five miles into eight. By the time the runner's high dies down, I'm drenched in sweat and starving.

I eat more than I usually would. With Nico's nutrition advice ringing in my brain, I go to a nearby diner to order a breakfast sandwich instead of making my usual eggs and black coffee. And on the walk home, I stop for a parfait at my favorite coffee house.

Whether it's the restlessness or the added calories, by the time I get home, I'm itching with the need to *do* something. I have six hours before my client appointment tonight.

An hour later, I'm back at the shelter where Nico and I volunteered.

"Hi there," says the front desk lady with a big smile. "How can I help you today?"

"Uh, I'm not really sure," I answer nervously. "I volunteered a few weeks ago and really enjoyed the experience, so I guess I'm back to see if I can help again."

She beams at me. "Well, we love to hear that. I can share your options with you, if you'd like." When I nod, she starts to list them off.

"It all comes down to your time commitment and experience level, really. You can either apply to be a foster parent—"

"I don't think I'm ready for that," I interrupt with a wince.

"That's quite alright, dear, plenty of people start with simpler options. You could take on more of an admin role, helping during our events or assisting foster parents with calling references and vets and things. *Or* you could apply to transport animals, or take them out for a day to get out of the shelter, or you could even just play with them out back—"

"That. That I can do."

When she gives me an amused smile at the outburst, I blush. "Sorry, I just don't have that much experience with dogs. I wouldn't trust myself to take them out of here."

"Perfectly understandable. And any little bit of help is monumental for the dogs, so we'll take anything you want to give us. Do you have some time now? I can take you in the back to pick out an afternoon play buddy."

I deflate in relief. "That'd be great, thank you."

When we walk through the kennels, it's a small pitbull that catches my eye. He looks so sad and so harmless that I feel comfortable taking him out back to the fenced in area by myself.

The front desk lady hands me a tennis ball and says, "He might not do much with it, but here you go. Have fun!"

She's not wrong. When I throw the ball, he stares after it for a moment, then gives me a side-eye and sits onto his haunches.

Huffing a laugh, I try with the tug of war rope. He doesn't bite into it.

But when I finally sigh and take a seat beside him in defeat, he promptly climbs into my lap with a tired exhale that only dogs are capable of.

I smile and scratch behind his ears. "Oh yeah? That's all you wanted?" When he curls into a ball, he's positioned so his cheek is on my thigh, gazing up at me with his tongue lolling out and a happy smile on his face.

"Well, aren't you the cutest thing I've ever seen," I murmur, stroking his head.

For minutes, we just sit there, me petting him and him

staring up at me with the sweetest lovesick puppy eyes I've ever seen. Eventually, his eyes close when he falls asleep, but that smile stays on his face.

I keep petting him. Even when my back cramps and my legs start to itch from the fake grass, I can't look away from him.

He wanted nothing from me. Nothing but love and attention.

If only life was that easy.

I was raised to believe a woman's value is in what she can offer a man. That I was only lovable—if love was even real—if I was *worth* loving. If I was attractive, if I lessened my man's stress, and if I provided in the way women were meant to provide. Only then would I be worth loving.

But this dog…even with this being our first meeting, he loves me already. For no reason. Nothing I gave him, nothing I did for him. He just met me with love.

*I wish it wasn't just dogs.*

Nico's face flashes before me.

Beyond those first few dates when he hired me for company, I don't think he's wanted anything from me. He's been trying so hard to get to know me, to make me comfortable enough to open up to him, and he's asked for nothing in return. He even took sex and intimacy off the table so I couldn't "pay" him in the way I've always understood my worth.

He's wanted nothing from me but me.

He's the *only* one I've ever felt that with.

My thoughts are interrupted by the front desk lady appearing before me. "You two seem cozy," she says.

"Oh, uh, yeah, he fell asleep pretty much instantly. I feel bad, I didn't really do anything for him."

She gives me a warm smile.

"Oh, honey. You gave him a safe space. You did everything for him."

---

I get ready for my date tonight on autopilot.

I see Mr. Clarke every six weeks like clockwork. I show up in his favorite red dress, we chat until something I say makes his dick hard, and then I pull the top of my dress down and he jerks off on my breasts. He never touches me. He just has a thing for degrading women with his semen.

I feel like I'm having an out-of-body experience when I knock on his hotel room door. I haven't felt in control of my actions since I started getting ready. It feels like my brain is trying to separate from my body.

"Daisy, it's so nice to see you," he says when he opens the door.

He's a nice enough man, I guess. I manage to return a smile.

"Hi, Mr. Clarke. How have you been? I've missed you."

*Autopilot. Everything is on autopilot.*

I listen to him yap about his job for twenty minutes. I think he's an executive at some technology company, I don't know. I've never been able to care that much. They don't want me to listen, anyway; they just want to talk.

*Nico wants to listen.*

By the time Mr. Clarke unzips himself, I can only stare at his dick, suddenly clueless about how I ever didn't run screaming from the sight of it.

"On your knees, Daisy," he says in a rough voice.

My eyes dart to his and widen.

"I can't," I breathe.

His movements pause. "What?"

I swallow thickly, even as my certainty solidifies. "I can't do this," I say, stronger this time.

To his credit, he looks concerned. "Are you...alright?"

I let out a humorless laugh. "No, I'm not. I am so far from alright."

His expression shifts to confusion, but I don't have time to explain. Grabbing my purse, I spin toward the exit. "I'm sorry about this. I'll have the agency call you."

The door has barely shut behind me when I'm pulling out my phone.

"Amara? We need to talk."

# TWENTY-SEVEN
## SCARLETT

My stomach is a twisted knot of anxiety by the time I step into the arena.

It's packed, the crowd so thick that I'd be surprised if it isn't sold out. Which means if Nico didn't leave me a ticket, I have no way of getting inside. *Is my gesture still romantic if I watch from my phone at the arena ticket booth?*

I try not to think too much while I stand in the Will Call line. And when I reach the front, I only allow myself one deep breath before asking, "Hi, is there a ticket for Scarlett Adler?"

The worker only grunts in response and turns toward his computer screen, his fingers tapping away on the keyboard. I don't breathe the entire time he searches. But then…

"Yup, one ringside ticket for Scarlett Adler."

My breath whooshes out of me. *He kept his promise. He really does want me here.*

I send the employee a grateful smile as I take the paper ticket from his hand. It takes me a few minutes to walk to my section, and another few minutes to wait for the hordes of people to find their seats.

Finally, I settle into my seat. I did enough research to know Nico is the co-main event tonight, so I'm not surprised that having his ticket puts me two rows behind the judges and event staff. I'm so close to the cage, I can see the blood stain on the mat.

Nerves once again flood my body at the thought that it could be Nico's blood later.

I suck in a deep breath, forcing myself to remember that Nico is a professional, that he's really good at what he does. That if I want to support him—*be* with him—I need to trust him.

"First fight?"

Turning, I take in the sight of the older woman beside me. She's smiling at me, and I get the sense that she's trying to be reassuring.

"It's always worse in your head, don't worry," she says comfortingly.

I return a tremulous smile. "Was I that obvious?"

She chuckles. "It's not you. I've just been in the world for a long time, so I can spot the newcomers."

Curiosity replaces some of my anxiety. "Do you know a fighter? Or did you fight?"

A loud bark of laughter comes from the older man sitting on the other side of her.

The woman rolls her eyes. "Ignore him. He's laughing because I'm famous in our family for crying over killing spiders." Her expression sobers. "My son is a fighter. We've attended every single one of his fights, which is a lot of fights over the years."

Just then, a deafening cheer rolls through the crowd. All around me, drunk fans are screaming and pointing at the TVs in the arena.

*I shouldn't have come. This is too much.*

But just as that thought registers, I hear, "Scarlett?"

I jerk in surprise and turn toward the voice. There's a guy standing in the aisle next to me, staring at me with a questioning expression. He's…gigantic. In height and in muscle. And combined with the buzz cut, I'd bet good money that he's military.

It takes me a second to remember that he said my name. My brow furrows. *How does he know my name?*

*Wait…he looks familiar. Why does he look familiar?*

"I'm sorry, do I know you?"

"Nico sent me," he says simply. "Said you'd probably prefer to watch from the back."

I let out a breathy laugh. "He's not wrong." I send the lady next to me a guilty wince. "No offense, but this place is insane."

She chuckles and pats my arm. "None taken, sweetheart." Looking past me at the guy standing in the aisle, she asks, "She's with Nico?"

I frown. "You know Nico?"

"She birthed the nut job," the big guy says. Stepping behind our row, he leans down to kiss the woman on the cheek. "Hi, Mom," he murmurs.

*Oh my God.*

*I just met a client's mother.*

And then I realize… This is Nico's brother. The one who gave me an IV when I was sick. That's why he looks familiar.

"You're Alexander," I say on an exhale.

The affectionate smile on his face softens when he turns to me and nods. "You look better than the last time I saw you."

I let out a breathy laugh. "Thanks to you. Did Nico pass on my undying appreciation, by the way? Because I'm pretty sure I *felt* like I was dying."

If I wasn't so good at reading people, I probably wouldn't notice the small tic in his mouth that tells me I earned a smile. His only obvious response is a gruff, "It was nothing."

"Agree to disagree," I tell him with a smile.

For a moment, he only blinks at me. Something tells me this isn't the type of man who would know what to do with me. Especially when he asks bluntly, "Do you want to follow me to the locker room?"

I'm standing before his question is even finished. "God, yes, please." Remembering his parents, I turn toward them. "Are you coming back, too?"

"Nah, they like to watch from the crowd," Alexander says, pressing another kiss to his mother's cheek. "They're maniacs."

She rolls her eyes, but she's smiling. "I like to get the full experience, sue me."

"We'll see them after," Alexander tells me. Then he jerks his head toward the back. "Come on, we're this way."

At the last minute, I remember to send a smile to Nico's parents. A *client's* parents. *What is my life?* "It was nice to meet you."

"You too, sweetheart. Have fun!"

I happen to glance up at the big screen, where a fight highlight is currently being shown. There's blood and sweat flying everywhere.

*This family's definition of fun is wild.*

It's too loud for us to talk during our walk through the crowd, but even when we reach the blocked-off area where Alexander has to flash a name tag to get through, he doesn't seem to be interested in conversation. Which is good, because I'm suddenly hyperaware of the fact that for the first time, I'm going to purposefully see Nico outside of our usual arrangement. And nerves are once again making themselves known.

But when we reach the room that says *Nicholas Price* on the door, there's no one inside.

"We just missed him," Alexander explains, correctly interpreting my look of confusion. "He saw you on the screen just as they called him to be on deck."

"Oh," I breathe. "So he's—?"

I'm interrupted by the sound of a cheer so loud, I can hear it even from back here. When I look up at the TV, I see what they're cheering about: Nico has entered the cage.

At the sight of him, every molecule of oxygen leaves my lungs.

Part of it is his physical appearance, of course. I normally see him wearing jeans and a shirt, so seeing him now, shirtless, his muscles glistening with sweat, is a shock to the system. But it's not just that. It's also the look of concentration on his face, and the intensity radiating off of him. The Nico I know is sweet, and funny, and usually focused entirely on making me comfortable.

The Nico on the screen is the one the rest of the world sees.

I can barely breathe as the camera zooms in on his face, the announcer screaming his name into the microphone. I'm suddenly very aware of what Nico told me once before, about how fighting can be dangerous if your head's not in the game. He seems focused, but maybe that's just his poker face.

*God, please let his head be in the game.*

"Is he—?" I clear my throat and try again. "Is he better than this guy?" Turning toward Alexander, I'm sure my desperation is obvious. "I mean, he's going to win, right?"

He nods, but it's his true lack of concern that eases my anxiety. "As long as he's the aggressor, he should be fine.

This guy usually waits until his opponents are tired before working for a submission."

"A submission?" I latch onto the word. "Those won't hurt him, right?"

There's a flash of amusement on Alexander's face. "No, those don't hurt." Then his expression softens. "He'll be fine."

As the bell rings that signals the start of the fight, I take a deep breath and decide to trust him.

Thankfully, it becomes obvious right away that Nico is going by Alexander's strategy. He rushes out of the corner, quick to throw out a combination of punches. He's pushing his opponent back, chasing him with punches and then kicks. They're not necessarily landing, but it's such an immediate flurry of aggression that it takes me by surprise.

Still, I'm holding my breath as I watch him. When his opponent finally pushes back with a combination of his own, I gasp, my pulse pounding harder.

*Please don't get hurt, please don't get hurt…*

Everything feels like it's in slow motion as the punch cracks into Nico's jaw. Sweat flies, the crowd cheers…

And Nico laughs.

Which makes the crowd even louder. And when Nico shoots forward with a vicious combination of his own, they get louder still.

"Does he always fight like this?" I ask in a breathy voice.

There's a huff of laughter beside me. "No. He's usually checked in and stone cold." Alexander glances toward me. "I guess something must've given him a morale boost," he murmurs quietly.

My heart stutters at that, but I tell myself it's just the adrenaline of watching the fight.

For the next few minutes, we watch Nico methodically

and continuously break down his opponent. I don't know the names of any of the moves, or what his strategy is, but even I can tell he's good at what he does. I can see it in the way his opponent's ribs redden from the repeated kicks, and from the flash of blood that tells me his face is cut.

Suddenly, Nico shoots forward and tackles his opponent to the ground. "Nice," Alexander murmurs. Shifting into another gear, Nico absolutely *lays into* his opponent. It's one punch after another, never slowing and each one being thrown harder than the last.

I clasp my hands over my mouth, barely breathing through the intensity. *He's going to win. Holy crap, he's going to win.*

And sure enough, with only thirty seconds left on the clock, the referee steps in and stops the fight. Nico wins.

A huge exhale of *relief* whooshes out of me. *Oh my God. Nico won. He's safe.*

"Well, that was unusual," I hear Alexander muse. When I turn to face him, he looks both pleased and surprised.

"What was unusual?" I ask.

When he faces me, there's a sparkle of curiosity in his eyes. "He rarely goes for the knockout," he explains. "He's usually a strike-to-the-end kinda guy."

"Oh," I exhale.

I wonder if this potentially being Nico's last fight was the reason for the knockout. And then I wonder if he's told his family about wanting to retire. Glancing at Alexander, I decide not to say anything just in case he hasn't.

When my focus shifts back to the TV, Nico's being interviewed by one of the announcers. He's grinning, visibly invigorated by his victory, and the crowd *loves* him. As much as Nico might feel like he fell into this career, it's clear that he was meant for it.

The next ten minutes are a blur. There's an interview, some pictures being taken, then the camera follows Nico's departure from the cage and his walk through the arena. I'm still staring blankly at the TV when it transitions to the announcers talking about the next fight.

But then the door to the locker room slams open. And Nico's here.

He stops in the doorway when my eyes lock on his. He's grinning, practically vibrating with excitement, and I can see in his gaze and brightened expression that he's happy I'm here. That he wants to pull me to him.

And yet, he still lets me make the first move. "Hey, Red," he says fondly. "You made it."

My vision blurs, and I let out a teary laugh as I rush toward him to throw my arms around his neck.

"Baby," he murmurs, so only I can hear. When he brushes a soothing hand down my hair, I squeeze him tighter. "Why are you crying?"

I pull back to look at him, my hands reaching for his face to confirm there are no injuries. "Because that was really scary," I admit with a laugh. "Are you okay? Is anything hurt? Why on *earth* would someone do this to themselves?"

Chuckles rumble around us, and I become suddenly aware of our surroundings. Nico's coaches and teammates have stepped into the room.

My face heats as I step back, but Nico grabs my hand before I can get too far.

I secretly love it.

"Good fight, Nico," Alexander says, stepping forward to extend his hand for a fist bump. "The takedown was nice."

Then his parents walk through the door, his mom rushing toward him for a hug. Begrudgingly, Nico lets my hand go to embrace her.

"Oh, honey, congratulations," she says warmly, joy radiating off of her. "That was incredible. I'm so proud of you."

The sentiment isn't aimed at me, but even *I* feel how much she genuinely means it.

*What must it feel like to have a parent say that? And mean it?*

As if she hears my internal thoughts, his mom looks at me and smiles. "Thank you for coming tonight. I can only imagine how much your support helps him during his fight camp."

And yeah, the sentiment hits hard. I don't have enough breath to respond, so I just give her a smile and turn toward Nico.

He's watching me, his heart on his sleeve. I can read every thought on his face.

Which only makes it harder to breathe. Because I think I might feel the same way.

"—yeah, I'll tell him. You got it."

We all turn toward the new voice and see a handsome man in a very sharp suit stepping into the room. He slides his phone into his pocket and looks at Nico.

"Good news, little brother, it looks like— Oh, I'm sorry. I didn't realize we had company." When he notices me, a charming smile curves his lips. He steps forward and smoothly reaches for my hand, his mischievous eyes never leaving mine as he lifts it to his lips.

Before he can say anything, I quirk an eyebrow and say dryly, "You must be Lucas."

Again, the whole room laughs. But Lucas doesn't seem offended. On the contrary: he seems pleased. And when Nico wraps an arm around my waist to pull me against his side, his expression shifts to amused.

"And you must be the lovely Scarlett," he says, stepping back. "It's a pleasure to meet you. Does this mean you'll be joining us at the afterparty?"

Frowning, I turn toward Nico. "Afterparty?"

Nico just smiles and shakes his head. "It's not what it sounds like. It's just a tradition we have for after my fights. The whole family goes out to eat at whatever restaurant is still open—usually a pub—and we gorge ourselves on food and drinks." I can hear the uncertainty in his voice when he asks, "Will you come with us?"

All the people in the room fade away, until it's only Nico and me.

"Do you want me to?" I ask quietly.

His gaze never leaves mine. "More than anything."

And that's when something unlocks inside me, and I let him all the way in. Whatever this thing between us is, I'm committed to it. I want it.

"Okay then," I say, smiling. "I'd love to join."

# TWENTY-EIGHT
## NICO

*I can't believe she's here.*

*I can't fucking believe she's here.*

I genuinely thought I was seeing things when I looked at the TV as I was pacing, waiting for my name to be called. Especially when I saw her sitting next to my parents, having a conversation with my mom. Because at that moment, it was so, *so* easy to picture her in my life. At the family dinner on a Sunday, or sitting on the sidelines at the gym. It was so easy.

I knew I couldn't see her before the fight, but hell, if I wasn't eager to hold her in my arms afterwards. It's why I went for the knockout. I didn't want to wait a second longer than I needed to.

And now she's here. With me. Saying she wants to stay with me.

*This is infinitely better than tonight's win.*

"Are you ready to get going?" I ask, trying and failing to tamp down on my deliriously giddy smile.

Her lips twitch with amusement. "Are *you* ready to get going?" When her gaze darts down to my chest, I revel in the sight of heat flashing in her eyes.

"What, you don't think I'd fit in shirtless in New York?" I tease.

"It's less the shirtlessness, and more the blood smeared across your skin," she says with a pointed nod at my chest.

"He'd still probably fit in," Lucas mumbles from where he's furiously typing away on his phone. When we turn toward him, realizing we're not the only ones in the room— *how did I forget we're not the only ones in the room?*—he looks up and asks, "So are we going? I reserved the private dining room for us."

I sigh, even though I know he's right. "Yeah. Let me just shower and get myself together." I turn toward Scarlett again. "You okay to wait a few minutes for me? We can send everyone ahead and then taxi over together."

In all honesty, I just want her to myself for a few minutes. Not that I'm fooling anyone.

"Yeah, of course," she says. "Take your time."

I don't take my time. I hurry through the entire process. If I was a little clearer on how things stood between me and Scarlett, I would've pulled her into the bathroom with me just to have her in my vicinity.

But as it stands, having her here, knowing she came tonight for *me*—not for a date, not because I'm paying her, but to be with me—it's a heady feeling. And it's strong enough to make it impossible to keep my distance from her once I step out of the bathroom and see her still sitting there, a happy smile on her face when she sees me.

"You look better," she says sweetly. "Feel better?"

I pull her to her feet and into my arms. "I felt better the second you walked into the room, baby," I murmur into her hair.

She hums, the sound content, as her arms tighten around my neck.

I can't quite find the courage to look at her while I say what's on my mind, so I tighten my hold around her waist and bury my face in her neck. "I'm glad you came tonight," I admit. Then I gather enough courage to add, "Am I allowed to say I missed you?"

I don't breathe as I wait for her answer. But then...

"I missed you too," she whispers.

*Thank fuck. That's one clarification on the relationship.*

I press a kiss against her skin, and then another. *God, I wish I could kiss her properly.*

But that's going to require a conversation, and now's not the time. Now, I want to simply revel in the fact that I have her here with me.

So I pull back and ask, "Will you stay with me tonight?"

And I swear, if kissing her feels half as good as the sight of the smile she gives me...I'm fucked.

"I'd like that."

But first: dinner with my family.

---

The taxi ride is a short one, but I eat up every second of it. As soon as we're in the car, I pull her tight against my side so there's no space between us. I can't stop touching her, can't stop pressing kisses against her skin.

After the tenth one, she giggles and asks, "Are you sure you're okay? You're awfully touchy tonight."

I sigh and fall back against the seat. "It's the adrenaline. It makes me a little punch drunk for a few hours." Peeking at Scarlett with one narrowed eye, I add, "It also means you can't hold anything I say against me, at least until tomorrow morning."

"Unfortunate, but I understand," she says, amusement lacing her tone.

"I kind of like you worrying about me, though."

She ducks her head to hide her smile, but I reach up to tuck a strand of hair behind her ear to see her better.

"I also kind of wish we were going back to my hotel right now," I admit quietly. "Room service and cuddling, maybe putting a movie on, sounds really good right about now."

Her mouth twitches with another pretty smile. "Cuddling? I didn't think grown men used that word."

"They do when it means having you in their arms," I murmur, my nose pressed to her temple. *God, she smells good.*

I have to force myself to sit back before I get too drunk on her. "But just to set expectations, there probably won't be any of that later anyway."

When she frowns in confusion, I explain, "Once we put a few burgers in me, I'll for sure be passing out as soon as we get home. I'm not going to be great company." Then I'm the one frowning when something occurs to me. "I just realized your time with me tonight is going to be mostly spent with my family. Shit."

Scarlett lets out a cute breath of laughter. "First of all, I kind of figured about the passing out thing. I came to watch and support you, not to make you entertain me. Second of all…" She shrugs, a softness about her as she says, "I like your family."

My chest warms at that. "Yeah?"

She bites down on her lip and nods.

"Try to keep that sentiment for the next hour, because I guarantee you, they're about to grill you," I say instead.

At that, a look of nervousness takes over. "Really? Shoot.

I have no idea how to talk to parents. I didn't think this through."

I press a comforting kiss to her temple and pull her closer. "Relax. Just be yourself. They'll love you."

Her nerves don't lessen. They actually increase by the time we reach the pub, because I can feel the way her muscles tense as we take a seat with my family. I give her hand a reassuring squeeze under the table.

"There you two are!" my mom exclaims gleefully. "We were just talking about how good you looked in your fight tonight."

"Well, don't let my presence stop you," I say, gesturing between us. "Continue."

She rolls her eyes with a smile. "As if you need a bigger head." Her gaze darts to Scarlett for a split-second, then back to me. "But in all seriousness, honey, you did look amazing. Did he get you with anything?"

I shake my head as I slide an arm along the back of Scarlett's chair. "Not really. One or two kicks landed, but nothing big."

She nods. "Okay, good." Then she turns her attention fully to Scarlett. "In that case, I'd much rather chat with Scarlett."

I give Scarlett a look that says *I told you so*, but I'm grinning. "I don't blame you."

Scarlett smiles at my mom, but I can see the stiffness in her shoulders. "I'm not that interesting, Mrs. Price," she protests weakly.

My mom waves her off. "Nonsense. Nico clearly being smitten with you makes that impossible."

"Christ, Mom," I groan with a wince.

She ignores me. "And none of that *Mrs. Price* nonsense. Call me Stephanie." Leaning forward, excitement shines in her eyes as she clasps her hands together. "Tell me something about yourself, dear. What do you do?"

I stiffen just as Lucas chokes on his beer. *Shit.* I should've anticipated this happening.

But mostly, I hate the way Scarlett's panicking. If I couldn't read her as well as I can, I might not have noticed, but it's obvious to me.

"I, uh—"

"Scarlett's in college," I interject quickly. Not just because it's my favorite pastime to remind Scarlett how smart she is, but also because mentioning academics is the easiest way to get my mother, the teacher, talking.

Sure enough, she perks right up. "Really? Where? What are you studying?"

The tiniest bit of tension releases from Scarlett's shoulders, but it's enough to make me breathe easier. "Um, I'm studying psychology online at ASU," she answers with a tremulous smile.

"Oh, they have a great liberal arts program." My mom nods along. "And psychology, that's amazing. Why did you pick that?"

Scarlett shrugs. "I guess I just like knowing why people do the things they do."

Lucas snorts from his place across the table. "When you find out, let me know. It would make my job a hell of a lot easier. What year are you in college?"

There's only a beat of doubt this time before she answers. "Senior. I didn't start until I moved to New York, so I had a two-year delay."

Lucas frowns. "But Nico said you're twenty-two. You're finishing your bachelor's in two years?"

A self-conscious shrug this time. "Two and a half."

He's laser focused on her now, his curiosity piquing. "Do you know what you want to do with your degree?"

"I haven't decided yet," she says quietly, taking a sip of her water.

"Have you ever thought about law? If you can get through a liberal arts undergrad that quickly, you'd probably kill it as a paralegal."

To my surprise, Scarlett says, "Briefly. Never say never, but legalese doesn't really interest me."

He huffs a laugh. "Fair." Then more to himself than to her, he adds, "I almost wonder what you'd score on the LSATs."

I see the split-second debate that starts in Scarlett's mind. She wants to say something, but her natural reaction is to hold back.

I'm waiting with bated breath, not just to hear what it is, but hoping she'll decide to say it out loud instead of having me nudge it out of her.

A big part of me wants to cheer when she steels her spine and says, "One seventy-one."

You could hear a *pin* drop around the table.

Because we all know that despite his jokes, Lucas is insanely smart. And even he didn't score that high on his LSATs.

"You scored a *one seventy-one?*" he asks, gaping. "What, just for fun?"

Scarlett shrugs again, a proud smile tugging at her lips. "I wanted to see if I could do it."

*Fuck*, she's impressive.

*I wish I could kiss her.*

*I wish she'd let me.*

Finally, Lucas shakes his head, a small smile on his

mouth. And his only answer to Scarlett's admission is an impressed whisper of, "Damn, girl."

I might not be able to kiss her, but I can't stop myself from leaning over to murmur in her ear, "You're so fucking sexy."

She ducks her head to hide her smile, but I see it anyway. Pressing a kiss to her cheek, I lean back into my own chair. But not before I feel Scarlett's hand clasp mine under the table.

In the end, it's that easy for her to win over my family. Dad and Alexander are the easy-to-please ones of the group, and with Lucas's respect in the bag, and Mom happily observing my—very obvious—affection for her, my family falls for her just as naturally as I have.

Not that I was ever worried. I know exactly how incredible Scarlett is. But I'm thrilled that *she* gets to see my family reach the same conclusion.

And I know she sees it because there's a palpable change in her after that. For the rest of the dinner, she's... comfortable. She smiles easier, laughs effortlessly, and adds to the conversation without doubting herself. For the next two hours, we laugh at embarrassing childhood stories, tease each other constantly, and chat about everything and nothing as we get to know Scarlett and as she gets to know my family.

I'm half in love with her by the time dinner ends.

When we leave the restaurant, I look at Scarlett and ask, "Should I call an Uber? Or do we want to walk?"

To my surprise, she steps closer and weaves her arm through mine. "An Uber would be nice," she says softly.

It's a ten-minute drive back to my hotel. Long enough for

me to freak out about what's happening, but not long enough for me to verbalize it. This whole night has been surreal, and I have no idea what Scarlett's expectations are from here. So I simply revel in the feel of Scarlett curling into my arms.

I keep my mouth shut when we're dropped off in front of the hotel, and as we take the elevator to my floor. I don't want to disrupt whatever's happening here.

But when we reach my suite, the uncertainty gets the better of me.

"Do you want something to drink?" I ask. "Or a shower? I can…"

I trail off when she slips into my arms, a happy sigh sounding from her lips when her cheek hits my chest.

"Can we just…sit for a minute? I've wanted to be close to you all night."

I'd have to be dead to not give in to her request. Wordlessly, I guide her over to the couch and take a seat. To my surprise, she settles in my lap.

"Hey, baby," I murmur, brushing her hair away from her face.

Then…she presses her lips to mine.

And time stops.

*Holy shit.* She's never kissed me before. That's one of her rules as an escort. But now…

She's *kissing* me.

I'm still in shock when she pulls back. Her eyes are wide, her expression unsure.

"Scarlett," I breathe.

Before I can say another word, she's kissing me again.

And this time, I kiss her back.

With a sound that feels suspiciously like a whimper, I slide my hand into her hair and give in to the kiss I've been fantasizing about for weeks.

Her lips are soft, and warm, and as perfect as I knew they would be. She feels like she was *meant* for me.

I pull her more securely into my lap, my arm going around her waist and her knees going to either side of my hips. I want her as close as possible. I don't know what this is, or how far this is going to go, but I want all of it for as long as I can have it.

I kiss her until I need air. Until we're both gasping, needing to take a breath but unable to put that much distance between us. It isn't until she shifts closer, her hips starting to rock against me, that I summon the strength to put a pause on things.

"Scarlett," I gasp. "Hold on, baby, wait a second."

She's nodding, even as she tightens her arms around my neck and pulls herself closer. "Okay, yes, sorry. I've just wanted to do that for so long."

I swallow a groan as my face falls to her neck. *Fuck, what hearing that does to me.*

"Have... Have you wanted to do it, too?"

My head snaps up at her small voice. "What? Of *course* I've wanted to kiss you. I just... I was following your rules." Exhaling, I brush her hair back as I look into her eyes. "I just want to understand where your head is at. You caught me a little off guard, Red."

She smiles at the familiar nickname, which makes my gaze drop once more to her not-red lips. It only now occurs to me that she may have planned this.

"Sorry," she whispers. "But also, I'm not really."

Laughing softly, I tuck a strand of hair behind her ear. "Yeah, me neither," I tell her softly, dropping my hands back to her waist.

But then the moment sobers, the air between us growing heavy with emotions and unspoken thoughts. She might not be able to tell me out loud what this means, but I can see it in her eyes. Can *feel* it in her kiss.

We're more than the escort/client we started as.

I don't know how *much* more, but for now, I'll take whatever she'll give me. So this time, when we kiss, *I kiss her.* With each brush of my lips and caress of my tongue, I tell her everything I've wanted to say since the night she walked into my life. The night she flipped everything upside down in the best way possible.

# TWENTY-NINE
## NICO

When I jerk awake on the giant hotel bed, the room is pitch black. It's still the middle of the night.

I'm not surprised that I couldn't stay asleep, even though I crashed as soon as we made it to the bed last night. After an MMA fight and a big meal, I didn't have a chance in hell at staying awake. Even Scarlett's company couldn't keep my eyelids from drooping.

But now, a few hours later, I'm wide awake.

And very aware of the fact that I'm alone.

*Goddamnit.* I really thought she'd stay this time. With a heavy sigh, I push the covers off me and stand. I won't be able to fall asleep for a while now so I might as well indulge in some more food.

But when I push the bedroom double doors open and step into the suite, I realize the balcony door is slightly cracked, the wind whipping the curtains inside.

And Scarlett's on the balcony.

A relieved breath whooshes from my lungs as I quickly make my way over to her. She's sitting on the lounge chair with her knees pulled up, wrapped in the hotel robe, a steaming cup of tea in her hands.

*She's the most beautiful thing I've ever seen.*

Maybe it's the sight of her, maybe it's the real and raw relief at finding that she stayed… Either way, I momentarily lose my breath. Especially when she smiles at me.

"You're awake," she says, surprised.

I step out onto the balcony and close the door most of the way behind me. "It's the adrenaline. Sometimes I wake up a few hours after I crash."

She makes an *oh* sound and I want to taste it. *Can I taste it? She kissed me earlier, does that mean I get to do that now?*

Hesitant but too eager to stem the urge, I step toward her, gaze locked on her mouth. Then I start to bend down, still unsure of myself. But when she doesn't pull back, and instead tilts her face up toward me, I press my lips against hers.

I want to *devour* her. Now that she's given me permission, I want to kiss her every second of every day. The way she tastes, the way she slides her tongue across mine…it's intoxicating.

But I'm also aware of the hot drink in her hands and so I stop myself from becoming too aggressive. Begrudgingly, I pull away and drop into the chair beside her. Wanting to stay close to her, however, I pull her feet into my lap.

"Why are *you* awake?" I ask as I begin to massage her feet.

She has the softest, sweetest smile on her face as she shrugs. "I couldn't sleep. Maybe it's adrenaline for me, too."

I let out a thoughtful hum, my gaze dropping to her feet as my thoughts start to roll through my 4 a.m. mind.

"I really liked having you there tonight," I say eventually. When I lock eyes with her, Scarlett's *beaming*.

"Yeah?" she breathes happily.

I nod, the realization that's been swirling in my subconscious finally crystallizing.

"It felt like I was fighting for something," I admit quietly.

Scarlett's eyes widen at that. I've been honest with her about my thoughts about fighting, so my confession feels just as big for her as it does for me.

And it *does* feel big. Big enough that I want to give her the rest of my thoughts, to make her see exactly what she means to me.

"I've felt...restless," I rush to explain, needing her to understand. "Aimless. Like I've been putting one foot in front of the other for no other reason than to keep going. But my heart wasn't in it." My gaze never moves from hers, knowing I'm showing her too much but being unable to regret it. "Until tonight. When I knew you were watching."

I realized it as soon as I threw the first punch tonight. That purpose I've been searching for all these months? In that moment, it hit me as hard as any opponent ever has. It wasn't fighting that I needed to fulfill me.

It was fighting for *Scarlett.*

I see her pulse hammer in her neck. She might be able to read me like a book, but I can read her, too. She likes what I'm saying. Maybe she still doesn't trust it completely, but at least she *wants* to.

I can't stand the distance between us any longer. Leaning forward, I pull her chair up against mine and drop my forehead to hers, her rapid breaths now sweet puffs against my lips.

"Is this real?" I ask in a whisper, my voice rife with emotion I no longer want to hide. I'm all in this. "Because if it isn't, tell me now. I'm so far gone for you already, and if you're not sure, I—"

My words cut off when Scarlett presses her lips to mine.

I'm unashamed of the whimper that escapes me as I weave one hand into her hair to return the kiss. But before I can deepen it, she pulls back to whisper, "It's real. I'm all in with you, too."

Relief crashes over me.

Gently, I take the mug from her hands and set it down out of the way. And then I guide her into my lap, sink my hands into her hair again, and kiss her with the full power of my feelings.

I don't know how I ever survived without kissing her. Her lips are soft, her taste enough to make me dizzy with want. I could kiss her for hours and never get tired of it.

But it's not just the way she takes over my senses. It's also the way she kisses me *back*.

She kisses me like she can't survive another second without it either.

Her hands fisted in my shirt, she pulls herself as flush to my body as she possibly can. I'm already tilting my head to deepen the kiss when her hips rock against me. And the second my tongue touches hers and she breathes the sweetest *sigh* into the kiss, I'm a goner.

Securing one arm under her butt, I carefully stand with her in my arms, my lips never leaving hers. I feel for the door and slide it open.

I love feeling Scarlett's legs tighten around my waist as I walk us into the bedroom. I love the way she wraps her arms around my neck and pulls herself closer with a happy hum. Our physical chemistry has never been a question, but this feels like so much more than that.

This feels *real*.

I can't bring myself to put any distance between us, even when I lay her down on the bed. With my weight settled comfortably on top of her, I continue to kiss her, wanting to stay in this moment forever.

But eventually, hips start to grind and our breaths come quicker. When Scarlett lets out a whimper before nipping at my bottom lip, all of my blood rushes to my cock.

"*Fuck*, baby," I groan against her lips. "What do you need? I'll give you anythi—"

Scarlett's hand covers my mouth. I pull back just enough that I can look down at her with a questioning gaze.

Vulnerability shines in her eyes. "I want to not think," she whispers.

Understanding dawns. This feels different for her, too.

I press a gentle kiss against her palm before pulling her hand away. Every time we've had sex, Scarlett's been the one in control. I was so cautious of her boundaries that I let her be the one to lead us. But that can be exhausting. I'm not surprised she's tired of it.

A part of me is taken aback that she trusts me with it, though. In the best way.

The weight of that trust, the *honor* of it, settles over me like the comfort of a blanket. Nothing has ever felt more important.

And I want so badly to give her everything she's asking me for. Reaching back with one hand to grab the neckline of my shirt, I pull it off over my head. Then, with my gaze locked on hers, I stretch it into a long line and move it toward her eyes.

I watch carefully for the moment she understands. If there's any part of her that doubts me, if I see even a flash of nerves, I won't do it. But when surprise is quickly followed by a relieved nod, I know I read her correctly.

Carefully, I tie my shirt around her eyes.

By the time I'm done, she's trembling. I press a gentle kiss to her collarbone and tell her, "At any point, if you want to stop, just tell me. No safe words, just open communication." I press another kiss to her jawline this time. "Can you do that for me?"

Her nod is instant and eager. "Yes," she breathes, already arching into my touch.

I lean back enough that I can look down at her body laid out under me. Her hotel robe has opened wide, so I can see the curves of her breasts, and the knot on her belt won't take much to undo. It's a heady feeling, having her give herself to me like this.

My gaze travels over her body, wondering where I want to start with her pleasure. Because she might be putting the power in my hands, but the only thing I give a shit about is making *her* feel good.

In the end, I decide to taste her before anything else. The memory of her shaking against my tongue is too potent to skip it.

The moment I touch the knot at her waist, Scarlett sucks in a breath. By the time I work it open and slide the sides of her robe apart, her hands are fisted in the sheets and her chest is heaving.

"Easy," I murmur, pressing a kiss to her hip bone. "I'm going to taste you, and I want you to stay still while I do it."

The moan she lets out is enough to make my cock throb. I have to reach down to squeeze it as I slide down Scarlett's body and settle between her legs.

*Fuck*, she's edible. I don't know how I went this long without her.

But when I look up the length of her body and see my shirt covering her eyes, I'm reminded of the reason. Of the trust she's put in my hands, the trust I fought for. When I finally lower my mouth to her body, it feels bigger than sex.

I *groan* into her skin when her wetness smears across my lips. I've barely even touched her yet, and she's drenched. With my hands pressing into her thighs, I start to lick her, my tongue tracing over every inch of her. I could *live* on the taste of her.

Especially when a gush of liquid hits my lips after I suck on her clit.

My groan gets lost in her skin, but I can make out her whimpered *Nico*. Can feel her fingers thread into my hair to pull me closer. Wrapping my arms under and around her legs, I band one arm over her stomach when she tries to arch into my mouth. With the other, I press my thumb to her clit as I lick down to her entrance.

Scarlett's legs squeeze around my head when I slide my tongue inside, and her hand tightens in my hair. Another whimper slips from her lips.

But I realize that I can't quite get deep enough, can't give her what she needs to come. So after a few moments of— selfish—pleasure, I pull back and press two fingers inside her instead.

"Oh my God, *Nico,*" Scarlett gasps, her back arching off the bed. "That's going to make me—"

"I know," I groan, fucking her with my fingers. "I'm going to make you come all over my hand, baby." I move my thumb to press a kiss to her clit and add in a murmur, "And then I'm going to lick it off like the sweetest fucking dessert."

Maybe it's the feel of my fingers and mouth working in tandem, or maybe it's my words that emphasize her loss of control—one of them makes her tremble beneath me.

As I watch the orgasm roll over her, I can't help but think about how much I'm going to enjoy figuring out which it was.

"That's it," I murmur in a soothing voice, waiting until

her body drops to the bed before I pull my fingers from her. I press another gentle kiss to her pussy before lifting up so I can really look at her. "You come so prettily, Red."

A puff of air whooshes from her lips and she starts to squirm. When her hands clench into fists, I get the sense that she wants to pull the blindfold off. But she also likes being under my hand—if the power of her orgasm was any indication—and therefore won't reach for it unless I tell her to.

As I crawl up her body, I decide a part of me wants that, too. But not before I...

Instead of sliding my wet fingers into my mouth, I touch the pads of them to Scarlett's lips.

"Open," I whisper.

The same way she did to me that first night we spent together.

Only now, everything's different.

She sucks in a surprised breath...and then wraps her lips around me.

Now *I'm* the one panting. "Fuck," I groan as I watch her suck the entire length of my fingers into her mouth. Her tongue glides over them, and I can *feel* the way she moans at her own taste.

I can't wait any longer. I need to feel her for real.

Lifting to my knees, I hurriedly push my boxer briefs down before leaning over the bed to grab my jeans. I pull my wallet out and then the condom, the action giving me enough time and brain power to wonder... *What would it be like to fuck her bare?*

But that question feels too close to the question of *can* she fuck me bare, so before my brain can spiral from the reminder of Scarlett's job, I quickly slide the condom on and settle over top of her again.

I'm just about to guide myself inside her when it registers how hard she's squeezing my arms. Not because she's nervous, but because she's still wearing the blindfold.

It's enough to make me slow down, to stop myself from getting lost in Scarlett's body. This is more than just fucking.

Slowly, I lower my head to kiss her. And the moment our lips touch, a relieved sigh rushes from her lips and her arms wrap around my neck.

*This.* This is what I wanted. To feel close to her. To feel like I'm…more. For her.

With our lips connected, I reach down and guide myself inside her.

We both moan into our kiss. *Fuck*, she feels good.

When I start to fuck her, it doesn't take long for our breathing to become so labored that our kiss becomes two opens mouths pressed together.

Eventually, I drop my face to her neck. "You feel so fucking good," I groan into her skin. Scarlett answers with a whimper, her nails scraping across my back.

At the feel of it, I have the desire to restrain her hands, too. I want her as lost to me as I am to her.

I reach back and guide first one arm, then the other, up and over her head. Locking our hands together, I press them into the mattress as I take her lips in another kiss.

"Feel me," I whisper against her lips. "Feel *only* me. Feel how gone I am for you."

Her hands tighten around mine as she kisses me harder. As if she *can* feel it.

It's only when our breathing becomes labored again that I let my lips drift from hers. I kiss along her jaw, down her neck, across her collarbone. Eventually, I go low enough to suck her nipple into my mouth.

Moaning, she arches into me for more.

With my hands still pressing down on hers, I worry her nipple with my teeth. And then I change my thrusts to grind down on her clit.

"Nico," Scarlett gasps, writhing beneath me.

When I switch to her other nipple and hold my focus on her clit, her squirming increases. She's close.

I'm so focused on how she feels under me that it takes a second to register that she says my name again. And again.

I let go of her nipple and slide up her body. "What is it, baby?" I murmur as I press a kiss to her shoulder.

"Kiss me," she gasps. "Please. I want you to kiss me while you f-fuck me."

Maybe it's hearing her curse, maybe it's the request itself. Whatever it is, her words have me freezing, and then rushing to fulfill her request.

I let go of her hands, one of mine sliding under her shoulder to the back of her neck to hold us together. With the other, I slip the blindfold from her eyes, and then I kiss her with the desperation that only a man is capable of.

The second my lips press to hers, she comes.

So do I.

The orgasm consumes me. With no space between us, I feel every wave of Scarlett's release, and I want to drown in it. I want to drown in *her*.

For a moment, we are one.

# THIRTY
## SCARLETT

I'm still trembling when Nico collapses beside me. It's a relief to see he's breathing as hard as I am, because it feels like my heart is beating a mile a minute.

Even after my orgasm has died down.

I've never had sex like that. I didn't even think it was possible. Is that feeling what I've been missing this whole time? That connection?

Maybe it's the post-orgasm bliss, or maybe it's the late hour. But I think I've lost the filter that usually keeps me guarded. Because I suddenly want to talk to Nico about it.

I don't fight the urge to curl up under his arm. When he squeezes me closer and presses a kiss to my temple, I sigh and wrap around him.

"I didn't know sex could feel like that," I admit quietly.

There's the briefest hesitation in the way Nico brushes his hand up and down my arm. But just as quickly, he relaxes and continues his touch. "Yeah?" he asks softly.

It feels good to be honest with him. "Does it always feel like that for you?"

This time, his hand freezes completely.

"Never."

His answer only makes me want to share more. Knowing I shared something special with Nico? It's intoxicating.

This time, my confession is whispered.

"I've never…trusted someone like that. I thought it would be scary, but it wasn't. It was…empowering."

It should scare me when Nico stops breathing, but it doesn't. Instead of hiding away from his reaction, I lift my head and peek up at him.

He looks both terrified and confused, somehow.

"What is it?" I ask him.

That wide-eyed look stays on his face when he meets my eyes.

"I just…" His throat moves on a swallow. "I mean, weren't you…married?"

It takes me a second to understand what he's saying. When I do, I don't know whether to laugh or cry.

I roll onto my back with a tired sigh. "Yeah, looking back, it sounds ridiculous. My only defense is that I was nineteen." Feeling suddenly embarrassed, I mumble, "Sorry, I shouldn't be talking about sex."

"No, it's not that," Nico rushes out. The bed rustles as he shifts his weight to balance on an elbow beside me. "I *want* to talk about it. I want to know what you're thinking about." His voice quiets with the slightest sign of nerves when he adds, "I meant it when I said I'm all in, Scarlett."

I melt at the affection in his voice. *What did I ever do to deserve this man's attention?*

"It's not a pretty story," I say in the smallest voice.

"I don't care," he responds instantly. "If it got you to be here with me then I'll be nothing but grateful for it."

The smile I give him is sad. "Try to hold on to that thought, okay?"

His only answer is to press a kiss to my hair before shifting to settle back against the headboard.

I briefly contemplate facing him, but quickly realize it will be easier not to look at him. I might be self-aware enough now to know my past wasn't my fault, but that doesn't mean I'm not ashamed of it on some level.

So instead, I lie on my back and stare up at the ceiling, watching the lights of the city flash around me. "I don't even know where to start."

Nico's hand begins a soothing caress on my hair. "Just start at the beginning." But when I continue to hesitate, he adds, "I mean, some of it, I can already guess. So you don't have to go into detail about the…old-fashioned values you were raised with."

I almost want to laugh at how politely he managed to phrase that. "Old-fashioned is putting it mildly."

"Yeah, I know that, too," he says with a sigh.

And I feel so raw from the sex, and blinded by the late hour, that I end up just blurting out the beginning.

"Is it considered old-fashioned if my parents arranged a marriage for me when I turned eighteen? Or is it just plain crazy?"

For a moment, everything is silent. Then…

"They did *WHAT?!*"

This time, I do laugh, but it lacks amusement. "Insane, right?"

Nico's face appears above me, his brow furrowed. Thankfully, his eyes are filled with pain, not pity.

"Scarlett, that's so fucked up. I'm so sorry you had to go through that."

I shrug, numb to the memory. And to the childhood that taught me that numbness is the only way to live in a house like that.

"Believe it or not, I didn't hate the idea when they first brought it up," I admit, thinking back to seventeen-year-old Scarlett receiving the news. "I mean, he was older and accomplished and good-looking, and a big part of me was flattered that he wanted to marry me. So I didn't exactly fight it when my parents explained what was happening."

Anger starts to roil in Nico's eyes. "How much older?"

I answer with a sad smile. Too old, and we both know it.

"Anyway, like I said, I didn't really mind the match," I continue, picking at a loose thread in the sheets. "He was nice, and I thought he was cute, and his family's connections helped my family. So I was happy to do it."

What I don't tell Nico is that my husband's "connections" were just rich people connections. He was the mayor's son, and my being tied to him opened doors for my parents that they wouldn't have had access to otherwise. There was nothing genuinely "helpful" about it.

"The wedding was nice, too," I say through a sigh, looking at the city's shadows flashing on the ceiling. "He knew I didn't like being the center of attention, so he organized a private wedding in the courthouse for us. No pictures, no crowds, just us. It was a sweet memory." Then the memory sours. "We weren't really *together* together before the wedding, but the day after we signed our marriage license, I moved in with him."

Nico's muttered curse doesn't escape my attention. I can see him dragging a hand down his face out of the corner of my eye. But he doesn't interrupt.

"At the time, I didn't really wonder why everything happened so quickly. I mean, I'd been raised with traditional values, like you said, so I knew the general order of things. I knew what his role was, and mine. None of it raised any red flags for me." Pulling myself to a sitting position, I slide back until I'm against the headboard. "The first six months were great," I say honestly. "He would buy me flowers, take me out to dinner, surprise me with pretty clothes. Even the—" I blush. "Even the sex was sweet. I felt taken care of."

I wrap my arms around my legs as the harder memories start to take shape.

"But then things changed. He started to work long hours, and he'd miss the dinners I'd make for him like I'd been told a good wife should. On weekends, he'd disappear to the country club or to whatever work events he didn't feel like telling me about. I started to focus mostly on keeping the house spotless, making better recipes, and—" I blink furiously as I force the words past my lips. "Making sure I was as attractive as possible for him."

This time, Nico's curse isn't muttered. He slides from the bed and starts to pace.

To an extent, I understand his frustration. I might still be working through some of the misogynistic values I was raised and conditioned with, but that doesn't mean I'm not aware of how terrible it is that an eighteen-year-old girl was skipping dinners and spending all of her money on lingerie, just to earn the love of a man who had already vowed to love her through sickness and health.

But now that I've started, I *need* to get the rest out. I've never been able to get the rest out.

"By the time I turned nineteen, sex was the only thing he wanted from me. It was the only way I could get him to pay attention to me."

What I don't say out loud is that this is where I got good at sex. I tried anything and everything I thought my husband might like, solely with the hope that impressing him in the bedroom might make him like me again outside of it.

It didn't work.

"Then one day, he came home drunk and horny. Which wasn't unusual, but that night, I was really sick with the flu. It was the first time I ever said no to him."

My stomach drops through the floor at the rest of the memory. At the way he grabbed me and said he didn't care, that he'd just bend me over real quick. At the way I got really scared and pulled away, and for a split second, I thought he might force it anyway. And even though he passed out on the couch instead, I still spent the night shell-shocked and trembling.

Nico doesn't need to know that part.

I force my mind back to the present. "I guess after that, he decided I wasn't worth the effort anymore. He stopped paying attention to me completely." I pause for a deep breath, still unable to look at Nico. "And then he started to come home smelling like perfume."

Looking back, I ignored the signs for way too long. Subconsciously, I knew he was cheating on me, but a younger Scarlett wouldn't let herself believe it.

Not when she was doing everything a woman was supposed to do for her husband.

"The day I found another woman's underwear in his pants pocket, I knew my marriage was over," I say in a small voice. "I knew it would only get worse from there."

For a moment, I'm thrown back to the memory of that night. To the way I froze in horror and realization. To the way I panicked and ran to my parents' house, desiring consolation from my mother. To the way she waved me off and said this is just what men do.

To the way she looked me up and down and said maybe he did it because it looked like I'd put on weight.

I thought that would be the worst part of the day, but the feeling of being shooed from my childhood home and realizing the only other place I could go was my adulterous husband's house was somehow worse. I felt so utterly alone, and I had no idea what to do about it. I had no friends, no other family, and I was completely tied to my husband.

I'm snapped out of my thoughts when Nico stops at the foot of the bed, wincing and rubbing his forehead.

"Okay, in full transparency, I'm trying very hard not to ask Lucas to find this piece of shit predator so I can put him six feet under. So, in the spirit of fighting that urge, please tell me you left him immediately and are no longer married."

"Well, actually, you might laugh at this—"

"I can guarantee I won't."

Sighing, I crawl to the end of the bed so I can reach for Nico's hand and pull him toward me. "Yes, I left him immediately. And no, I haven't seen or heard from him since." More for myself than him, after a moment, I add, "My parents, either."

Sometimes I wonder about never hearing from my parents. I don't know what I expected their reaction to be about me leaving, but I expected *some* kind of communication in three years. Maybe that was just my childish hope, though. Maybe by running off, I embarrassed them to the point of wanting to disown me.

Nico drops onto the bed with a pained exhale. "Fuck, baby. I'm sorry. I mean, I'm not, because they suck, but..." He looks down where his thumb traces over the back of my hand. "I would've chased you," he adds quietly.

My chest warms at that, the smallest smile touching my lips. I believe him.

The moment lightened, Nico asks curiously, "So, what exactly is the funny part?"

I huff a laugh. "The funny part is that when I went home and started to angrily dig for more signs of his cheating, I found a marriage license in his office. But it wasn't my name that was on it."

Nico's brow furrows. "He was married before?"

"Not just that. When I got curious and looked up the woman's name, I found out that she had filed for divorce. And that it was still ongoing, which meant *they* were still married."

His confusion grows. "Can you be married to two people at once?"

I shake my head. "No. Which meant that *my* marriage wasn't legitimate. I guess he faked the ceremony and paperwork for my sake and hid the fact that he had a wife from a neighboring state." I look down at our hands and shrug. "Not great for my trust issues, but it did make my escape easier."

Nico mutters something that gets lost in his hand dragging down his face. "Christ. I have no idea how to process this."

I can't bring myself to look at him as I say, "I get it. It's a crazy story. But...hopefully you can see now why I don't trust easily."

Nico lets out a snort. "After that? I wouldn't blame you if you never trusted the male species again." But then his expression softens, and he shifts closer. "Thank you for sharing that with me. I know how big of a deal that was for you." He leans forward to cup my cheek and touch his forehead to mine. "Thank you for trusting me," he whispers.

And despite everything in my life that's taught me to be cautious—a childhood with people I'm not sure ever loved me and a marriage to a husband who only wanted me for superficial reasons—somehow, it feels right to trust Nico.

# THIRTY-ONE
## NICO

Waking up with Scarlett in my arms is a feeling I never could've prepared myself for. Especially when I look down and see her smiling in her sleep.

I pull her closer, feeling a rush of relief that she didn't leave early like last time.

"Has anyone ever told you you're an incredibly cuddly sleeper?" comes her muffled, sleepy voice.

I grin even though she can't see me. "Has anyone ever told you that you snore like a cartoon character?"

She freezes. "You're lying."

I muffle my laughter. *I* am *lying.* "Nope. You had both the big snorts and cute little wheezes down pat."

Another pause.

And then she rolls onto her back with a sigh. "Welp, I guess it can't be worse than the sound of me vomiting for hours."

I snicker down at her as I lift onto one elbow. I love that she's comfortable enough to joke about imperfections now. "To be fair, not much would be worse than that."

Finally, she lets a smile emerge. She stares at me, and I stare back.

"So…what do we do now?" she asks.

I grin. "Now…I feed you." Scooping her into my arms, I jump from bed and stride down the hallway to the kitchen. "Eggs and bacon okay? Or do you have a breakfast food request? They usually only stock the fighter fridges with basic food, but I can go out to get something if you want."

"Eggs would be great," she says with a smile as I set her on the barstool. "Thank you."

I smack a kiss to her cheek before turning to the oven and grabbing the skillet. "So polite. Now, how do you like your eggs?"

"Scrambled, please."

"Do you want toast with it? I think they put some bread in here—"

"No toast."

Her answer is so flat and instantaneous that I find myself turning around with raised eyebrows. Scarlett looks just as surprised by the speed of her answer.

"Umm, no toast, please," she rephrases carefully. "I'm still full from that burger last night."

*Baby steps, I guess.*

Once the pan is hissing with the eggs I dumped in it, I decide… *Fuck it, I'm just going to ask.*

"So, are you busy today? Or can you hang out for a little bit?"

*Translation: are you working today?*

Her hesitation makes me tense up. But then she says, "I'm not busy. At all, actually."

I paste a charming smile on my face that even Lucas would be proud of and turn around. "Want to come with me to a suit fitting then?"

She blinks at me. "Uhh…sure." Then she shakes her head and asks, "You have the most *random* ideas for dates, Nico."

I lean back against the counter with a grin. "Who said it was a date?"

But when I see a flash of doubt in her eyes, I quickly step forward to lean across the counter and take her lips in a kiss. "You should assume everything is a date from here on out," I murmur.

I love the way she relaxes at that. So much so that I kiss her again.

"So, what's the suit for?" she asks when I go back to an almost-burnt breakfast.

I quickly scoop the scrambled eggs out of the skillet. "I have this gala I have to go to for the UFC. Figured it's a good time to get a new suit."

Then something occurs to me, and I spin around.

"Come with me," I blurt out.

Her eyes widen. "What?"

Suddenly giddy about the idea, I tug her off the barstool and into my arms. "Come with me. Be my date."

Her confusion shifts to nervousness. "Nico…I don't think that's a good idea."

"Why not? They're not that bad. And it will be way more fun with you there." But when her tension finally registers, I try to dial back my excitement. "What's wrong?"

She can't meet my eyes. "I just…I don't think you should be seen with an escort."

I blink at her.

"Okay, first of all, you're not an escort when you're with me." *We'll deal with the unspoken part of that statement later.* "Second of all, why would anyone think you're an escort?" I narrow my eyes playfully at her. "Are you telling me I couldn't pull a woman as hot as you?"

It successfully breaks the tension, thank God. Her lips lift in a small smile.

But then reality intrudes, and it drops from her face. "I'm just saying, at a place like a gala, there's a chance we run into someone who knows I'm an escort. I *want* to go, but it's too risky."

"So I'm supposed to just hide you away for the rest of my life? Excuse my language, but fuck that. I'm not okay with that."

She sighs and pushes away from me. "You can say that all you want, but that's just not the world we live in, Nico. People are going to judge you for being with me."

"So I don't get a say in this?" I demand, my voice tinged with frustration. "If it's my risk then I'm the one who gets to take it."

"Of *course* it's your decision. I just—" She lets out a frustrated exhale of her own. "I hate the idea of hurting you or your career."

Immediately, all fight goes out of me. A warm feeling starts to grow in my chest.

Taking her in my arms again, I tilt her face up and press a light kiss to her mouth. "You're sweet for worrying. But let's leave that to me, okay? Let me handle that if it comes up."

She still looks skeptical, but eventually I get a small nod. It makes me grin and kiss her again, this one more forceful.

"So...suit shopping?" she asks when I sit her back on the barstool.

"We could go dress shopping, too," I offer as I plate our breakfasts. "If you want."

I have no idea where her head is at while she mulls it over. After a moment, she says, "A new dress is probably a good idea. But I'm not dress shopping with you."

I give her an affronted look. "Why not?"

She shrugs, smiling slightly. "Because it would take away from the big reveal. And a lady always makes an entrance."

I want to argue with her about the way she worded that, but suddenly all I can think about is Scarlett doing a grand dress reveal.

I have to clear my throat once, twice, before I'm capable of speaking. "Whatever you think is best."

Before I can say anything else, I notice her eyes dropping to my chest. I'm shirtless, wearing only joggers, so her gaze travels over my muscles, heat flaring in them with every inch. I quirk an eyebrow and wait for her to voice her thoughts.

"I wonder if you'll look hotter in a suit than you do right now."

I almost choke on my own spit. Scarlett flirting isn't anything new, but there's something new about *this*. She seems…liberated. Comfortable.

"You think I'm hot, Red?" I ask casually, wondering where she's about to take this.

Her eyes lift to meet mine. "I think you're the hottest man I've ever met. I always have."

A breath whooshes out of me. *This is definitely something new.*

I know I'm right when she stands and slowly walks around the counter, her eyes never leaving mine. When she stops in front of me, I'm barely breathing.

And then she leans forward to press a kiss to my chest, and I stop breathing entirely.

"Normally," she starts with a hum, "your jeans and a black t-shirt is my favorite look." I watch in awe as she places her finger to the place she just kissed and slowly starts to drag it down my body, over every ridge of every muscle. "But I'll admit…this casual *shirtless and barefoot in the kitchen* look is much more appealing than I anticipated."

I swallow roughly. "Yeah? If I had known that's all it would take to get you in my kitchen, I would've done it a lot sooner."

She lets out a tinkling laugh, the sound sweeter than this moment feels. Especially considering she's not looking at me, but following the path of her finger as it finally reaches my joggers.

"I had no idea it would," she says. Finally, she tilts her head up to meet my eyes.

Her pupils have blown completely black.

"I think it's the kitchen," she says, a tinge of breathlessness in her words. "You *in* the kitchen. You making me breakfast, taking care of me..." I watch her throat flex with a swallow. "I've never... I mean, I never *wanted* to...here."

It takes me a second to decipher what she's saying. But then it clicks.

She's never had sex in a kitchen.

I wonder if she's ever had sex—*real* sex, not sex with clients or shitty ex-husbands—anywhere but a bedroom.

And as I look down at her, as I take in every detail of her heated gaze—the pulse pounding in her neck, her chest moving with rapid breaths—I realize I was right about this feeling different. She *does* seem liberated. And comfortable enough with me to ask for something new.

I brush a strand of loose hair away from her face, letting out a thoughtful hum. Because I am nothing if not willing to give Scarlett anything she asks for.

"Then we should...*here*."

# THIRTY-TWO
## SCARLETT

I have no idea what's gotten into me. I have *never* come onto a man this brazenly.

But something feels different. It's Nico, yes, but it's also something in *me*. After last night, I feel comfortable with him, and comfortable in my own body.

And I want to explore it.

Desire rises like a tidal wave inside me. I want *everything* with Nico, so much so that I can't figure out what I want first. But he's standing there, looking so delicious, and suddenly, all I want to do is please him. So, I move to drop to my knees.

Nico stops me.

I look up at him in surprise, but that's the only thing I have time for because in the next second, he takes my mouth in a kiss.

And he's *feral*.

He wastes no time parting my lips with his tongue, then sliding it deep inside to taste me. His hands lift to cup my face, to angle me in a way that allows him to deepen the kiss further.

I *moan* into the kiss.

My hands come up to grab onto him, to grab onto *something*, because my knees are too weak to hold me up. I've never been kissed like this.

But before I can slide my arms around Nico's neck, I'm spun and bent over the kitchen counter.

The air fills with the sounds of our heavy breathing. My hands are braced on the marble, Nico standing behind me with his hands on my waist. I have no idea where he's going to take this, but I'm excited to find out.

Slowly, his hands travel down my body, over my hips and down to my thighs. The only thing I'm wearing is the t-shirt Nico gave me last night, so he hits bare skin almost immediately. When his hands start their path back up my legs, this time sliding under the hem of the shirt, I start to tremble.

"I'm having a very hard time deciding how I want you first," he growls.

But then his touch pauses, and he lets out a groan.

"*Fuck*, baby, I can't stop thinking about how you tasted last night. I need to—"

He doesn't finish his sentence, he simply drops to his knees behind me, grabs my ass cheeks in each hand, and opens me to him. At the first swipe of his tongue, I collapse onto the counter with a surprised moan.

The kitchen isn't the only thing that's new for me. This position, having someone *behind* me…that's new, too.

Not all escorts have the rule, but many won't allow a man behind them. Doggy takes away a woman's ability to see what the man is doing. The main concern is condom removal, but the position itself is so vulnerable that it's usually better to just take it off the table entirely.

With Nico, that vulnerability *is* the appeal.

Just like last night, I can't see what he's doing, I can only feel. I have no control over my body or what he's doing to it. I'm left completely at his mercy.

Right now, that feeling is what's about to make me come.

I scratch at the counter, searching for something to grab to ground me as the pleasure mounts. Nico still has me pressed open, giving me nowhere to hide, and his tongue is doing things I've never even dreamed of. By this point in our relationship, he's already mastered how I like to be touched, so he's not holding back. He licks and sucks me until I'm a whimpering mess, and then when a *please* slips out, he groans and slides two fingers inside me.

I come on his tongue instantly.

When Nico eventually stands, I'm still trembling, trying to catch my breath. Another whimper slips out when I feel him press a kiss to my lower back.

"I'll never get over how good you taste," he groans. "If I wasn't dying to fuck you, I'd stay on my knees for another hour." He slides his t-shirt up my body and over my head to bare the rest of me, leaving another kiss on my shoulder as he does it. "I'd see how many orgasms I could coax out of your pretty little cunt."

A breath whooshes out of me as my head drops between my shoulders. I *never* thought I'd enjoy being talked to like this.

Nico's arms come around me then, his hands going to each of mine to plant them on the counter.

"Stay right here, baby," he growls in my ear. "Don't move an inch."

And then he's gone, to who knows where. My brain isn't functioning enough to figure it out.

A minute later, he's standing behind me once again. It vaguely registers that he throws his wallet beside me, but then he's pressing between my shoulder blades and flattening the upper half of my body. I whimper when my nipples hit the cold counter.

"Is this what you wanted?" Nico asks over the faint sound of fabric rustling. "For me to take whatever I want, whenever I want?"

I'm panting as I nod. I want him so badly I can barely breathe.

Nico's satisfied hum reaches my ears just as the tip of his cock touches my clit. I moan as I turn my face into the counter.

"I think I like having you at my mercy like this," he muses, sliding his length up and down my skin. I can tell I'm drenched because he moves easily. On one pass, he almost slips inside, only correcting himself when I suck in a breath.

He's waiting. Or teasing. I have no idea, but the anticipation is killing me. It's like he's trying to figure something out. I'm just too keyed up to understand what he's—

His palm cracks lightly against my ass cheek.

I lift my head with a gasp…then *moan* as pleasure melts into my skin.

"Fuck, Scarlett," he grits out. This time, when he spanks me again, I lower my face to the counter with a needy sound I don't even recognize and shift my legs farther apart. "*Fuck.*"

When he enters me, it's with a hard, impatient thrust. No more of the slow, teasing Nico; now, he's a man whose sanity has unraveled.

The way he fucks me drives the breath from my lungs. It's hard and fast and I have zero control over any of it. The only thing I can do is widen my stance and try not to drown in euphoria.

Especially when he spanks me. And again, harder.

"We're going to have to draw all new boundaries for

you," Nico growls, the hand on my hip digging into my skin as he continues to fuck into me. "We'll have to find all those hidden kinks, won't we?"

I can only moan in answer. The memory of my escort boundaries doesn't even feel like it was in this lifetime.

Another wave of pleasure is already swelling inside me when I feel Nico's hand in my hair. He wraps the strands around his fist once, twice, then slowly pulls my head back until I'm drawn taut like a bowstring before him, his tongue licking up my neck to my ear. His touch is forceful, but with the heat of his body against my back, I can also feel the gentleness that I've grown so familiar with. That is letting me live out this fantasy for the first time in my life.

"You ready to come, baby?" he asks, the tinge of desperation in his voice giving away how affected he is and making me shiver. This feels just as intense for him as it does for me. I nod as much as I'm able.

"You're not going to fake it, are you." He doesn't ask it as a question. Doesn't give me the *choice*.

"No," I gasp, shaking my head frantically. "Never."

"Good girl," he growls, his thrusts growing more powerful. "Now...come on my cock for me."

When his hand slides between my legs, it barely takes five seconds. Between the command, the ownership with which he's fucking me, and his slippery fingers on my clit, I'm driven to heights of pleasure I didn't even know existed. I'm lost in another reality as the orgasm rolls through me, and I cry out for him.

Nico finds his release at the same time. His hips stutter, a broken groan tearing from his chest as he fills the condom.

*I wonder what sex without a condom will feel like.*

It's a testament to how much Nico just blew my mind that

the foreign thought doesn't alarm me. Instead, I turn my face toward Nico, needing the comfort of his kiss.

He obliges instantly. The hand that was wrapped in my hair loosens, and he cups my head as he takes my mouth in the sweetest kiss. When it ends, I collapse on the counter with a sated sigh.

Nico collapses on top of me, though he holds up most of his weight. "Jesus Christ," he groans, his hot breath on my neck. "I was *not* prepared for you this morning."

I only sigh happily again and wiggle my hips, absorbing the feel of him still inside me. "You seemed to do just fine, though."

"Trust me, it took all my willpower," he says on an exhale, pushing up onto his hands. He presses a quick kiss to my shoulder before pulling away from me.

I can't stop smiling as I straighten. Waking up in Nico's arms already made for a great morning, but now? I'll be thinking about today for a very long time.

---

Unfortunately, reality intrudes quicker than I want it to. And some of that giddiness fades.

After our suit-shopping expedition, Nico leaves to go back to Philly. The gala is only five days from now, so we probably won't see each other before then. We'll have to stick to phone calls.

That distance is what allows my anxious thoughts to creep back in.

Specifically, my decision to go to the gala.

I meant what I said to Nico: I *want* to go. I love the idea of being on his arm, of finally getting to go on a date with him where money isn't involved.

It's the rest of it that's making me hesitant.

Because the truth of the matter is, I'm fairly likely to run into someone who knows me. I've seen countless high-powered men in my three years as an escort, and while I tried to stay away from athletes as much as possible, that doesn't mean I don't have connections to the men around them. Not to mention, the gala is in my city. I wouldn't be surprised if I ran into a client just based on proximity alone.

And yet…Nico seemed so excited—and so *not* worried—that I can't quite convince myself to back out.

It's his excitement that keeps my doubts at bay for the rest of the night. Instead of thinking about how this gala could go badly, all I'm thinking about is how good Nico looked in his suit today. And how I'll need a beautiful dress to match him.

It's how I find myself at my favorite dress store the next day.

Every other dress I've bought in this store has been with other men in mind. And regardless of what happens with Nico in the future, I don't want to recycle those dresses for a date with him. I want to look better than I ever have. I want to look…like *his*.

"Daisy! How nice to see you again." Lisa, my personal shopper for the store, appears in front of me with a smile. "What are we shopping for today?"

I return the smile. "Hi, Lisa. I need a new dress for a gala next weekend." I look around the store, nibbling on my lip. "And it needs to be stunning."

Her eyes light up at that. I don't know if she's guessed what I do—what I *did*—but she knows *stunning* means *expensive*.

She knows my best colors already, so she brings mostly gold and green dresses over to the dressing room, along with a flute of champagne. She nails my vision almost immediately, same way she always does.

"He must be a special one," she comments, looking at me in the mirror. "This might be the most flattering dress you've ever let me put on you."

I huff a laugh. In the past, I tried to keep a little air of modesty and intrigue with my dresses. They always looked beautiful, of course, but they were always *just* simple enough that they didn't feel obvious. It was my way of distancing myself from my escort persona; if I wasn't wearing a racy dress, I didn't feel like a woman who found her worth in men.

But when I spin in front of the mirror and get a glimpse of the back of this dress, nothing could be further from my mind.

"It's perfect," I breathe. "I finally feel…like myself."

Lisa tilts her head with a smile. "And isn't that the most powerful type of outfit for a woman…"

*Powerful.*

I've been using that word in my subconscious the past few weeks. Do I feel powerful?

I don't know. I feel beautiful, but not in the way my mother used to make me feel, or Amara, or any of my clients. I feel beautiful in a… Yes, in a powerful sort of way.

Because of Nico.

I grin at Lisa. "I'll take this one."

# THIRTY-THREE
## NICO

I look around for the hundredth time, searching for a flash of red lips or blonde hair. *I wish I knew what she was wearing.*

It's the night of the gala and I'm standing on the steps of The Glasshouse, surrounded by limos, press, and people dressed to the nines. I wanted so badly to pick Scarlett up so we could arrive together, but the timing just didn't work out. After my fight last week, a lot of PR opportunities have come up, the organization seeing my win as the start of my climb for the top. I've just been too nervous to say the words *I'm retiring* to put a stop to it. Even the things I'm tasked with tonight are just me unable to say no to Lucas's ideas.

So now, instead of picking Scarlett up myself, I'm forced to wait for her at the front of the building, nerves and anticipation roiling in my gut.

And then I see her. And every ounce of nerves, fear, uncertainty…all of it disappears.

I watch, breathless, as she steps out of the black car. My gaze travels from her heels to the thigh-high slit in her dress that reveals her long legs, up the gold dress to her face. No red lipstick in sight. Her blonde hair is pinned up to expose her neck and shoulders, her makeup—and dress—all working together to create a showstopping outfit.

*Christ.* She's the most beautiful woman I've ever seen.

I try not to bolt across the steps to her, but my impatience must be obvious because there's amusement on her face when I finally reach her.

"Scarlett," I breathe, taking her hand as the driver closes the door behind her. "You look…"

She smiles warmly. "So do you."

I kiss her then. I can't *not* kiss her. Especially seeing she isn't wearing the red lipstick that so clearly became her armor.

Just as quickly, I stand back to look at her again. "Fuck, baby, you could've warned me."

She lets out a tinkling laugh. "What would be the fun in that?"

I spin her in a circle to take in the full dress, and I swear my knees nearly buckle.

"*Scarlett*," I breathe.

It's backless.

She's wearing a gold, backless dress with a slit up one thigh and a thin silver chain hanging down her spine.

"Do you like it?" she asks in a shy voice.

My eyes shoot to hers as she completes the spin. "Do I *like* it? Baby, I don't think I'm worthy of even walking behind you, let alone next to you."

I'm not kidding, either. How a woman like Scarlett ever gave me a chance is, at this moment, completely beyond me.

Smiling, she steps closer to adjust my tie and smooth down my suit. "Funny. That's exactly what I was thinking about you when I saw you in this suit." I only get to feel a brief moment of pride before she's stepping closer and pressing her lips to my ear. "I also kept thinking about all the things I want to do with this tie later."

My face drops to her neck with a groan, my hands going immediately to the soft silk of her waist. "Are you going to torture me all night? Because I do technically have some work to do."

I smile at the sound of her giggle. "I'll be good, I promise. I just wanted to get that one out."

Pressing a kiss to her shoulder before I pull back, I tell her, "We won't stay long. I just have a few people I need to talk to. And then you have the whole weekend to torture me as much as you'd like."

I love the way her eyes light up at that.

"Okay," she says with a soft smile. "Let's go, then."

I whisk her up the stairs, keeping my arm around her waist as the cameras flash and the occasional question is called out. I'm not a big enough athlete to warrant serious attention, but these reporters are always looking for the next juicy story. And Scarlett has captured their attention.

"Come on, they're not allowed inside," I murmur in her ear.

I feel the way she breathes a sigh of relief once we're inside the ballroom. I quickly grab two flutes of champagne off a nearby waiter's tray for us.

"So, what's the plan for this thing?" she asks after taking a small sip. "I know how they usually go, but I wasn't sure if there's something different you need to do."

I down half the glass in one swallow, needing the hydration after seeing Scarlett. "This one should be pretty easy. We'll people watch for a little bit, maybe mingle with a few sponsors Lucas told me to charm, and then it's time for speeches and dinner. Not that we need to be here for that. I'm only here for the networking."

When she looks around, I notice some tension in her shoulders. *Is she…nervous?*

"Everything okay?" I ask with a small squeeze of her hand.

Her eyes dart back to mine, a smile appearing on her lips. "Yeah. Just…taking it all in." After a beat of hesitation, she asks, "Is Lucas here?"

"He said he was going to try to make it. He's working on some acquisition that's been eating up his time lately, so I wouldn't be surprised if I got a text at 2 a.m., saying he lost track of the time."

Some of the tension goes out of her shoulders when she smiles. "And Alexander? Does he have any ties to your career?"

I snort. "Not unless you count using me as a punching bag when we were kids." Downing the rest of my glass, I add, "He would never come to a place like this. Too fake, too loud, too overwhelming." I only hesitate for a moment before giving Scarlett another piece of me. "He has a hard time with crowds," I admit quietly. "Ever since he came back from his last deployment, he tries to stay away from loud, large groups of people. He can do restaurants in small doses, but he has to be familiar with the place." I clear my throat around the squeeze of my chest, the ache I feel because I can't take my brother's pain away. "He's doing better, but…"

I feel Scarlett's touch on my arm and turn toward her, grateful for the comfort.

"He's lucky to have a family that cares enough to know him that well," she says. "Others may have left him to flounder."

I show off a half-grin, trying to break the seriousness of the moment. "Nah. Lucas is too annoying to let him drown like that."

She must sense my need for distraction because she slides her arm fully through mine and squeezes me close.

"So, about that people watching… Do you have any crazy stories about anyone in here?"

---

An hour later, I'm tipsy on the whiskey I've switched to.

And on Scarlett's laughter. The woman hasn't stopped laughing since I started talking.

I don't think she's even buzzed because she's still nursing her first glass of champagne. I tried to get her something else, but she declined so quickly that it made me wonder if she's using it as an accessory more than anything.

So if it's not the alcohol making her laugh, I have to think she's enjoying herself.

I can't stop staring at her. She's radiant tonight. She looks *happy.*

I find myself once more clearing my throat. I can't *breathe* around this feeling tonight.

But when Scarlett smiles at something I say, and then looks at me and that smile grows… I can't tamp down on this feeling any more than I can stop myself from breathing.

"I have to admit, I'm a little surprised there's dancing at this party."

I snap out of my haze and try to focus on her. "What's that?"

She gestures at the center of the ballroom, where a few couples are swaying together. "I'm surprised there's dancing. I wouldn't think MMA fighters would be keen on dancing."

I sniff. "Speak for yourself, Miss Snooty Booty. Fighting is basically just dancing." When she lets out a snort of laughter and mouths *Snooty Booty?* I shrug and say, "It's a

*Happy Feet* reference in our family. Mostly used to describe Lucas."

"Ridiculous," she says with a chuckle. Then she quirks an eyebrow at me. "So, you know how to dance?"

*Shit. I may have taken this joke too far.*

"I mean, I don't know the waltz necessarily, but—"

"Great." She places her glass on a nearby table before grabbing my hand. "Then you don't mind dancing with me."

I sigh, knowing the jig is up, even as I let her pull me along. "Scarlett, I was just kidding…"

She stops on the dance floor and spins toward me. "I am fully aware, Nico. You're not the only one who can read people."

She must notice my hesitation because she gives me a soft smile and guides one of my hands to her waist and takes the other in her hand.

"I know you were kidding, but it really is similar to fighting," she explains quietly. We're swaying before I can even form a conscious thought about *I don't know what the fuck I'm doing.* "If I had to guess, it's closest to judo. That's the one with the foot sweeps, right?"

My eyebrows shoot to my hairline. "O-kay. How did you know that?"

She shrugs, looking proud of herself. "I may or may not have done a little extra research."

I look down at her, unable to do anything but admire her.

And that feeling in my chest grows.

I have to swallow around it, as it fights to end up on my lips. I might drown from this feeling.

I try to staunch it with a kiss. Bending down, I press my mouth to hers, reveling in the way her arms wrap around my neck, and she sighs happily into the kiss. I could hold her forever and never tire of it.

When I pull back, it's only to put the smallest amount of space between us. I clear my throat. Again. "Scarlett..."

She looks up at me with a smile on her lips and stars in her eyes. "Hmm?" she says with the sweetest little hum.

*Shit. I* need *to tell her.*

"Scarlett, I—"

"Nico, there you are!"

The moment shatters into a thousand tiny shards of glass.

Startled, I jerk back.

"Sorry to interrupt, my boy, but I might not get a chance to talk to you later," comes a voice from beside me. Turning, I realize it's one of the sponsors Lucas sent me to talk to. "Do you mind if I steal you for a few minutes? It won't take long."

Blinking, I look down at Scarlett. "Uh...sure. I guess."

She gives me—and then the man beside us—a polite smile as she steps back. "It's alright, I can wait. Work is work."

"That it is," the man says with a deep chuckle, throwing one arm around me. "And this one is one of the hardest workers of them all."

Looking around the ballroom, I search for a place to lead Scarlett so I don't have to leave her in the middle of a gala surrounded by sharks. When I spot an open spot at one of the bars, I flash an apologetic smile at the man and say, "Just give me one minute. Let me grab her a drink, and then I'll join you."

He waves me off as he turns toward the group I'm assuming he came from. "Of course. We'll be waiting over here."

Ushering Scarlett over to the bar, I quickly order her another glass of wine. "So no one offers to buy you a drink while I'm gone," I tell her with a wink.

She shakes her head with a smile. "Guess I'm not as unreadable as I thought."

I press a kiss to the corner of her mouth. "Not to me," I murmur.

When I pull back, I glance around as I ask, "You sure you're okay here for a minute? I'll be quick, but…"

"Nico, this is exactly the kind of crowd I *can* handle," she says with a light chuckle. Taking a sip of her wine, she waves me off. "Go work. I'll be waiting right here when you're done."

I let out a heavy exhale. "Okay. Call me if you need anything."

And when I turn away from her, I tell myself the drop I feel in my stomach is because our dance was interrupted.

Nothing else.

# THIRTY-FOUR
## SCARLETT

I watch Nico walk off, feeling like a bubble of sunshine wants to burst in my chest.

I have to fight the urge to giggle or squeal into my wine. I have no shot at hiding my giddy smile.

It's all Nico's doing, of course. I never thought I could enjoy an event like this, not surrounded by people I used to schmooze and being assaulted by memories of a similar place I'd rather forget. On paper, I shouldn't be having the time of my life tonight.

And yet...I am.

I glance around the ballroom, already wishing Nico were back.

*Is this what it means to truly enjoy a person's company? Wanting them around constantly because they make everything better?*

I stifle a laugh at the thought. *Enjoying* Nico's company is putting it lightly, I think. It's more likely that—

"You know, I would've had you as a girl who likes white."

Stiffening, I turn toward the voice at my side.

He's young and attractive, clearly an athlete in a room like this. With a charming grin on his face and a tie-less, casually unbuttoned white shirt, it's also clear he's on the prowl.

I've never met him before, so I smile politely and ask, "I'm sorry?"

He nods at the glass in my hand. "You're drinking red wine. I would've assumed white."

"Oh. Uh, no."

He tries again. "Can I buy you a glass of white? Maybe you'll like it better."

*God, I'm so sick of men.*

The thought is so jarring that I have to act like I'm wiping my mouth with a bar napkin to hide my laugh. When I've finally composed myself, I send him another polite smile and say, "Oh, that's okay, thank you. I'm fine with this one."

"Well, how about a cocktail instead?"

I somehow manage to smother my sigh. "Look, I appreciate the offer. But I'm actually here with someone."

Of course that's the answer that gets through to him.

"Ah. Sorry, I didn't realize you were already booked tonight."

I turn toward him with a frown. "Excuse me?"

He gestures between us with a shrug. "I said I didn't know you were booked. I thought you were…how shall I say it? Networking."

My spine goes ramrod straight, dread dripping down the bones.

*Shit. Shitshitshit. This is exactly what I was afraid of.*

"I think you have the wrong idea," I say stiffly. And then, a little desperately, I add, "I'm here with Nicholas Price."

Hotshot seems amused by this information. "Nico?

Really? Damn, I didn't think he'd actually make the call. I figured he'd be too much of a nice guy."

I try to ignore the comment by taking another sip of my wine, wishing I could *will* this guy away. I don't like how this conversation is going.

He doesn't seem to be bothered by my lack of interest. My skin crawls with the way I can feel him look me up and down. I suddenly hate this dress.

"Damn, why didn't the agency show me your picture?" he murmurs. "You fit my criteria perfectly. You sure you can't fit me in before Nico comes back? I promise I'll be quick."

I whip my head toward him with a glare before I can think better of it. "I'm sure you would be."

He lets out a loud laugh. "Ouch. I didn't think whores had time standards. Figured you'd just want the quick buck."

And maybe it's that word, or maybe it's the fact that it's being used in a conversation with Nico's name in it, but I'm suddenly desperate to get out of this situation and away from this guy.

"Look, I'm not here for what you think I am," I say forcefully, my frustration obvious. "I'm here as Nico's g-girlfriend—"

But my voice cracks on the word. I've never used it before, never even *thought* about using it, and Nico and I haven't discussed it—

Hotshot's eyes go wide, glee and something a little more cruel flashing in them.

"*Girlfriend?* That's hilarious." And when he sees my doubt, my *fear*, that cruelty sharpens. "Oh, you sweet summer child. You *do* think he's serious about you."

His sarcasm makes anger boil in my veins. I latch onto it, preferring it to this terror.

"You have no idea what you're talking about," I bite out.

It doesn't sway him one bit. In fact, it makes him double down.

"I'll do you a favor, Pretty Woman," he says in a low, dark voice. It's only now that I hear the slurred edge of his words. "I'll tell you the truth, before you get in too deep. There's no way a man like Nico Price would date a prostitute. He's too pure, too traditional."

With every word, the knife slices deeper. Because he's saying everything I've been secretly worried about, but too scared to voice.

And then he leans back, gives me a once-over of disgust, and cuts the final blow.

"And you're...well, you're a whore. Nothing but a hole for lonely men to fuck."

*I think I'm going to puke.*

I want to scream, hit him, tell him to take it back. I want to find Nico and beg him to tell me none of it is true.

Instead, I plaster a smile on my face that even my mother would be proud of and say, "Yes, I am. And as I said, I'm spoken for tonight. Excuse me."

I don't know how I manage to stand and walk off without tripping over my feet, but I do it. Heading in the direction I saw Nico disappear, I tell myself I just need to find him. When I find him, everything will be alright.

It has to be.

# THIRTY-FIVE
## NICO

It doesn't take long to discuss the sponsorship opportunity. And yet, it feels like it takes too long.

By the time I'm promising to have Lucas look over the contract this week, I'm already itching to get back to Scarlett. I know she's fine on her own, but I think *I'm* the one who hates being without her.

I breathe an internal sigh of relief when three of the four men make excuses to leave for the dining hall. I'm just about to make an excuse of my own when the fourth man, a man I don't recognize, asks me, "So, are you enjoying your time between fights?"

I smile politely and nod. "I'm always eager to get back to fighting, of course, but yes, the downtime has been much needed."

I don't understand why he laughs and says, "I bet Daisy's keeping you plenty busy, huh?"

I frown in confusion. "I'm sorry?"

The man nods in the direction we came from. "Daisy. Your date?"

When I still can't make the connection, he nods and says,

"Ah, did she tell you a different name? Makes sense. Amara's girls like to switch things up. She was Daisy the nights I had her."

That's when it registers. This man knows Scarlett as an escort.

Dread fills my stomach like a lead balloon. *Fuck. Why did I never think this would happen?*

This is exactly what Scarlett was afraid of. She *knew* this could happen. Maybe she even knew it would fuck me up.

I was just too much of a naïve idiot to consider what this would mean.

Or how it would feel.

Because this man has hired Scarlett. Has seen her naked. Has *fucked* her.

I can't find the words to respond to this man. Who doesn't seem to notice, because he just keeps talking.

"Yeah, I was disappointed to leave her behind when I moved to the West Coast. Based on the way things were going, I thought I'd be able to entice her to move out, but... guess the money wasn't enough for her." He chuckles, the sound almost fond. "I can't fault her for being her true little gold-digger self."

Instantly, rage fills my body. How *dare* he talk about Scarlett that way.

*That* the man finally notices. Lifting his palms up in a gesture of surrender, he says, "Sorry, no disrespect meant. It was just always the vibe I got from her."

*I can't believe my fucking ears.* "You got a *gold-digger* vibe from her?"

The guy actually seems bewildered. "Well...yeah. She's an escort." Seemingly in a rush to make me understand, he adds, "Has she pulled the kissing act with you yet?"

I gape at him. "The what?"

He huffs a laugh. "I guess not. No, it's this little tug of war game she plays. Says she doesn't kiss clients, even holds off for a couple weeks, and then she ropes you in by kissing you to make you feel like you're special." He sighs. "I hate to admit it worked on me. The girl's good."

And suddenly, I can't listen to any more.

It's too much. The knowledge that this man has been intimate with Scarlett, that what he's describing is, on paper, the same experience I've had with her. The weeks of fear that I'm falling for the oldest trick in the book, combined with Lucas's warnings that I *am* falling for the oldest trick in the book. All of it twists into a ball of panic that's threatening to explode.

"Excuse me," I mumble. I turn away before waiting for an answer.

I manage to stumble back into the ballroom, my gaze desperately darting through the crowd for a glimpse of Scarlett, even though I have no idea what I'm about to say to her.

When the crowd clears, and she finally appears in my line of sight, the knot in my chest loosens slightly.

Until I see her talking to Tyler. The guy who referred me to the agency. And he's got a hungry look on his face I know all too well.

I'm still pushing past people when she walks away from him. It distantly registers that she seems relieved to see me, but I'm too locked on Tyler to fully consider what that might mean. Thankfully, the moment his gaze meets mine, and he sees the murder in my eyes, he strides off without a word.

Scarlett stops in front of me. "There you are—"

"What was that?" I demand, too sharply, still looking after Tyler.

She jerks back in surprise. "What? Nothing."

My eyes narrow, my focus finally locking on her. "Don't lie to me, Scarlett. This doesn't work if we're not honest with each other."

Her hesitation is obvious. And maybe if I didn't feel so on edge, I might be able to see what it's hiding. But I am, and I can't.

"Okay, fine," she says slowly. "He propositioned me."

I don't even blink. "And?"

Her brow furrows. "And what?"

"And what did you say?"

At that, her eyes go wide. "What did I *say?* What kind of question is that?"

"A logical one," I retort. "You said it yourself: we were going to run into former and potential clients of yours tonight. So. What did you *say*, Scarlett?"

Fear flashes in her eyes, but I'm too lost to my own to do anything about it. "I said no," she says in a small voice.

"Why? He didn't offer enough?"

Scarlett jerks back as if she's been slapped. "*What?*"

I know I should stop. I *know* I should stop. I should take a deep breath and talk myself down from this ledge. But I'm spiraling, and the alcohol running through my veins isn't helping. My feelings for Scarlett are making my fear that hers aren't real grow to insurmountable heights. I can't *breathe*.

I step closer, my voice dropping to a too-harsh whisper. "Was any of this real? Or have I been a game to you this whole time? Poor, naïve Nico, falling for the high-class escort. And paying for the privilege."

Her eyes widen more as they search mine, her chest heaving. "It isn't like that—"

I don't let her finish, because all I can picture is another man kissing her. "God, you must've gotten a real kick out of making me pay to watch you vomit all night long. That was probably a first in escort history, huh? Did you laugh about it with your madam?"

"Why are you doing this?" she whispers, tears shimmering in her eyes. "What happened when you left?"

I slide my hands into my pockets and say stiffly, "I ran into one of your clients. *Another* one, apparently."

Her gaze darts over my shoulder, a nervousness appearing in her expression. "I'm sorry that happened," she says slowly. "But I've never lied to you about who I am. And I *told* you this could happen."

I let out a humorless laugh. "Warning me I might run into someone who's tasted your pussy is a little different than finding out I've fallen victim to the same scheme as who knows how many other men, Scarlett." Then something occurs to me, and I bite out, "If that's even your real name."

Hurt colors every inch of her features, but I'm too blinded by my panic to truly see it. "What are you talking about? What scheme?"

I lean closer. "Are you honestly telling me you've never used your little no-kissing rule to string men along for more dates?"

*Christ*, her acting skills are next level. She doesn't even look guilty.

"You think I did that as a *ploy?*"

I shrug and lean back. "I have no idea. Honestly, it would be a damn good one."

She still just looks shell-shocked. "You're so wrong, Nico. I don't even know what that would accomplish."

"You mean other than making men feel special when you finally do kiss them?"

She gapes at me. "I have *never* kissed a client."

This time, my laugh is loud and filled with too much pain. "How am I supposed to believe you? This entire time, I've been the one who's been pursuing this relationship. How do I know what's true if I don't even know how you feel about *me?*"

When hurt flashes in her eyes, my immediate reaction is to wrap her in my arms, to comfort her and fight off the pain.

But...I can't.

Because right now, in this whiskey-fueled moment, all of my worries from the past few weeks, all of the warnings and doubts I've tried to shove down, they all come bubbling to the surface.

And I'm too terrified of the thought of losing her to fight them back.

"I...I never meant..." Her words are unsure and do nothing to lesson my panic.

When her eyes dart over my shoulder once again, I can't stop myself from blurting out, "Trying to figure out which one of your clients you should admit to?"

Her gaze snaps back to mine. When she doesn't respond right away, just studies me, I squirm for the first time.

"I don't care who you just ran into," she says, lowering her voice. "Because it doesn't matter. He *lied* to you. He probably saw you kissing me and got angry that I never kissed *him.*"

A small trickle of doubt drips down my back. My fear is still too big to handle, but for the first time since I left her at the bar, a little bit of critical thinking cuts through the haze of red.

*Was the guy lying?* I didn't even consider the option. Between the panic that he might be telling the truth, my feelings for Scarlett, and then the sight of her with Tyler, I jumped straight to *Scarlett* being the liar.

For a moment, I can only look at her. I'm still vibrating with uncertainty, still too on-edge to think clearly.

In the end, the only thing I can admit is a broken, "I don't know what to believe."

Instantly, Scarlett straightens her spine. All emotions disappear from her eyes, a wall shuttering between us as she plasters a mask over her face. It's the same expression she used to give me in the beginning when she was shutting me out.

"Well, I guess that decides everything, then," she says with a forced polite smile. "Have a good night, Mr. Price."

And then she turns and disappears into the crowd.

# THIRTY-SIX
## SCARLETT

I can't get out of the ballroom fast enough.

Tears blur my vision, and for the first time since my mother put me in heels at the age of thirteen, I stumble. I have to catch myself on a nearby table to steady my trembling legs.

Swiping furiously at my cheeks, it takes me a second to realize it's still early in the night, and that the front of the building is still swarming with people and paparazzi. I won't be able to get out of here without attracting attention.

I bolt down a blocked-off hallway instead. When I find a bathroom at the end of it, I let out a stuttered exhale of relief, then push through the door and collapse on the chaise lounge inside.

Finally alone, I give in to the tears.

Sobs wrack my chest, the hurt exploding like fireworks. Nico's words ring in my ears on repeat.

*God*, I am such an idiot. A stupid, delusional idiot. I thought I would find comfort and reassurance when I sought him out. Instead, I learned the truth about how he sees me.

I shake my head, the tears running freely. I can't believe I let myself hope, let myself *feel*. Nico was never going to see me as anything more than an escort.

*Because I'm nothing more than an escort.*

I let out a wet, humorless laugh. The scolding I'd be receiving from my mother right now would be one for the ages.

*This is what you get for thinking a man would like you for anything more than what you can provide for him. It's your own fault for letting yourself get carried away by some ridiculous fairytale.*

And yet…I *tried* not to get carried away. I fought so hard not to fall for the dream that Nico spun. The dream that I could be my own person, a woman valued beyond the size of my waist and the services I can provide on my knees. That I could be a *human being.*

I should've known it was all a fantasy. Clearly, even Nico didn't believe it.

Leaning back, I suck in a deep breath, trying to calm myself. I need to get out of here. I don't want to run into Nico again, but even more, I just want to get home. I want to curl up in a ball and forget these past few weeks even happened. I want to go back to my life before Nico and his pretty dream.

*My life before Nico.*

I don't know why that thought startles me. I may have been empty before him, but at least I had a grasp of reality. I knew who I was and what my purpose was. I knew what my days would look like.

Now, I don't know anything.

I mean, where do I even go from here? I haven't worked in over a week, haven't fully committed in over three. I've been too busy falling for Nico's lie, venturing outside of my apartment to discover interests that don't matter. *Wasting* my time.

I should've just stayed with what I knew.

With timing only the universe is capable of, the door opens. And Amara walks into the restroom.

"Scarlett," she says softly. "I thought that was you."

I swipe at my cheeks, feeling them burn with embarrassment. "What are you doing here?"

"Networking," she says simply. She hesitates for a moment, then takes a seat beside me and brushes a strand of hair out of my face. "I didn't expect you to be here, cara. Who are you here with? And how did they upset you? You know if it's a client—"

The sheer ridiculousness of the comment—of this *moment* —has me laughing bitterly. "You have no idea how complicated that question is, Amara."

I feel her studying me. "It doesn't look that complicated, Scarlett," she says with tenderness in her eyes. "And it's not like I haven't already guessed."

My brow furrows as I turn toward her. "What does that mean?"

The only thing I told her was that I needed to take a hiatus. She pressed, of course, but I told her I needed a break, both physically and mentally. That after three years of working consistently, never taking time off, I was burnt out.

In hindsight, maybe framing it as a leave of absence instead of just quitting was my subconscious telling me things with Nico were too good to be true.

Amara sighs and drops her hand. "Scarlett, I've been in this business for twenty years. I *worked* in it for ten. I am not blind to the temptation of certain clients." She gives me a knowing look. "Not to mention, I know what they all look like."

My gaze drops to my hands in my lap.

"Look, I get it, okay? You're young, the lifestyle is

intoxicating, the *men* are intoxicating—you're not the first girl to fall for a client's bullshit. These men, they…" I see the moment Amara goes into her own memories. "They spin these stories, make us fall for their lies, and then the second we don't fit the type of woman they want, they leave us in the dust."

My eyes slide closed, a tear running down my cheek. It sounds insane to describe Nico in this context. Of all the men I've met, all the assumptions I've made about people…he's the absolute last one I ever would've thought would fit into this category.

Amara gives me a pitying look as she brushes a hand over my hair. "I hate to say it, but every girl will have one of these. We all go through it. There's always one man who manages to convince us that they're not like our other clients, that they love and respect us. It's practically a rite of passage."

But that only makes the tears flow quicker. "I thought he was different," I whisper.

"Oh, cara…" Amara wraps an arm around my shoulders, and when she pulls me against her, I both hear and feel the sigh that wracks her body.

For what feels like forever, she just holds me. And then in a broken whisper, she says, "I'm so sorry, Scarlett."

I don't know what she's apologizing for, so I just curl into her embrace.

But her apology continues, her words full of regret and guilt. "I'm sorry you're in pain. I'm sorry he hurt you. And I'm *so* sorry I put you in this position."

I pull back slightly with a confused sniffle. "What?"

Amara's eyes take on a sheen as she says, "I know this will sound ridiculous coming from a madam, but I've only ever wanted the best for you. That day we met, I really did want to help you. I only mentioned the agency because you were stressed about money. I never meant that you needed to—"

Her voice cracks as my stomach drops. *You never needed to sell your body for money.*

I can't even really hold it against her. Looking back, Amara never pressured me to get into the dark side of the agency. But after one too many offers from clients—and one too many days where I felt worthless already—I was the one who got myself into it.

The sound of Amara clearing her throat snaps me back to the present. "But even when you started sleeping with clients, I still thought I could help you," she says, the desperation in her voice obvious. "I thought, *I can give her the weak, submissive men, and they'll help her to feel more empowered.* I thought, even with all the toxic bullshit we go through as women, that there might be some part of this job that could show you how strong and beautiful and incredible you are." A tear runs down her cheek. "But I think I was wrong. I did more harm than good. And I am so, so sorry, cara. Please forgive me."

I slump into her arms again. Understanding some of Amara's reasons for the past three years does bring me some level of relief, but I would never blame her for who I became or what I went through. I take full accountability for everything that's happened in my life that led me to this moment.

I squeeze her in a hug. "It's not your fault," I whisper. "I have nothing to forgive you for."

And so, we sit there, two women wrapped around each other, existing in a world that we've had to learn hard lessons to survive in. Finding comfort in each other, instead of the men we can't rely on.

Eventually, we pull back and wipe at our tears. "Let's get

out of here," Amara says. "Fuck these men. I say we go home, break open a ten-thousand-dollar bottle of champagne, and talk shit about them while we do facials and pedicures. What do you think?"

"That sounds like the perfect Friday night," I say with a watery laugh. "I'm in."

I move in front of the bathroom mirror to quickly fix my appearance. Thanks to my expensive products and perfected routine, most of my makeup is still in place. Eye drops and a little bit of concealer dulls the proof of my tears, but there's not much I can do about the swelling. And even though a new coat of lipstick fixes my mouth, the fact that it was smeared because of Nico's kisses brings a rush of tears all over again. I have to blink them back before they can fall.

Amara's gentle touch turns me to face her. Lifting my chin so I'm forced to meet her eyes, she says firmly, "Just to be clear, *you* are the most beautiful, sought-after woman in New York City. Bar none. Any man would kill to have you spit on them. Forget Nicholas Price. I don't know what he said to you, but I want you to know he's wrong. *You* are the most worthwhile jewel in this entire city."

I try for a smile, but it doesn't work.

# THIRTY-SEVEN
## NICO

I want to run after Scarlett the second she disappears from my sight.

Not that I would know what to say if I caught up to her. I'm still confused and hurt and terrified of the idea that I may have been played.

But my heart doesn't understand any of that. All it knows is that I hate the sight of Scarlett walking away from me.

I take one step after her, stop, then take another.

*Fuck it.*

Uncaring about the people I bump into, I bolt after her. She's in heels and in need of a ride; she shouldn't be hard to catch up to. I just need to talk to her, beg her to make sense of the mess of thoughts in my head. I'm sure we can figure it out. We just need—

I explode onto the front steps, breathing too heavily. My eyes dart around, looking desperately for Scarlett's blonde hair or gold dress. She's the most beautiful woman in the world; she should be stopping traffic everywhere.

She's nowhere to be found.

I let out a muttered curse and look back at the gala's entryway. *Did I pass her?*

Twenty minutes later, I've reached the conclusion that she's disappeared.

Also, that I am completely *fucked*.

Because now that she's out of my sight, I have no way of finding her. Beyond sending her three texts—that go unanswered—I have no idea where she lives or where she might go.

With another bitten-off curse, I spin toward the bar and order a double whiskey. I have no idea what to do from here.

When Lucas finds me an hour later, I'm sufficiently drunk.

"Whoa," I hear his voice from behind me. "What the fuck did I miss?"

I lift my glass toward him with a crooked smile. "Nothing. Your timing is perfect. I was just about to take this shot." I wave at the bartender. "Can I get one more for my brother, pretty please?"

"Uh, actually…" Lucas takes the glass from my hand, and I send him a glare. He waves the bartender off and says, "Just a water, when you get a chance."

"Spoilsport," I grumble. But my head is already starting to spin, so I don't have the energy to argue.

"I'll repeat my question, Nico. What did I miss? What happened to you?" He looks around in alarm. "Did something go wrong with the sponsor?"

I snort, the pounding in my head increasing tenfold. "You mean the sponsor who's seen my girlfriend naked?"

At that, his eyes widen. "Him and Scarlett?"

I tip my imaginary hat. "That would be the one."

Lucas mutters a curse of his own and throws the shot back.

"Exactly what I said," I mutter with a groan.

"Wait a minute. How did that even come up?"

I scoff. "If you're asking from a business standpoint, don't worry. The sponsorship is still intact. They're sending it over in the morning for you to review."

"I'm not asking because of *that*," Lucas snaps, exasperated. "I'm just trying to figure out what *you're* dealing with. Was Scarlett here?"

I can only nod miserably.

"So, you brought Scarlett as your date and the sponsor recognized her. And then what?"

I stare at him in shock. "What do you mean, *then what?* He was her client!"

Lucas's expression shifts to confusion. "So? You knew she was an escort."

"It's not just— Forget it, you wouldn't understand." I chug half of my water. "You hated that I was with her anyway."

He sighs. "Nico, I didn't hate that you were with her. I was just worried she was playing you."

I let out a humorless laugh. "Welp. Turns out, you were spot on."

Lucas's brow furrows as he spins the whiskey glass between his fingers. "It doesn't make any sense. I saw you two together. That girl was smitten with you."

I let out a drunk hiccup as I stand. "Well, that's just where we are. I'm going to get out of here."

"Where are you staying? You're not going home, are you?"

I freeze as I'm pulling a few bills out to tip the bartender. *Shit, I had planned to stay at Scarlett's tonight.*

Lucas sighs. "Alright, let's just go back to my hotel. You

can sleep this off and then figure out how to have an actual conversation with Scarlett tomorrow."

"She won't return my texts," I mumble. "And I have no idea where she lives."

He slaps me on the back and starts to lead me toward the exit.

"Lucky for you, I'm a problem solver."

---

I wake up with the hangover from hell.

Groaning, I roll onto my back. Unsurprisingly, Lucas put me on the couch last night after I raided the mini bar in his room.

"Morning, sunshine," I hear him call out from the kitchen area. "Sleep well?"

I can only summon the energy to flip him off in answer.

But it isn't until I blink open my eyes and spot my suit draped across the nearby chair that all the memories from last night come flooding back.

*Scarlett, looking like the most beautiful woman I've ever seen.*

*Meeting one of her clients face to face.*

*Finding out I've been played by the woman I had fallen for.*

Suddenly, I want to puke for more than just alcohol reasons.

Lucas's sympathetic look distantly registers as I bolt for the bathroom. As I heave the entire liquid contents of my stomach into the toilet, I can't help remembering the last time I watched someone vomit all night long.

Once my stomach is empty, I collapse back onto the cold bathroom tile with a pained breath.

*How did I let things get this fucked up?*

I thought I'd been getting through to her, peeling back her layers by giving her a safe environment to do so. How had I been so wrong?

*I need to talk to her.*

It's the only thing I can think of as I drag myself back to the hotel room. Confusion or not—heartbreak or not—I want to hear the truth from Scarlett's lips. I just need to figure out how to find her.

When I stop in the kitchen and reach for the coffee machine, Lucas is giving me a blank look. I merely quirk an eyebrow at him in question.

"So…weird thing happened this morning," he starts. "Your accountant called me."

I finish pouring out the coffee and spin toward him with a snort. "Why? Did he assume I've been robbed because a hooker sweet-talked me out of a ridiculous amount of money?"

I still can't read the look he gives me, but he's not amused. "Not exactly."

And then he spins his laptop toward me.

I take a sip of coffee before moving closer. Squinting, I try to make sense of the numbers on the screen.

"Fifteen thousand? What's that charge for?"

"It's not a charge, Nico," Lucas says carefully.

When I look closer, I realize he's right.

It's a deposit.

"Who—? Wait, is that from a sponsor? I didn't think—"

And then I see the note beside it.

And my stomach falls straight through the floor.

*Maybe one day I'll be able to give and receive affection without a dollar sign, but for now, this is where I'm at. Thank you for being patient with me these past few weeks; I appreciate it more than you'll ever know. I held onto your money because it never felt right to use it. In hindsight, it was because I always knew my feelings for you were real.*

*So, I'd like to give it all back, in the off chance that yours are real, too.*

*I'm so excited to see you at the gala tonight.*

*xoxo*

*Scarlett*

I think I start to hyperventilate. I get dizzy as soon as I straighten, and I have to grab the back of the kitchen chair to steady myself.

*Fuck. Fuckfuckfuck.*

There's only one reason Scarlett would give back all the money I spent on her.

"I'm a goddamn idiot," I breathe.

Lucas leans back in his chair as he studies me. "It would look that way, yes."

I don't even have the energy to smack him for the comment. I just turn my attention to him with slack-jawed shock.

"What the fuck am I supposed to do now?" I ask, my tone pleading. "She was planning to give all the money back, and I—"

*Christ. I made her feel like a money-hungry prostitute.*

"I need to go see her." Suddenly, everything feels urgent. I can't let Scarlett spend another second thinking I don't see her as the most incredible woman in the world. That I *always* felt that way, and that I just got really fucking scared and stupid for a second.

I go to pull my shirt on, but with that motion I get a whiff of my own booze and misery-fueled stench. When I wince and drop the shirt, the pause in my panic brings a big dose of reality to the moment.

I collapse onto the couch in defeat. "I have no idea where she lives."

Lucas rolls his eyes at that. "I told you, I already solved that problem. Go shower before you make the poor girl pass out from your stench."

My brow furrows. "You *solved* that problem? What does that mean?"

He lets out an exasperated sigh and leans back in his chair. "It means I have a private investigator on my payroll, and I asked him to find Scarlett's address."

I gape at him. "You *what?*"

"What, so doing a google search is immoral, but hiring an escort isn't? Pick your battles, little brother."

It only takes one reminder of Scarlett's face as she walked off last night to make my decision.

"Send me the address."

# THIRTY-EIGHT
## SCARLETT

When I leave Amara's apartment the next day, I don't feel any better—or have any more answers—than I did last night.

But the exhaustion of staying up has my brain moving through mud, therefore dulling my thoughts. So, I can't bring myself to regret going home with her instead of being alone. The only thing that ends up being annoying is having to put my gala dress back on before I call an Uber.

I probably could've just stayed in the lounge clothes Amara lent me to sleep in, but a weird part of me wanted to wear a walk-of-shame outfit. I might not have had sex last night, but if I'm going to feel like an escort, I might as well look like one.

Even though I don't think I'll ever be an escort again.

I'd already subconsciously made the decision the night I ran out on my last client, but now I'm sure of it. Even though things are over with Nico, I can't go back to that life. I need to be more than I was.

I need to decide who I am.

Odd that I needed a man to show me that my mother may have been wrong.

Exhaustion pulls at my bones when my Uber finally pulls up in front of my apartment. It's late, later than I wanted to get home, and all I want to do is sink into a hot bath and sleep for a week.

But when I find Nico sitting on the steps of my building, that exhaustion disappears. Suddenly, my skin is crackling with electricity.

I have no idea why he's here, and more importantly, I have no idea how he knows where I live. However I felt about Nico before, at this moment, I'm going to treat him like any other man: with my guard up and my brain on full alert.

He spots me as soon as I climb out of the car and hurriedly stands to his feet. It isn't until his eyes drag over my body and his face goes pale that I realize what he's seeing.

He thinks I was with a client last night.

Instantly, anger infuses my veins. I was too surprised and hurt last night to register anything else, but now, with Nico standing, judgmental, in front of me? I'm pissed off all over again.

My steps slow as I near him, adding a little extra sway into my hips. *Let him look.*

"Mr. Price," I say with a sweet purr. "To what do I owe this pleasure?"

His throat moves on a rough swallow. "Can we talk?"

I cock my head to study him. "I assume whatever it is you want to talk about isn't something you want to be public knowledge so...should we go inside?"

He looks...nervous? His gaze drops down to my dress again before he nods.

Maybe I should care more about Nico seeing my apartment for the first time right now, especially since this was supposed to happen very differently in our original after-gala plans. No one's ever been in my apartment besides Amara. It should feel more vulnerable, shouldn't it?

But I'm so focused on Nico, so frustrated and curious about what he's doing here, that none of those feelings register. I unlock the front door and sweep into the apartment without any hesitation.

"Would you like anything to drink?" I ask over my shoulder. "I have water, water, or water with ice. Take your pick."

When I pull a bottle from the fridge and spin to face him, he's wide-eyed, looking at me in a way he never has.

*Fair enough. I feel a little crazed right now, too.*

"So…what can I do for you, Mr. Price? Here to book another night?"

That seems to snap him out of it because he takes a few big steps forward into the kitchen.

"Don't call me that," he begs. "Don't talk to me like I'm a client."

"But you *are* a client," I remind him with a quirked eyebrow. "You paid me for every date, remember?"

"Only because it was the only way to get you to talk to me!" It explodes out of him, and for a moment, I wonder which outburst was his true subconscious: this, or the one last night.

I can't tell, and that's the problem.

"Men don't usually pay me to *talk*, Nico." The name slips out of me before I can think better of it.

"Then men are fucking idiots," he snaps back. Then he sighs. "And I'm one of them."

I narrow my eyes at him before taking a sip of my water, my chest tightening. "No argument there," I mutter, more to myself than anything.

With a shake of his head, Nico says, "Okay, look. We need to talk. About last night."

I slowly close my water bottle and place it aside. Then I lift myself up on the counter, crossing my legs in a way that the slit of my dress exposes my thigh.

"Fine. Pay me."

Nico's eyes widen. "What?"

My stare never wavers. "You just said it was the only way to get me to talk. So pay me."

"Scarlett, that's not what I—"

"Pay me or get out."

I think my words—and my tone—startle both of us. I have *never* ordered a man around. I've always done my best to smooth things over, to make any situation I'm in as stress-free as possible. Even as an escort, demands have never been a part of that.

But there's something welling up inside me, something demanding to be heard.

Nico must see it in my face, because even though he looks like he wants to push back, even though it takes him a few seconds to make the decision, in the end, he reaches into his pocket. Pulling out a wad of cash, he slams it on the kitchen counter.

"There. Now let's talk."

My heart can't decide how it feels about this. By default, it felt right to demand the money, but I think a small part of me was still hoping that last night was a fluke, that Nico really does care for me.

But I take one look at the cash and square my shoulders, stepping right back into my escort heels. I let a seductive smile slide across my lips as I uncross my legs and spread them.

"So, how can I help you, Mr. Price?"

This time, it's frustration that flashes across his face at the name. Stepping forward, he places his hands on my knees and tries to push them together. "Scarlett, stop it."

I manage to maneuver us so instead of my legs closing, I can wrap them around the backs of his legs to pull him into the V of my thighs. "But this is so much more *fun* than talking," I say in a playful whine. Guiding his hands up my thighs, I lean forward to speak against his lips. "Don't you remember how good it feels to touch me?"

His hands reach my hips, and his grip immediately tightens. I watch as he squeezes his eyes shut, clearly struggling.

"Don't," he says in a harsh whisper. "Just…please, don't."

"Why not?" My tone is flat and emotionless. "You practically said it yourself, I'm just a whore. This is what I do."

In an instant, Nico's entire demeanor changes.

His eyes shoot open and lock onto mine, hurt and palpable regret swirling in their depths. His face goes slack, as do his shoulders and his grip on me. All of a sudden, he looks exhausted.

"I didn't mean that," he says firmly, but with a sadness I feel all too well. "I swear to God, Scarlett, I didn't mean that. And I'm so fucking sorry that I said it. I—" He looks away, his throat bobbing on a swallow. "It threw me off when I ran into that guy, and I took it out on you. I *never* should've said those things to you. You didn't deserve it, and I hate myself for hurting you with it."

I study him for a moment. I already knew Nico's freakout was a reaction to running into a client, but what I don't know is whether the things he said were thoughts finally spoken, or something else.

In the end, I simply keep the emotionless tone and come back with the truth.

"Doesn't really matter. You were right."

There's a flash of anger in his eyes. "The *fuck* I was. You are not a whore."

I roll my eyes at him. "Nico, I literally sleep with—"

"You are not what you *do*, Scarlett."

It isn't his outburst that stuns me into silence, it's the conviction with which he says it.

He must see something in my eyes because he immediately softens.

"You are so much more than you give yourself credit for," he says, the longing in his expression making my skin tingle all over. "You keep putting yourself in this box because you're scared to see yourself as anything more. Because your parents and some fucked-up situation three years ago landed you in this twisted lifestyle that you won't let yourself get out of. I want to get you out." There's a twinge of desperation in his voice now. "Please, Scarlett, let me get you out. Let me convince you that you're more than this, that you're smart and kind and perfect all on your own."

I want to believe him. I *want* to believe I'm more than just a man's accessory.

But we already went down this road, and I don't trust Nico enough to believe him again.

I meet his eyes and hold them as I ask quietly but without wavering, "Why would I do that when, at the first sign of trouble, you accused me of lying to you and acted like a completely different man than the one I've come to know?"

The breath he sucks in is audible. I don't know what he expected me to say, but it wasn't that.

Slowly, he lets out a big exhale. "Okay. Okay, let's talk about that."

I straighten where I'm still sitting on the counter. "Fine. Let's."

Seeming to read that I need a little bit of space for this, he backs up against the opposite counter and slides his hands into his pockets. His words are careful when he speaks.

"You know I ran into your client last night. Which wouldn't have been a big deal, but he said something about you that really bothered me." Guilt flashes in his eyes. "And instead of asking you about it, I reacted emotionally. I fucked up." He glances away as he mutters, "It didn't help that I saw you with Tyler, either."

"Who's a piece of shit, by the way," I snap at the reminder. "Are you friends with him?"

Nico looks up, startled. "What? No. He's just another fighter out of Philly; we run in the same crowds." He frowns. "Why is he a piece of shit? Did he…say something else to you?"

I want to laugh. "Oh, *now* you're protective? Because let me tell you something, Nico: he made me feel like shit, but *you* made me feel worse."

He stares at me, speechless. I've never let myself be anything but the agreeable girl, even with Nico.

And it feels *good* to unleash on him a little.

His throat moves on another rough swallow. "You're right. I was a total piece of shit, and I'm so, so sorry. I never should've said what I did to you."

Maybe the hardest part of this is that I suspect he means it. He does feel bad for freaking out at me, because the way he acted, it isn't like him at all.

My words are quiet when I ask, "Then why did you?"

He takes a big step forward, seemingly done with giving me space. Cupping my face in his hands, he tips his forehead to touch mine.

"Because I got really fucking scared that you didn't feel about me the way I feel about you," he whispers. "Because…" He pulls in a shaky breath. "Because I realized I was falling in love with you, and the absolute worst thing I could think of was finding out I was just a client to you."

My heartrate triples. *He was falling in love with me?*

I have no idea how to respond to that. How am I supposed to respond to that? I've never felt this strongly about someone before, never had someone feel this strongly about *me*.

Nico must not expect a response because he straightens, hands still cupping my face.

"Give me another chance, baby," he begs, his voice raw with emotion that brings tears to my eyes. "Let me make it up to you. Let me love you the way you should be loved."

"You hurt me." It bursts out of me. I didn't realize how badly I needed to say it until it's out there.

Regret flashes in Nico's eyes. "I know, and I'm so—"

"A big part of me is screaming to forgive you." He goes quiet when I cut him off, and the rest of it rushes out of me. "That I should accept your apology so we can smooth everything over and continue as if none of this happened. That would be the easiest thing…for *you*."

He's hanging on to every word, but he stiffens on that last one. He knows something is different.

"But another part of me," I continue, quietly but with conviction, "a much smaller, newer part I'm embracing, is telling me to throw you out of my apartment. Because you hurt me. You broke my heart last night, and I don't want to forgive you. Not yet."

The moment the words are out of my mouth, a sense of calm settles over me.

Because for the first time in my life, I'm making a

decision for me. Not for my mother, or for whatever man I'm standing in front of, but *me*.

Maybe I should be more wary of Nico's reaction to my words. After all, I was taught to be scared of a man's displeasure. But I'm not surprised when he eventually nods and drops his hands from my face.

"I understand." After a moment, his eyes lock with mine once more, glassier than they were a minute ago. "Part of me wants to get on my knees and beg for your forgiveness. But... another part of me is proud of you for telling me no."

Before I can react to that, he leans forward to press a kiss to my temple, the gesture making my heart ache. And then he's turning and walking away.

But he stops as he opens the front door. "Just so you know, this isn't a goodbye. I *will* earn your forgiveness." And there's ironclad conviction in his gaze when he adds, a little softer, "I'm not giving up on us, Scarlett."

# THIRTY-NINE
## NICO

For two weeks, I hate myself.

To be honest, I've hated myself ever since I got Scarlett's wire transfer, when I realized just how badly I fucked up at the gala. But after seeing the look on Scarlett's face when she kicked me out of her apartment...that self-hatred reaches a new level.

Thank God I don't have any more fights coming up because my workouts are dog shit after that. I go through all the motions, and I do everything my coaches tell me to do, but my heart's not in it. Because if Scarlett isn't in my life, nothing else matters.

I think it's the reason I end up calling Lucas to come by the gym.

I'm cooling down from a session when he walks in. He nods at my striking coach, who just finished holding pads for me, and gives me a curious eyebrow raise.

"What's up, Nico? Why am I here?"

I jerk my head for my coach to follow us into the gym office. When I shut the door behind them, they're both on alert.

"I'm done," I announce. "My contract is up. I'm done fighting."

Lucas and my coach look at each other, then look at me, then look at each other again.

"I feel like you should take this one," my coach says.

Lucas fixes his full attention on me as he leans back in his chair and rubs a hand over his mouth.

"Is this because of Scarlett?"

My coach makes a silent *ohh* sound and leans back in his own chair.

"Yes and no," I answer honestly. "Yes, because she triggered the realization, but no, it's not *because* of her."

"Okay, then… Walk me through it, little brother."

I let out a heavy exhale and collapse on the office couch. "My heart's not in it, Lucas. It hasn't been for a while. I fell into this shit, and I've been doing everything physically possible to get as good as I possibly can, but none of that changes the fact that I *fell* into this career." I look at my coach. "I'll never make the Top Ten. You know it, I know it — It's not a self-deprecating thing; it's just the God's honest truth. And I have no interest in making it to the top, either. All I wanted, all I *ever* wanted, was to see how far I could take this thing. And now that I have my answer, I'm ready to be done."

Coach lets out a chuckle, but it doesn't sound like he's laughing at me. He almost looks fond as he says, "Only you could make it to the highest level of fighting *just for fun*."

My shrug is stiff. "Sorry. It felt like a waste not to try."

He stands, smiling, and claps me on the back. "Nothing to apologize for, son. Our hearts want what they want, and there's no shame in that. You never needed my blessing, but if you're done, I'll support you."

I give him a grateful smile. "I appreciate you, Coach."

325

He pats me on the back again before walking off with a casual, "When you start looking for your next job, keep in mind, I could always use a business partner. Just saying."

*Yeah*, that had occurred to me. Retiring doesn't only mean not fighting, it also means I need a new income stream.

"So, explain to me how Scarlett plays into this," Lucas says, interrupting my thoughts. "You haven't heard from her?"

I shake my head miserably. I texted her a few times, simple messages that stressed how much I love her and how sorry I am about everything. But she has yet to respond.

Maybe I'm being delusional about earning her forgiveness. After all, she was locked down so tight the last time I saw her, I truly couldn't get a read on her when she kicked me out.

Lucas's tone is careful when he says, "I'm going to ask you something, but I don't want you to be angry with me for asking it."

My brow furrows in confusion, but I nod.

"If Scarlett doesn't take you back, if you never see her again...do you still want to retire? Because it kinda sounds like you want to quit fighting so you can have more time to spend with a woman who isn't yours."

My head falls back against the wall with a tired exhale. I haven't wanted to think about a scenario where I don't get Scarlett back, but Lucas's question is valid. It's why I called him and not just my coaches.

I take a minute to envision a future without Scarlett. It sucks, but I force myself to consider what it would look like. Do I still want to fight? Do I still want to kill myself for the joy of getting in the cage and potentially climbing the rankings? Would I still have the heart for it?

*No.*

The answer comes so quickly that relief floods my body. I was about eighty percent certain of my decision when I called Lucas in, but being asked the question so bluntly and having the answer come so quickly is a relief in itself.

"I would still want to retire," I tell Lucas, lifting my head to meet his eyes. "I don't want to do this anymore."

He studies me for about two seconds. Then he nods and says, "That's all I needed to hear. When I get the call for contract renewal negotiations, I'll tell them you're done."

I slump into my seat. "Thanks, man."

"You have any idea what you're going to do for money? Or is this your way of saying you're going to need to crash on my couch for a bit?"

I let out a bark of laughter. "As if you don't live in a two-story penthouse apartment with four bedrooms and an entirely unused guest suite."

"I'd still put you on the couch," he says with a sniff.

I'm smiling as I shake my head. Regardless of everything with Scarlett, this conversation has taken a huge weight off my shoulders.

But then Lucas sobers and asks gently, "So, what are you going to do about Scarlett?"

I let out a heavy exhale, trying to expel the sadness that fills me at the mention of her name. "I have no idea. I don't want to push her, but at the same time, I don't know if I'm capable of letting her go. She's...everything. And she *deserves* everything." I drag a hand down my face. "I guess that's the frustrating part. Regardless of if she forgives me, I wish she knew that. She should know how amazing she is."

"So then tell her," Lucas says simply.

I blow out another breath. "I can't keep blasting her with texts every day. That's repetitive and annoying, and I need to make more effort than that."

"Then tell her in a way she'll believe." Lucas leans forward to brace his forearms on his knees. "Nico, you told me she opened up to you in a way she never has to anyone else. You know more about her than anyone else. *Show her* why you think she's amazing and how you feel about her."

At that, an idea sparks. It might not be enough to earn her forgiveness, but that's not the main goal anyway.

Getting Scarlett to see herself the way I see her, the way I *truly* see her…that's the goal.

I lock eyes on Lucas. "Do you have time to take a long lunch? I could use your help with some brainstorming."

He doesn't even hesitate. He just nods and says, "Let me call my assistant. I'll cancel the rest of my day."

# FORTY
## SCARLETT

My days after the gala are bizarre in a thousand ways. I had already decided to quit working as an escort after Nico's fight, but it isn't until my conversation with Amara that I truly come to terms with it.

It's disappointing to realize how much of my life I centered around men.

For one, I have to figure out what to do with myself when I'm not in class. Without clients, I have nothing to plan my daily schedule around. I can sleep in late, run my errands whenever I want; I can spend an entire day—or night—rotting on the couch watching movies. I'll need to figure out a job eventually, but the one good thing about being a high-end escort who didn't leave her house for years is that I have more than enough money saved to keep me comfortable for a while. I can spend this time finding my new normal.

The other bizarre change is not having any obligations. Without any men in my life, I have no "reason" to workout, or get my roots touched up, or go clothes shopping.

Until I realize I miss doing those things.

So, I start doing them again. But this time, I do them for myself.

Instead of bleaching my roots so I'm the perfect shade of blonde from root to end, I ask for a shadow root and some dimension in my strands. Instead of just running on the treadmill for two hours, I sign up at a local Pilates gym to try out some classes. Instead of starving myself on a banana and a flavorless green shake, I swallow my guilt and experiment with new breakfast dishes that include carbs and actual sustenance.

I feel like an entirely new person, living an entirely different life.

I also make it a goal to visit one new place or try one new thing every day. I'm sick and tired of living out of my apartment, spending the day in dread and the night in depression. I want to experience life, not just let it pass me by. One day, I visit the Banksy museum. Another day, I make it my mission to find the best slice of New York pizza. I even do a solo date to a restaurant I've been dying to try. I finally take a tour of the Statue of Liberty, and then go back again three days later when I can't stop thinking about Ellis Island.

Thank God Nico came along and shook up my world. Regardless of how things ended with us, that's one thing I'm grateful for every single day. If it wasn't for him, I wouldn't have had the courage to start venturing out on my own like this. He gave me a starting point, made me remember my interests that I had completely forgotten about.

But that doesn't mean I don't get sad when reminders of him appear.

Every day, I'm conflicted about my feelings for him. I miss him, probably more than I want to admit, but oftentimes, after I think of him, I remember our fight at the gala, and I'm hit with a wave of sadness and hurt. It's hard to reconcile that with his apology.

I just wish I knew which ones were his real feelings. I *want* to believe he only pushed me away because he got scared, but…it's hard. Whether it's because of my long-standing trust issues or not, it's hard to trust his words.

And then one day, I open my front door to find a wrapped present on my doorstep.

I don't know what I expected, but it wasn't a book on the psychology of love. And paired with it is a little handwritten note that says,

> *I love you because you're the smartest person I know.*
> *P.S. Don't tell Lucas.*

I let out a teary laugh as I read it. I've never been made to feel like my brain was something to be proud of. So hearing that Nico might love me for it…

I swallow roughly. It's too much to hope for.

But two days later, there's another gift waiting for me. This time, it's the t-shirt Nico gave me the night I got sick. The one I loved wearing because it smelled like him.

It still smells like him.

This note says,

> *I'd love you through every sickness. It would be my honor.*

I slump against the doorway, the memory of the time Nico took care of me crystallizing in my mind. I wondered that night if it meant he could love me, but it was too bizarre of an idea at the time to really consider it. Now I wonder if that was the first sign.

For the next week, there's a gift waiting on my doorstep every other day. They don't always come with notes, but the ones that do make me shed a tear.

A yoga mat for my workouts, because he loves me for how strong I am. Concert tickets to another Hans Zimmer show. A pink dog collar with a note that says,

*I love you for your kindness. The way you love rescue animals tells me everything I need to know about your heart.*

I always thought gifts from men would be clothing or jewelry. Any other man would've made the assumption that I can only be impressed by diamond earrings or expensive heels. But not Nico.

Nico's gifts aren't expensive, they're *thoughtful*. They show me he not only paid attention to me, but that he also loves what he saw. He loves me for the qualities I never thought were lovable.

With every gift, my anger at him thaws.

But the day I open my door to an envelope, it melts completely.

There's a Polaroid inside. When I look closer, I realize it's a picture from the night of his fight, when we were out at dinner with his family. With the angle it's taken from, I'm guessing his mom was the one who took it when we weren't looking.

I choke on a sob at the picture.

It's of Nico and me. We're sitting at the table, and I'm

smiling about something as I look down at my lap. I look *happy*. I've never seen a picture of myself where I don't look either poised or anxious, but in the picture Nico's mom snapped, I look like I wouldn't want to be anywhere else in the world.

And then there's Nico.

I've never seen what love looks like on a man. I never had an example growing up, and God knows my own relationships never included true love. Not the way it looks on Nico.

It's in his eyes, in the way he's looking at me. His arm is braced on the back of my chair, giving me space while also being close to me. And he's *staring*. The sparkle in his eyes looks like it could be a painting. And he's smiling at me, in a way I'm familiar with but have never truly considered.

He loves me.

*Of course* he loves me.

Even before these gifts and notes, I knew it every time we were together. He showed me when he listened to me, when he cared enough to do things for *me*.

I feel a tear run down my cheek as I turn the picture over. There's a handwritten note on the back that just says,

*I love you. I'll always love you. If loving you through this picture is the only thing I deserve, I'll still consider myself the luckiest man in the world.*

It's in that moment that I realize…I love him.

Throughout all of this, he was patient with me and made me feel safe. He took the time to show me *why* he loves me because he knew I needed to hear it. He made me laugh when I needed some lightness in my day. And if the way he loves his family is any indication, he loves with his whole heart. He's the kindest man I've ever met.

And he's everything I've ever wanted but was too scared to hope for.

Sliding the picture very carefully into my wallet, I quickly grab my keys and close the door behind me. I need to see him. I don't care about our fight at the gala. I see now that it was his fear talking when he said what he did. Knowing he loved me, knowing what it *feels like* to love someone, I can't blame him for reacting the way he did. I don't want to.

Maybe that's the biggest thing I've learned from Nico. That when you love someone…trusting is easy.

And I'm ready to trust him.

# FORTY-ONE
## NICO

Someone's knocking at my front door.

It's 9 p.m. on a Tuesday, and I'm sitting on my couch, trying to distract myself by scrolling mindlessly on social media. Unfortunately, I keep getting clips from last week's *Dancing With The Stars* episode, which just makes me think of Scarlett. The sound of the knock is a welcome distraction.

When I look through the peep hole and see Scarlett, I do a triple take.

*She's here? Right now?*

It never occurred to me that she might come back to me. Even as I packaged the gifts, and handwrote the notes, I never let myself think about a future with her in it. It was too painful, too much to hope for.

But now... Now, she's standing at my front door.

I have no idea which way this is about to go, but after taking a deep breath, I open the door.

"Scarlett," I breathe.

She looks different. She's wearing jeans and a t-shirt, for one, and her hair looks like it might be a different shade. And she's only wearing a little bit of makeup—no red lips.

"Hi, Nico," she says with a careful smile. "Can we talk?"

I almost trip over my feet to stand aside and wave her in. "Of course. Come in."

I can't take my eyes off her as she steps into my apartment. I'm trying desperately to get a read on her, on why she's *here*, but she's on guard enough that I can't quite make it out. The one thing that makes me feel better is that she doesn't seem angry.

Stopping in the middle of my living room, she spins and asks casually, "So, how has your week been?"

I must still be in shock because I immediately answer, "Good, it's been good." And then her question—and the oddness of it—registers, and I shake my head. "This feels too reminiscent of our first few dates; it's kind of blowing my mind a little."

Scarlett lets out a laugh. "You're right, I'm sorry. I'm a little nervous."

That finally gives me the sign I need to move a little bit closer to her. "Why are you nervous?" I ask, my tone softening.

Her eyes are big, her nerves obvious now. "Because I've never done this before," she whispers.

*God, I just want to hug her.* "Done what, baby? Why are you here?"

Sucking in a breath for courage, she looks up into my eyes. "To ask you if you meant what you said in all those notes."

"Of *course* I did." It rushes out of me as I step forward and take her in my arms. "I meant every single word, Scarlett."

She gives me a tiny nod, but I'm just thankful she's accepting my embrace. "And just to clarify, did you mean what you said the night of the gala?"

"*No.* Scarlett, I swear on my brothers' lives that I didn't mean any of that. I…" I swallow roughly and admit, "I was just in love with you and terrified." Then, quieter, "It was my insecurities talking, and I hate myself for ever letting you hear those words."

Another nod, but this time, she wraps her arms around my neck.

"Okay, then. I love you, too."

I'm pretty sure my heart stops. *Did she just…?*

"You…you what?"

She lifts up onto her toes, a sweet smile on her face, and whispers the words against my lips. "I love you, too, Nico."

I kiss her then. I can't *not* kiss her.

I press my lips to hers, pouring every ounce of love, relief, joy, and apology into the kiss. Maybe it's because I haven't been able to kiss her for the longest time, or maybe it's because I wasn't sure I'd ever be able to kiss her again, but nothing has ever felt more important than this moment.

I don't let her go, even when the kiss finally ends. I might even pull her closer. Touching my forehead to hers, I breathe, "God, I missed you. I hated not talking to you. Not touching you. Not seeing you."

She shifts even closer, her smile still in place as she melts against me. "I missed you, too," she says quietly. "So much."

I could stay like this forever, but a moment later, she pulls back slightly and says, "There's something I need to tell you." Before I can panic over *that*, she says quickly, "I'm not an escort anymore."

Surprise mixes with relief. But what comes out is a breathless, "Thank fuck." I attempt an apologetic look. "I'm sorry, I don't want to start off a relationship with rules, and I *especially* want you to tell me to fuck off when it's appropriate, but I'll be honest: I don't think I could have handled you sleeping with other men."

I wince at my own words and try to defend myself. "I mean, *maybe* I could come to terms with it if it was a sexual empowerment thing, but I'm 99% sure you hated it, so I feel like I can—"

Her hand covers my mouth. She's smiling, looking at me adoringly. And I relax a bit.

"You would've been well within your rights to ask me to stop, Nico. I don't think I could have handled you with another woman, either."

I perk up at that, a grin sliding across my face as I pull her hand away. "No? Interesting. I wonder what jealous Scarlett looks like."

She quirks an eyebrow. "Flirt with another girl and find out."

My laughter is loud, my chest filling with warmth as I tighten my arms around her. "I would never. I only have eyes for you, Red."

A hum leaves her chest as she beams up at me and wraps her arms around my neck again. "Good." But then her smile slips and she says in a soft voice, "I'm sorry I didn't tell you earlier."

I grow serious at her words. Before I can respond, she hurriedly adds, "I *should* have told you. Especially since I pulled back on clients weeks ago. As soon as I started having feelings for you." She looks up at me, a plea in her eyes. "I'm sorry I ever made you doubt that I had feelings for you," she whispers.

A breath rushes out of me. "Oh, baby, no…" Taking her face in my hands, I tilt it up so she can see the truth in my eyes when I say, "That was never your burden to carry. My doubts were *my* issue. You never need to apologize for my own blindness."

When she sniffles, still looking unsure, I press a kiss to her lips. "Because I *was* blind," I say softly, my forehead touching hers. "You made your feelings obvious in a dozen different ways. I was just too scared to pick up on them."

Thankfully, that seems to reassure her, because she pushes up on her toes to kiss me again.

"I bet none of them were as obvious as that picture your mom took of us," she says with a light laugh.

I quirk an eyebrow as I pull her over to my couch. "Agree to disagree on that. Baby, you told me your real name on our fourth date."

It's cute, how stunned she looks as I tug her into my lap. "Wow. I guess you're right. For all I knew, you could've been a serial killer."

I nuzzle into her neck, wondering if I can cancel my plans for the next century to keep her here. "A serial killer who gets off on making your fake orgasms real? Doubtful."

"Oh my God." She covers her face with her hands, her shoulders shaking with a silent laugh. "I still can't believe you caught that."

"It was how you could tell *my* feelings were growing," I murmur into her skin.

Scarlett lets out a happy hum as she turns to snuggle into me, and we sit quietly, absorbing finally being together.

But after a moment, I straighten with a sigh. "On the topic of quitting jobs… I officially retired."

Her eyebrows shoot to her hairline, breath catching. "Really?"

I nod, lifting one hand to tuck a strand of hair behind her ear. "You made me realize my heart wasn't in it. I made the announcement yesterday."

"I guess we kind of helped each other out, then," she says softly.

I return her smile, my heart threatening to explode from this much love. "I guess so."

But a moment later, I let out a loud laugh when something occurs to me. "So, we're both unemployed now?"

Scarlett huffs a laugh in return. "I guess so."

"Well, at least we have that fifteen grand to live on for a little while..."

# SCARLETT'S EPILOGUE

*Six months later*

I can smell the dinner Nico's cooking before I even open the door.

It took me a while to get used to it. When I first moved in, I slipped right back into the habits I'd adopted during my first marriage. I cleaned religiously, and I had dinner on the table by the time Nico would get home.

On our fifth day of living together, Nico hid all the cleaning supplies and physically removed me from the kitchen.

Nowadays, we split the household chores. When Nico cooks, I clean up after. We both do surface-level cleans, but I prefer to do the deep cleans. We've created a partnership, instead of living by roles defined by gender stereotypes.

Nico looks up when I walk into the apartment. He's standing at the kitchen island, chopping vegetables with a dish towel thrown over his shoulder.

Nobody prepared me for how hot the domesticated look is.

"Hey, baby," he greets with a smile, putting the knife down to wipe his hands. "You're home early."

"Professor let us out early," I say, dropping my bag in the entryway. Before walking over to Nico, I squat down next to our couch and scratch behind the ears of our sleeping dog.

The same dog that stole my heart that day at the rescue clinic.

"Hi, Kimbo," I coo, smiling when his tail starts to thump against the cushions. "Did you give up on begging Daddy for scraps?"

"More like he filled up on scraps he conned from me," Nico mutters. "I swear, his puppy dog eyes rival yours."

I straighten and make my way over to my boyfriend. When I reach him, I tuck into his arms in a way that feels more natural than breathing. "I have no idea what you're talking about," I say with an innocent smile.

"Yeah, okay," he mutters. But he's smiling as he presses a kiss to my hair.

I don't think I'll ever get enough of this easy intimacy between us. Out of all the things I love about being with Nico, this is the thing that has made me feel the safest.

"How was your day?" he murmurs against my temple, tightening his arms around me. "Did you have the meeting with your academic advisor?"

Giddy about the topic, I pull back enough to meet his eyes. "I did. We made a plan for the classes I'll enroll in next semester, and we pulled all my application materials together that masters programs usually need."

His eyes light up instantly. No one gets more excited for my academic success than Nico Price. "Yeah? That's amazing."

I suck in a deep breath. "Now I just need to take the GRE and figure out where I want to apply."

He softens at that and pulls me into his arms again. "I'm so proud of you, baby," he murmurs, nuzzling into my neck.

I melt into his embrace, a happy smile forming on my lips. I'll never get tired of his unconditional love.

"And how was *your* day?" I mumble into his chest.

I both hear and feel his warm chuckle. His hand brushes over my hair as he says, "It was good. Spent the morning having Lucas walk me through the gym's legal stuff so I can finally get added as a partner, and then I held pads for one of the guys getting ready for his pro debut. Not much different than my usual day, honestly."

At that, I pull back so I can look up at him again. "Do you ever miss the fighting part?"

He smiles and shakes his head as he reaches to tuck a strand of hair behind my ear. "Never. The only thing I ever miss is *you* during the day."

"Such a charmer," I try to tease. Pushing up onto my toes, I press my lips to his.

With a soft groan, he takes control of the kiss. His arm around my waist tightens and his other hand sinks into my hair so he can tilt his head and deepen the connection. The moment his tongue slides across mine, I surrender with a breathy moan.

The only reason we break apart is because the oven timer goes off. If it weren't for that, Nico likely would've been two seconds away from lifting me onto the counter. Ever since we moved in together, his hunger for me seems to have grown.

Before I met Nico, I sometimes wondered about what a sex life would feel like after working as an escort. If I'd ever flash back to clients, or if I'd ever truly be able to enjoy sex without my baggage.

I wish I could've told myself that I'd never even *think* of my past. That having sex with a partner you love and trust more than anyone else is an incomparable experience.

Plus, he consistently knocks every other thought from my head.

Nico pulls away with a sigh to turn off the timer. "I'm half tempted to cancel this dinner tonight."

"No, you're not," I say with a chuckle. "You love when we host your family."

Another sigh, this one coupled with a fond smile. "Yeah, you're right."

I watch as he pulls a pan from the oven. "Do you want me to help?"

"No, I do not," he says as he returns to chopping vegetables. "Your only job is to sit there and look pretty. Do you want a glass of wine?"

That warmth in my chest bubbles over.

"Yes, but I can get it," I say, shifting around him to grab a wineglass from the cabinet. But before I pull out a bottle of wine, I press another kiss to the corner of his lips.

"I love you," I whisper with a smile. Every day, I wish there was a better way to say that, that some words existed that might express even a shred of my love and appreciation and gratitude for this man, but I haven't yet found them.

It doesn't matter, though. Nico knows. I see it in the way he smiles at me, and the way he takes my lips in a kiss of his own.

He opens his mouth to say something, but before he gets the chance, there's a knock on the door.

His head drops with an annoyed exhale. "I'm getting pretty sick of these interruptions."

I giggle as I place my wineglass on the counter. "Don't

worry, we'll have all the time in the world tonight," I tell him in a sultry whisper as I pass by him.

"I'm going to hold you to that, Red," he growls.

# NICO'S EPILOGUE

I have to stop myself from proposing at least once a week.

Especially when I'm standing in the kitchen, watching her laugh with my parents. She fits in so seamlessly with my family, it's hard to imagine I ever lived a life without her.

I wanted to intertwine our lives as soon as we made things official. It felt like I'd been waiting my whole life for Scarlett, and I didn't want to spend another day without her. But this was new for Scarlett and she was still discovering herself. The last thing she needed was a man suggesting she move in with him—the day after they got together.

Although that's not to say I didn't fall to my knees in relief when she broached the subject a few weeks later.

Now, I get to wake up to her smile every morning and fall asleep with her in my arms every night. I get to ask her every single day how her classes are going, and what she's researching on her own, just because she's so excited to learn new things. I get to watch her laugh with my parents during our monthly family dinner. And fall more in love with her every time.

"Dude," Alexander grumbles from his seat at the island. "You're staring again."

I huff a laugh and go back to the salad I'm almost done assembling. "I'd say I'm sorry, but…"

He rolls his eyes and takes a swig of his beer. "But you're not. Yeah, we know." Then he frowns and kicks Lucas in the shin where he's silently sitting on the barstool next to him. "What's up with you? You haven't said ten words since you walked in here."

Lucas seems to shake from a trance. He *has* looked distracted tonight. He keeps looking at his phone, which wouldn't be unusual if it wasn't followed by him frowning and then looking off into the distance.

"Me? Oh, I'm just giving your communication style a try," he says, waving Alexander away. "Maybe you're right; maybe grunts are more effective than words."

Alexander and I look at each other, then back at Lucas.

"Alexander has a better chance at becoming a beauty queen than you do taking a vow of silence," I say dryly.

It earns me an angry grunt from Alexander.

Lucas slumps forward onto the counter with a defeated breath. "Okay, fine. I'm distracted."

We wait patiently for the explanation, but nothing could prepare us for the moment he straightens and says angrily, "I got my *ass* handed to me in court today."

I gawk at Lucas. Alexander's beer freezes on the way to his lips.

After a moment, I turn toward Alexander and say, "I don't know if I'm more surprised at the fact, or hearing him *admit* the fact."

"Definitely the second," Alexander mutters.

"Ugh, *focus*," Lucas says with a rare glare. "This is serious. I haven't lost like this since…actually, I don't think

I've *ever* lost like this. The guy absolutely wiped the floor with me."

"So…what happened?" I ask carefully.

Lucas blows out a frustrated breath. "Opposing counsel's private investigator got their hands on some case-ending information." He frowns and grumbles, "Information my client *should* have shared with me, but thought he could hide. Apparently, the PI managed to dig it up anyway."

I bite down on my amused smirk. Alexander doesn't bother hiding his.

"If *my* team didn't even know about it, how the fuck did this PI find out?" Lucas complains. "Where was he even looking?"

"Why do you assume it's a he?" I ask, only half-joking. "Women are probably way better at sleuthing."

Lucas snorts. "If it's a woman, I'd like to meet her. I could use her on my team."

Just then, Scarlett appears in the kitchen. "A lot of animated discussion going on over here," she comments as she reaches for the side dishes. "What are you boys talking about?"

While she's close enough, I quickly press a kiss to her hair. "Lucas got humbled by a woman today."

Scarlett's eyebrows rise. "Really? Wow. Can I meet her?"

Lucas rolls his eyes and opens his mouth to retort, but we hear my mom call out, "I would also like to meet her!"

The apartment fills with laughter. Even Alexander cracks a grin.

"You guys are bullies," Lucas grumbles, reaching for one of the side dishes. But he still affectionately hip checks Scarlett on his way to the dining table. "I'm never being vulnerable with you again."

By the time dinner is over and the pastries Lucas showed up with have been consumed, I'm eager to be alone with my girlfriend again. And Scarlett can read every thought in my head because she's smiling when I shut the front door a little too forcefully behind Lucas and Alexander.

"You don't think they'll be offended you kicked them out?" she asks with a laugh as I stalk toward her. "Between this and the teasing—"

"No more talking about my brothers," I grumble, pulling her down onto the couch with me. "I've shared your attention enough for one night."

She curls up in my lap with a happy sigh. "You always have my attention."

"I'm happy to hear it," I say, wrapping my arms around her. I drop my cheek to her head as one hand starts to brush along her thigh.

When she yawns, I pull back to look at her. "Tired?"

She nods and snuggles closer. "It's just been a long month. It'll be a relief when my semester is over."

I start to massage her back. "You've been working hard. You should take a break after finals, actually do something to relax."

"*You* should relax, too," she says, poking me in the side. "I bet you're putting in just as much time at the gym as you did when you were fighting."

I don't disagree with that. Because she's right; after I made the decision to retire, I took all of the time and effort I'd spent on myself for my career, and I redirected it to the gym and its fighters. I don't know if being a gym owner is going to be my long-term career, but for now, it's a relief to have something I feel *good* about doing.

"It's peak fight season. It'll slow down soon," I explain.

When Scarlett lifts an eyebrow, I add, "I mean, you're right, but *also*…it's peak fight season."

Scarlett settles back against my chest. "Maybe we should plan something relaxing next month. We could both probably use it."

For some reason, a conversation comes to mind when she says that. One I had with Lucas and Alexander all those months ago in the back of a Mexican restaurant. The original proposed solution to all my problems.

Before Scarlett came along.

"Maybe we should go on vacation," I suggest casually.

Scarlett freezes for a split second, then laughter fills the air.

"Amara kept pushing me to take a vacation when we first met," she says in an amused voice. "It was going to be my last-ditch effort to find some semblance of happiness."

For a moment, I can only blink at her. I knew a lot of our connection stemmed from us both living a lonely existence, but I never would have imagined we were attempting the same solutions for it.

It makes me that much more grateful we found each other.

Wrapping my arms around her once again, I say, "As glad as I am that you *didn't* take that vacation, I do actually like the idea of taking one now."

Scarlett lets out a thoughtful hum. "I do too. Sitting on the beach with a book in my hand and dinner reservations to look forward to sounds like paradise." She tilts her face up to brush her lips against mine. "Especially if you're with me."

"That sounds amazing," I murmur as I return the kiss-that's-not-a-kiss. "I'm in."

I feel her lips curl up. "Where should we go then?"

I'm smiling as I kiss her again. "I believe someone once suggested Greece?"

*I wonder if I can hold onto this ring long enough to propose to her there...*

# ACKNOWLEDGMENTS

This book was such a spicy good time. After my last book put me through the emotional wringer (I say that lovingly), it was a relief to return to my roots of spice and down-bad men. I hope you enjoyed this one as much as I enjoyed writing it.

As always, my first *thank you* goes to my husband. As much as it pains me to admit, I wouldn't be able to write any of my books without you. I'm grateful every day to have you in my corner.

The second *thank you* goes to my forever godsend: my editor, Kenzie. I've been saying it since book number one (this makes nine): I'm so amazed by your ability to take my three star drafts and turn them into five star books. Your brain is insane and I mean it when I say there would be no Nikki Castle without you. Thank you for being the best editor slash therapist a girl could ever ask for.

To my beta readers and friends: Sarah, Brittany, and Nicole. Thank you for doing a last minute beta read (will I always be so chaotic? who knows) and helping to shape this story into its best possible version. But more importantly, thank you for being the most supportive friends I could ever ask for.

To my family, friends, readers, everyone who has read and supported my stories: *THANK YOU.* I say this during every release but without you, a book is just some ink on a dead tree. Thank you for loving these stories as much as I do.

# ALSO BY NIKKI CASTLE

# ABOUT THE AUTHOR

Nikki Castle is a wife and dog mom from Philadelphia who writes spicy love stories about alpha MMA fighters and the women that melt their badass, playboy hearts. She's a full-time romance author during the day and spends her evenings running a Mixed Martial Arts (MMA) gym with her husband, who is also a retired fighter.

Nikki has been writing in one way or another since she was a teenager. She pursued an English and Philosophy degree in college, and finally decided to sit down and fulfill her longtime dream of writing a novel when quarantine began in 2020. "5 Rounds" was her first book—and it was supposed to be her only book. Now, she's a full-time author who can't imagine a life in which she's not crafting love stories.